THE ASHES OF LONDON

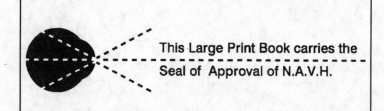

THE ASHES OF LONDON

ANDREW TAYLOR

THORNDIKE PRESS
A part of Gale, Cengage Learning

GALE
CENGAGE Learning·

Farmington Hills, Mich • San Francisco • New York • Waterville, Maine
Meriden, Conn • Mason, Ohio • Chicago

GALE
CENGAGE Learning®

LIBRARY OF CONGRESS CATALOGING-IN-PUBLICATION DATA

Names: Taylor, Andrew, 1951 October 14- author.
Title: The Ashes of London / Andrew Taylor.
Description: Large print edition. | Waterville, Maine : Thorndike Press, 2017. |
  Series: Thorndike Press large print mystery
Identifiers: LCCN 2017001850 | ISBN 9781410498298 (hardback) | ISBN 1410498298
  (hardcover)
Subjects: LCSH: Great Fire, London, England, 1666—Fiction. |
  Murder—Investigation—England—London—Fiction. | London
  (England)—History—17th century—Fiction. | BISAC: FICTION / Historical. |
  GSAFD: Mystery fiction. | Historical fiction.
Classification: LCC PR6070.A79 A94 2017 | DDC 823/.914—dc23
LC record available at https://lccn.loc.gov/2017001850

Published in 2017 by arrangement with HarperCollins Publishers Limited

Printed in the United States of America
1 2 3 4 5 6 7 21 20 19 18 17

For Caroline, as always

AUTHOR'S NOTE

On 1 September 1666, London was the third largest city in the European world, after Paris and Constantinople. Estimates vary but its population probably amounted to around 300–400,000 people.

The city had three great centres of political power, strung along the north bank of the Thames — just as they are today. The wealth of the merchant classes was concentrated in the walled medieval City between the Tower in the east and St Paul's Cathedral in the west. A mile further upstream, beyond Charing Cross, was the sprawling Tudor and Stuart palace of Whitehall; this was the King's principal London residence and the heart of the government's executive powers. Beyond that lay Westminster, where Parliament sat in a former royal palace.

The river linked these centres of power and offered the easiest way to travel from one to the other. Around them, the suburbs expanded steadily. London Bridge — at this time, the only bridge below Kingston, ten miles upstream — linked the City to Southwark, itself as large as many seventeenth-century cities, on the south bank of the Thames. The river was also the main artery for trade, both domestic and foreign.

Charles II regained his throne in 1660 amid scenes of almost universal jubilation. In the previous twenty years, hundreds of thousands had died in the Civil War between Crown and Parliament, including Charles's own father, executed with a nice sense of symbolism in front of his own Banqueting House at Whitehall Palace. Afterwards, sustained by the army, Oliver Cromwell ruled the country with ruthless and bloody efficiency. When Cromwell died in 1658, however, the Commonwealth rapidly crumbled, and a restored monarchy seemed the only practicable way to heal the country's divisions.

Six years later, the jubilation had subsided. The King's profligate court horrified and angered his more sober subjects. Religion was a constant source of conflict — the Anglican establishment, restored with the King, nursed a deep distrust of the dissenting Protestants who had formed the core of

Cromwell's support. Both parties loathed the Catholics, who in popular imagination were associated with conspiracies at home and implacable, devious malignity abroad. The government was chronically short of money, which hampered its policies at every turn. To make matters worse, the plague struck repeatedly at the capital — in 1665, its most virulent outbreak, the mortality rate was an extraordinary one in five.

Still, somehow, London grew and prospered. Then, on 2 September 1666, the Great Fire began to burn in a baker's shop in Pudding Lane, deep within the densely populated heart of the old City.

■ ■ ■ ■

I
Ashes and Fire

4–8 SEPTEMBER 1666

■ ■ ■ ■

CHAPTER ONE

The noise was the worst. Not the crackling of the flames, not the explosions and the clatter of falling buildings, not the shouting and the endless beating of drums and the groans and cries of the crowd: it was the howling of the fire. It roared its rage. It was the voice of the Great Beast itself.

Part of the nave roof fell in. The sound stunned the crowd into a brief silence.

Otherwise I shouldn't have heard the whimpering at my elbow. It came from a boy in a ragged shirt who had just pushed his way through the mass of people. He was swaying, on the brink of collapse.

I poked his arm. 'Hey. You.'

The lad's head jerked up. His eyes were wide and unfocused. He made a movement as if to run away but we were hemmed in on every side. Half of London, from the King and the Duke of York downwards, had

13

turned out to watch the death throes of St Paul's.

'Are you all right?'

The boy was still unsteady. I took his arm to support him. He snatched it away. He hunched his shoulders and tried to burrow between the people in front.

'For God's sake,' I said. 'Stand back. You'll fry if you get closer.'

He wriggled to the other side of the woman next to him. The three of us were in a row, staring between the shoulders and elbows of the men in front.

The largest part of the crowd, including the royal party, was in the churchyard north-east of the cathedral. But the boy and I were in Ludgate Street, west of the portico. I was on my way to Whitehall — indeed, I should have been there an hour ago, for I had been summoned by Master Williamson, who was not a man to keep waiting.

But how could a man tear himself away from this spectacle? It was beyond imagination, beyond belief.

We were safe enough here at present, as long as we kept our distance. Some of the buildings between us and St Paul's had been demolished in the hope of making a firebreak, which gave us a view up the hill to the cathedral. But I wasn't sure how long

14

we could stay. The heat and the smoke were already searing my lungs and making it hard to breathe.

Though the fire had now leapt the Fleet Ditch to the north and to the south, Fleet Street itself was still clear, at least for the moment, so there was no danger of it cutting off our retreat. The flames were travelling at about thirty yards an hour, much the same rate as they had since the fire started early on Sunday morning. But you could never tell. The wind might change again. Sparks might carry a hundred yards or more and find something else to act as kindling. The fire followed its own logic, not man's.

Streams of molten metal were now oozing between the pillars of the portico and down the steps of the cathedral. It was a thick silver liquid, glinting with gold and orange and all the colours of hell: it was the overflow of the lead pouring from the burning roof to the floor of the nave.

Even the rats were running away. They streaked over the cobbles in waves of fiery fur, for some of them had already caught fire. Others were too old or too frail or too young even to flee, and they were baked alive in the heat. I watched three rats trapped in the silver rain, where they struggled and squealed and shrivelled and died.

Despite the lateness of the hour, despite the pall of smoke that blanketed the city, it was as bright as midday. By this stage — eight or nine o'clock on Tuesday evening — the cathedral glowed from within like an enormous lantern. It dominated its surroundings even in destruction.

I glanced to the left, beyond the woman beside me to the upturned face of the boy. The glare made him look less than human: it drained the life away and reduced him to a sharp but flattened representation, like a head stamped on a coin.

There was always a fascination about a fire, but this one elbowed aside all the others. I had been watching the city burn since Sunday morning. I had known London for as long as I had known anything. In a sense I was seeing my own history going up in smoke.

To my surprise, it was oddly exhilarating. Part of me was enjoying the spectacle. Another part thought: And now everything must change.

No one had really believed that the flames would reach the cathedral. St Paul's was commonly held to be impregnable. Squatting on its hill, it towered over the City and suburbs as it had for centuries. It was huge — nearly six hundred feet long. The spire had fallen in the old Queen's time, and it had never been replaced. The tower remained, however, and even the body of the church, from the new portico in the west to the pinnacled choir in the east, was more than a hundred feet above the ground. The walls were so massive that nothing could penetrate them.

Besides, everyone said that the Divine Hand was protecting St Paul's, for the fire had had ample opportunity to attack it. Its school, just to the east, had already been consumed, along with its great libraries; I had spent much of my youth there, and I did not much mourn its loss. But, until this evening, the flames had swirled around the church itself, leaving it untouched. St Paul's, they said, had always been more than a church, more than a cathedral: it stood for London itself. It was the soul of the city. It was invulnerable.

I was wearing my second-best cloak, which I had taken the precaution of soaking in the Thames before coming here. I had learned the hard way that any protection from the heat and the fumes was better than none, and a cloak could hardly make me hotter than I already was.

An almighty roar burst from within the building. A gout of fire gushed upwards above the choir. Flames spurted through the window openings. Hot air surged towards the watching people. The crowd fell back.

'Oh dear God,' the boy said in a high, agonized voice. 'The crypt's gone up.'

One of the men in front threw down his hat and stamped on it. He flung out his arms and howled. His friends tried to restrain him. It was Maycock, the printer.

It's an ill wind, I thought. At least that will please Master Williamson.

Maycock and many of his fellows had stored their more valuable books, papers and cases of type in the crypt of the cathedral, St Faith's, which served as their parish church. They had left nothing to chance: they had barred the doors with locks and bolts; they stopped up every opening that might possibly admit a spark or a draught. Even if the church tumbled about their heads, they thought, their books in St Faith's would be safe below ground for all eternity.

But they and everyone else had reckoned without the strong, capricious wind. It had set fire to goods in the churchyard. It had blown sparks from there, and from burning buildings nearby, onto the roof of the choir. The roof had been under repair for months

— so exposed timbers covered places where the lead had been damaged, and these had been baked by the bone-dry summer. The sparks danced towards them, and in that hot air it was not long before the first flames appeared.

The wind fanned the flames, which ignited the network of beams supporting the roof. Seasoned oak burned almost as hot as sea coal. The heat had ruptured the vault beneath and the great stones had tumbled down into the choir and the nave. The inside of the building had been full of wooden scaffolding, which had acted as kindling. In a matter of minutes, the whole interior was alight.

Somehow the fire had reached the crypt. The rain of falling stones from the vault must have punctured the floor of the choir. The books and paper stored below in St Faith's had exploded in a gush of flame.

Already the temperature where we were standing was increasing.

The woman beside me stirred. 'Pray God no one's in there still.' Her voice was so close to my ear that I felt her breath on my skin.

It was surely impossible to survive the heat inside the cathedral. It was bad enough out here, and it was getting worse. Anyone inside must be dead or dying, like the rats.

Maycock the printer collapsed. His friends seized his limbs and dragged him away. Their going left the boy, the woman and me in the front rank of the crowd.

'Look! Look — the roof!'

She flung out her arm and pointed. Her face glowed as if she had seen a vision of eternity. I followed the line of her finger. From where we were standing, we could see the south-west corner of the cathedral, where the little church of St Gregory nestled against the nave.

The roof fell in with a rumble that was audible above the crackle of the fire. There was a high, wordless cry.

The boy broke away from the crowd and ran towards St Paul's.

I shouted at him to stop. The fire swallowed the sound. I swore and went after him. The heat battered me. I smelled singeing hair and charred flesh. My lungs were on fire.

The boy had his arms outstretched — towards the cathedral? Towards something or someone inside?

My legs were longer than his. After twenty or thirty yards, I seized his shoulder and spun him round, knocking his hat off. I wrapped my right arm around him and dragged him backwards.

He struggled. I tightened my grip. He hacked at my shins. I cuffed him hard about the head, which quieted him for a moment.

Sparks showered over us, driven by the savage wind that was driving the fire itself. Both of us were coughing. A sliver of flame danced on the front of the boy's shirt. I swatted it with my hand, but another appeared on the loose sleeve. At last he woke to the danger he was in and cried out. I tore off my cloak and wrapped his thin body in it to smother the flames.

The crowd parted as I dragged him away from the heat. I pulled him into the partial shelter of a mounting block outside a shuttered tavern on the City side of Ludgate. I slapped his face, first one cheek and then the other.

He opened his eyes. He brushed the cloak away and bared his teeth like an angry cat.

'God's blood,' I said. 'You little fool. You could have killed us both.'

The boy scrambled up and peered towards St Paul's.

'There's nothing you can do,' I said, shouting to make myself heard above the roar of the fire and the crashes from the disintegrating building. 'Nothing any of us can do.'

He fell back against the mounting block. His eyes were closed. Maybe he had fainted again. I peeled the cloak away and sat him on the step. The shirt was no longer smouldering, though the neck was ripped.

The boy was still coughing, but less violently than before. Even here, some way from the fire, it was as bright as midday, albeit the sort of flickering, orange brightness you would expect when Armageddon was raging and the end of the world was nigh.

For the first time, I saw him clearly. I saw a black smudge of soot or dirt on the thin neck. I saw the gaping shirt and the hollow below the collarbones. I saw the sheen of sweat on his chest, coloured by the fiery glow in the air.

And I saw two perfectly rounded breasts.

I blinked. St Paul's burned, the crowd jostled and the air was full of sounds of explosions, roaring flames and collapsing buildings. But in that moment all I saw was the boy.

The boy?

I pulled aside the neck of the shirt.

No, this wasn't a boy. It wasn't a girl, either. From the waist up at least, it was a young woman.

Her eyes were open and staring into mine.

I let the shirt drop. She stood up. The top of her head was below my shoulder. She snatched up my cloak to protect her modesty. Despite the crowd we might have been alone, for everyone was looking towards St Paul's.

'What are you doing?' she said.

She didn't sound like a beggar or a woman of the streets. She sounded like the lady of the house addressing her maid. A lady who wasn't in a good temper, and a maid who had committed some gross error.

'What do you think?' I said. 'Saving your life.'

As if to prove my point, there was a sharp crack from the cathedral and a fragment of the portico's pediment fell with a crash that shook the ground. The blocks of stone fragmented into a cloud of rubble and dust.

'Where are you from?' I said. 'Who are you? And why are you —'

She began to move away.

'Stop — that's my cloak.'

I lunged at her hand and pulled her back. She raised my hand towards her lips. For one mad moment I thought she was about to kiss it. An expression of gratitude for saving her life.

I glimpsed the whiteness of her teeth. She bit the back of my hand, just behind the lowest knuckle of the forefinger. The teeth dug deep and jarred against tendon and bone.

I screamed and released her.

She ran through the crowd on Ludgate Hill with my cloak floating about her shoulders. I stood there, watching her and nursing my hand. I was desperately thirsty. My head ached.

During the Fire, I saw much that seemed against custom and nature, against reason and Divine ordinance, much that seemed to foreshadow still greater disasters yet to come. *Monstra,* as the scholars called such things, meaning wonders or prodigies or evil omens. The destruction of St Paul's was one of them.

But when I fell asleep that night, I did not dream of flames and falling buildings. I dreamed of the boy–woman's face and the wide-open, unfocused eyes.

CHAPTER TWO

Ashes and blood. Night after night.

I was thinking of ashes and blood when I woke from a fitful sleep on the morning after the Fire reached St Paul's. I knew by the light that it was early, not long after dawn.

Not the hot ashes of the city last night. Not the blood from my hand, after the boy–girl had bitten me.

This blood had been dripping from a head. As for the ashes, they had been cold. A weeping man had rubbed them into his hair.

All this had given me nightmares when I was child, and for months I used to wake screaming, night after night. My mother, usually the mildest and most obedient of wives, had berated my father for allowing her son to see such things.

'Will they do it to me one day?' I had

asked my mother. Night after night.

Now, on a summer morning years later, I
heard a ripple of song from a blackbird. The
bed creaked as my father shifted his weight.

'James?' he said in the thin, dry voice of
his old age. These days he slept badly and
rose early, complaining of bad dreams.
'James? Are you awake yet? Why's it so hot?
Let's walk in the garden. It will be cooler
there.'

Even here, on the outskirts of Chelsea, the
sky was grey with ash, the rising sun reduced
to a smear of orange. The air was already
warm. It smelled of cinders.

After I had dressed, I removed the bandage from my left hand. The bleeding had
stopped but the wound throbbed painfully.
I rewrapped the bandage and helped my
father down the narrow stairs, hoping we
would not wake the Ralstons.

We walked in the orchard, with my father
leaning on my right arm. The trees were
heavy with fruit — apples, pears and plums
mainly, but also damsons, walnuts and a
medlar. The dew was still on the grass.

My father shuffled along. 'Why is it so
black?'

'It's the Fire, sir. All the smoke.'

Frowning, he turned his face up to the sky. 'But it's snowing.'

The wind had moderated a little overnight and had shifted from the east to the south. The air was full of dark flakes, fluttering and turning like drunken dancers.

'Black snow,' he said and, though the morning was already so warm, he shivered.

'You grow fanciful, sir.'

'It's the end of the world, James. I told you it would be so. It is the wickedness of the court that has brought this upon us. It is written, and it must happen. This year is sixteen hundred and sixty-six. It is a sign.'

'Hush, Father.' I glanced over my shoulder. Even here, such talk was dangerous as well as foolish, especially for a man like my father whose liberty hung by a thread. 'It isn't snow. It's only paper.'

'Paper? Nonsense. Paper is white. Paper doesn't fall from the air.'

'It's been burned. The stationers stored their paper and many of their books in the crypt at St Paul's. But the Fire found a way to it, and now the wind brings these fragments even here.'

'Snow,' the old man muttered. 'Black snow. It's another sign.'

'Paper, sir. Not snow.' I heard the exasperation in my voice and wished I had said

27

nothing. I sensed rather than saw the dismay in my father's face, for signs of anger or irritation upset the old man, sometimes to the point of tears. I went on in a gentler voice, 'Let me show you.'

I stooped and picked up a fragment of charred paper, the corner of a page with a few printed words still visible on the scorched surface. I handed it to him.

'See? Paper. Not snow.'

My father took the paper and held it close to his eyes. His lips moved without sound. Even now he could read the smallest print by the dimmest rushlight.

'What did I tell you?' he said. 'The end of the world. It's another sign. Read it.'

He held out the fragment to me. The paper had come from the bottom of a page, at the right-hand corner. There were five words visible on it, taken from the ends of two lines on the page:

. . . Time is
. . . it is done.

'Well?' He stretched out his arms to the black flakes swirling in the dark sky. 'Am I not right, James? The end of the world is nigh, and Jesus will return to reign in majesty over us all. Are you prepared to face your God at His judgement seat?'

'Yes, Father,' I said.

Since May, my father and I had lodged in a cottage within the fenced enclosure of a market garden. We shared the house with the gardener, his wife and their maid. On fine days, the old man sat in the garden and shouted and waved his stick at marauding birds and small boys.

Mistress Ralston, the gardener's wife, was willing enough to take our money, and I made sure that our rent was paid on the nail. She complained about the extra work, though the maid did most of it, and she did not like having my father about the place during the day. She put up with us for the money. Of course, she said, if Master Marwood's health worsened, that might be another matter. She and Master Ralston could not be expected to nurse the sick.

I had chosen this place when my father was released on my surety, and for three reasons. The country air was healthier. The lodgings were cheap. And, most importantly, the garden was remote enough from London to reduce to insignificance the possibility that someone would recognize him; yet it was not too far for me to go daily to and from London.

My father was a marked man. When the King had been restored, six years earlier, Parliament had passed an Act of Indemnity, which pardoned all who had fought against the Crown in the late insurrection. The only people excepted from this blanket pardon were the Regicides, those who had been directly instrumental in the execution of the King's father at Whitehall.

My father was covered by the Act, for he had not been named as a Regicide. But he had thrown away the King's clemency after the Restoration, and by his own choice, and now we suffered the consequences. I loved my father, but sometimes I hated him too.

My mother had hoped I would have a different life. It was she who had cajoled my father into enrolling me at St Paul's School. She had dreamed that I might become a preacher or a lawyer, a man who worked with his mind and not his hands. But she had died a few years later. My father, whose business was declining, withdrew me from the school and bound me to him as his apprentice. Then came his last act of folly, after the Restoration, and he and I were entirely ruined.

After breakfast, I told him I must go to Whitehall.

'Ah, Whitehall,' the old man said, his face

brightening. 'Where they killed the man of blood. Do you remember?'

'Hush, sir. For God's sake, hush.'

But I did not go to Whitehall. Not at first.

I had intended to walk there, but the road to Westminster, Whitehall and the City was choked with Londoners fleeing on foot and horseback, in coaches and wagons. With them they carried the elderly and sick; some of the latter showed signs of the plague, which still lingered in the town.

Others were encamped in fields and orchards along the roadside, erecting makeshift tents and shelters or merely sitting and weeping or staring vacantly towards the smoke of the Fire. Shock had made them numb.

It would take me at least an extra hour, I calculated, to fight against the current of people and walk towards London. So I went down to the water and hailed a pair of oars to take me downriver. It was an expense I could ill afford but a necessary one.

The Fire had been good to the watermen, for everyone wanted a craft of any sort to take them and their possessions to safety. They would pay the most inflated fares without a moment's argument. Overladen craft, large and small, wallowed in the water.

The Thames, even this far west, was as busy as Cheapside had been until the Fire had reached it.

But, as with the road, the traffic tended to be away from London. I haggled with the boatman, reasoning that he would prefer to have a boat with a fare in it than one that was empty when he returned to collect more refugees and their possessions.

We made good speed, with both the current and the tide on our side. The Thames was as grey as dirty pewter and littered with charred debris and discarded possessions, particularly furniture. I saw a handsome table, floating downstream, its legs in the air with a gull perched on one of them.

As we neared Whitehall Stairs, I told the waterman not to pull in but to continue downstream as far as St Paul's. I had a curiosity to see what was left of it. Part of me wondered if the boy–girl would return there, too. Something had drawn her toward the cathedral as the rats were fleeing from it, something so powerful that she had ignored the Fire.

From the river, London was a horrifying sight. Above the town hung a great pall of smoke and ash. Beneath it, the air glowed a deep and sultry red. The sun could not break through, and the city was bathed in unnatural twilight.

From Ludgate to the Tower there seemed nothing left but smouldering devastation. The close-packed houses, built mainly of wood, had melted away, leaving only fragments of blackened stone and brickwork. Even here on the water, with a stiff breeze blowing up the Thames, we felt the heat pulsing from the ruins.

Every now and then the dull crump of an explosion boomed across the water. On the King's orders, they were blowing up buildings in the path of the flames in the hope of creating firebreaks. There was an explosion somewhere between Fleet Street and the river.

The waterman covered his ears and swore.

'We can't pull in, master,' the waterman said, coughing. 'God save us, you'll fry if you go ashore.'

A shower of cinders passed us, some clinging to my sleeve. I brushed them frantically away. 'What about downstream?'

'It's the same all the way down — and hotter than ever — they say it's the oil burning in the warehouses.'

Without waiting for my order, he pulled away from the north bank and rowed us out to midstream. I stared at St Paul's. It was still standing, but the roof had gone, and both walls and tower had a jagged, shimmering quality, like outlines seen under flowing water. Columns of smoke rose from still-burning fires within the blackened shell. It wasn't a church any more. It was more like a giant coal in an oven.

It was impossible that the boy–girl could be within twenty yards of it or more. No living creature could survive that heat.

'Whitehall,' I said.

CHAPTER THREE

The palace of Whitehall sprawled along the river to the south of Charing Cross. It was a warren of buildings, old and new, covering more than twenty acres. It had a population larger than that of most villages.

There was no panic here, but there were signs of unusual activity. In the Great Court, workmen were loading wagons with goods, which would be removed to the safety of Windsor if the Fire spread further west.

I enquired after my patron, and learned that he was in his private office in Scotland Yard, an adjacent complex of buildings which lay on the northern side of the palace. Master Williamson also worked in far grander lodgings overlooking the Privy Garden; but when his business was shabby and private he walked across to Scotland Yard and conducted it in the appropriate surroundings.

Williamson was engaged, so I was forced to kick my heels in the outer office used by clerks and messengers. One of the clerks was making a fair copy of a report on the Fire for the *London Gazette*. Among his other responsibilities, Williamson edited the newspaper and ensured that its contents were as agreeable as possible to the government.

He himself ushered out his visitor, a portly, middle-aged gentleman with a wart on the left-hand side of his chin. The stranger's eyes lingered on me for a moment as he passed by.

Williamson, still wreathed in smiles, beckoned me. 'At last,' he said, the good humour dropping like a falling curtain from his face. 'Why didn't you wait on me yesterday evening?'

'I'm sorry, sir. The Fire delayed me and —'

'Nevertheless, you should have come. And why the devil are you so late this morning?'

Williamson's Cumbrian accent had become more pronounced. Though he had lived in the south, and among gentlemen in the main, for nearly twenty years, his native vowels broadened when he was irritated or under pressure.

'The refugees blocked the road, sir.'

36

'Then you should have started earlier. I needed you here.' He waved at the clerk who was working on the report for the *Gazette*. 'That idiot cannot write a fair hand.'

'Your pardon, sir.'

'You've not been in my employ for long, Marwood,' he went on. 'Don't keep me waiting again, or you will find that I shall contrive to manage without you.'

I bowed and kept silent. Without Williamson's patronage I would have nothing. And my father would have worse than nothing. Williamson was under-secretary to Lord Arlington, the Secretary of State for the South, and his influence spread throughout the government and far beyond. As for me, I was the least important of Williamson's clerks, little more than his errand boy.

'Come in here.'

He led the way into his private office. He said nothing more until I had shut the door.

'Did you go to St Paul's last night as I commanded?'

'Yes, sir. I was there when the crypt went up. The cathedral was beyond rescue within an hour, even if they could have got water to it. The heat was terrible. By the time I left, molten lead was trickling down Ludgate Hill.'

'Was anyone inside?'

I thought of the boy–girl running towards the building when the Fire was at its hottest. I said, 'Not as far as I know, sir. Even the rats were running away.'

'And what were the people in the crowd saying?'

'About the cause of the Fire?'

'In particular about the destruction of the cathedral. They say it has angered the King as much as anything these last few days, even the damned Dutch.'

I swallowed. 'They attribute it to one of two things, sometimes both. The —'

'Don't talk in riddles.'

'I mean, sir, that they say the two causes may be linked. For some say God is showing his displeasure at the wickedness of the court' — better not to blame our profligate and Papist-leaning King in person, for walls had ears, especially in Whitehall — 'while others attribute the Fire to the malignancy of our enemies. To the Pope or the French or the Dutch.'

'It won't do,' Williamson said sharply. 'Do you hear me? The King says it was an accident, pure and simple. The hot, dry summer. The buildings huddled together and dry as kindling. The east wind. An unlucky spark.'

I said nothing, though I thought the King was probably right.

'Any other explanation must be discouraged.'

The King's ministers, I thought, were between a rock and a hard place. Either they had merited God's displeasure through their wickedness or they were so ineffectual that they could not prevent the country's enemies from striking such a mortal blow at the heart of the kingdom. Either way, the people would blame the Fire on them and on the King and his court. Either way, the panic and disaffection would spread. Better to change the subject.

'Master Maycock, sir, the printer,' I said. 'I saw him yesterday evening at St Paul's. He was like a man possessed — he had his goods stored in the crypt, and they went up with the rest in the Fire.'

Williamson almost smiled. 'How very distressing.'

There were only two licensed newspapers in the country, for the government permitted no others. Maycock was responsible for printing *Current Intelligence*, which was the upstart rival to the *London Gazette*, the newspaper that Master Williamson ran.

'If only Maycock had done as Newcomb did, and moved his goods out of the City,'

Williamson said with a touch of smugness. Newcomb was Williamson's printer.

'Newcomb's lost his house, though,' I said. 'It was by Baynard's Castle, and that's gone.'

'I know,' Williamson said in his flat, hard voice. 'I already have it in hand. I have in mind some premises in the Savoy for him, if all goes well. If God wills it, the next *Gazette* will be Monday's. We shall lose an issue but at least that means we shall not be able to publish the City's Bill of Mortality this week. People will understand that — there's more important work to do than waste time compiling lists of figures. Besides, I'm told that the death count has been remarkably low. God be thanked.'

I understood Williamson perfectly, or rather I understood what he did not say. There might well have been dozens of deaths, perhaps hundreds, in the areas where the unrecorded poor huddled together near the river, near the warehouses of oil and pitch that burned as hot as hellfire. The Fire had broken out there early on Sunday morning, when half of them would have been in a drunken stupor. Others had died, or would die, from the delayed effects of the Fire — because they were already ill, or old, or very young, and the distress of fleeing from their homes would destroy them.

But it would not serve the King and government to worsen the sense of catastrophe unnecessarily. The *London Gazette* was usually published twice a week. The missing issue would cloak the absence of a Bill of Mortality for the week of the Fire. In the circumstances, its absence would be unremarkable. The Letter Office — another of Williamson's responsibilities — had also been destroyed, so even if the *Gazette* could have been printed, it could not have been distributed through the country.

'A terrible accident,' Williamson said. 'That's what you say if you hear anyone talking about it. We must make sure nothing in the *Gazette* or its correspondence suggests otherwise.' He brought his head close to mine. 'You're sharp enough, Marwood, I give you that. But if you keep me waiting again, I'll make sure you and your father go back to your dunghill.'

As if to lend emphasis to his words, a distant explosion shook the window in its frame.

'Go back to work,' he said.

CHAPTER FOUR

Cat drew the grey cloak over her head. The fine wool smelled of the fire, but also something unpleasantly musky and masculine. The face of the thin young man whose cloak she had stolen was vivid in her mind, his skin almost orange in the light of the flames.

She was still breathing hard from running through the streets, from pushing her way through the crowds. She had looked back often as she fled, and sometimes she was sure she glimpsed his face. But, thanks be to God, he wasn't there any more.

She crouched and tapped on the window shutter.

Three taps. Then a pause. Three more taps.

Light flickered in the crack behind the shutter. The window was no more than eighteen inches wide, and not much taller. The sill was barely six inches above the cobbles. The ground level had crept higher and higher over the centuries.

Something flickered in the crack of light. Three answering taps. Then a pause. Three more taps.

She moved deeper into the alley. It wasn't dark — even here, beyond the walls. The Doomsday glow filled the narrow space with a murky orange fog that caught at the back of her throat and made her want to retch.

No one had taken refuge here yet. No one human. The mouth of the alley was concealed by an encroaching extension from the shop on the other side of it. Unless you knew it was there, you wouldn't see it.

But the rats had known where the alley was. They were fleeing the burning city in their hundreds of thousands. She felt movement around her feet and heard a distant squealing.

The ground was paved with uneven flags, which were covered with cinders, scraps of paper and charred fragments of wood and cloth that crunched like black gravel beneath her shoes.

At the end of the alley was a pointed archway recessed in the wall, the stone frame for an oak door studded with nails. She had seen it by daylight: the wood had blackened with age and was as hard as a stone wall.

In the distance came the sound of three explosions. They were blowing up more of the houses in the path of the fire.

There came a faint scraping sound from the other side of the door. Then silence. Then another scrape. No lock, thank God. Only two iron bars, as thick as a man's arm.

The door swung inwards. A crack of light appeared on the other side, widening with the opening door. She slipped through the gap. Immediately she turned, closed the door and dropped the latch in place.

'Mistress . . .' The whisper was a hiss of air, barely audible.

'The bars, Jem.' Cat's eyes hadn't adjusted to the gloom yet. 'Quickly.'

The flame wavered behind the grille of the closed lantern as he placed it on the floor. Shadows fragmented and glided over the wall. The air was foul, for the cesspit of the house on the other side of the alley had leached through the foundations of the wall.

Jem scuttled to the door. Iron grated on stone. He had rubbed grease on the bars to make them move easily and as quietly as possible. She watched, clutching the grey cloak about her throat.

When the door was doubly barred, he turned to face her. She heard his breath, wheezier than usual perhaps because of the smoke. Sometimes his wheezing grew so bad that they thought he would die of it. 'Scratch me, I wish he would,' Cousin Edward had said last winter. 'It's like listening to a death rattle.'

'Mistress, what happened?'

She brushed aside the question with one of her own: 'Where are they?'

'Madam's retired. Master's in the study. Master Edward's not back yet. The dogs are loose.'

If the dogs were in the house, then the servants had gone to bed too, all but the watchman and the porter.

Jem bent down for the lantern. As he picked it up, the shadows merged and swooped to the vaulted ceiling, sliding over stone ribs and bosses.

Now she was safe, or as safe as she could be for the time being, Cat was aware that she too was breathing raggedly, and that she was drenched with sweat. It was hot even in here.

He lowered his voice still further. The flame flickered as he mouthed the words, 'Did you find him, mistress?'

Tears filled her eyes. She bit her lower lip, drawing blood. 'No. And St Paul's is lost. I

45

saw part of the portico fall and crumble into dust.'

'If Master Lovett was there, he will have escaped.'

'We must pray he did.' Her words were pious, but her feelings were more complicated. Was it possible to love her father and fear him at the same time? She owed him her devotion and her duty. But did he not owe her something as well? She wondered why Jem cared for him, the man who had once beaten him so hard that it caused the lameness in his leg.

'Remember, I cannot be sure it was him I saw this morning.' Jem brought the light closer to her. 'Your clothes, mistress. What happened?'

'It doesn't matter. Light me upstairs.'

The house was built mainly of stone and brick — a blessing in these times, Master Alderley had said at dinner, though he also urged his family to mark that God tempered the wind to those who took thought for the morrow — and it lay at a safe distance beyond the City wall near Hatton Garden. The place had belonged to the monks in the old days and it had been much altered since then. It was old and rambling, with stairs that spiralled to chambers that were long gone and to great vaulted cellars half-full of rubble.

Jem led the way, holding the lantern high. They mounted a flight of steps and passed through another door.

Claws clattered on stone. The mastiffs met them in the passage. One by one, they pushed their moist muzzles at Cat. They pressed against her, sniffing and licking her outstretched hand, eager for her familiar touch. By day the dogs lived in a special enclosure in the yard, and by night they patrolled the house, yard and the garden.

'Thunder,' she whispered into the darkness, 'Lion, Greedy and Bare-Arse.'

The dogs whined softly with pleasure. Cat drew a deep breath. Now the worst was over, she began to tremble. It was unlikely she would be discovered now. For most of the time, the nightwatchman stayed at the other end of the house, away from the kitchens and close to the study and the cellar that Master Alderley had adapted to be his strong room. The dogs would warn them if he was about, and his lantern and his footsteps came before him when he patrolled the other parts of the building. As for the porter, he slept in the hall, on a mattress laid across the threshold of the front door. He would not move from there until Edward returned.

The passage led to the kitchen wing. They crossed a narrow hall with a row of small, shuttered windows, descended a few steps and turned sharply to their right. Then came a spiral staircase that climbed through the thickness of the wall, lit only by the occasional unglazed openings that gave glimpses of the sullen glow above the burning city. These stairs smelled strongly of the stink of the Fire, unlike the lower regions of the house. They taxed Jem's strength, for he was short of breath as well as lame.

Cat's chamber was a small room facing north towards the hills of Highgate. The heavy curtains were drawn across the window, blocking the glare of the Fire, which was visible even on this side of the house.

Jem lit her candle from the flame in the lantern.

'Why has my father come back?' she said.

'He does not confide in me, mistress.'

'They will kill him if they find them. He must know that.'

He bobbed his head in acknowledgement. She wondered if he knew more than he was saying.

'Thank you,' she said. 'Good night.'

Jem lingered, his face unreadable in the gloom. 'They say in the kitchen that Sir Denzil will dine here tomorrow.'

She bit hard on her lip. This on top of everything. 'Is it certain?'

'Yes. Unless the Fire prevents it.'

'Go,' she said. 'Leave me.'

He turned and hobbled from the room.

Once the door was closed, and she was quite alone at last, she could allow herself to cry.

CHAPTER FIVE

It was a mark of Sir Denzil's importance that Aunt Olivia sent Ann to help Cat dress for dinner. Cat did not have her own maid to attend her, a fact that underlined her anomalous status in the household.

Ann, Aunt Olivia's own maid, spent what seemed like hours working on Cat's appearance. Most importantly, she wound a bandage beneath Cat's breasts with padding set in it in order to create the impression that Cat had far more of a bosom than God had at present seen fit to provide. Cat was already a woman — she would be eighteen next birthday — but sometimes it seemed to her that she and Aunt Olivia were different creatures from one another.

The maid worked in silence, frowning constantly, and tugging at laces and bandages as if Cat were an inanimate object incapable of feeling pain and discomfort. Afterwards, she showed Cat her reflection in Aunt Olivia's Venetian mirror. Cat saw a richly dressed doll with slanting eyes and elaborately curled hair.

Ann brought her down to the best parlour. She left Cat stuffed and trussed like a goose for the oven, to wait on the pleasure of Uncle Alderley and Sir Denzil Croughton.

The parlour smelled of fresh herbs with a hint of damp. The dark wood of the floor and the furniture had been waxed to a dull sheen. A Turkey carpet glowed on the table underneath the windows. There was a small fire of logs, despite the unnatural warmth of the season, for the room was chilly even in summer.

She stood by the table and idly turned the pages of a book of airs that lay there, though she could not have sung a note to save her life.

Her mind was elsewhere, wondering whether she could slip outside again tonight, with Jem's help, and how it might be contrived.

She heard steps on the flags outside the door and shivered with distaste. Her hand froze in the act of turning a page. She knew who was there even before she turned: she would have recognized that slow, heavy step in the middle of a crowd.

'Catherine, my love,' said Cousin Edward.

The Alderleys never called her Cat.

She turned reluctantly and gave him the curtsy that good manners required.

He bowed in return, but with an element of mockery. 'Well! You are quite the court beauty today.' He sucked in his breath to show his appreciation and walked slowly towards her, watching her face. 'How you have grown!' He moved his hands, sketching an exaggerated version of her shape. 'A miracle! Scratch me, my dear, I think this must be the effect of Sir Denzil. The power of his charms is acting on you from afar.'

She closed the book. She said nothing because that was usually wisest with Edward.

'And what are you reading?' He stretched out his hand to the book. 'Ah — studying your music. How delightful. Shall I beg you to sing to the company after dinner? I'm sure Sir Denzil would be enchanted.'

She was tone-deaf, and Edward knew it.

He lowered his head and she smelled the wine on his breath. 'Of course I myself am already enchanted without the need of song.'

Cat edged away from him. He followed her, penning her close to the table and blocking her retreat. She turned away and affected to stare through the window at the green geometry of the garden and the hot, heavy sky. He was a big man, nearly six foot, and growing fat, for all he was barely five-and-twenty. He looked like a pig, she thought, and had the same voracious appetites. Most of the time he ignored her, which was infinitely better than the times when he baited her instead. Lately, she had been aware of his eyes on her, watching, measuring.

'This miracle.' He moistened his lips. 'This sudden change to your appearance. Why, you are all of a sudden grown so womanly. It is quite remarkable.'

He laid his hand on her shoulder. His touch was warm and slightly moist. He tightened his fingers.

'Skin and bone, sweet cousin,' he said. 'Like a child still. And yet . . . and yet . . .'

She pulled away from him.

He brought his head closer to hers, and again she smelled the wine on his breath. 'I saw you last night.'

Startled, she looked up at his flushed, familiar face.

'Creeping back to the house,' he said. 'You'd been out by yourself, hadn't you, walking the streets like any tuppenny whore. You little Puritans are all the same, primness and virtue on the outside and the filthiest wickedness within. I saw you from the window of the tavern by the gate. Slipping like a thief into the alley. Who let you in? That crippled knave of yours?'

Cat had hated Edward Alderley for some time now. She was a good hater. She hoarded the hatred as a miser hoards his gold.

The latch rattled on the door. Edward snatched away his hand and stepped back. Cat smoothed her dress and turned to the window. She was breathing rapidly and her skin prickled with sweat.

Olivia came into the room. 'Let me look at you, child. Now turn to the side.' She nodded. 'Good. Your colour is much better than usual, too.' She turned to Edward. 'Don't you agree? Ann has worked wonders.'

He bowed. 'Indeed, madam. Why, my cousin is quite the little beauty today.' He smiled at his stepmother. 'No doubt the work was carried out under your guidance.'

Uncle Alderley came in with Sir Denzil.

The ladies curtsied, and Sir Denzil bowed elaborately, first to Olivia and then to Cat. He was a small man with a lofty periwig and unusually high heels to his shoes.

'Ah!' he said in a high, drawling voice, directing his remarks impartially at the space between the two women. 'A feast of beauty!' He turned to Master Alderley and touched his lip with his forefinger, an oddly childlike gesture. He wore a diamond ring on the finger. 'Truly, sir, I am a veritable glutton for beauty.' He looked directly at Cat for the first time and said without marked enthusiasm, 'and soon I shall have the pleasure of eating my fill.'

The ungainly compliment fell like a stone in a pool. There was a moment's silence.

'Well, sir,' Aunt Olivia said to her husband. 'Shall we go in to dinner?'

Power, Cat thought, resides in small things.

If anything confirmed Uncle Alderley's position in the world, it was the fact that, while the City was burning to ashes on his doorstep, he himself was dining at home quite as if nothing were amiss. The food was as good as ever when he entertained a guest he wished to please, and the servants just as attentive. They used the best cutlery, the two-pronged forks and the knives with rounded handles that fitted snugly in the hand; Aunt Olivia had insisted on having them; they had been imported from Paris at absurd expense.

There was a message here for Sir Denzil Croughton, and perhaps for Master Alderley's own family as well: the Fire could not destroy Master Alderley or his wealth; he was, under God and the King, invincible.

They dined as usual at midday. There were five of them at table — Master and Mistress Alderley at either end, Cat and the honoured guest side by side, and Edward sitting opposite them. There were four servants waiting at table. To Cat's surprise, Jem was among them, dressed in an ill-fitting suit of the Alderleys' black-and-yellow livery.

'What's this?' Master Alderley said, as Jem appeared at his shoulder.

'Did I not tell you, sir?' Aunt Olivia said. 'Layne is nowhere to be found, so we must make shift the best we can with Jem.'

'What the devil does Layne think he's about?'

'I'm sure I don't know.'

'I'll have the fellow whipped when he returns.'

'Just as you say, sir.' A good hostess, Olivia noticed that Sir Denzil's nostrils were twitching. 'Would you care to try the carp, sir? I made the sauce myself, and I pride myself on my sauces.'

Sir Denzil looks like a fish himself, Cat thought. Quite possibly a carp.

All the dishes had been prepared in their own kitchen, for Aunt Olivia scorned to send out for food; she was far too good a housekeeper. Besides, few cook shops were still open, and the few that remained were inundated with custom.

In Sir Denzil's honour, there were three courses. To his credit, he responded manfully to the challenge. He dug deep into a fricassee of rabbits and chickens, returned again and again to the carp, ripped chunks from the boiled leg of mutton, and swallowed slice after slice of the side of lamb. The food passed through his mouth so rapidly that he seemed hardly to chew it at all.

'Is that a lamprey pie?' he asked Aunt Olivia in a voice that rose almost to a trill. 'How delightful. Yes, perhaps I will take a little.'

Two pigeons, a dish of anchovies and most of a lobster went the way of everything else. By this time Sir Denzil was slowing down, though he compensated by increasing his consumption of wine, revealing an unusual capacity for canary, of which he must have drunk close to half a gallon. By this stage, his colour was high and there was a certain glassiness in his eye that reminded Cat irresistibly of the carp as it had been when it first arrived in the kitchen.

They drank the health of the King and confusion to his enemies. Prompted delicately by Aunt Olivia, Sir Denzil proposed two toasts, first to his hostess, who smiled graciously and accepted it as her due, and then to Cat, who stared at the table and wished to God she were anywhere else but here.

Sir Denzil crooked his finger at her, and the diamond ring sparkled. 'You see, my dear, I wear your ring. And I shall send you mine as soon as it has been reset.'

This ring, this token of love, was a polite fiction. Cat had understood from Master Alderley that he himself had provided both rings, for Sir Denzil was short of ready money and tradesmen were not enthusiastic about allowing him credit. The rings were designed to be symbols of the betrothal. Master Alderley had sent this one to Sir Denzil only yesterday.

The conversation was mainly of the Fire, of course, and of the King and the court.

'There are grounds for hope,' Sir Denzil informed them, his piping voice muffled by a mouthful of lobster. 'I heard the King himself say so this morning. If the Duke of York can hold the Fire at Temple Bar, then Whitehall is saved.'

Olivia touched her throat. 'Are we safe here?'

'Lord Craven's men have turned back the

flames at Holborn Bridge,' Master Alderley said.

Sir Denzil waved his fork. 'You need not trouble yourself in the slightest, madam.'

'I'm advised that the worst is over,' Master Alderley said. 'Even Bludworth has at last begun to pull down houses. Only in Cripplegate, but it's a start.'

'I fear the Lord Mayor is an old woman, sir,' Edward said.

'Very true, sir,' Sir Denzil said. 'Only a fool would have failed to realize that creating firebreaks was the only way to hold the fire. Bludworth's indecision has cost us half the City.'

'He was afraid he'd be sued by the tenants or the freeholders if he pulled down their houses,' Master Alderley said. 'Or both. It comes down to money. It always does.'

'The City must thank God for the King and the court,' Sir Denzil said. 'Without their cool heads and brave deeds, it would have been far worse. That's the trouble with these aldermen and merchants and so forth. In an emergency, they are no better than children. They cannot even save themselves and their ledgers.'

'That isn't true of all of the aldermen,' Master Alderley said drily. 'Fortunately.'

The change of tone put Sir Denzil in mind of the company he was in. 'Of course, sir. And thank God for it. Now if only you, not Bludworth, had been Lord Mayor, it would have been a very different story, I'm sure.'

'Who would be a Lord Mayor?' Master Alderley said. 'It's a great deal of expense and a man has little return on his investment, as well as much risk. For Bludworth, it will mean ruin.'

'Will you take a few anchovies, sir?' Aunt Olivia said, judging that it was time to change the subject. 'My niece made the sauce according to a French recipe, and I'm sure she would value your opinion.'

Sir Denzil tasted it and nodded. 'Delicious. Did you know, madam, I have a Frenchman in my kitchen now? I hope you will all dine with me soon. I fancy you will not be disappointed. He has cooked for Monsieur d'Orleans, you know, and several gentlemen have tried to steal him since I brought him over from Paris.'

Cat stole a sideways glance at Sir Denzil. A streak of sauce ran down his chin and onto the collar beneath. He dabbed it with his napkin.

Dinner was nearly over, but no word of the business that had brought Sir Denzil here had passed between him and Master

Alderley, apart from the matter of the rings. Cat suspected that the terms of the betrothal between herself and Sir Denzil had not yet been finally agreed, but of course nothing would be discussed at table before the women. But somehow it seemed tacitly accepted that the principle of the thing had been established. She tried to imagine what it would be like to see Sir Denzil consuming food and drink at table every day of their married life. Her imagination baulked.

'You must ask my cousin Catherine to sing to you after dinner,' Edward said, leaning over the table towards Sir Denzil.

'Yes, indeed,' Sir Denzil said, taking up his glass and frowning into it, as if surprised to find it empty again. 'I shall be charmed, I'm sure.'

Jem limped forward to refill the glass.

Edward glanced at Cat, smiling, just for a second. 'One cannot listen to my cousin's voice and be unmoved.'

Olivia said: 'What a pity, Sir Denzil, that the pleasure must be postponed for a little while. Master Alderley tells me that you and he must withdraw after dinner.'

Master Alderley grunted.

Olivia leaned towards Sir Denzil, affording him an agreeable prospect of her breasts. 'And are you considered musical, sir?'

'Indeed I am, madam. All the Croughtons are.' He toyed with a spoonful of apple pie. 'After all, is not music the food of love?' At this point he realized that it was perhaps impolite of him to stare so long and so fixedly at Mistress Alderley's bosom while talking of love. He put the spoonful of pie in his mouth and transferred his gaze to Cat.

'How I long to hear you singing duets,' Edward said. 'It will be quite ravishing.'

When at last dinner was over, Master Alderley withdrew to his study with his guest leaning heavily on his arm and humming 'Drink to Me Only with Thine Eyes'. Edward made his excuses to the ladies and left the house.

'So,' Olivia said as she led Cat into the parlour. 'In a while, you will be Lady Croughton.'

'Must I be, madam?'

'Yes.' Olivia sank gracefully into a chair and took up her embroidery. 'Your uncle has quite made up his mind. Sir Denzil has no money but he has the ear of the King and those about him. But you must not let it worry you. The marriage will not come to pass until the winter. Master Alderley needs a little time to make sense of Sir Denzil's affairs and deal with the settlements. Sir Denzil is not a man to take liberties beforehand, I think.' She smiled in a sly way that brought out her resemblance to a cat. 'And perhaps not even afterwards. The one thing you must do when you are married to Sir Denzil is to feed him well. Take my advice, my dear — a good cook and a well-provided table will save you a world of grief.'

'But I don't want to marry him.'

'You're not so foolish as to long for love? You're far too sensible, child. Love and marriage are two quite different things.'

'I don't want to marry anyone.'

Olivia stabbed the needle into the silk. 'You must do as you're told,' she said. 'You cannot stay here for ever, doing nothing but getting your fingers inky and scratching your meaningless lines on scraps of paper.'

'But they are not meaningless, madam. They are plans — they are designs of buildings that —'

'Fiddle-Fiddle.' Aunt Olivia's temper was rising. 'It is not an occupation for a lady. Besides, your uncle has been very kind to you in making this arrangement. He wants to see you comfortably settled, as you are his poor sister-in-law's only child, and you may be in a position to help him and your cousin once you are married. You should remember that it cannot have been easy for him to manage — after all, Sir Denzil knows who your father is. Everyone does.'

CHAPTER SIX

When Cat was very little, the Lovetts had a dog. He was a nameless animal of no breeding but infinite patience. The dog reminded her of Jem in more ways than one. One of her earliest memories was of toddling in the garden of their house in Bow Lane, hand in hand with Jem, with the dog on the other side of her.

It was difficult to say exactly what Jem did at Barnabas Place. In the old days, he had worked for her father as a confidential clerk and manservant. When their troubles came, her father had sent him with her to her aunt in Champney. Later Jem had escorted her to Uncle Alderley's.

Jem had been old even then, but his breathing had been better and his joints not so rusty. He was not valued at Barnabas Place. He slept in the loft above the stables, along with the man who killed rats, emptied slops and did other unpleasant necessities.

He ate in the back kitchen and did what he was told to do. Apart from board and lodging he did not receive a wage, though Cat occasionally gave him a few pence or even a shilling or two.

'It isn't fair,' Cat once said to him. 'You're always working, always doing something for someone. They should pay you.'

'The master gives nothing for nothing.'

'But you give him something.'

'You don't understand, mistress. I am nothing. To your uncle, I mean. His worship wouldn't miss me if I were not here, so why should he pay me? If he thinks about it at all, he knows I will stay whether I'm paid or not, because he knows I have nowhere to go. He pays nothing for nothing. That's how he's become rich.'

Early in the evening of the day of the dinner, after Sir Denzil Croughton had been assisted to his coach, Cat went in search of Jem. She found him in the little yard behind the washhouse. He wasn't wearing the Alderley livery any more. He was in his ordinary clothes and preparing lye, the mixture of ashes and urine that was used for soaking badly soiled laundry. It was a woman's job usually but the washerwoman had lost the two girls who usually came in to assist her; presumably they and their families were somewhere among the flood of refugees.

The walls of the yard were high, trapping the hot air below the heavy grey sky. The grey was tinged with an orange glow. Even here, the ground was flecked with ashes. Cat watched him at work for a moment before he saw her. He was stirring the mixture in a half-barrel, stooping over his work with the sweat streaking his shirt and running down his arms. His thin grey hair hung limply to his shoulders.

When she called his name, he turned his head. His face was red with heat and exertion, shining with sweat. He stared unsmilingly at her.

Cat wrinkled her nose. 'Come in here. I can't talk to you there.'

She turned and went into the barn. She heard his dragging footsteps behind her. She stopped and faced him.

'How can you bear it?' She spoke at random, for her head was hurting and she found it hard to gather her thoughts. 'The smell. The heat.'

He shrugged, and she realized that for him it was not a question worth answering. 'Is there news of Layne?' he said.

'Not that I've heard. Why?'

'Sometimes I wonder about him, mistress.' He stared at her. 'He likes to know where you are.'

'Layne does? Why in God's name?'

'I don't know. But I've heard him asking your aunt's maid, more than once, and I've seen him watching you. I think he searched my box the other day, though I can't be sure. If he did, he might have found —'

'I can't worry about Layne now,' Cat interrupted. 'I want to go out tonight. I'll need clothes again.'

Jem shook his head.

'An old shirt — a pair of breeches. That's all.'

'No, mistress.'

'But there must be something you can find. There's a chest of rags for the poor, isn't there? You'll find something in there, I'm sure. I have a cloak now — the one I found yesterday.'

'It's too dangerous.'

'That's not for you to decide. Do you need money? Would that make it easier?'

'I won't help you.'

'Why not?'

He looked at her. Their eyes were on a level. 'Because it's not safe.'

'What does it matter?' she said. 'I must see my father. They are going to make me marry Sir Denzil. I'd rather die.'

Jem ignored that. 'I shouldn't have let you go last night,' he said. 'The City is a madhouse on fire.'

She stamped her foot. 'You'll find me clothes. And you'll wait at the door and let me in when I come back.'

'No.'

'I command you.'

'I'm sorry, mistress.'

Cat advanced on him. 'I can't do this without you.'

He stood his ground. 'You won't know where to begin. He can't meet you in St Paul's now.'

'I'll find him. In Bow Lane, perhaps.'

'But there's nothing left in Bow Lane.'

For a moment she grappled with this idea, that the house where she had grown up no longer existed. 'Nearby, then.'

'He could be anywhere, mistress. If he's still alive.'

'Of course he's alive.' She glared at him. 'Can you send word to him?'

'No. He always sends word to me. Safer that way.'

'How?'

Jem shuffled, easing the weight on his lame leg. 'I was told not to tell you.'

She scowled at him. 'My father hasn't seen

69

me for six years. He forgets I'm not a child any more. So do you, but with less reason.'

He stared at her for a long moment. 'There's a man,' he said at last. 'He brings me a letter sometimes, or sometimes just a message. And he takes them from me in return. Yesterday he told me that you should go to St Paul's, that your father would find you there in Paul's Walk.'

'Who is this man? Where can you find him?'

'I don't know, mistress.'

She glared at him. 'You must know something.'

He hesitated and then said slowly, 'He lives somewhere near Cursitor Street. I think he might be a tailor. I saw him sometimes in the old days.'

'Then I shall go there and look for him. If my father isn't with him, then perhaps he will know where he is.'

'I won't let you,' Jem said. 'It would be folly. Let me see if I can find him. Better still, be patient until he sends word.'

'No. I shall go. You must help me.'

Jem shook his head. 'It's too dangerous. If they find your father in London, they will put him on trial for treason. And anyone they find helping him.'

She raised her hand to slap his face.

Slowly she lowered it. 'Why are you being so obstinate, old man? One word from me, and they will turn you out on the street.'

'Then say it,' he said. 'The one word.'

The long evening drew at last to a close.

Uncle Alderley and Cousin Edward had been into the City and then as far west as Whitehall. At supper, they were full of what they had seen. The Fire was diminishing, though it was still burning steadily and there was always the danger it would reach the great powder magazine in the Tower, particularly if the wind veered again. The great exodus from the City had continued. Perhaps seventy or eighty thousand people had fled. They were flooding into the unburned suburbs, to Houndsditch and the Charterhouse, to West Smithfield and Clerkenwell, and even to Hatton Garden, where they were lapping around the walls of Barnabas Place itself.

'They are like people in a melancholy dream,' Master Alderley said. 'They simply cannot understand what has happened.'

The refugees camped wherever they could. The park at Moorfields was packed with them — more than twenty acres of ground covered with a weeping, moaning, sleeping mass of humanity. Some had gone over the river and set up camp in St George's Fields, where the ground was marshy even in this sweltering summer, and evil humours rose from the ground at night. Others — the more active or the more terrified — had gone further still, to the hills of Islington.

'God knows where it will end,' Master Alderley said. 'Once people leave the City, why should they come back?'

Alarm flared in Olivia's face. 'But what shall we do, sir?'

'You need not worry, my dear. They will always need money wherever they go. I have taken precautions. So we shall do very well, whatever they do with London's ashes.'

She leaned over the table and patted his hand. 'You are so wise, sir.'

Master Alderley withdrew his hand at once, for public displays of feeling disturbed him; but he was not displeased with this show of wifely admiration.

'Is Layne back?' he demanded.

'No, sir.'

'Then we shall have to turn him off. I know you brought Layne into the household, but I cannot have a servant who will not attend to his duty.'

'It may not be his fault. Perhaps the Fire has delayed him. Perhaps he has had an accident.'

Master Alderley frowned. 'We shall see. In the meantime, we must find another man to wait at table. I don't wish to have that cripple again.'

'No, sir. Of course not.'

'We saw Sir Denzil,' Edward said in a moment. 'He was attending the Duke of York.' He turned to Cat, which meant that his father and his stepmother could not see his expression. 'He and I drank to your betrothal, cousin, and to the speedy arrival of an heir to Croughton Hall.'

'That would suit us all very well,' Master Alderley said. He gave Cat a rare smile. 'We shall have you wedded by Christmas and brought to bed of a fine boy by Michaelmas next year.'

'So be sure to cultivate this French cook of his, cousin,' Edward murmured, too low for his father to hear. 'French cooks are always men of infinite subtlety and resource. I am sure Sir Denzil's will know how to set his master on fire for you.'

After supper, Olivia took Cat up to her own bedchamber to discuss the wedding, its location, who should be invited, and what she and Cat should wear.

Ann came to undress her mistress while they talked. Olivia sat at her dressing table wearing a bedgown of blue silk trimmed with lace, with four candles reflected in the mirror and throwing their murky light on her face. The warm air was heavy with perfume.

The subject was of absorbing interest to Olivia, and the discussion — the first of many, no doubt, she said with a smile — went on for longer than Cat would have believed possible.

Cat's eyes strayed to the great bed that stood in the shadows, surmounted by a canopy. She imagined Uncle Alderley — so staid, so old, so disgusting — heaving and twisting and grunting there. The thought of it, together with the perfume and the suffocating sense of femininity that seemed to fill the room, made her feel ill.

Olivia did not belong with Uncle Alderley. She could not enjoy his attentions, Cat thought, though in public she behaved with impeccable obedience towards her husband. But Cat had heard their raised voices through closed doors.

Was this what marriage meant? This unnatural union? This heaving and twisting and grunting? A public show of devotion concealing private quarrels and secret lusts?

Ann left the room to fetch hot water.

'Well?' Aunt Alderley said. 'Is it not exciting? You have so much to look forward to. They say Croughton Hall is very fine.'

Cat sat forward in her chair so she could see the reflection of her aunt's face wavering in the mirror. 'Madam,' she said, 'I don't want to be married to Sir Denzil. I mean it. Is there no way — ?'

'But, child, you must let those older and wiser guide you.'

'He doesn't please me.'

'So you've said. But it's nonsense, my dear. Liking will come later, if God wills it, as it does in most marriages. You must not concern yourself about it now. Remember, he has everything to recommend him, including the fact that your uncle is in favour of the match.'

'But he's so —'

Aunt Alderley shook her head. 'Not a word more, my dear. You're overtired, and this makes you say foolish things. Besides, this horrible Fire has upset us all.'

There was a tap on the door, and Ann entered with a jug of steaming water.

'We'll discuss the question of jewellery later,' her aunt said in a brisk voice. 'But now, my love, you must go to bed. You have great circles under your eyes. Shall Ann come with you and undress you?'

'No, madam. But thank you.'

When she was released, Cat climbed the stairs to the floor above the main bed-chambers, candle in hand. She had walked this way so often that she could have done it in the dark.

Every now and then she passed a window that gave glimpses of London glowing like a bed of coals in the night. It seemed to her that the fire was less bright than it had been, as if its fury were gradually dying. Occasionally there were muffled explosions. The work of demolition continued.

For an instant, a vision of a new London rose in her mind, growing from this bed of coals: a town of great piazzas and avenues, of lofty churches, and of fine buildings of brick and stone. She would get out her drawing box and her papers when she was safely in her room. She would map an outline of this new and glorious city. The box had been a gift from her other aunt, Great Aunt Eyre; it reminded her of a time when she had been happy.

Cat raised the latch on her door and entered the chamber. Once inside, still with the candle in her hand, she inserted a wooden wedge above the latch so it could not be raised from the outside. She had fashioned the wedge herself, from a splinter of kindling, using a knife she had sent Jem to buy.

She put down the candle on the table under the window and tugged the laces that tied the bodice of her dress.

There was a chuckle behind her. She sucked in her breath and spun round.

'Pray let me assist you, my sweet.'

Edward was standing almost at her shoulder. For a moment it was as if he had materialized from nothing, like the evil spirit he was. Chasing after that came the realization that he must have been waiting for her in the gap between the side of the big press and the corner of the wall.

He smiled at her. He wore his bedgown of padded silk trimmed with fur. Around his head he had wound a silk kerchief. He looked younger without his periwig, more like a bloated version of the boy he had once been.

The boy who had pulled her hair and put a dead crow in her bed.

'Go away,' she said, retreating. 'I shall scream.'

'Scream all you like, my love. No one will hear.'

He seized her as he spoke. His left arm circled her head and the hand clamped over her mouth and nostrils as he pulled her towards him. His right arm wrapped itself around her waist.

She struggled for breath. She kicked his shins but her soft indoor shoes made no impression on him.

Her left hand swept over the table and touched the candlestick. She picked it and jabbed the flame of the candle into his cheek. The light died. He swore. His grip tightened.

'Hellcat,' he whispered.

Darkness came. And pain.

CHAPTER SEVEN

Nothing lasts for ever, Cat thought, for was there not always death to make an end of it?

She lay in the darkness. She was on her back still, her legs apart, her dress rucked up, for what was there to be modest about any more? The pain in her body was acute but strangely remote, as if it belonged to someone else, someone she had once known well and now was a stranger.

Sometimes a church clock struck the hour. That was strange too, the very idea that this devastated city still contained churches with clocks and bells that told the time.

Churches among the ashes of the dead.

Gradually other thoughts drifted into her mind. She could go to Aunt Olivia, praying to God she would not find Uncle Alderley tossing on top of her in the canopied bed.

But Olivia would say that those things

were only to be expected, that this was what gentlemen always tried to do to pretty maids, and even to less pretty ones. She would say that Cat should have taken better care of herself, and above all she would say that it was Cat's fault.

It was the way of the world. Men always tried to make love to women. That was what Olivia had said in the spring, when she had turned away a servant who had got herself with child. Cat had argued that the man should bear at least some of the blame.

'But it was her fault, Catherine,' Olivia had said, 'just as it was Eve's. A woman leads a man into sin, that's what your uncle says, and of course he is right. The girl should have managed it better, and now she must live with the consequences. And there's an end to it.'

Would they throw Cat into the streets, a defiled woman to live in the gutter as best she could? Probably not — they would simply pretend it had not happened. Master Alderley had his heart set on her marrying Sir Denzil, and Master Alderley was not a man who changed his mind once it was made up.

Another thought struck her. If she told her uncle and aunt, would they even believe her?

As a child Cat had been thrown from a horse and landed awkwardly on a heap of stones. This had been almost a year before she first had her courses and her body began to change. But after the fall, she had bled from the place where women bleed at that time of the month.

Cat felt herself but could not feel anything except pain. If there were no token of blood to show that she had lost her virginity, then why indeed should they believe her? In that case, it would be her word against Edward's. Her word was worth nothing. But in his father's eyes, Edward could do no wrong. She was merely the unwanted niece, a relation by law but not by blood, the child of a man whose name was not mentioned. To the Alderleys, her only value was as something to be traded, bought and sold.

Something to be robbed. Something to be defiled.

Even Jem had abandoned her. He would not help her — besides what could a crippled servant do? He would argue caution in all things, just as the foolish old man always did.

Time passed.

Never forget, never forgive.

Quite suddenly she knew what she would do. The decision arrived ready-made, needing no thought. It was there because nothing else was left to her.

The click of the latch made Cat catch her breath. She opened the door and listened.

The sounds of Barnabas Place settled around her — the creaks, the pattering of rodents, the whispering of draughts. The air was stuffy and still very warm.

She held up the candle, which accentuated the gloom. Her eyes adjusted slowly. This was the darkest hour before dawn. But the Fire still tainted the night sky. An uncurtained window at the end of the landing framed a sullen red glow.

With the bundle under her arm, she stepped from her room and closed the door. She wore her plainest dress. Her shoes were in the bundle, together with a leather bag containing a few small possessions, among them her box of drawing instruments.

Over her shoulders was the grey cloak she had stolen last night from the young man at St Paul's. She felt a momentary pang of guilt. He had tried to help her, after all — had perhaps saved her life when she had panicked and run towards the cathedral in search of her father. She couldn't remember much of what he had looked like, apart from the fact that he had been so thin you could see the skull beneath the skin. Also, he had heavy, dark eyebrows that belonged on a larger, older face.

Movement sent spikes of pain deep inside her body. She passed under an archway, turned right and hesitated at the head of the main staircase. Her candle was the only light.

These stairs led down to the balustraded landing, with rugs on the floor and sconces on the polished wood of the panelling, and with ornate plaster mouldings on the ceiling. All the magnificence was invisible.

Olivia's chamber was down there, with the canopied bedstead. Beside it was Master Alderley's closet, which had a bed in it, as well as a table, a large inlaid cabinet of Dutch manufacture and a number of presses. The third chamber was empty.

She listened, but all was quiet.

Cat continued down the landing to the archway to the spiral staircase. She found her way by touch, by memory, and by the variations in the darkness of shadows beyond the candlelight. She paused at every step and listened, though she desperately wanted to hurry. This, in reverse, was the route she had used last night, when Jem had brought her up to her chamber.

On the floor below, a door led to the side

landing beyond. Unlike the main landing, which was within the shell of what had been the prior's lodging in the days when the old monks had lived at Barnabas Place, this landing gave access to a different range at right angles to it. Her own chamber was in the upper floor of this building.

The landing took the form of a passage running along its outside wall, with four doors at intervals on the right-hand side. All these doors were closed. She slipped down the passage to the third door. Here she paused, and listened.

The sound of deep, rhythmic snoring reached her. She put down the bundle. She crouched until her cheek touched the ground. A current of air flowed through the gap under the door. But there was no light in the chamber beyond.

Cat stood up, wincing as another spike of pain stabbed her. The other rooms on this landing were unoccupied; they were furnished as bedchambers for the guests that so rarely came. At one time, Edward had slept in the third bedchamber in the main range, but his habit of returning in the early hours, usually drunk, had irritated Master Alderley beyond endurance; and in the end he had ordered his son to move into this wing.

She pushed her hand into her dress and took the knife from her pocket. She raised the latch.

The door opened silently — Olivia would not tolerate a squeaking hinge in any house of hers. The snoring increased in volume. Cat became unpleasantly aware of a fetid smell that reminded her of the wild beasts in the menagerie at the Tower.

Shielding the candle flame, Cat advanced into the darkness beyond. What little light there was showed her the curtains drawn about the bed. It also caught on someone standing beside it in the dark — a dwarf-like man with a great wig; and for a nightmarish instant she thought that Sir Denzil Croughton was waiting for her. The candlestick dipped in her hand, and she almost let it fall. Then reason reasserted herself: what she saw was Edward's periwig on its stand.

The snoring continued. Cat drew back the curtain and held up the candle so its light shone into the bed.

Edward was lying on his back. For an instant she didn't recognize him: he had taken off the silk handkerchief he wore at home when he was not wearing his wig. His naked scalp was as bald as a newly peeled potato and not unlike one in shape. He had thrown off the covers in the heat. He wore a white linen nightgown, open at the neck.

The snoring stopped without warning. In the sudden, dreadful silence, Edward was looking at her. She saw his eyes, with twin flames burning in them, one for each pupil, reflecting the candle.

Cat did not think. She jabbed the knife at the nearer eye. The tip snagged for a moment when it touched him, then it dug into the eyeball, which wobbled beneath the pressure like a boiled egg without its shell when you speared it with a knife.

His body bucked in the bed and he let out a scream as high-pitched as a girl's. His arm swung up towards her. She reared back. The candle tilted in her hand. The flame caught the edge of the bed curtain.

The blood looked black in this light. It gleamed like liquid ebony.

The flame ran up the side of the curtain and gave birth to another flame, and then to a third.

Edward writhed on the mattress, wailing and crying, his hands covering his face.

Cat turned and ran. The candle was in her hand, by some miracle still alight, though the flame was dancing and ducking like a wild thing.

Behind her, the screams continued, the flames rose higher, and the chamber grew brighter and brighter.

'Mistress . . .'

She gasped and dropped the bundle.

The whisper came from her left. She heard the laboured breathing mingling with her own. Down here in the cellar, with the stench from the cesspit oozing through the wall, it was very quiet. You could hear and see nothing of what might be going on in the rest of the house. The screams. The flames.

'Jem.' She was panting, and the words came singly, in fits and starts. 'What are you doing?'

'Waiting for you, mistress.'

He stirred beside her in the darkness. She raised the candle. His pale face was at her elbow.

'You said you wouldn't help me,' she said.

'I am not here to help.' His breath wheezed. 'I feared you would come. I'm here to stop you. Have you not thought? Your father may well be dead.'

She stooped for her bundle. 'Something's happened. It changes everything.'

'Nothing's changed outside. It's as dangerous as ever.'

She said bluntly, 'It's more dangerous here. Edward took me by force.'

'Took you . . . ?'

The horror in the old man's voice gave her a perverse pleasure. She said, 'He was waiting in my bedchamber tonight. He raped me.'

'But you're still a child.'

'Not any more, you fool,' she snapped, forgetting in her anger to lower her voice. 'And so I went to him as he slept and I stabbed him in the eye.'

She felt his hand on her arm. A sob rose from her throat.

'Is he dead?' he asked.

'I hope so.' She took a deep breath and said in a rush, 'I must go — go anywhere, anywhere but here.'

'Then I'll help you.'

'There's nowhere. Nowhere safe.'

'But there is.'

She turned and blundered against him. His arms went around her. She was trembling but she did not cry.

'Child,' he said. 'Child. You must go alone. I would slow you down. Go to Three Cocks Yard, off the Strand. The house to the left of the sign of the green pestle. Ask for Mistress Martha Noxon. She's my niece, and they have no knowledge of her here. Give her this, and she will know you. Perhaps your father will find you there.'

Jem pressed something into her hand. It was small and smooth, curved, cold and hard.

'Put it in your pocket.' He gave her a little push. 'And go. Go now.'

Somewhere in the distance was a faint, ragged baying, growing in volume. Thunder, Lion, Greedy and Bare-Arse were giving tongue.

CHAPTER EIGHT

I could not afford to anger Williamson any more than I had already done. I worked late that day and made sure I was at Whitehall early on the following morning, which was Thursday, the fifth day of the Fire.

The news was good. The wind had slackened and veered north, which made it easier for those fighting the Fire. There were reports that the Duke of York had halted the westward march of the flames at the Temple. God willing, the mansions of the Strand would be spared, and so would Whitehall itself. The fires were still burning vigorously elsewhere, but their relentless advance had been largely stopped.

I was already at work when Williamson came up to the office in Scotland Yard. I knew he was on his way for I had seen him from the window in the court below, deep in conversation with the portly gentleman with the wart on his chin. I expected him to be in a good humour because of the news about the Fire, but his face was grim and preoccupied. As soon as he came in, he called me over, commanding me to bring him the list of fatalities.

He scanned it quickly. 'Good. No new ones overnight. God has been merciful.' He lowered his voice. 'But talking of death, Marwood, there's one that isn't recorded here.'

He paused, as if to consider some weighty aspect of the matter far beyond my understanding. I was used to that, for Williamson employed such tactics to build a sense of his own importance — in his own mind, perhaps, as much as in the minds of others.

'We have a body,' he said. 'I think you'd better see it now.'

We clattered down the stone stairs, setting off a crowd of echoes, with Williamson leading the way. On the ground floor, he demanded a lantern from the porter. While we waited he turned to me.

'A patrol went up to St Paul's at dawn,' he said in a low voice. 'It's like an oven in there, even now. A beggar told them there was a body in Paul's Walk. In what's left of a chantry chapel on the north side.'

'Where the ballad-seller used to have a

stall?' I asked.

The cathedral's nave, Paul's Walk, had become a cross between a market, a public resort and a place of assignation in recent years. The ballad-seller made most of his income from his secondary trade, which was pimping.

Williamson nodded. 'Two of the guards left their powder behind and went in and pulled him out.'

'A victim of the Fire, sir?'

'He's definitely not the stallholder. And he can't have been there long. Someone would have noticed him before the Fire.'

'But why's he here, sir?' Surprise stripped the appropriate respect from my voice. 'At Whitehall?'

The question earned a scowl. The porter brought the lantern. Williamson gestured to me, indicating that I should light the way for him.

We descended by another staircase into the cellarage. I had never been here before — the palace was so vast and so rambling that I knew only a fraction of it, and none of it well. A low passage stretched the length of the range. Small gratings were set high in the left-hand wall to let in a modicum of light and air. On the right was a row of doors, all closed.

Williamson took a key from his pocket and unlocked the door at the far end. We entered a windowless chamber with a low barrel-vault of bricks. It contained no furniture apart from a heavy table in the centre of the room. The cellar smelled strongly of burning, as everywhere did now, as well as of sewage and damp.

On the table lay a large, untidy bundle draped with a sheet.

'Uncover it,' Williamson said.

I set down the lantern and obeyed. The man was naked. He was on his side, facing me.

'God in heaven,' I said.

He lay awkwardly on the table, for his arms were behind his back, which pushed his shoulders forward and twisted his body to one side. It was as if he had been frozen in the act of trying to roll off the table.

He had matted, shoulder-length hair, which was grey with ash and perhaps with age as well. There wasn't much flesh on him. His head poked up and forward like the prow of a barge.

'Who is he, sir?'

'I don't know.'

Williamson took up the lantern and directed its light towards the body. The skin was powdered with ash. Seen from close to, it looked yellow beneath the dirt, like parchment. It was shrivelled and blistered. The heat would have done that. The body didn't stink. But that didn't necessarily mean the death was recent, I thought, because the heat would have mummified it.

The man's chin had caught on the table, and his mouth was open, which gave him the air of surprise. His lips were pulled back, exposing the remaining teeth. A bruise on the temple had grazed the skin.

'Was he naked when he was found?' I asked, for it seemed to be my place to ask questions.

'No. His clothes are there.' Williamson nodded at a bundle on a bench that stood by the wall.

'Perhaps he was trapped inside when the cathedral caught fire.'

Williamson shrugged. 'Turn him over,' he ordered in a casual voice, as if telling me to turn a page or a key.

I couldn't rid myself of the idea that the soul of the dead man was floating about the roof of the cellar and watching us. I gripped the corpse's shoulder with one hand and his hip with the other. The flesh was cool and yielded slightly to my touch. It felt like a slab of boiled brawn. I pulled the body towards me, gradually increasing the pressure.

The corpse lacked the rigidity of the recently dead, which made it unnervingly unpredictable. It was also much heavier than I expected. It reached its tipping point and fell with a thump on to its front.

The arms poked up.

'You see?' Williamson said softly.

We stood side by side, staring at the hands of the dead man in the light of the lantern. The thumbs were tied together with a length of cord, so tightly tied that they had turned black.

'Why just the thumbs?' I said. 'Why not tie the wrists?'

'I don't know. But look there, Marwood. The back of the head.'

There was a small wound in the neck, just below the skull.

'Stabbed from behind,' Williamson said. 'Up into the brain. By someone who knew what he was about.'

I held my peace. So it was murder, that much was clear. The Fire acted as a cover for many crimes, so why not murder among them? What wasn't clear to me was why Williamson was so interested and, above all, why he had brought me here to see the body.

'It's the clothes that matter,' Williamson

said abruptly.

He had wandered over to the bench. He held up a torn shirt, then a coat and a pair of breeches with the same pattern. I joined him. The heat had darkened the material, charring it in places, but it was still possible to make out the broad vertical stripes on the material of both coat and breeches. Black, perhaps, and yellow.

'A suit of livery?' I said.

'Yes.'

A badge was fixed to the collar. Williamson rubbed it with his fingertip. I peered at it. A pelican was feeding her young with flesh plucked from her own breast.

'He's one of Henry Alderley's men,' Williamson said. 'The goldsmith — you must know of the man. That's his device, and his livery. That's why the body has been brought here. That's why we must know who killed him. And above all that's why we must go carefully.'

The King had gone by barge to the Tower, inspecting his ruined capital on the way. From there he intended to ride to Moorfields, to address the crowds of refugees. Master Williamson would have liked to go with him.

Instead, he was obliged to walk to Barnabas Place in Holborn to see Henry Alderley about a dead servant, with me in attendance on him. It was much hotter here, even in the unburned streets, than it had been by the river. In the normal run of things, he would have taken a coach, but the streets were so congested with traffic that this was impracticable. He was not habitually an active man and his face was soon shiny with perspiration.

These were strange times. There had been riots last night, and rumours of food shortages. Foreigners had been attacked on the assumption that they had been responsible for the destruction of London, purely by virtue of their being foreign. The King had summoned the militias of neighbouring counties, ostensibly to help fight the Fire but also to keep order if the riots spiralled out of control.

But even in the middle of this crisis in the nation's capital, Master Alderley was still a man of importance, not just a goldsmith and an alderman of the City. His wealth was enormous, and the King himself was said to be one of his principal debtors.

So Williamson naturally wished to treat Master Alderley with due respect. But I was puzzled, all the same. Why come himself at a time like this? He was not a justice. He was not a lawyer. He was not a courtier.

Williamson frequently glanced over his shoulder, as if worried that I might slip away, leaving him alone among the refugees and the desolation. This was probably the first time that he had left Whitehall since last week. He must have known in theory what the Fire had done to London, but the reality of it took him by surprise.

We skirted the remains of the City, avoiding the worst of the destruction. He was visibly shocked by what he saw: the smoking ruins, the blackened chimneystacks rearing out of the ashes, and the sluggishly moving crowds of homeless people encumbered with possessions and with the weaker members of their families.

These horrors affected me, too, but I had my own worries to distract me. Williamson had no reason to trust me, let alone like me. I had worked for him only since the beginning of the summer. The connection between us had come about in a most unexpected way, and he could not have welcomed it.

In May, I had petitioned the King for the third time, begging that His Majesty might in his infinite mercy see fit to release my father from the Tower. He had been imprisoned since the suppression of Venner's Rising in 1661. Though my father had not taken part himself in this abortive attempt to seize London on behalf of King Jesus, he had been a known Fifth Monarchist before the Restoration, and the authorities had seized treasonable correspondence that implicated him in this new rebellion. Since my father was a printer by trade, the conspirators had asked him to print a proclamation announcing the change of monarchy from the terrestrial to the divine. Fool that he was, he had agreed.

The Fifth Monarchists took their beliefs from the second chapter of the Book of Daniel, in which the prophet interpreted King Nebuchadnezzar's dream of a great image made of gold, silver, brass, iron and clay. Daniel prophesied on this evidence that four kingdoms would rise: and that then would come a fifth kingdom, which would break into pieces and consume all the others, and that this kingdom would last for ever. My father and his friends had had no doubt whatsoever that this fifth monarchy would be that of King Jesus. To bring this about they had been the implacable foes of the King in the late civil wars, and had done much to bring about the execution of Charles I.

Unfortunately the King's death had not ushered in the reign of King Jesus after all. Instead it had led to the Commonwealth, which had soon become a military dictatorship under Oliver Cromwell. Cromwell, a king in all but name, grew increasingly hostile towards his former allies among the Fifth Monarchists. A year or two after his death, the monarchy was restored amid great popular acclamation in the person of Charles II.

My father had not given up hope, and the burning of London could only encourage this. Despite everything, he was still waiting for the destruction of terrestrial empires, still waiting for King Jesus and the reign of heaven on earth. And I was still trying to keep his mouth shut about it.

The King had not responded to my petition for clemency, which had come as no surprise since he hadn't responded to the other two. But, ten days later, Master Williamson had written to me and commanded me to wait on him at Scotland Yard.

Yes, he said, His Majesty in his infinite mercy had decided that my father could, on conditions, be released into my custody. The first of these was that he should live in retirement and undertake not to meet those of his former associates still at large. There was no question, of course, of his house, business and possessions being restored to him. The second condition was that I should stand surety for his good conduct.

The third condition was that I should enter the employment of Master Williamson, and undertake any tasks that he might see fit to give me.

When disgrace had fallen on us after Venner's Rising, I had been nearing the end of my apprenticeship to my father. In other words, I had the knowledge and the skills of the trade. That was one reason why Williamson wanted me to liaise with Master Newcomb, the printer of the *Gazette,* to make sure that he did not cheat the government.

He had given me other tasks, however, from the very beginning. My years at St Paul's School had not been altogether wasted — I had an education that most other apprentices lacked. So he set me to copying letters. Taking notes. Running errands. Even talking to people on his behalf, sometimes when he did not wish his interest in them to be known.

But why take me with him now, when he went to call on one of the richest men in the kingdom?

Why me?

CHAPTER NINE

Barnabas place was not far from Holborn Bridge, where my Lord Craven's men had brought the Fire to heel yesterday. The streets around it were mean, but the house itself was ancient and of considerable size. It also appeared to be built largely of stone, which must be a great comfort (Master Williamson remarked) in these inflammatory times.

I rapped on the great gate with the hilt of my dagger. Williamson stared about him, his mouth twisting with distaste. Refugees had swollen the crowd of beggars and supplicants that usually gathered at a rich man's gate.

I knocked again. This time a shutter slid back and a porter asked me what we wanted.

'Master Williamson is here on the King's business. Tell Master Alderley he is here.'

The porter let us in, shaking his staff at

two women, one with a baby wrapped in a shawl, who tried to slip in after us to beg for alms or find shelter. He showed us up a short flight of steps and into an anteroom.

All this was to be expected, but for some reason the porter was not at his ease. His eyes were restless, and he could not wait to leave us alone. After he left the room, we saw him whispering to another servant, and then both men turning to look towards the room where we were.

Moments passed. I stood by an oriel window overlooking a small courtyard. Williamson paced up and down, occasionally pausing to make a pencilled note in his memorandum book. It was strangely quiet after the hubbub of the streets. The thick walls of Barnabas Place made it both a sanctuary and a prison.

'Why in God's name is Alderley keeping us waiting?' Williamson burst out, his Northern accent particularly marked.

'Something's going on, sir. Look.'

While I had been at the window, nearly a score of servants had gathered in the yard; they waited, uncharacteristically idle for the time of day, moving restlessly to and fro, and holding short, murmured conversations with each other. There was a furtiveness about their behaviour, and a strange air of uncertainty.

At that moment the door of the anteroom opened and a young lady entered. Williamson and I uncovered and bowed.

'Mistress Alderley,' Williamson said. 'How do you do?'

She curtsied. 'Master Williamson. I hope I find you in good health?'

Her dark eyes flicked towards me, and I felt an inconvenient jolt of attraction towards her.

'Sir, my husband begs your indulgence, but he is delayed,' she went on without waiting for a reply. 'He will come as soon as he can, I promise. A matter of minutes.'

'But he's here?'

She was older than I had first thought, a shapely woman with fine eyes. Her charms were not moving at the same rate as the calendar. She looked tired.

'Yes, sir, he is,' she said. 'And you must pardon the delay. We have had such —'

She was interrupted by another knock at the gate. Murmuring excuses, she slipped from the room in a rustle of silks.

We heard her voice outside, raised in command, and that of the porter and of a stranger. A little later a man clad in black crossed the courtyard under convoy of the porter. They went almost at a run, scattering the servants as they passed.

'I know that man,' Williamson said, joining me at the window. 'It's Dr Grout, isn't it?'

'A physician, sir?'

'Of course. What did you think I meant? A doctor of theology? He treated my Lady Castlemaine when she had the French pox. She swears by him.'

Mistress Alderley returned. 'Forgive me, sirs — we are at sixes and sevens.'

'Someone's ill?' There was a hint of panic in Williamson's voice, for stone walls were not a barrier to all evils, only to some of them. 'Not the plague, I hope? Not here?'

'Not that, sir, God be thanked.' A muscle twitched beneath her left eye. 'Something worse. My stepson, Edward, was attacked last night. In this very house. In his own bed.'

Williamson sat down suddenly.

'God's body, madam. Will he live?'

'It's in the hands of God, sir, and Dr Grout's. Poor Edward was stabbed in the eye. He has burns as well — his bed curtains were set on fire. He lies between life and death.'

'Have you caught the man who did it?'

'We believe so.' Mistress Alderley sat down opposite him and gestured with a hand heavy with rings at the window to the courtyard. 'It was an old servant, a malcontent. He was roaming the house last night at the time of the attack. My husband will soon have the truth out of him.'

'Madam,' Williamson began. 'There is something Master Alderley must know about another —'

He broke off. There was a commotion in the courtyard below. Two burly servants were manoeuvring an old man out of a narrow doorway sunk below the ground. The captive's hands were tied in front of him. His face was bloody. His hair lay loose on his shoulders. He wore a shirt and breeches. His feet were bare.

'He set fire to the house, too,' Mistress Alderley said. 'We could have burned to death in our beds.'

The servants pulled the old man up the steps and dragged him across the cobbles to a ring set in the opposite wall. They strapped his wrists to the ring. The younger servant tugged at the buckle to make sure it was secure.

His colleague brought out a trestle, placed it between the old man and the wall, and forced him to his knees. He seized the shirt at the neck and ripped it apart, exposing the victim's thin, curving back. The vertebrae stood out like a bony saw.

Williamson and Mistress Alderley joined me at the window. No one spoke.

Another man approached the little group in the yard. He wore a dark suit of good quality and looked like a discreetly prosperous merchant. He carried a whip in his hand, from which hung nine tails, each tipped with steel.

'Who's this, madam?' Williamson said.

'Master Mundy, sir. The steward.'

Both Williamson and Mistress Alderley had automatically lowered their voices.

There was a hush in the yard. Apart from Mundy, no one moved. He took the bound man by his hair and twisted his head so he might see the whip with its dangling tips of steel, so that he might understand that this would be no ordinary whipping.

Mundy released the old man's head. He stood back and waited.

The seconds stretched out and seemed to grow into minutes. I found I was holding my breath. At last a figure emerged from the shadow of an archway on the far side of the yard. With the exception of the man stretched over the trestle, the servants straightened their bodies and turned towards him.

He was middle aged, tall and spare,

dressed with a sober magnificence. He walked to the trestle and stood by it.

The scene in the courtyard now had a theatrical quality — even a religious one, as if some quasi-sacred ritual, sanctified by law and custom, was about to be enacted. Master Alderley was entirely within his rights to take a whip, even a cat o' nine tails, to a refractory servant, particularly one under suspicion of a grave offence. Was he not master in his own home, where his word was law, just as the King was master in England, and God was the master of all?

But something chilled me in the sight of Alderley on one side of the trestle and Mundy swinging the whip in the other. Their victim, tied like a pig before slaughter, was small, ragged and grey.

Alderley's lips were moving. The window was closed. His words were inaudible in the anteroom above the courtyard.

The steward bowed to his master. In a flurry of movement, he swung the whip high and brought it down on the wall just above the ring to which the victim was tied. Mortar sprayed from the masonry in tiny puffs of dust. The steel tips did not touch him. But the old man bucked against his bonds and tried to rear up.

Williamson watched, his face rapt. 'You're

sure he assaulted his master's son?'

'It's a certainty, sir.' Mistress Alderley glanced at him. 'Besides, if it had been a stranger, the mastiffs would have had him.'

It was not her words that gave me pause. It was something in her voice and in that swift, sideways glance at Williamson's face.

She wants him to believe what she says, I thought. It's important to her.

'Why?' Williamson said. 'Why would he commit such a crime against man and God? Was the motive robbery?'

Mistress Alderley was staring out of the window again. 'He's an ill-conditioned, awkward fellow, sir, with a head full of wicked notions.'

'Then why's he in service here?'

'He served a connection of my husband's first wife, a man who took up arms against the King and committed all manner of evil in the late disturbances. Master Alderley only took him in for charity's sake, for otherwise he would have starved.' Again that sideways glance at Williamson's face. 'And look what his kindness has brought upon us.'

I flinched as the first blow of the whip landed on the old man. The victim screamed, and the sound penetrated the glass of the window. His body lifted and twisted. Spots of blood appeared across his back and side. They coalesced into streaks and then into broadening crimson lines.

Mundy glanced at his master, who nodded. I wished I could look away. But I could not.

The whip fell again, the steel tips of the thongs raking across the skin. It left the victim shuddering, gasping for breath.

A spot of blood touched the sleeve of Alderley's coat. Mundy waited while his master took out a handkerchief and dabbed at it. Then Alderley stepped back and nodded again to the steward.

The whip fell for the third time.

'It's an example for the other servants, too,' Mistress Alderley said, swallowing hard; perhaps she didn't like this spectacle any more than I did. 'Afterwards he will go before a magistrate, of course, but Master Alderley says that none is to be found at present, because of the Fire. They've all fled.'

The servant's back had been reduced to a raw red mess, flecked with white where the bones beneath the skin had been exposed. Alderley held up his hand. Mundy backed away, the whip held over the crook of his arm. The semicircle of watching, murmuring servants retreated, moving away from the steward as if the thing he carried were infectious.

The flogged man was arching his back and gasping for breath. Alderley bent down and said something in his ear. If it earned a reply, it did not satisfy him, for once again he moved away and signalled to Mundy.

'I wish to God this were not necessary,' Mistress Alderley said, turning away from the window.

The whip fell for the fourth time.

The body bucked and slumped over the trestle, the head drooping down as if its own weight had become intolerable. The cobbles beneath the body glistened with blood.

It was a body now, I realized, not a man. I felt ashamed and soiled, as if by witnessing what had happened I had somehow condoned it.

Williamson shifted from one foot to the other. 'It's a bad business, madam.'

'Indeed, sir,' she said softly.

Mundy came forward and bent to examine the mess of blood, tendon and bone stretched across the trestle. He glanced up at his master and gave a tiny shake of the head. A shudder rippled through the watching servants.

Alderley gave the steward an order, dabbed his sleeve again and walked across the courtyard without another glance at the body. He paused beneath the oriel window, looked up and bowed. He passed inside, and a moment later his heavy footsteps sounded outside the door of the antechamber.

He bowed again, without servility, to Master Williamson, acknowledged his wife's curtsy and, having glanced at me, ignored me altogether.

'I'm grieved that you saw that,' he said. 'My apologies.'

'My dear.' Mistress Alderley did not look into his face. 'Did the wretch confess at last?'

'Yes,' Alderley said loudly. 'At the very end. The damned ingrate — he cheated the gallows. And left my poor son at death's door.'

'I must go to Edward,' said Mistress Alderley. 'Would you give me leave to withdraw, sir?'

'Of course. I shall join you as soon as I may.'

I rushed to open the door for her. She fluttered from the room with a swift, assessing glance at me by way of thanks.

'My wife has told you our troubles, sir?' Alderley said to Williamson. 'Dr Grout is with poor Edward now.'

Dr Grout could not say for sure whether or not Edward would recover. At all events he would lose the sight of his right eye. There was the risk of infection, too. His right arm was very badly burned. His pain and distress were terrible to witness. But for the grace of God, the fire in his chamber might have spread further and the entire house would have gone up in flames. They could all have been burned to cinders in their own beds.

Williamson presented his condolences as if they were as cumbersome as a box of stones. His Northern tongue did not slip easily into the flowery speech of the South.

'Now, sir,' Master Williamson said. 'I must not delay you at such a time. But one thing cannot wait.'

I returned to the window, to avoid giving the impression that I was eavesdropping. Blood had pooled around the trestle. The servants had already dragged the old man's body from the courtyard.

'Is one of your manservants missing?'

The blood had dried to a rusty red on the cobbles. As I watched, a boy came into the yard with a broom and a bucket. He emptied a silver arc of water over the trestle and the cobbles around it.

'What?' Alderley said, frowning. 'How in

the world did you hear that, sir? I take it
you mean Layne?'

Below me, a man appeared with four
mastiffs on leashes, two to each hand. He
paused to say something to the boy. Meanwhile, the dogs lowered their heavy heads
and licked the bloody water with enthusiasm.

'Layne?' Master Williamson abandoned
his attempt to approach the subject delicately. 'I've no idea of his name, sir. All I
know is that we have found a man wearing
your livery in the ruins of St Paul's. It pains
me to tell you that he was murdered.'

CHAPTER TEN

On my second visit to Barnabas Place, two days later, I went alone, trudging through warm ashes among the ruins. The heat was still intense.

There were many other people in this wasteland, some looking for their families or what was left of their homes; others scavenging for valuables. I had heard stories of men who had found artificial mines of metals in this lost city — pools of solidified lead, lumps of iron, even veins of silver and gold. Truly, this was another New World, where a man with few scruples might find riches as well as horrors, privations and sorrows.

'Not here, sir,' the porter said when he opened the wicket to me. 'His worship went to Westminster two hours ago.'

'Then Mistress Alderley?' I said, and I felt a faint and foolish current of excitement pass through me. 'Is she within?'

The porter went to enquire. After a few minutes he returned and showed me into the room with the oriel window through which I had seen a man flogged to death.

Time passed. I had no means of measuring it, but at least half an hour must have passed before I heard the Alderleys' steward, Master Mundy, ordering that a horse be brought round. A small, richly dressed gentleman crossed the courtyard below, his face concealed by a hat in which were two ostrich feathers; they were dyed purple and bobbed up and down as their owner walked beneath them.

Shortly afterwards, a manservant appeared and conducted me into the body of the house.

'Who was that below?' I asked. 'The gentleman who just left.'

'Sir Denzil Croughton, sir.' The man added, with a hint of vicarious pride, 'His worship's niece is betrothed to him.'

'So he's a regular visitor, then?'

'She's away in the country.' He shot me a glance, and I thought there was an air of caution about him now, as if he had said too much. 'Sir Denzil calls for news of her, and also to enquire of his worship's son. This way, sir.'

The servant led me down flagged passages

116

to a richly furnished parlour overlooking a small garden, and told me to wait. I resigned myself to the loss of another half hour but it was only a moment before Mistress Alderley glided into the room, with her own maid behind her.

'We met on Thursday,' Mistress Alderley said. 'I remember — Master Williamson's clerk. Your name?'

I gave her my best bow. 'Marwood, madam. James Marwood.'

'I don't know when my husband will be back. But perhaps I can help you.'

She sank into a chair and waved to me to sit opposite her. Such remarkable condescension, I thought: was she always like this or was it a show for me?

The maid settled with a pile of mending at the other end of the room. She glanced briefly at me and her face twisted as if she had a mouthful of vinegar.

'First, madam, Master Williamson commanded me to ask how Master Edward Alderley does.'

'A little better, thank you. He still lives. Dr Grout is with him now. He says we must thank God the knife did not penetrate the brain.'

I dipped my head in mute gratitude for this mercy. 'You are as yet no wiser about the reason for the attack?'

'Our old servant was unhinged, a malcontent with his head full of blasphemous notions. Such madmen are two a penny after the late war. We must try to forget Jem, sir, for we can never understand him.' She paused and added in a lower voice, 'We were most grateful for Master Williamson's kindness in the matter. It was Providence indeed that sent you both to us on that day.'

I admired her delicate way of putting it. Though Alderley had been quite within his rights to beat a servant, particularly on such gross provocation, it was a little unfortunate that the guilty man had actually died under the lash. At least Williamson, a witness of unimpeachable veracity and with useful friends, had been there at the time. He had smoothed away much of the awkwardness with the authorities, pointing out that the culprit had probably died from his illness and old age rather than the beating, and also making the point that his death had been a kindness to the villain himself, for it had saved him from the rigours of imprisonment, a trial and public execution.

'There was also the other servant who died, madam. At St Paul's.'

'Layne?' She spoke faster and more loudly now, as though this was a subject she preferred to talk about. 'Yes — what a terrible thing, sir.' Her voice acquired a touch of emotion that would not have been out of place in a playhouse. 'Alas! Poor Layne! There was a man who fully repaid our trust. My husband and I were most distressed by his death.'

After the coroner's inquest, Layne would go quietly to his grave. Alderley had offered to pay for the burial, Williamson had told me, and the thing would be done decently.

'I suppose it was for the sake of the few pence in his purse?' Mistress Alderley leaned forward. 'Have you news of the murderer? Has someone laid information?'

'I'm sorry, madam. Not that I have heard. The times are so out of joint that nothing is as it should be. But Master Williamson understands your indignation, and he wondered if he might serve you in any way.'

'How very kind of him.' Her eyes narrowed, for perhaps she knew that no one offered something for nothing. 'But surely nothing can be done? Unless a witness comes forward, how could we lay the rogue who killed Layne by the heels?'

'You may be right.'

'I wonder if it could have been the lunatic.' She noticed my puzzled expression. 'Jem, the man who attacked my stepson. After all, he attempted murder inside this house, so perhaps he had already committed one outside it.'

'It is a most ingenious suggestion, madam.' It was a convenient explanation too, and one that would resolve the business without troubling the Alderleys too much. 'Tell me, pray, who is Layne's next of kin?'

'A brother, I believe. He's in the West Indies, serving as an able seaman on one of the King's ships. Why?'

'Are Layne's belongings still here? His box?'

'Yes. My husband has taken charge of it until the brother comes home.'

'Master Williamson wondered whether I might inspect the contents in case there is something to suggest the identity of the assailant. It's just possible, you see, that the murder was not something that happened by chance.'

'I believe Master Mundy — our steward, you know — has already gone through the box and made a list of what was in it. Would that do?'

'It would be better if I saw it myself — no doubt Master Mundy was listing the contents rather than considering their possible significance.'

'Neatly said, sir.' She gave me another of those subtly unsettling smiles. 'You should be a lawyer. But perhaps you are?'

In another life, I might have been. I shrugged the flattery aside with a smile, though I was warmed by it, for flattery rarely came my way. 'What of the other man's box?'

'Jem's? I think we have it still. I would have burned it but Master Alderley would have none of it. My husband is a stickler for following the due processes of law. There is a niece or a cousin in Oxford, I believe, and he has instructed Master Mundy to write to her.'

'In that case, perhaps I might see Jem's box as well.'

'Of course, sir. Master Mundy shall be your guide.'

She was looking at me as she spoke, and I was looking at her. Suddenly the words dried up. A silence settled between us, as uncomfortable as it was unwanted. I stirred, and the chair beneath me creaked twice. The sound was deafening in the silence.

Mistress Alderley looked away, in the direction of her maid, who still sat with her head bowed, sewing industriously. 'Ann? Take Master Marwood to Master Mundy. Tell Master Mundy to give our visitor every assistance in his power.'

Master Mundy, a grave man aware of his own importance, led me down to the servants' part of the house. It was strange to think that, two days earlier, this sober and upright gentleman had beaten an old man to death with a cat o' nine tails.

'Was there not a printer in the City named Marwood in the old days?' Mundy said as they were descending the stairs. 'A Republican, I think — a Fifth Monarchist?'

'Perhaps, sir. I cannot say.'

'I believe he was imprisoned when the King came into his own again. No connection of yours, then?'

'No, sir. I come from Chelsea.'

I had grown used to deflecting such questions, for Marwood was not a common name. I had Mundy's measure now. He had the manner of a gentleman but now he worked as a rich man's steward. There were many such in London — men who had lost their estates and who now clung all the more tenaciously to the airs of their former stations.

I followed the steward to a locked room near the kitchens of Barnabas Place. Here, on slatted shelves, were kept the trunks and boxes of the servants. Mundy indicated two of them on the bottom shelf. They were crudely made from deal boards nailed together, with the corners strengthened with thin strips of metal. Each was about two feet wide, and eighteen inches high and deep.

He left me to lift them onto the table that stood under the small window at the end of the room.

'I cannot understand why you need to inspect them,' he said. 'It is quite unnecessary. I have made full inventories.'

'I must follow my orders, sir. I am commanded to search them, and I must do as I'm bid.'

A crude letter L had been burned with a poker into the wood beneath the lock of the nearer box. Mundy turned the key in the lock, lifted the lid and stood back.

I examined what was inside. A servant's box was his private life enclosed in a small space; everything else — his time, his labour, his clothes, his loyalties — belonged to his master; but the box was his. Apart from a few clothes, Layne had possessed a winter cloak, a pair of gilt buckles, a horn mug, a knife with a blade ground almost entirely away, a pipe, a pouch containing a few shreds of dry tobacco and an astrological almanac, printed octavo.

I picked it up and glanced at the title page. 'Was he a Dissenter?' I asked.

Mundy drew himself up. 'Sir, all members of this household attend the Established Church and follow its forms and usages.'

'How long had he worked for Master Alderley?'

'Two or three years. Mistress Alderley hired him when her husband was in France.'

'And you were satisfied with him?'

'By and large, yes. He was clean and sober in his habits. I would not have suffered him to stay if he had been otherwise.'

'Was he liked in the household?'

'I suppose so.' Mundy shrugged, indicating that such matters were far beneath his exalted sphere. 'As far as I know.'

'What was he doing abroad on the Tuesday?'

'He went out after dinner. The master sent him to Whitehall with a ring he'd had reset for Sir Denzil Croughton.'

I looked up from the book. 'The gentleman who is betrothed to Master Alderley's niece?'

'The ring was a gift from Mistress Lovett to Sir Denzil, a token of their betrothal. In fact I warned Mistress Alderley it might be unwise to trust a servant with such a valuable jewel.'

'So when Layne didn't return that evening, you thought he might have run off with it?'

'Indeed.' Mundy drew himself up, pursing his lips. 'A not unreasonable supposition, you must agree.' His voice was solemn, nasal and monotonous: a voice to drive his listeners either asleep or distracted. 'But in fact Layne had given it into Sir Denzil's own hands. Sir Denzil was wearing it when he dined here on Wednesday. And I saw it again on his finger not an hour ago, when he called on Mistress Alderley.'

'So Layne must have reached Whitehall?'

'Yes. It was the last time he was seen.'

Until, I thought, his body was found amid the ruins of Bishop Kempe's chantry chapel in the nave of St Paul's.

'It must have been the Catholics,' Mundy burst out. 'They need no reason to murder honest Protestants.'

He unlocked the other box, Jem's. This one too had its owner's initials burned beneath the lock. I had been a printer's apprentice once so I knew enough to appreciate well-proportioned letters. These ones were neatly squared and equipped with serifs.

'Could they read and write?' I said.

'These two?' Mundy shrugged. 'You can

tell by their marks on the boxes. Layne could read, more or less, but he could barely write his own name. Jem could write well enough if he had to, and he could read as well as I can. He'd come down in the world. Because of his wickedness, no doubt.' The steward raised the lid of the box. 'He kept a strange collection of rubbish. But it's only to be expected. The man was strange enough himself.'

On top was laid a shabby serge coat. Beneath it was a small silver cup, a Bible with print so tiny and poorly set as to be almost unreadable, a cracked clay bowl with a ragged ochre line running around the rim, and a child's doll about five inches long, crudely carved from a single piece of wood. The doll's face was flat with tiny, blunt features gouged into it. The eyes were black dots. The mouth was a faded red line. It wore a dress of ragged blue cotton.

Mundy poked the cup. 'This has some value. Jem must have brought it with him from his old place. Or perhaps he had it from his own kin — I heard it said that long ago his father was a clergyman, but they turned him out of his curacy for his godless ways.'

'Mistress Alderley told me he had once

worked for the family of her husband's first wife.'

'Indeed. Mistress Lovett's kin.' He frowned. 'Best forgotten.'

'Why?' I said.

Mundy put the cup back in the box. 'Are you finished here, Master Marwood? I have people waiting.'

'One moment, sir.'

I returned to Layne's box, partly because I sensed that Mundy was trying to hurry me away. I took up the almanac. I lifted it up to the window and turned the pages against the light, to examine the paper more closely.

As my father's son, I knew at once that the paper was French, which was normal enough for any book. The watermark, a version of the bunch of grapes, told me that it came from a well-regarded mill in Normandy that used only rags from pure white linen in its manufacture. The type was sharp and clean, probably from a newly cast case of type, and it had been set by a man who knew his business.

The binding told the same story. All in all, this was not a book that you would expect to find in the box of a servant who struggled to write his own name.

I closed the almanac and put it into

Layne's box, tucking it under the cloak. Something stabbed my finger, and I withdrew my hand with a cry of pain.

'What is it?' Mundy said.

I squeezed the pad of the index finger on my right hand, and a tiny ball of blood appeared on the tip. 'Something sharp.'

I licked the blood away and pulled aside the cloak. A batten had been nailed across the bottom of the box, bisecting it from back to front, in order to strengthen it. One of the nail heads stood proud of the wood, and its edge was jagged — and sharp enough to pierce the skin. There were two other battens parallel to it, to the left and the right. It struck me that the central one was made of a different wood from the others. It was newer, coarser grained and slightly thicker. The nail heads attaching it were new and rough, whereas those on the other side were dark with age and deeply embedded into the soft wood.

I knew a little about hiding places. In his prime, my father had been something of a carpenter, like many printers, and sometimes he had had a need to conceal papers and other small objects. I took out my knife and used the blade to lever away the central batten from the base of the box. The nails securing it were much shorter than the size of their heads suggested.

'Master Marwood! I cannot allow you to damage the property of one of our servants, even if —'

Mundy broke off as, with a twist of the blade, I wrenched up the baton. Beneath it, gouged into the base of the box, was a shallow and irregular depression about four inches long and two inches wide. It contained a piece of paper, folded into a flat package.

I picked it up. The paper was unexpectedly heavy. Something shifted within its folds. A guinea fell out. Then another; then a third, and then three more. I picked one up and held it to the light from the window. The gold shone like a miniature sun. The guinea had been minted this year: 1666.

'You had better add these to your inventory, sir,' I said.

I took up the paper, smoothing it out before I rewrapped the gold inside it. There was something written on the inside in a neat, clerkly hand.

Coldridge. PW.

I rubbed the paper between finger and thumb and held it up to the light. Even before I saw part of the bunch of grapes, I knew that it was probably an endpaper torn from the almanac I had just examined.

Six new guineas. An expensive almanac. A servant who had been barely literate at best. Two, neatly written words: Coldridge. PW.

I asked to see Mistress Alderley again before I left Barnabas Place. I was shown into the parlour. She was writing at the long table while her sour-faced maid sewed by the window.

She looked up. 'Did you find anything?' she said abruptly.

'Very little, madam.' I glanced at the maid, whose head was lowered over her work, and said quietly, 'Layne had six guineas concealed in a hidden compartment of his box.'

'What of it? His savings, I suppose.'

Perhaps she was right, I thought, though it was a great deal of money for a servant to have. The guineas had shown no signs of use. Their hiding-place had not been made long ago, for the scars in the wood had not darkened with age.

'There was something written on the paper that held the guineas.'

She sat up, suddenly alert. 'Yes? What?'

' "Coldridge PW". Does it mean something to you?'

She shook her head, the interest draining from her face. 'Why should it?'

'According to Master Mundy, Layne

wrote but little and poorly. So perhaps Jem wrote it. But in that case, why was it in Layne's box?'

I waited but she did not reply.

'On Thursday you told Master Williamson that Jem once served a connection of your husband's first wife,' I said.

She stared at me, as if surprised and even irritated that I should have raised the matter. 'Yes — he served the father of my husband's niece, Mistress Catherine Lovett. She's his niece by marriage, not blood, by the way — the child of his first wife's brother. Jem served her father, when they lived in Bow Lane off Cheapside. Afterwards he went with Catherine to her aunt's house, and then he came with her here.'

'May I speak to Mistress Lovett, in that case?' I said. 'As Jem was once a servant of her father's she may know more about him.'

'That's not possible. My niece is away at present, staying with friends in the country. She finds the summer heat intolerable, especially with this Fire, and her uncle decided a change of air would be good for her.' Mistress Alderley took up her pen and lowered her head over her letter. 'Perhaps you can ask her about Jem when she returns. Pray remember me to Master Williamson

when you see him, and thank him for his
kindness to us.'

II
ASHES AND WATER

6 SEPTEMBER — 31 OCTOBER 1666

CHAPTER ELEVEN

Hot and filthy, Cat had arrived in Three Cocks Yard in the early hours of Thursday, 6 September. The Fire was still raging but the wind had changed, swinging from the east to the south and slackening in force. She was aware of that even as she stumbled through the crowds. During the Fire, everyone was aware of the wind.

She had nothing but the clothes she stood up in, the small bundle she had carried with her, and the object that Jem had pressed into her hand when she fled from Barnabas Place. She was still in pain from Cousin Edward's attack — a dull, continuous soreness, punctuated by stabs of agony that made her gasp. Her thighs and her arms were tender with bruises.

On any other night, Three Cocks Yard would have been dark and silent at this hour, the houses barred and shuttered. But nothing was normal now. The sky reflected the Fire, casting a lurid glow over the yard. A heavily laden wagon filled half the space.

Mistress Noxon's house was beside the apothecary's, which Cat knew by the sign of the pestle swinging in the air above the shop. The front door was standing open. Two porters were manoeuvring a pair of virginals down the steps, with a young gentleman scurrying about them like an agitated terrier.

Behind them, in the hall of the house, was a small, handsome woman of middling height and generous proportions. Unlike the men, she was perfectly calm. In her hand was a sheet of paper.

'And that's thirty-five shillings for the dinners ordered in, sir,' she was saying in a sharp voice that cut through the racket in the yard. 'If I don't have it on the nail as well, you'll have to leave the rest of your furniture to cover what you owe.'

She caught sight of Cat as she was squeezing past the wagon. She motioned her to wait and continued to deal with the young gentleman. A large, red-headed manservant staggered down the stairs with a crate in his arms.

'Don't take that out, John, not until he's paid his reckoning. Leave it in the back of the hall.'

The servant did as he was told. He saw Cat and stared at her.

'Don't stand there dreaming,' the woman snapped. 'Bring down something else.'

At last, when the young gentleman had paid his bill and left with his wagon, she came down the steps from the front door and beckoned Cat forward.

'Who are you?'

'Mistress Noxon?'

She ran her eyes over Cat, taking in the bundle under her arm. 'Who's asking?'

'Jem sent me.'

'Oh yes? Jem who?'

Cat fumbled in her pocket and brought out the object that Jem had given her. It turned out to be a dark, smooth, flattish stone in the shape of an oval, which might have been picked up on a shingle beach. There was a white line of another mineral embedded in it, orange in this light. It made a wavering M if you had a mind to see one there.

M for Martha? Mistress Noxon took the stone, stared at it for a moment, and slipped it in her own pocket.

'Mistress Lovett,' she said softly.

'Yes.'

'You need somewhere to lodge.' It was not a question. 'How long?'

'I don't know.' Cat swallowed, for her mouth was terribly dry. 'I have a little money. Not much.'

Mistress Noxon ran her eyes over Cat, inspecting her as if she were a prospective purchase. 'Mistress Lovett can't stay here. Nor can any young lady. This is a house where single gentlemen lodge.'

Cat turned to leave by the street door, which still stood open.

'You don't have to go,' Mistress Noxon said. 'But if you stay, you stay as a servant and you work for your keep.'

'I'm not afraid of hard work.'

'You will be by the time I've finished with you. Well? Do you stay as a servant or do you go as a lady?'

'I stay.'

Mistress Noxon folded her arms across her bosom and stared at her. 'As a servant.'

Cat dipped a curtsy. 'If it please you, mistress.'

'Close the door, then, and come down to the kitchen.' Mistress Noxon led her into the house, calling up to the manservant, telling him to bar the door. In the kitchen, she said, lowering her voice: 'In this house, your name's Jane.'

'Yes, mistress. Has Jem talked of me? Did he say he might send me to you?'

Mistress Noxon brought down the flat of her hand on the table. 'You're not to mention him. If you want to stay, you will be Jane and nothing but Jane and you will do as you're told and not ask foolish questions.'

'But I should tell you why I —'

'I don't want to know,' Mistress Noxon said. 'It's better not.'

The house in Three Cocks Yard had been bought as a speculation by a wealthy Oxford haberdasher. It stood with three neighbours in a flagged court, from which a narrow alley led down to the Strand on the northern side, not far from Temple Bar.

The principal apartments were let to single gentlemen. There were three lodgers. At present, only Master Hakesby was in residence. He was a draughtsman, an elderly man of uncertain temper. He was working on a design with Dr Wren, the architect and mathematician whom the King had appointed as one of his Commissioners for the rebuilding of London, which made him automatically an object of fascination to Cat.

The haberdasher had installed Mistress Martha Noxon as housekeeper. She had formerly been in his service as his wife's chambermaid and, if Margery's insinuations were to be believed, as his own paramour. Margery did most of the cooking but Mistress Noxon considered her too slatternly to wait at table. There was also a manservant named John and a ten-year-old boy, who was more trouble than he was worth and slept in a sort of kennel by the kitchen chimneystack.

The servants were told that Jane was a stranger from a village near Oxford, and that she was a remote connection of Mistress Noxon's. They knew that this was probably a lie, and that the young woman called Jane was a mysterious intruder in their world, but they were too afraid of Mistress Noxon to ask questions or tell tales.

Cat did the work she was given. She kept her mouth shut when she could. When she couldn't, she roughened her voice and tried to imitate the inflections and turns of phrase that the other servants used. They thought she gave herself airs, but they left her alone for fear of Mistress Noxon. There was even an unexpected pleasure in being Jane, not Cat: in being someone else.

The work was often hard but it was not strange to her. She had been brought up not only to run a household but to do the various tasks, from cooking to cleaning and beyond, that she might set a servant to do;

this was good for the soul, for it kept a woman humble, which was pleasing in the eyes of God and man; it was also prudent, for it enabled one better to direct and instruct one's own servants.

For Cat, what was strange and unpleasant was not so much the work itself but to learn how a servant felt as she scrubbed a floor that belonged to someone else. It was a different feeling from that of someone whose family owned the floor.

When Cat thought about her former life it seemed remote and somehow foreign to her, as if it belonged to a different person. But she was too tired to do much thinking. The work was exhausting, but that was good because sometimes it stopped Cat from remembering what she had done to Edward, what he had done to her, and what her life had now become.

She was so heavy with weariness that she usually fell asleep as soon as she climbed into bed in the attic she shared with Margery. But she had bad dreams, haunted by Cousin Edward, and by the fear that she was carrying his child. On the first night, she woke both herself and Margery with her screams.

Two days after Cat's arrival, Mistress Noxon summoned her to her little room by the kitchen. The skin around her eyes was pink and puffy.

'You should know that he's dead. My uncle.'

'Oh mistress.' Cat's eyes filled with tears. Jem.

'Tell no one. There will be no mourning. We don't know him, and we never did. You understand? The man was such a fool. I never met such a one in all my days.'

But Mistress Noxon kept the stone that Jem had sent her by Cat in her pocket, together with her money, her keys, her rings, and other precious things.

Cat wept herself to sleep that night — as quietly as possible, for fear of waking Margery again. Without Jem, she had no one who cared for her unconditionally and completely. Without Jem, she was alone. Unless her father found her.

According to the gossip of servants, if a woman did not take pleasure in an act of copulation, she could not become pregnant by it. Cat did not believe this, not least because she could not understand how any woman could take any pleasure whatsoever from such an assault on her body even if it were not forced on her.

Besides, she had seen animals about the

business in the farmyard and fields of Cold-ridge. For females at least, copulation had more to do with grim necessity than pleasure.

The fear that she might be pregnant remained. She could think of nothing worse than carrying Edward's ill-begotten child. She became even more afraid of this than of being taken up for Edward's murder.

She had made her calculations. She thought it probable that Edward was still alive. Had he been killed, the news would surely have penetrated even to Three Cocks Yard by now, even to the basement kitchen that was the centre of her life. The Alderleys were such a prominent family that the intelligence would have spread throughout the town faster than the Fire itself.

You could not hide a murder, even in a house like Barnabas Place with high, thick walls, though you could hide lesser crimes. Assault and battery, for example. Or rape.

At the beginning of her fourth week at the beck and call of Mistress Noxon, she had pains in her groin and the blood began to flow. Some men believed that a woman's monthly courses were full of evil humours, that they blackened sugar, made wine sour and turned pickled meat rancid. Men, Cat thought, were such fools that they would believe anything. Mistress Noxon provided the necessary cloths to deal with the blood, and even an infusion of valerian and fleur-de-luce to ease the pain.

Cat welcomed the discomfort and inconvenience. If she had fallen pregnant, it would have been necessary to find a way to kill the baby.

Gradually, Cat became aware that there was another difficulty in the shape of John, the manservant. He was a tall, broad-shouldered lad, a country boy at heart, with red hair, bright blue eyes and a slab-like face whose colour and approximate shape made Cat think of a leg of mutton before it had gone in the oven. Margery, the cook, thought he was the finest young man that the world, let alone London, had to offer. John had been quite happy to accept this adoration and even to repay it at his convenience with small doses of affection.

But then Cat had come to Three Cocks Yard and, despite her best efforts to be plain Jane, to be colourless and dull in every particular, John found her of absorbing interest. He was not a man to whom words came easily, but he had other ways of making his feelings known. He blushed when she came into the room. He would appear

at her shoulder when she was emptying the slops and take the pots from her in his enormous hands. Once, when the kitchen boy showed a tendency to be impudent to her, John clouted his ear with such force that the boy's feet lost contact with the ground.

One consequence of this undesired and unrequited devotion was that Margery hated Cat.

Chapter Twelve

At last, nearly six weeks after the Fire, the rain came.

Cat stood by the attic window of the house and squinted over the surviving rooftops and the jagged outline of the ruins at the stump of St Paul's tower.

There had been showers since the Fire, and dull days with heavy grey skies, but the heat of summer had mingled with the heat of the Fire and lingered long after it should have ended. This rain was different. It poured from the sky in thick silver rods like water through a colander.

It was much colder, too. That was less welcome. Cat went down the steep stairs, little better than a ladder, to the second floor, and worked her way down to the basement. The kitchen was full of the smell of bread. The baker's boy had called in her absence.

'What kept you?' Mistress Noxon said.

'Daydreaming again? It won't do. Not in this house. I had to open the door myself to the boy.'

Cat curtsied and apologized. She had learned humility lately, along with her new name, which she answered to like a dog. A dog called Jane. They had not been easy lessons.

'Draw the beer now.'

She left Mistress Noxon laying the tray for her to take upstairs. She had often felt the rough edge of Mistress Noxon's tongue. At first, it had made Cat furious — how dare the woman speak to her in that way, especially when they were alone? Later, she accepted it as necessary.

Her circumstances had changed and so must she. In time, she learned to distinguish when Mistress Noxon was truly angry, when she was irritable for a reason that had nothing to do with Cat, and when her anger was entirely mechanical, administered for Cat's good, in the same way that Cat's nurse used to administer a regular purge to her.

She filled the beer jugs from the barrel in the scullery and took them back to the kitchen.

'Take the tray now. Master Hakesby's up. The barber's coming to shave him, and he'll want his breakfast before that.'

Cat tapped on Master Hakesby's door, and he told her to enter. He was partly dressed and in his gown, a handkerchief around his shaven head. He was seated at the table by the window and already at work.

'Put it on the chest,' he said without looking up. 'And pour some beer, will you?'

She obeyed and brought the cup over to him. He took it without looking at her. She strained to see what he was working on. There was a small sheet of paper before him. He was using ink but not a ruler or compasses.

This is an idea, Cat thought, something that comes in the night and needs to be pinned down before it vanishes in the daylight.

A cruciform shape. A church, then. An octagon where the four arms meet: probably a great dome, like St Peter's in Rome. And, from the transepts, curving outer lines stretching to nave and choir, softening the right angles where the transepts meet with the long axis of the church.

Was it St Paul's? A new St Paul's?

Master Hakesby took a mouthful of beer. He spilled a few drops on the table and dabbed at it with a handkerchief. He looked up but she didn't think he saw her, not properly. 'What is it, Jane?'

'Nothing, sir.'

'Then go away.'

The next day, after the great rainstorm, was a Tuesday. In the afternoon, Cat was set to washing and waxing the floor and panelling of the parlour. Mistress Noxon came into the room before the task was half done.

'You're to go to St Paul's,' she said. 'For Master Hakesby. It's urgent.'

Cat stared at her. Since her arrival here she had not gone further than the Strand.

'There's no one else to send.' Mistress Noxon ran her finger along the curved mouldings of the door panels, automatically checking for dust. 'You know the way?'

Cat nodded. She had grown up in Bow Lane, east of St Paul's, and the streets from Charing Cross to the Tower had been part of her childhood.

'John's in Westminster or I'd send him. Margery gets lost if she pokes her head out of the door. So that leaves you.' There was no need to add that the kitchen boy couldn't be sent because he was a halfwit, and Mistress Noxon wouldn't go herself because it would be beneath her dignity. 'Besides, it's time you went further abroad. You need air. You're as pale as a death's head.'

'What am I to do?'

'Master Hakesby wants a portfolio. It's the small green one on the table in his chamber.'

'I know.' Cat knew everything there was to know about Master Hakesby's chamber.

'You'll find him in Convocation House Yard. Do you know where that is?'

'Yes, mistress.'

'Show this paper to the men on the gate, and they will let you in. Give the portfolio into his own hands, mind — he was most particular about that — and take care to keep it clean. Be off with you. And keep it dry. Hold it under your cloak.'

It was still raining, though less heavily than before. Wrapped in the grey cloak she had stolen from the man at St Paul's, Cat walked through the ruins of London. After Temple Bar and the first few houses of Fleet Street, there was nothing to be seen but devastation.

Even now, six weeks afterwards, London was a desert from the Temple to the Tower. You could see from one end of the City to the other. All that was left of the greatest city in the country, apart from mounds of ash and rubble, were gutted churches and blackened spires, fragments of stone and thickets of unstable chimneystacks. In places the heat had been so intense that stones had calcined and become an unnatural white in colour.

The change in the weather had affected everything, and not on the whole for the better. The rain had turned the pale ashes into a dark grey sludge that clung to your shoes and pattens and stained your clothes. It was growing colder, too. Everyone said it was going to be a bad winter.

Cat crossed the Fleet Ditch, which was choked with sooty debris. Tendrils of smoke rose up from the labyrinth of ruins on either side of Ludgate Hill, for rubbish still smouldered, and fires burned slowly in deep, almost airless cellars.

At Ludgate, the mounting block was still there, marked by the flames, but one of the few features recognizable from before the Fire. She supposed she should feel guilty about the thin young man for repaying his attempt to help her by biting his hand and stealing his cloak; but a sense of guilt was one of the luxuries she could no longer afford.

In a moment Cat reached the spot where she had stood on the night of St Paul's destruction. Had her father been inside? Had he been among the nameless dead? She wanted to know, one way or the other. Her lack of knowledge unsettled her. Even after he had fled abroad at the Restoration, she had known he was living somewhere beyond the Channel. Occasionally letters from him would come, sent care of an unknown friend and then passed to Jem, who would slip them into her hand.

She paused to look at the ruined portico. By a strange paradox, it had been her father's pride. He had been a mason by trade. Before the war he had worked on the cathedral under the direction of Master Inigo Jones. True, Master Lovett hated the Church of England and all its works, including St Paul's. But she had seen him stroke the stones of one of the columns as a man strokes a favourite dog. He had talked, almost against his will, of the novelty and the elegance of the portico's design.

A porter passed close to her, brushing his hand over her hip. She moved quickly away. In the old days, she had not been a servant and she had never walked alone in the streets. Now she had become a target for passing men of all ages, for their touches, squeezes, attempted kisses and lewd suggestions. She wondered at this, at the curious lack of discrimination that men showed in their lusts.

In Convocation House Yard, a crowd was gawping at the bodies propped against the wall. St Paul's had given up a number of its dead because of the Fire, for tombs had burst open in the heat and flagstones cracked apart. Some corpses were little more than skeletons. Others were clothed in dried flesh in various stages of decay, a few with fragments of clothing and shrouds clinging to them. The souvenir hunters had been at work, and there were bodies that had lost fingers, toes, hands or feet; one lacked a skull.

Pride of place, according to Mistress Noxon, went to Bishop Braybrooke, who hadn't been seen in public since 1404. His mummified corpse had tumbled down to St Faith's in the crypt underneath the choir. Here he was in person, propped on his feet against a blackened wall to await his second resurrection: he was quite intact, with many of his teeth, a red beard and hair, though his skin was like leather.

A fence had been erected in the angle between the cloister containing the ruined Chapter House and the south wall of the nave. Its gate was guarded by a watchman with a large dog. He took Cat's paper and peered at it, his lips moving. She had already examined it — it was a general pass, signed by Master Frewin, the Chapter Clerk, and was so thumbed and greasy that it had clearly been used many times before.

Even with the pass, however, the watchman did not let her in. He made her state her business and told her to wait. He sent a boy to fetch Master Hakesby. The dog, which was chained to one of the gateposts, strained towards her and forced her to recoil, to the obvious entertainment of its master.

With a sudden stab of loss she thought of the mastiffs she had left behind her. Now Jem was dead, she missed none of the human inhabitants of Barnabas Place, with the possible exception of Aunt Olivia, but she yearned for the dogs, for their protection and their uncritical affection.

Thunder, Lion, Greedy and Bare-Arse. Especially Bare-Arse.

The boy returned. With him came Master Hakesby. He was a tall, shabbily dressed man with his own grey hair. Everything about him was thin, from his long feet to his head, a distorted cylinder of bone perched on narrow shoulders. Cat curtsied. He held out his hand for the portfolio.

'Come with me,' he ordered. 'I may need other drawings as well, and you can fetch them. I shall enquire of Dr Wren when he comes.'

The watchman pulled on the dog's chain, drawing him to one side so Cat could pass through the gateway. She followed Master Hakesby across a yard that stretched from the outer wall of the cloister towards the west end of the cathedral.

An open tent stood to one side of the yard. Workmen were sorting a miscellany of objects heaped against the wall at the back. Cat glimpsed an iron-bound chest with a curving lid. Propped against it was a marble bust of a periwigged gentleman that could not have been long from the sculptor's chisel. There was a blackened memorial brass of a dead cleric and a carved throne of painted wood surmounted by an episcopal mitre.

'Come along,' Master Hakesby said over his shoulder. 'Dr Wren is away, but he sent word he will be here at any moment and he wishes to see this most particularly.'

Blocks of stone stood in the open air, some of them carved. It occurred to Cat that, if they did not repair St Paul's, the ruins would become, if nothing else, a vast quarry.

Master Hakesby led her into a shed, about fifty feet long, which had been built against the exterior of the cloister. Two clerks were standing at a long, high desk and entering items into ledgers that lay open before them. Behind them was a ledge with a jumble of boxes and books on it. At the other end of the shed was a table to which a sloping surface had been attached with iron clamps. Hakesby walked over to it.

'Don't touch anything,' he said, glancing back over his shoulder. 'Stand over there and dry yourself by the brazier.'

Two plans were laid out on the slope, their corners held down with fragments of fire-burned stone. There were pens and ink laid out beside it, together with the tools of a draughtsman's trade — compasses and rulers, set squares and dividers, pencils and pens.

Master Hakesby set down the portfolio and examined the contents. Afterwards he returned to his drawing board. She watched him, straining her eyes to see what he was working on. Not St Paul's, she thought. This was more than any church. She made out lines that crossed each other in a pattern. Not a grid: more complicated than that. Streets? A city? London itself?

Was it his own design or one of Dr Wren's? Or both? She had heard Master Hakesby say that Wren had too much work to handle all the detail himself, and besides he frittered away too much of his time in Oxford or in meetings at Whitehall or with prospective clients. Master Hakesby was his draughtsman, almost his partner, though the designs were usually in Dr Wren's name. The hand holding the pen trembled. Hakesby steadied it with his left hand. He paused, took a deep breath, and continued his work.

Cat was growing uncomfortably hot by the brazier. She loosened the cloak about her shoulders.

At the same moment, Master Hakesby's hand twitched, seemingly of its own volition. The side of it brushed the inkpot, which toppled over. Ink glided towards the portfolio. He swore. The inkpot rolled over the edge of the table and fell to the floor, leaving a trail of drops to mark its passage.

Cat darted forward. The cloak fell from her shoulders. She scooped up the portfolio and the sheets of paper lying beside it.

Master Hakesby looked at her. His lips worked but no words came out. Cat put the portfolio on a stool and crouched to pick up the inkpot. There was a rag on the table, which she used as best she could to wipe up the spilled ink.

Hakesby was still staring at her.

'Sir,' she said, softly so the other men would not hear her. 'What is it? Are you ill? Shall I —'

'Be silent.' His lips twisted into a scowl.

She was looking at the plans, which were similar to each other. 'It's London, sir, isn't it? Or part of it. But — but a different London.'

His eyebrows shot up. 'How do you know that?'

She nodded at the geometric mass of fortifications in the lower right-hand corner, by the north bank of the river. 'Because that's the Tower, sir — it says so. And the Thames, from there to London Bridge, and —'

'You can read?'

'Yes, sir, and write a fair hand.'

She had known serving women who could do both, there was no reason why she should not be one of them. She came a step nearer, and still holding the inkpot.

'But all this is different, sir. The Tower's not that shape. And that space to the west, where eight roads meet — what is that?'

'It is a plan of London as it might be. Not London as it is.'

'Dr Wren's London?'

'And mine, as well,' Master Hakesby said, scowling. 'Indeed, as much mine as his, if

158

the truth be known. A vision of what this city might be.'

His right hand, which was resting on the table, began to tremble again. He covered it with his left hand, pressing it down. He glanced at Cat and saw the curiosity in her face.

'Sometimes it does that,' he snapped. 'And when it does, I cannot do this.'

'Do what, sir?'

He gestured at the slope, at the plans, at the tools of a draughtsman's trade.

She held his gaze for a moment. Then her eyes strayed back to the two plans. They showed the same south-eastern section of the City. She made out pencilled measurements and notes on one of the plans. Perhaps, she thought, Master Hakesby was making a fair copy of a rough draft. She yearned to study it, to make the building take shape from its design.

There were new voices in the yard, and a man laughed outside. The shed door opened, crashing against the wall. Two men entered.

Dr Wren, his face smiling and a little flushed.

And Uncle Alderley.

Cat's mind filled with a cloud of disbelief. Uncle Alderley did not belong in this new world of hers where she was a servant and a fugitive.

Master Hakesby snorted. 'You'd better wait, though I doubt there'll be much work today. Not my kind of work, at least.'

'There is a curious volume you must see, sir,' Dr Wren was saying to Uncle Alderley. He was a younger, smaller man than Master Hakesby, finely dressed and fine of feature; a gentleman. 'We found it in a tomb in Paul's Walk. They say it's well nigh as old as the cathedral itself.'

Cat lowered her head and set the inkpot on the table. The gentlemen strolled towards the ledge behind the clerks' desk at the far end of the shed. She did not dare look at them. Trembling, she turned away, took up a rag that Master Hakesby had been using as a pen-wiper, and rubbed the ink-stains on her fingers.

'This one, sir,' Dr Wren said to Uncle Alderley. 'Pray examine this initial capital, with the curious picture entwined within it.'

She risked a swift, sideways glance. Dr Wren had opened a huge, charred book, bound in leather and metal. Uncle Alderley was looking down at it. He had his back to her.

A terrifying possibility possessed her. Cousin Edward might be with them. He might walk through the doorway from the yard at any moment.

'Master Hakesby?' Wren said. 'Would you be so good as to show Master Alderley our discovery? You can unravel this monkish scribble better than I can.'

While the men's backs were turned, Cat slipped along the side of the shed and through the open door to the yard. She ran to the gate. The dog, distracted by the ribald shouts of spectators around the bodies propped against the cloister wall, let her pass unhindered. She lost herself in the crowd and walked westwards through the ashes and ruins of the City.

The rain had grown heavier while she was in the shed. As she walked, it streaked her cheeks like tears and soaked the shoulders and skirts of her dress. She had forgotten to retrieve the grey cloak.

CHAPTER THIRTEEN

'Upstairs, Jane,' mistress Noxon said with a jerk of her head.

It was a fine morning and a little sunshine had penetrated the walled enclosure at the back of the house in Three Cocks Yard. Cat was pegging out washing on the line — small, delicate items, handkerchiefs and cuffs and the like, which Mistress Noxon preferred to see washed and ironed under her own direct supervision.

'Shall I finish this, mistress?'

'Leave it. Master Hakesby wants you. Are your wits on holiday?'

Cat straightened her cuffs and went upstairs. She was wary — she had had no conversation with Master Hakesby since she had fled from Convocation House Yard two days before. She knocked on the door of his chamber and was told to enter.

He was standing by the window, little more than a tall, stooping shadow because of the sunlight behind him. Beside him was Dr Wren. Cat dropped a curtsy to the space between the two men. Neither of them paid her any attention.

'I must have the new measurements by this afternoon,' Dr Wren said. 'I'm quite determined to do this at least as it should be done. The King wants it too, I know.'

'Will you speak to him about the rest, sir?' Master Hakesby said. 'About the city?'

'I'll try. I doubt it will do any good though. That was clear enough when we met the gentlemen from the Privy Council and the Common Council.' Wren's face was pale and tired. He spoke with cold deliberation, as if the words were painful and needed careful extraction. 'However much the King desires a new London, he hasn't the money, and nor has the City; and I don't believe the City has the will for it, either. All they want to do is make money. No surprise in that — all I had from Alderley the other day were fine words. As long as he gets his interest on his loans he could not care a straw. They are all the same. They look to their profits, and they cannot see much further than the end of the next quarter.'

'But the Custom House, sir,' Master Hakesby put in, frowning. 'There's no difficulty there?'

'I hope not, if we play our cards right. After all, it is a symbol of the royal power in the heart of the City, and the King is alive to the importance of that. But we cannot delay drawing up the design, for he may change his mind. I must take the revised plans to Whitehall after dinner, so pray make the calculations as soon as possible and transfer them to the fair copy. Could you do it here? I'm sure the girl will bring you what you need. I'll call for them on my way this afternoon.'

Hakesby bowed.

'When you send the girl out,' Wren went on, 'would you ask her to get more sand, too? My shaker is empty, and I smudged a letter I wrote last night most barbarously. Who has your business?'

'Finching's, by Temple Bar.'

Wren took up his stick. 'And black-lead for the pencil.' For the first time he looked directly at Cat. 'Make sure you keep the paper clean and dry on the way back. Take particular care not to crumple or mark it in any way.'

She curtsied, keeping her eyes down.

'Are you sure she'll do?' Wren said. 'She looks barely more than a child.'

'Jane is older than she looks, sir. Quick in apprehension, reliable, and also most deft in her movements.'

'If you say so.'

Hakesby and Cat listened in silence to Dr
Wren clattering down the stairs. They heard
two voices rising and falling below, his and
Mistress Noxon's, and then the bang of the
front door.

'Why did you run off the other day?'
Hakesby said.

'Your pardon, sir.' The lie came smoothly.
'I was wanted here. Mistress Noxon said I
was not to dally at St Paul's.'

'If I were less addlepated, I should have
brought your cloak home with me today.
You left it in Convocation House Yard.
Another day. Now, as to the paper, it's for
fine work, and we shall need two quires of
it. Take this spoiled sheet and show it to the
stationer. The size and quality must be
precisely the same.'

She took the sheet. She noticed how his
fingers trembled so much that the paper
wavered in the air.

The day that followed was happier than any
Cat could remember in the weary years
since she had left her great-aunt's house in
Champney and come to live with the Alderleys.

When Cat returned from the stationer's,

she found Hakesby bent over the long table which stood at right angles to one of the tall windows. He was working on a set of figures. His left hand rested on his right hand, steadying it. She did not dare ask what was wrong with him. Perhaps he was unduly attached to spirits, though she had seen no bottles about his chamber. But one of Uncle Alderley's clerks had been so afflicted and, according to Edward, had died raving in the back yard of an alehouse.

He looked up and asked her to show him her purchases.

'Good,' he said. 'Can you make ink?'

'Yes, sir.'

'Then you shall make me some now. Enough to fill that jar.'

He pointed at another table in the corner of the room. Beside the empty jar were oakgalls, copperas and gum arabic.

'Use the rainwater in that pot. It's purer and flows better.'

She set to work, absorbed and happy, and went to and fro between Master Hakesby's parlour and the kitchen, gathering what she needed for the work. There was already ink on the table by the window. She wondered if he were testing her.

Hakesby continued with his figures. After half an hour, he came over and inspected her progress. The making of ink was not something you did in five minutes.

'Leave that for a moment. I shall try an experiment with you, and we shall see how you do. You told me the other day that you can read and write.'

'Yes, sir.'

He took a book from a shelf, opened it at the title page and set it on the table. He pointed at the title. 'Then what does this say?'

She bent over it. '*I quattro libri dell'architettura di Andrea Palladio.*' She stumbled over the unfamiliar words but pressed on, syllable by syllable. '*Ne' quali, dopo un breve trattato de' cinque ordini, & di quelli avertimenti, che —*'

'Enough.'

'Your pardon, sir, I do not know Italian, and —'

'But you know it is Italian, and that is something I did not expect. Now we shall try another experiment.'

He took up the sheet of spoiled paper she had taken as a sample to the stationer's and told her to mark out lines of varying lengths in black-lead with the help of a ruler, taking care that the line should be as fine and faint as possible.

Cat sat at the table in the window, with

the paper resting on the slope that Master Hakesby used. As she worked, she was aware of him moving about the room, inspecting the progress of her ink manufacture, consulting a memorandum book, and tugging at his long fingers as if they pained him.

He must have been watching her for, when she had finished, he was at her shoulder immediately.

'Good. Now take up that pen — no, not that one, the one there with the finer point to it. It needs trimming. When you've done that, ink in the lines.'

This took much longer. There was no room for error. She finished the task at last, but not entirely to her satisfaction.

'A slight blot to the end there,' Master Hakesby said, 'and that line below is not quite as regular as I would like — but otherwise well enough. Now write beside it with the same nib, and in letters as small and neat and delicate as you can, the words: *Christopher Wren delineavit.*'

Cat looked sharply at him. 'I don't understand, sir.'

'That doesn't matter. Do it.'

The words crept across the paper.

'Good. A clerkly hand. Where did you learn these skills?'

'When I was young, I served an old lady who lived in the country.' The lie came fluently, because Cat had prepared it while she was working. 'My mistress taught me, and I helped her, especially when her eyes began to fail. She had travelled in Italy when she was younger, and she had an interest in all this.' She gestured at the plans on the table. 'Then she died, and I came up to London.'

In a sense, the story was true enough, as stories went, though not the whole truth; the lady had been Cat's Great Aunt Eyre. Before her death, she had given Cat the box of drawing instruments. They were of Italian manufacture, the box inlaid with ivory.

'She taught you well. So today you will help me a little more.' Hakesby's fingers fluttered. 'With this.'

Master Hakesby was working on a design for the Customs House on the Thames. The old building, more than a hundred years old, had been gutted in the Fire. The plans were almost complete, but the previous day Dr Wren had introduced refinements to the all-important south elevation overlooking the Thames, which necessitated the making of a fine copy of that portion of the plan, together with the insertion of the revised calculation of measurements affecting the whole structure.

Speed was everything, Hakesby told her, for the King would soon be inundated with designs for new buildings; and he who was first in line was in the best position possible, particularly if his face was known and liked at court, as Dr Wren's was. Indeed, the King had promised as much. On the other hand, in Master Hakesby's experience, the promises of kings were not always to be relied on.

The design was ready when Dr Wren returned after dinner. He cast an eye over it, while Hakesby stood beside him. Cat was still in the room, waiting to be dismissed.

'This hand isn't yours, Master Hakesby.'

'It's the maid's.'

'What?' Wren stared at Cat. 'The girl did this? This one?'

'Jane writes a fair hand. Better than mine today, since my ague has come on again.'

For the first time, the Doctor seemed to see Cat clearly. He was a handsome man, she supposed, with particularly fine eyes. He turned back to Hakesby. 'The work will do. It will do very well. We shall give her sixpence for her trouble.'

Dr Wren's words fell into the deep pool of memory. For an instant, up from its dark depths, came other words and the gleam of another sixpence. And with them, conjured from a place beyond death, came Great-Aunt Eyre herself at Coldridge, the house in Suffolk.

'You have done well, child,' Aunt Eyre said, peering at the paper in her hand, for she was growing short-sighted. 'It is very prettily drawn, and you have an arch that is most like Domitian's in Rome, erected to his brother Titus. Here's a silver sixpence. Mind you guard it well.'

When Cat came down from Master Hakesby's chamber, she found Margery in the scullery, clearing up after dinner. The other maid gave her a look of barely concealed dislike.

'Mistress is in her room,' she said, tossing her head. 'She wants you.'

Judging by the redness of her eyes, Mistress Noxon had been crying. By the time Cat came to her, the tears were dry and sorrow had given way to truculence.

'I've had a letter,' she announced. 'From a man called Mundy, at Barnabas Place. Calls himself Alderley's steward. Sounds as stiff as a broom handle but much less useful.'

Cat could not speak. Her happiness was sponged away. Fear made it hard to breathe.

She could not escape the Alderleys — first at St Paul's and now this.

Mistress Noxon's voice seemed to be coming from far away. 'The letter was sent to my old house in Oxford, and then sent on here. It's about my Uncle Jem's box. They want it collected.'

'So they don't know I'm here?' Cat whispered.

'Whatever gave you that idea, you foolish girl? This fellow Mundy says I have to collect it, otherwise it'll go on the bonfire. I'm sure there'll be nothing in it worth the having. John will have to take a handcart. It's the waste of at least half a day for him, which is so vexing.'

Cat began to tremble, and she steadied herself against the kitchen table. 'Will they learn that you live in London?'

Mistress Noxon shook her head. 'Not if John tells them he's to take the box to the Oxford carrier.'

'Pray God there's no difficulty.'

Mistress Noxon's face became very red. 'You forget yourself, Jane. Why should there be a difficulty? Anyway, it's no concern of yours. He was my uncle, was he not? Now tell me this — what have you been doing upstairs all day?'

'Helping Master Hakesby.'

'It won't do, do you hear me? Doing what, pray?'

'He sent me out on a commission —'

'I know that!'

'And I made ink for him, mistress, and I did some drawing.'

Mistress Noxon snorted. 'If Master Hakesby wants you to work for him, then he must pay for you. And mark this, Jane, I'll have no lewd behaviour in my house. Go and help Margery. You've been idling about all day, and it's spoiled you for your proper work.'

CHAPTER FOURTEEN

They found the second body six weeks after the first, early in the morning of 18 October.

The first I knew of it was when Williamson arrived at the Scotland Yard office and called me into his room. He told me to shut the door. I knew from his voice that he was in a bad temper.

'Body in the Fleet Ditch,' he said to me without preamble. 'Take a barge and go and fetch it. The officer who reported it will go with you — Lieutenant Thurloe. He'll give you any details you need on the way. Take a pen and I'll dictate a warrant for you.'

'Has he been murdered, sir?'

Williamson ignored the question. Either he had taken too much wine last night or, more probably, he had had the rough side of someone's tongue this morning. 'Bring it back and have them put it where the other one was. That servant of Alderley's.'

'And what about the copy for the *Gazette*?

Shall —'

'Just do as I say, will you? Or find another master. It's all one to me.'

Half an hour later, I walked down the stairs from the office with Williamson's warrant, signed and sealed, in my pocket. At the half-landing I met a gentleman on his way up. I stepped aside to allow him to pass me.

The newcomer was huffing and puffing, his face red with exertion. He glanced at me with irritation in his face, as if I shouldn't have blundered into his path. I recognized him. It was the gentleman with the wart on his chin.

The first time I had seen him he had been coming out of Williamson's office the day St Paul's was burned. The second time was on the following day, just after they had brought Layne's body to Whitehall.

Here he was again. And here was another body.

Thurloe was small and square-built, with the scar of a sword wound on his cheek. He served in the Lord General's Regiment of Foot Guards, which had a different character from the other guards regiments, since it had once formed part of the New Model Army of the Commonwealth.

We took one of the palace barges down-river to the Fleet. It was the fastest way to get there and also the most convenient means for bringing back a corpse. Two soldiers came with us, carrying a bier.

The oarsmen rowed hard against an in-coming tide. They were sullen, for they knew the nature of the errand; none of the watermen cared to transport a dead body, and some accounted it unlucky. The water was choppy. It wasn't a comfortable journey.

'How did you find the body?' I asked Thurloe as we went downstream.

'Haven't you seen my report?'

'No, sir. Besides, I'd rather hear it from you.'

He shrugged. 'We found him a little upstream from the footbridge over the Fleet by Bridewell. One of my men saw the body — he was floating among the rubbish. No hat or shoes, but still in his coat, stockings, breeches and shirt. We pulled him out. He hadn't been robbed — nearly two shillings in his purse and there's a ring on his finger. His clothes aren't much but you could raise a few shillings on them.'

'Anything else in his pockets?' I asked.

'A pocket Bible.' He glanced at me. 'It's not a bridge that many use after dark. Too ill-lit. Besides, that way into the City is notorious for thieves.'

Our barge reached the mansions that lined the river frontage of the Strand. Seagulls swooped around us, and their harsh, sad cries filled the air.

'Could the man have wandered there without knowing its reputation?' I said.

'Unlikely, unless he was a stranger.'

'Any wound?'

'Not that I saw.'

'A drunk taking a shortcut home? Perhaps he slipped, hit his head and fell in the Fleet.'

'I suppose it's possible he was after a Bridewell Bird,' Thurloe said, picking at the question as if it were a scab, despite his reluctance to indulge in conjecture. 'That could have brought him there.' A note of disapproval entered his voice, a hint of the Puritan. 'He didn't look that sort of a man, but you can never tell. Lust is universal. The Devil makes sure of that.'

My mind filled with an image of Olivia Alderley. A married woman I hardly knew, and so far above me in station that she might as well have been living on the moon. I told myself not to be a fool and pinched my thigh as hard as I could to distract my wandering thoughts.

'But I don't think he was alone, sir.' Thurloe gave me a sardonic smile. 'Because his thumbs were tied together.'

Bridewell Dock came into sight. It was here that the Fleet flowed into the Thames. The battlemented walls of Bridewell reared up in front of us, set a little back from the sloping bank of the river on the left side of the lane running down to the dock.

Once a royal palace, it now housed vagrants, foundlings and women of the streets, known collectively as Bridewell Birds. Their sexual favours came cheap. The Fire had coated the pink brick of the buildings with a patchwork of grey and sooty black; most of the roofs had fallen in. Some of the former inhabitants still clung to the shell of the place, for they had nowhere else to go.

We disembarked and walked up the lane. The guards followed us at a distance with the bier. Immediately opposite Bridewell, at its northern end, was the bridge over the Fleet. On the other side was the postern through the wall of the City. The fire had destroyed the gate itself but the postern's stone archway remained, framing the lane beyond. The two soldiers whom Thurloe had left to guard the body were leaning against a wall. They straightened when they saw us. One of them pushed a small earthenware bottle into his pocket.

The soldiers were standing in the angle where a house met the wall of a yard. Behind them, on the ground in the corner, was a long bundle covered with a patched sail. A dozen bystanders watched from a distance, drawn by the combination of red coats and a dead body.

'Uncover him,' Thurloe ordered. 'And shield us from those vultures.'

The soldiers peeled away the sail and held it up as a makeshift curtain. It swayed in the breeze. I stared at the body. The man was lying on his side, facing us, with his arms wrenched behind him. He was short and skinny, with unexpectedly fleshy lips around a large mouth, much like a frog's. He wore his own hair, which was thin and grey. His chin was thick with stubble. There was bruising on the temple.

I pushed aside the flap of his grey coat with the toe of my shoe. The breeches were held up with a broad belt.

'Papist!' one of the bystanders yelled. 'Damned French Papist.'

At a sign from Thurloe, the bier was placed on the ground beside the body. The guardsmen lifted the dead man by his shoulders and knees. The bound arms made it difficult for them. The soldier at the head lost his grip. The corpse's head smacked on the wet cobbles.

The soldier carrying the legs gave a yell and jumped back. The lower half of the body tumbled off the bier. The canvas curtain fell to the ground. The corpse's mouth gaped in a pink and foolish grin.

Thurloe swore. 'Free his arms,' he said. 'Get him on the bier.'

'He's not dead!' someone shouted from the little crowd, which was growing larger. 'Hang him!'

A soldier cut the strip of leather that tied the thumbs. He and the comrade dragged the body onto the bier as if it had been a sack of carrots.

'Kill him!' cried another. 'Kill them all.'

Thurloe glanced over his shoulder. His men were already turning towards the crowd and drawing into a knot to protect the corner where the body lay. Their hands rested on the hilts of their heavy swords.

For the first time I felt a frisson of fear running up my spine. The crowd had swollen to almost twenty people, most of them young men. The larger the crowd, the more stupid it became.

Thurloe turned his head and spat at them.

I looked down at the body. Its head had been thrown to one side when it was tossed on the bier. The face was on its side, looking away from me.

'Are they right?' I said. 'Is he a Papist?'

'No sign of it if he is. Anyway, those scum don't think, damn them. They don't think anything at all.'

The sparse hair of the dead man had re-arranged itself so the back of the neck was visible. There was a line of blood on the skin.

'A moment, sir.'

I knelt by the body and probed the back of the skull with my fingers.

'Best not to linger,' Thurloe said. 'Come on.'

'He wasn't drowned. Look.'

There was a wound in the back of the neck, just below the skull. The man had been stabbed, the blade driving up into the skull. If there had been much blood, the water had washed it away.

'Your eyes are sharp, sir,' Thurloe said. 'Now let us be off.'

Whoever did this thing, I thought, he knew what he was doing, and his method was the same as that of Layne's killer. So were the bound thumbs. I noticed something else — a row of pins, four of them, stuck in the collar of the coat so that only their heads were visible.

Thurloe looked at the crowd and lost

patience with me. 'You can stay if you want, sir. At your peril. You two. Take the bier in front. The rest of you behind — down to the dock.'

Nobody said anything as we crossed the footbridge, marched down to the dock and loaded the bier onto the barge. The bystanders kept their distance. Once we were over the bridge, they dropped away, one by one.

Thurloe and I took the stern seat under the awning.

'I beg your pardon, sir,' he said. 'But there comes a point with a crowd like that when a man must fight or go.'

'You're right,' I said. There was no point in quarrelling with him. The oarsmen pulled out into the river. 'I wish we knew who he was,' I went on. 'Someone must know.'

'There's a good chance you do, isn't there?'

The barge rocked slightly as the bier was manoeuvred aboard.

'What do you mean?'

'It's in my report,' Thurloe said, as if I were to blame for not having had a sight of it beforehand. 'There was a name in the Bible. The ink had run but you could still read it: Jeremiah Sneyd.'

Sneyd. The name was very faintly familiar to me, and I knew the memory of it was lodged somewhere in my childhood.

'Were the bound thumbs in the report as well?' I asked, suddenly wary.

'Of course they were.'

'Who did you report to?'

'My captain. Then I was brought before a man called Master Williamson.'

CHAPTER FIFTEEN

It was dark before I returned to Chelsea, to our lodgings with the Ralstons. Now the nights were growing longer, I found it harder to ignore the inconveniences of living so far from London. The roads were dangerous. The watermen were reluctant to venture this far upstream after nightfall. Those who would, charged accordingly.

Much of the day had been taken up with conveying the body to Whitehall and arranging to have it lodged in the cellar of Scotland Yard. If Williamson had been there when the barge had reached Whitehall, the job could have been done in half the time.

In Chelsea, I found my father dozing by the fire in the kitchen.

Mistress Ralston jerked her head at him. 'He's not been himself today.'

I shrugged. My father hadn't been himself for five years or more.

'Look at him, twitching like that. He mutters to himself like a cage full of monkeys.'

'He's old, mistress. We shall be the same one day, no doubt. If we're spared that long.'

'He was crying earlier. Master Ralston said it put him off his meat.'

'I'm sorry for it,' I said.

'And he was going on and on about walking to Whitehall with you. But saying it was winter. The Thames was frozen over.'

Oh no, I thought. Not this.

'Someone was crying fit to burst, he said, and you started crying too.'

Yes, I thought, I remember it all too well. I was a child again, holding my father's hand and on our way to Whitehall. The sky had been as mottled and grey as a piece of ageing meat on a butcher's stall. There had been little noise apart from the keening of the gulls, the shuffling of feet, the jingle of harness and a low rumble of deep voices like distant thunder.

'And all the time, he was weeping fit to burst,' Mistress Ralston went on. 'It's not a comfortable thing to have in a respectable house.'

It hadn't been comfortable at the time, I wanted to say, so why should it be comfortable now? In Whitehall, there had been soldiers, both cavalry and foot. The nearer we had come to the palace itself, the denser the crush of people. But the crowd had not been merry like townsfolk on a holiday or restless and loud like apprentices on the rampage or even sombre like a congregation around a preacher.

Mistress Ralston worked herself into a passion of righteousness. 'I tell you what, sir, my husband's had enough. That's what he said to me. He's a fair man but there's only so much that flesh and blood can bear.' She sniffed. 'In particular when it's not your own flesh and blood.'

I knew that Master Ralston was no more than a convenient mouthpiece for Mistress Ralston in these matters. I said, 'My father's not usually so bad. I'll help him upstairs.'

But Mistress Ralston wasn't finished. She drew me away from the fire. 'He was praying aloud in the middle of the garden this afternoon. Bareheaded, and no coat. It was raining.'

'His wits wander. But there's no harm in him.'

'I don't know about that.' Mistress Ralston lowered her voice still further. 'Anyway, it wasn't just prayers. It sounded next best thing to treason, what he was saying. I can't have that sort of loose talk, not in my house. It sets tongues wagging, and you know it does. I'd be sorry to lose you, but Master

Ralston says the pair of you will have to go if it continues.'

She wasn't sorry at all. She was probably looking for an excuse to get rid of us. Since the Fire, there was a shortage of accommodation even this far from London, and she would be able to charge a new tenant far more than we were paying her.

I woke my father, took him outside to relieve himself and then helped him up the steep stairs to the chamber we shared.

Movement and fresh air temporarily revived the old man. 'Babylon,' he murmured as he climbed, hauling himself up by the rail fixed to the side of the stairs. With each stair he reached, he produced another name. 'Persia. Greece. Rome.'

'Yes, Father.' I had heard these words often before. 'Hush. Save your breath for climbing.'

'And then at last the Fifth Empire, thank the Lord.' He raised his voice. 'The mighty shall be cast down, and become as dust at the feet of the righteous. Praise the Lord.'

'What did I tell you?' Mistress Ralston called up from the kitchen.

I persuaded my father out of his clothes and into his nightgown. The old man knelt to say his prayers, insisting that I join him. Once in bed, he looked up at me.

187

'Shall we sing a Psalm, James?'

'No, not tonight,' I said quickly.

My father had an unexpectedly high voice. Once it had been sweet and true, but now he could not hold a note. When he sang, he sang so fervently that his voice was audible at the far end of the orchard.

He opened his mouth.

'Tell me, sir,' I said. 'Did you know a man named Sneyd?'

The question distracted him. He shook his head violently, rolling it to and fro on the pillow. 'No, no. I know no one.'

'Hush.'

'Except my God. And you. I don't know Jeremiah Sneyd, I'm quite sure of that.' Master Marwood's eyelids fluttered. 'Perhaps I used to, but I can't remember, not at present. I can't remember anything now, my dear.' He closed his eyes, screwing them tightly shut as a child does. 'Except that Jesus will save me, praise be to God.'

I kissed my father's forehead, picked up the candle and tiptoed from the chamber.

Sneyd, I thought. Jeremiah Sneyd. He knew the man's name was Jeremiah.

CHAPTER SIXTEEN

I listened to the rain on the window and wished that someone would give me a cup of warmed wine or at least stand me by a fire. After months of near-drought, the rain had fallen almost unceasingly for the last week. I had walked from Chelsea to Whitehall and my clothes were damp. My left shoe had sprung a leak. My stockings were streaked with mud and ash.

'You were late again,' Williamson said.

'Your pardon, sir. I came by the road, and the way was difficult because of the rain.'

'Then come by river. Or move closer to Whitehall.' Master Williamson paused to gather his thoughts. 'What is it, Marwood?' he said in a quieter voice. 'You look more like death than a head on a spike.'

'My father was restless last night, sir, and I had no sleep.'

'You know that's nothing to me. He's

lucky to be alive and in his own bed. How is he?'

'His own wits wander a little further every day, and every day they take longer to return. He's harmless enough but our landlady doesn't like it.'

'Then find other lodgings.'

'It won't be easy. Especially now, because of the Fire. Would you, sir, be so kind as to . . . ?'

'If I have time, and if I think you deserve it, I may consider the matter.' Williamson pushed back his chair and gathered together the papers on his desk. 'Now — I can spare you only a moment — my Lord Arlington is waiting, so we must be brief. This man from the Fleet.'

'Sneyd, sir,' I said softly. 'Jeremiah Sneyd.'

'Perhaps. If the Bible was his. There's a Sneyd who used to live with his wife near Cursitor Street. He was once recorded as a Fifth Monarchist. It's not a common name. Go and see if it was him that turned up in the river. Don't say you've come from here, of course — say your father was asking after them.'

Williamson marched to the door, looking at me as he passed with a flicker of malice on his face. 'Perhaps they'll talk to you when they hear your name. Or the widow will, if it's the man we want.'

I opened the door and stood aside. So that was why the name of Jeremiah Sneyd had been familiar to me, and to my father. I would wager good money that he and my father had attended the same meetings.

'You can pray together,' Williamson said.

Cursitor Street was a narrow thoroughfare east of Chancery Lane. I asked after the Sneyds at a chop-house on the north side, but drew a blank. This did not surprise me, for I guessed that they were not the sort of people who had the money or inclination to frequent such places. I tried a butcher nearby with no more luck, and then a cookhouse, with the same result.

Then I remembered the four pins in the dead man's coat. I went into a tailor's shop and asked if he knew a man named Sneyd.

'Sneyd?' cried the tailor, who was cross-legged by the window, sewing a waistcoat. 'Of course I do. But where is he? Faith, he could hardly have chosen a worse time to stay away.'

'He works here, sir?'

'He does piecework. Nothing too fine or delicate. His eyes aren't up to it.' While he was speaking, the tailor continued to drive his needle in and out of the fabric. 'But he's usually reliable, if nothing else.'

'You were expecting him today?'

'Yesterday. I sent word to his lodging, saying I had something for him. But I've heard nothing.'

'Where does he lodge?'

'Ramikin Row, off Took's Court. The third turning on the left, past the pump. It's the house by the sign of the three stars.' The needle paused for a moment. 'If you find him, tell him that he needn't bother coming back.'

The house had seen better days. It tottered over the street, each of its storeys jettied out a little further than the one below. There was a shop selling rags on the ground floor. I asked there, and the shopman sent me up the rickety stairs to the top floor.

'Mind how you go, master,' he called after me. 'Sneyd's as sour as vinegar these days.'

I was glad to be out of the rain. The house was let out by the room, and many faces peered at me on my way up. I knocked on the door of the attic at the back and a woman opened it almost at once, though only by a few inches.

'Mistress Sneyd?'

'Who's asking?'

She was probably in her forties but she

looked older. She was toothless and her face had fallen in. The skin around her eyes was red and swollen. She was respectably dressed in a plain black gown of serge, though the material had faded with age.

'My name's Marwood,' I said.

There was a spark of recognition in her face.

'My father is Nathaniel Marwood.'

'The printer? But I thought —'

'That he was in prison? No, mistress. They let him out six months ago.'

'I'm glad. But why are you here?'

'I am looking for Master Jeremiah Sneyd.'

'He's not here.' She began to close the door. 'Anyway, he does not concern himself with such things as he did before, he —'

I planted my foot between the door and jamb. 'Forgive me, mistress. I mean no harm to you.'

The pressure on my foot relaxed. The door swung back into the room.

'What does it matter?' she said, her eyes filling with tears. 'What does anything matter? You might as well come in.'

The room was furnished only with a truckle bed, a small table by the window, and two stools. The floor was bare and swept clean.

Her lip were trembling. 'Truly the ways of

the Lord are mysterious.'

'What's wrong, mistress?'

She twisted her hands together as if washing them in invisible water. 'Nothing. This miserable life.'

She fell silent. For a moment neither of us spoke. I knew that Williamson wanted me to keep her in ignorance of her husband's fate and suck her dry of whatever she knew. I couldn't do it.

I took a deep breath. 'Mistress Sneyd, is your husband a small man, without much fat on him, and with long grey hair and a large mouth?'

She nodded, her eyes widening.

'And he has a row of pins in his coat, and he carries a Bible in his pocket with his name inside it?'

'Something's happened to him.' She took my arm and shook it, as if she would shake the truth out of me. 'He's dead. Oh merciful God, he's dead, isn't he?'

'Yes.'

'How?'

'He was found in the Fleet Ditch by one of the patrols.'

It seemed wiser not to mention the stab wound, not at this point, or the bound thumbs, but to allow her to assume that her husband had drowned. I expected the poor woman to throw her apron over her head and wail. Or to fling herself onto her knees and pray to her God. Or even hit me. Instead, she turned slowly away and sank down on one of the stools by the table. She stared out of the window. After a moment she began to polish one of the lattices with her fingertip.

I sat opposite her. 'I'm sorry. You must have been worried when he didn't come home.'

She sniffed but gave no other sign she had heard. I couldn't see her face. The finger went round and round, squeaking slightly on the glass.

'This is the second day he's been gone, isn't it? When did he go out? Wednesday evening?'

'Yes,' she said. 'If only he'd listened to me, he'd still be alive. He should have kept away from old comrades. Like your father.'

'Which comrades?' I said. 'One in particular? Someone he'd served with? A soldier?'

She looked at me now, and her hand dropped away from the window. 'Someone from the old days. One who believed in God as he did.'

'A Fifth Monarchist,' I said softly.
She nodded.
'And who was this comrade, mistress?'

'He wouldn't tell me. He said he'd been sworn to secrecy, and that it was better that I should not know. Me! The wife of his bosom.' She gave a short, bitter laugh. 'As if he could not trust me.'

The woman was so distressed that she hardly knew what she was saying. I asked her more questions. Answers spilled out of her, though not in the order of my asking, and sometimes the answers were to questions I had not asked at all.

Gradually I pieced together a story. The unknown comrade had sent a message near the end of August, asking her husband to meet him one evening. Master Sneyd had returned from the meeting, full of mysterious excitement, but he would tell his wife nothing of what had transpired. There had been other meetings, she thought, and her husband had seemed happier in himself than she had seen him for a long time.

'Not since Oliver seized power. Fifteen years or more. God forgive me, I rejoiced to see him so cheerful.'

I understood the timing of that all too well, for as a child I had seen a similar pattern in my father. After the execution of the King, the Fifth Monarchists had nursed high hopes that theirs would be the dominant voice in government, and that they would make England a godly country, fit for Christ's return. But Oliver Cromwell had had a different idea of God and other plans for England. He had swiftly destroyed their hopes and consolidated his own power.

'This man, this comrade,' I said. 'Do you —'

'Master Coldridge?' she interrupted.

'What? I thought you didn't know his name.'

'Then you didn't listen properly. How like a man.' Anger revitalized her, and I glimpsed the woman she usually was, without this load of grief weighing her down. 'I said he wouldn't tell me. But I knew. I knew by the letters he sent on. They went to Master Coldridge.'

The flare of vitality died away. She wiped her eyes with her apron.

'Letters? What letters?'

'He'd been taking them down to the letter office for years. He thought I didn't know.'

'Where did they come from?'

'How should I know? It must have been when he was out at work or with his friends. He made money by it, I know that. Not much but something.' Her voice trailed away. Her fingers plucked at her apron.

I was losing her. I tried one last question: 'This Coldridge: do you think he served with your husband in the late war? What was your husband's regiment?'

Mistress Sneyd looked wildly at me. 'Colonel Harrison's.'

That answered more than one question. Harrison had been another Fifth Monarchist. He had commanded the escort that brought the captured King to Windsor not long before his execution. The son of a butcher, he had been a brutal and notably efficient officer; he had also been named as a Regicide, and had been the first man to be hanged, drawn and quartered after the King's return.

'But why do you want to know this?' Her voice was thick with suspicion. 'Are you one of them, another dangerous dreamer from the old days? Or are you a spy?'

'I'm a friend, mistress. I cannot say more.'

'You foolish men,' she said. 'With your secrets and your spies and your killing and your burning. You cannot truly believe that God wants such things of his creatures? Can you not let us live in peace?'

CHAPTER SEVENTEEN

After I left Mistress Sneyd, I should have gone back to Whitehall and talked to Williamson. But I needed to think about what I had learned.

I walked up past Staples Inn and into Holborn. My head churned with uncomfortable thoughts. Mistress Sneyd had ordered me from her sight, cursing me for the news I had brought her. The best she could hope for now was a life of drudgery. As for the worst, that depended on Master Williamson and his masters.

It was possible that the government would order Mistress Sneyd's arrest after I had made my report. If the worst came to the worst, I thought, they might also think it prudent to place my father in custody again. I had little doubt that another dose of confinement would kill him. But he was an obvious target for their suspicion. He was not only a Fifth Monarchy man but he had also known Sneyd.

Anything to do with Fifth Monarchists concerned the authorities. They must be aware as well as I was that Fifth Monarchy men had always held 1666 to be a year of great importance, for 666 was the number of the Great Beast in the Book of Revelation. Besides, when all the numeral letters in the Latin tongue were written down in diminishing numerical value, they made MDCLXVI, which was 1666. My father was quite sure that this extraordinary numerological phenomenon must portend some great event in that year. He was also certain about the form this would take: after the Beast would be the Second Coming of the Messiah, and King Jesus would reign over us all for ever and ever.

Which meant, of course, our sovereign lord King Charles II must be none other than the Great Beast. And, to make way for King Jesus, he must, like his father, be killed.

At the end of Fetter Lane, I waited at the crossing for a break in the traffic. The rain was heavier than it had been. I needed to find shelter and something to eat. An empty stomach wouldn't help me think.

It struck me then that I wasn't far from Barnabas Place. It lay a little further eastwards, north of Holborn. The image of Olivia Alderley's face swam into my mind. I had a sudden urge to see her, or at least to be near her. More to the point, I remembered a tavern outside the gates of the house. I might as well take shelter there as anywhere and combine food for the soul with food for the belly.

The tavern was at the sign of the Three Feathers. I took a seat near the end of the long table and ordered ale and soup. I had a view through the tavern window of the closed gates of Barnabas Place. I watched the rain splashing into the puddles among the cobbles in front of the gateway. Half a dozen beggars were finding partial shelter under the great arch. I thought about Olivia Alderley, my father and the Great Beast until my head began to hurt.

I had almost finished eating when there was a commotion across the road in front of Barnabas Place. One leaf of the great gates opened. Two servants shouted at the beggars and shook their fists.

In the middle of this confusion, a large, red-headed man trundled a barrow under the arch and pushed it in the direction of Holborn. He was easy to see partly because of his size — well over six foot. His hair was loose, and spread below the brim of the brown hat and over his shoulders. The jolting of the cobbles made his progress slow. He stared about him as he went, like a countryman new to town.

He passed close to the window where I sat. He was wheeling a box on the barrow. A servant's box by the look of it, and unexpectedly familiar. Below the lock, two neatly formed capital letters had been burned into the wood.

I had seen the box in Barnabas Place with Master Mundy at my shoulder. It had belonged to Jem, the servant who had attacked his master's son and been flogged to death before my very eyes. Mistress Alderley had told me that her husband had written to Jem's relation, asking her to remove the box. So, on the face of it, there was nothing strange about this.

Nevertheless, on impulse I threw down the money to pay my score and went out of the tavern. Keeping well back, I followed the red-headed man. He crossed Holborn, pushing his barrow briskly over the road with a confidence that suggested he was more used to London than he had at first appeared, and turned into Fetter Lane.

The box was the last trace of the man who had attacked Edward Alderley. There had been a poignancy about its contents — the

silver cup, the doll and unreadable Bible —
but nothing among them to suggest that
Jem had nursed murderous inclinations
towards his employers.

Fetter Lane ran southwards to Fleet
Street. The first half was much as it had
always been, though sootier than before. But
the Fire had reached the southern half of
the lane and wrought its dark transforma-
tions on the buildings there. To the right,
undamaged London continued westwards
into the suburbs. But to the left there
opened a prospect of the blackened City
wall, with the ruins of St Paul's rising starkly
on its hill beyond Ludgate.

To the east, there was nothing but ashes
and ruins for nearly a mile and a half —
from here in Fetter Lane, west of the City
boundary, to the Tower of London.

The desolation struck me like a blow, fresh
and painful, as if all this destruction had
been newly made yesterday, and as if this
were my first sight of it. It was grief, I think,
nothing more or less. I knew it was absurd.
But I had noticed this reaction in others as
well as in myself: that we mourned for our
ravaged city as if for a mother; or as Mistress
Sneyd grieved for her husband. The sorrow
came in waves, just as it had when my own
mother died.

Ashes and ruins. Tears pricked my eyelids. I swore aloud, for such grief was of no earthly use to me, and two clergymen, passing in the opposite direction, gave me disapproving looks.

'Drunk,' said one, speaking in a normal voice as though I were a block of wood incapable of hearing anything, let alone understanding it.

'Or mazed,' said the other.

'Or both,' said the first, with the air of one covering all eventualities.

Ashes and ruins? Nothing left from here to the Tower?

I stopped so abruptly that one of the clergymen almost bumped into me. Before the Fire, most of the principal carriers had been based at one or other of the City inns, where the wagons left almost daily for all parts of the kingdom. I was sure that Mistress Alderley had said that Jem's relation was a woman living in Oxford. The Oxford route was exceptionally busy — the court had moved there last year because of the plague and stayed there for months; it had returned to London only a month or two after Christmas. The wagons left the City by Newgate, crossed Holborn Bridge, and travelled westwards into the Oxford road.

But most of the City's inns were no longer there.

At the foot of Fetter Lane, the red-headed man was turning right in the direction of Temple Bar and the Strand.

So where the devil was he going? It was possible that an Oxford carrier now left from somewhere in Fleet Street, say, or the Strand. Possible, but scarcely convenient. A set of stables in Holborn would have made much more sense, or even further west, and there were plenty of inns that would have welcomed the business. Or perhaps Jem's box was to be stored somewhere in London before it went to the carrier.

Possible, yes, but not what I had expected. It was a kink in the probable, like a break in the pattern of one of the Alderleys' Turkey carpets.

At the bottom of the lane, I crossed to the other side and turned into Fleet Street. It was more crowded here and the red-headed man wheeled his barrow in the direction of Temple Bar. He was now nearly a hundred yards ahead, but it was easy to keep him in sight because of his hair and his height.

A small, ragged boy collided with me, as if by accident. I swore. In the corner of my eye, I glimpsed movement on my other side.

A second boy was approaching, keeping well back.

I snarled at them. I reached for my purse with one hand and the hilt of my dagger with the other.

The pickpockets sheered away like startled magpies rising from carrion. They darted across the roadway, narrowly escaping collision with the horses of a wagon lumbering towards the City.

My hand still on my dagger, I backed against the wall while my breathing returned to normal. Sometimes the pickpockets operated in packs, and a second attempt would be made on a potential victim while he was recovering from the first. I glanced westward down Fleet Street.

The man was gone.

I swore again. The incident with the boys must have taken less than a minute. The man and the barrow could not have gone far. I started walking again, more quickly this time. I looked into shops, into taverns, and into the mouths of alleys.

I asked two people, a manservant and a cook boy, whether they had seen a red-headed man with a barrow. The servant ignored me, for he saw my hand on my dagger, and hurried past. The cook boy shook his head, waited in vain for a penny and spat on the ground to relieve his feelings.

The best possibility, I decided, was a lane scarcely wide enough to take a cart. It led to a paved court with a pump in the corner. It was a modestly prosperous enclave. The houses formed a terrace; they were not large, but they were newly built and with brick frontages. One had an apothecary's shop on the ground floor, another a jeweller's, and a third a superior establishment selling china imported from France and Germany. I paused by the pump and pretended to be making a note in my pocketbook.

In the centre of the terrace was a gate which led, no doubt, to the private yards and cesspools behind the houses. If the man had gone anywhere in this court, it was probably through that gate. I looked up at the windows, which looked blankly back at me.

After a moment, I returned to Fleet Street, crossed the road and went into a tavern. When the waiter came, I threw caution to the winds and ordered a jug of wine. As soon as the waiter returned, I asked the name of the court opposite.

'Why, sir,' he said, wiping greasy hands on a greasy apron. 'That's Three Cocks Yard.'

CHAPTER EIGHTEEN

I had not been inside St Paul's since the Fire. Now, when I left the tavern, I knew it was time to go there. Perhaps it was because I was now a little drunk. Perhaps it was because I wanted to postpone my interview with Master Williamson.

I had not made a conscious decision to avoid the place. My reluctance was instinctive, unexamined and unexplained, part and parcel of the mysterious grief for my lost London.

The closer I came to the cathedral, the more ruinous it looked. Convocation House Yard had been fenced off, as had the remains of the cloisters and Chapter House. Carpenters had sealed the doorways and the Dean and Chapter had appointed watchmen to patrol the exterior by day and night. There had been attempts to loot graves in the first day or two, and the authorities were doing their best to put a stop to it.

A stonemason's boy directed me to the cathedral's office of works. Here I negotiated with the watchman guarding the entrance to a temporary enclosure between cloister and nave, within the wider enclosure of the yard. Williamson had given me a general pass that vouched for me as a clerk attached to Lord Arlington's office. Eventually this proved powerful enough to persuade the watchman to send for the Clerk to the Chapter.

Master Frewin, an anxious-looking gentleman in his fifties, eyed me with a frown. 'You want to go into the cathedral? But why?'

When in doubt, a bare-faced but unassailable lie was the simplest policy. 'My Lord Arlington wishes me to make an inspection, sir.'

'But God knows, there have been inspections enough. And Dr Wren and his colleagues have advised His Majesty of the condition of the fabric.'

'Indeed, sir. But now his lordship has commanded me to make notes on one or two particular points.'

'Such as?'

I stared at Master Frewin. 'He does not wish me to discuss that.'

I knew that my damp and shabby clothes did not inspire respect. But a confident manner and an air of borrowed authority had served me well in the past. I watched the emotions chase over the clerk's face — irritation, doubt, calculation and even a touch of fear.

'Very well,' he said at length. 'But I warn you, it's dangerous. Walls collapse without warning. The floor is treacherous in many places. We've lost several men already. If you venture in there, you take your life in your own hands — you understand that?'

I bowed. 'Are there men working in there now?'

'Of course.' Master Frewin rubbed his forehead. Now he had decided to capitulate, his manner became almost confidential. 'Come this way, and mind where you tread. We are trying to clear the rubble away, for we cannot do anything with that there. We are still waiting to hear whether they will repair or rebuild. It is a perfect nightmare.'

'You are to be pitied, sir.'

Frewin's voice rose to a wail. 'The King says one thing, the Dean another, and God knows what goes on in the Lord Mayor's head, if anything. Dr Wren would build a new Jerusalem if he had the chance, but where's the money to come from? And all the time I'm obliged to do what I can to keep the place safe.'

'One thing first, sir. I am commanded to enquire about the body that was found in Bishop Kempe's chantry after the Fire.'

'Layne? Master Alderley's manservant? Poor devil.'

'Did you see him?'

'Oh yes. I saw all the dead. It was often hard to know whether the Fire killed them or whether they were centuries old.'

'Had you seen Layne before?' I asked. 'In life?'

He shook his head. 'I didn't know him from Adam. Master Alderley asked me the same question when he came here the other day with Dr Wren.'

While we were talking, Frewin had led me across the yard piled high with salvaged stones to a large shed built against the cloister wall, where a number of men were at work sorting and recording salvaged materials. He pulled aside a heavy leather curtain on the back wall. An opening had been punched through the masonry, and a new door inserted in the opening. Beyond it were the remains of the north walk of the cloister. The ruins of the Chapter House were visible through the windows on the right, which had lost their glass.

'This way, sir. On the left at the end. That was once the cathedral's south door.'

Part of the door, a blackened mass of wood and iron, still hung on its hinges. It had been propped open with a baulk of timber. Beyond it was the long, roofless nave.

I paused in the doorway, assaulted by the din. Three labourers with hammers and chisels were at work nearby, shearing away blocks of dressed stone from the rubble core of fallen walls. Under the crossing, a gang of labourers was singing a drinking song in time with the scrapes of their shovels. Someone was shouting near the west end of the nave, where the modern portico had been attached to the main body of the church in the previous reign.

A network of paths had been cleared through the rubble. Men dragged barrows laden with stones and other debris. Each barrow required two or three men to move it, and their iron-shod wheels grated on the ground. The air was full of swearing and grunting and groaning.

'Bedlam, sir,' Master Frewin said. 'I never thought I should live to see such a thing in St Paul's. God knows, it was bad enough under Oliver, but when the King came into his own again, we hoped the good times had returned with him. What fools we were.'

There were tears in the man's eyes. More grief. I looked up, to avoid his face. The blackened pillars and crumbling walls rose to the open sky, heavy with rain clouds.

'Why?' Master Frewin said. 'What's it all for?' He turned and stumbled along the cloister walk, leaving me in the doorway.

Now I was here, I had to force myself to enter the church. I walked up to the crossing. The great pillars that held up the tower were cracked and leaning. The roof remained over the high altar at the east end, but it was particularly dangerous in that part of the building because of the collapse of the choir floor into St Faith's in the crypt below.

Surely they could not rebuild this? The Fire's destruction had ravaged a building that had already been tottering. During the war and under the Commonwealth, the authorities had encouraged the physical decay of the cathedral, as well as challenging its sanctity. Cromwell had stabled a regiment of cavalry in the cathedral, and the troopers had ridden their horses up and down the steps to the choir. My father had cheered.

Huge though the cathedral was, it was difficult to move around it easily — partly because of the rubble, and partly because the workmen filled what open space there was. I zigzagged through the ruins to what was left of Bishop Kempe's chapel in Paul's Walk. This was just west of the crossing, on the north side of the nave. Even before the Fire, the chantry had been in a decayed condition. Some of its stones had been stolen. The statues that had filled the niches had been decapitated or entirely destroyed.

Little was now left of the chapel or its past history. I scrambled over a heap of stones to reach it. There were still fragments of carving, some with traces of faded paint attached to them. The altar block was there, though it had been thrown off its dais. The heat had cracked it in two. I wondered whether the pimp and his ballads had survived the Fire.

This was where Layne's body had been found, his thumbs tied behind his back, squeezed between the altar and the chantry wall.

Someone was shouting behind me, near to the temporary screen at the west end of the nave. One of the workmen was ordering his dinner.

The manservant must have been killed on the very night that the Fire had destroyed St Paul's. Otherwise the corpse would have

214

been found sooner. The church had been full of people seeking refuge before that for both themselves and their possessions.

'And a jug of ale,' the workman shouted, his voice hoarse. 'Make sure it's cold, Richard. None of your lukewarm slop like last time.'

I wasn't listening to what the labourer was shouting. My mind was concentrating on Layne's murder and the night of the Fire in Paul's Walk. But I heard the sounds of his words, and some part of my mind imposed a meaning on them.

Make sure it's cold, Richard. Cold, Rich. Coldridge.

I looked down Paul's Walk at the man who wanted his dinner.

Words made patterns.

Coldridge PW, I thought. Coldridge, Paul's Walk.

I walked back through the cloister ruins and pushed aside the leather curtain. I was in a hurry to be gone — I needed to report to Master Williamson at Whitehall, and I had already lingered here too long.

Master Frewin was nowhere to be seen in the shed that served as a workshop. I approached an elderly draughtsman stooping over his board, and asked where the Chapter

Clerk might be found.

He straightened his spine and rubbed his eyes. 'He's probably in his private room.'

'Then would you say farewell to him, sir, on my behalf and give him my thanks? My name is Marwood, on business from Whitehall.'

'He'll not be long, if you care to wait.' The draughtsman waved a bony finger with an untrimmed nail at the end of it. 'He works over there, and his inkpot is still uncovered.'

I followed the direction of the finger. I saw Master Frewin's stool and desk, not five yards away, with a flight of wooden steps rising up the wall behind it. At the top of the steps was a door, which I assumed led to Master Frewin's private room.

I also saw a cloak. It was hanging on a rusty nail that had been hammered between two stone blocks of the wall between the draughtsman's stool and Master Frewin's. The cloak was grey, made of wool but lightweight — not for winter use. It was on the shabby side.

Frowning, I walked over to it and fingered the material. It smelled of burning, as did almost everything at present.

A shock ran through me, as if I had fallen into cold water. There was a long rip on the left-hand side of the lining, where a cut-purse's knife had gone astray in the summer of the plague.

I lifted it from the nail and turned back to the draughtsman. 'Sir — this is mine, I believe.'

The man inclined his head courteously. 'I believe not, sir.'

'But I'm sure of it, sir.' I held up the cloak. 'I don't know how it came here, but see this tear here — I remember it well.'

The last time I had seen the cloak was when it was protecting the modesty of the young woman who had repaid me by sinking her teeth into my hand.

'You are mistaken, sir. I know that for a fact.' The draughtsman came towards me and, with unexpected firmness, took the cloak and hung it back on the nail. 'An easy mistake. One grey cloak is much like another, just as all cats are grey in the dark.' He looked past me and over my head. 'Ah. And here is Master Frewin on the stairs. You may make your farewells in person.'

Sometimes I hated my father almost as much as I loved him.

He brought down troubles on his own head, and also on the heads of those around him. In Oliver's time, and before that, he had been a stationer. He had been a printer in a small way, living and working in Pater Noster Row. He had inherited the press and the business from his father-in-law, to whom he had been apprenticed.

We had been comfortable enough when I was a child, despite the war. But my father did not prosper when Oliver Cromwell became Lord Protector. He blamed this partly on my mother, on the grounds that God was punishing her, and us, for trying to persuade him that Cromwell's rule would bring peace and stability to the realm, and that this was all that mattered.

'But there is no peace worthy of the name,' my father had said at the deathbed of my little sister, who had died of a vomiting fit before her first birthday, 'other than God's peace. Thanks be to God. Stop your wailing, woman. You should weep tears of joy for her.'

When the King returned, my father had been too honest to change his opinions and too foolish to hide them. This Charles Stuart, he was wont to tell me, was a man of blood like his father, a spawn of the Devil, a lover of foreign whores and a Papist in Protestant clothing. He reminded me that we had seen one king's head removed from his body. God willing, there was no reason why we should not see another lose his head.

Even then, I had known that it would be only a matter of time before my father's opinions brought him into conflict with the authorities. When they arrested him at last, he was a hale, middle-aged man. When they let him out, five years later, his body was feeble and his wits wandered.

Unfortunately it wasn't just his wits that wandered. When I returned from Whitehall that evening, Mistress Ralston was waiting in the kitchen.

'The old man's outside somewhere. The Lord alone knows where.'

'In the garden?'

'Perhaps.'

I reined in my anger, for she made him sound like a straying dog. 'When did he go out, mistress?'

'As it was getting dark.'

I glanced at the pegs by the door. 'Without his hat? Without his cloak?'

Mistress Ralston shrugged. 'I'm not his mother. He's a grown man.'

I turned to go.

'Master Ralston's not pleased,' Mistress Ralston said. 'You'll have to take your father away. He's decided. You are paid up until next Friday so you can have until then.'

It was cool outside, and the air smelled of

the river. A light rain was falling, soft as a caress. The stars were out.

My eyes adjusted to what light there was. The market garden was laid out with great regularity, for Master Ralston was orderly by nature. I paced slowly up and down the long, straight paths, navigating by memory as much as by sight. As I walked, I called my father's name.

On either side were raised beds where, in their seasons, Master Ralston cultivated soft fruits, herbs and all things fit for salads. I came at last to the orchard that took up more than a quarter of the garden's area. Apple, plum and pear trees had been espaliered against a south-facing wall, and the standards were lined up with the regularity of Ironsides on parade.

'My son. My son.'

My father was sitting on the sodden ground and leaning back against the trunk of one of the standards.

'This is an apple tree,' he said, through chattering teeth.

'Yes, Father. But you must come back into the house.'

'An apple tree. Whereof Eve did eat, and therefore was forever cursed, as were all the generations of man that grew from her womb.'

'It grows late, sir. Let me help you up.'

His limbs were stiff. He clung to my arm and I hauled him up with some difficulty. Despite his frail body, he was surprisingly heavy. I guided his wavering footsteps back to the cottage. The kitchen was in darkness when we got there, for the Ralstons had retired for the night and taken the candle with them.

There was still a red glow from the banked-up fire. I lit a taper from an ember and by its light found our candle on the dresser.

'The King is coming,' my father said.

'Yes, sir.' I lifted a chair into the ingle and guided him to it. 'Sit down.' I fetched his cloak and draped it over his shoulders. 'You must not go out in the dark. Besides, the weather is turning colder. You must wear your cloak when you venture outside, sir, and your hat.'

'Yes,' he said. 'Of course. You needn't concern yourself.' He sounded almost his old self, brisk and assured.

I said, 'Tell me, sir, were you ever acquainted with a man named Coldridge?'

'Coldridge? No.'

'Or did you ever hear tell of a man with that name?'

'No.' He leaned forward in the chair, and

221

I sensed that I had lost him again. 'But I'll tell you something, if you like.'

'What?'

'The King is coming.'

'I think not.' I filled a cup from the kettle, which still contained a little lukewarm water. 'Drink — it will warm you.'

He struggled to rise. 'The King —'

I pushed him gently back into the chair. 'What would His Majesty want with plain folk like us? Or we with him? Drink, I pray you.'

My father took the cup but did not drink. 'The King comes to all, James, high and low.'

A suspicion crept into my mind. 'Which king, sir?'

'Why, I do not mean that man of sin, Charles Stuart, the son of the man of blood. I mean King Jesus.'

That night I had little sleep. I lay in bed, listening to the snores of my father beside me.

Towards dawn I dozed for a while, my mind drifting into that borderless territory between the past and the present where dreams and nightmares walk. I was a child again, and going to Whitehall, walking towards a gateway that stood between tall towers. The brickwork was chequered black and white. Despite its size, it was quite overshadowed by a building at right angles to it, a slab of stone and glass that reared up on the left.

There were more walls on the right so the people were hemmed in on all sides except the way they had come. The soldiers lined the walls and clustered particularly thickly in front of the tall building. Their helmets and breastplates gleamed. Their red sashes were stripes of blood.

A man said: 'He's there already, Master Marwood.'

'Where?' my father asked.

The man jerked a thumb at the big building, which was behind him. 'In there. The Banqueting House.'

'When will they do it?'

'No one knows.' He nodded at a stage draped in black that projected from it. 'But that's where.'

Time passed.

I grew colder and colder. The crowd was never still and I was so small and restless that men kept treading on my feet or knocking against me. I was hungry. The very name of the Banqueting House made my mouth water. The great ladies and gentlemen would be inside, and the soldiers' captains and colonels, dining on joints of meat served on gold plates and dripping with gravy.

The air filled with the chimes of many clocks. My father chafed my hands to warm them. He gave me the heel of yesterday's loaf to take the edge off my hunger, and cut me a piece of hard cheese with his horn-handled knife.

'You've been good,' he said. 'You must be brave now, child, for the sake of King Jesus.'

CHAPTER NINETEEN

John towered over Mistress Noxon. His cheeks were flushed, and his chin poked out. 'I tell you, mistress, he were following me.'

'Nonsense. Put it in the corner there for the time being, beside the dresser.'

He set down Jem's box on the kitchen floor and straightened, smoothing his hands on his breeches. He gave her the key for the box. Only then did he say, 'He were, though.'

For John, usually so silent, this was eloquence. Cat, who had been staring at the familiar box, turned her eyes on him. He blushed and smiled at her.

'Who was?' Mistress Noxon said.

He dragged his eyes away from Cat. 'Skinny fellow. From Barnabas Place, then all the way down Fetter Lane, then in Fleet Street.'

'Someone walking in the same direction.

Nothing strange in that.'

The chin poked out a little more. 'I know when a man's watching me, mistress.'

'Why would anyone watch you?'

'Green coat?' Margery said.

Mistress Noxon shot her a look of outrage for presuming to interrupt.

But John was nodding. 'Yes, that's him.' He swung back to Mistress Noxon. 'See, mistress? Margery saw him too.'

Mistress Noxon frowned. 'How? You've been in the house all day.'

Margery said, 'I went upstairs for a clean apron, mistress. I chanced to look out.'

She had been watching out for John, Cat guessed, that was why. That's what love did — it made a fool of you.

'What did you see?' Mistress Noxon said.

'A young man, mistress, in a green coat. Not a one you'd pay much attention to in the normal run of things.'

'Well dressed?'

Margery shook her head. 'A clerk, maybe, or a shopman. I couldn't see his face because of the brim of his hat. But John's in the right of it, he wasn't a big man.'

'I could have snapped him in two like a twig if I'd a mind to,' John said.

'He stopped by the pump,' Margery went on, bent on making the most of this opportunity. 'Wrote something in a book he had in his pocket.'

'He's up to no good,' John said with finality. 'Sneaking after me like that. Next thing we know he'll murder us all in our beds.'

'That's plain foolish, John,' Mistress Noxon said. 'And you know it is.'

'I know what I saw, mistress. And it weren't just me. It were our Margery too. She saw him.'

Mistress Noxon stared at the faces of the servants around her. 'Very well. Tell me if you see this fellow again.'

'Like a twig,' said John, smiling at Cat and nodding vigorously. 'I could snap him like a twig.'

'This won't get Master Hakesby's supper on the table, will it?' Mistress Noxon snapped. 'Come on — to work, you idle rogues.'

Later, when supper had been cleared away, when John had gone to his straw mattress in the lean-to in the yard, and Margery, complaining of a headache, had hauled herself up the stairs to bed, Mistress Noxon came out of her private room.

Cat was on her hands and knees before the hearth, shovelling ash.

'Just as I thought,' Mistress Noxon said in

a low voice. 'Nothing in the box, nothing but rubbish, and not much of that, either. Which is not to be wondered at. I'm sure those knaves at Barnabas Place took anything of value before my poor uncle was in his grave.'

Cat stood up, brushing her dress.

Mistress Noxon had an old coat over her arm and a collection of objects in her hands. She dumped them on the kitchen table.

Cat looked at what was left of Jem. The silver cup, tarnished and dented, that Jem had been given at his christening. The serge coat he wore on Sundays. The Bible he read every evening, holding it up to his eyes. The bowl that Cat's mother had thrown onto the rubbish heap at the Bow Lane house, and Jem had taken in because it still had some use in it. And Hepzibah, the doll Jem had made for Cat when she was so little that she had believed Jem to be her father.

'Names have meanings,' Jem had told her, for he knew such things from another life and could translate words from Latin, Greek and even Hebrew. 'Hepzibah signifies "my delight is in you". Also it means the one you protect.'

She had sensed even then that he had not been talking about the doll but about her.

'That's everything,' Mistress Noxon said.

'Can you believe it? That a man should leave so little behind him.' She hesitated, and then lowered her voice. 'Do you happen to know if he had anything else?'

'There should be an almanac,' Cat said. 'He always had an almanac. I bought him one every year.'

Mistress Noxon sniffed. 'He believed such foolishness? All those prophecies? You'd have thought the astrologers would have warned us about the Fire beforehand, instead of saying they did afterwards. And they should have warned my uncle about —' She broke off, and turned her head away from the candle on the table. 'Well, that's all over with. He believed all manner of nonsense, and so for that matter did your father.' She jerked her head at the objects on the table. 'Is that doll yours?'

'It was, mistress. He made it for me. And when I grew too old for it, he said he would have it.' Cat swallowed. 'He said he would keep it for my children.'

'You'd better take it, then.'

'I won't have any children.'

'Take it.'

Cat picked up the doll, wrapping her fingers around its familiar shape. There were tooth-marks on Hepzibah's head, for Cat had found the taste of her strangely comforting.

'You haven't got a box for your things,' Mistress Noxon said, making it sound like an accusation, for every servant should have a box. 'I suppose you might as well have this when I've emptied it.'

CHAPTER TWENTY

'What man?' Cat said.

'A young man,' Master Hakesby murmured. 'He took one look at the cloak and was instantly persuaded it was his. But I told him it was not, and in the end he went away. But I thought it wise to bring it back today — he seemed to have taken such an inexplicable fancy to it, after all. It should have occurred to me to bring it before — with weather like this you must have a use for it.'

He held up the grey cloak and draped it over Cat's arm. They were standing in the doorway of Master Hakesby's room and talking in low voices. Dr Wren had honoured Master Hakesby with a visit. He was sitting at the table by the window and computing columns of figures.

'But what sort of man was he, sir?' Cat said. 'His appearance? His station in life?'

Hakesby glanced curiously at her, and she

knew she had made a mistake: she had forgotten that she was here as a servant; she had spoken to him in her natural voice, as if he were her equal.

'A clerk, perhaps?' he said. 'I asked Master Frewin about him afterwards — the Clerk to the Chapter, you know; it was he that the young man came to see. Master Frewin said he was one of Lord Arlington's men come to inspect the fabric.' Hakesby's right hand began to tremble. He thrust it out of sight into his pocket. 'Not that he was there long enough to see very much at all. Master Frewin thinks he was sent merely to keep us on our mettle, to remind us that the King and the court have their eyes on us.'

'Master Hakesby?' Wren glanced up, and his eyes fell on Cat. He frowned. 'If you have a moment, would you be so good as to cast your eyes over these calculations?'

Cat was dismissed. She dropped a curtsy and left the room. She carried the cloak up to the attic she shared with Margery and then returned to her afternoon duties. The rest of the day passed in an uncomfortable daze, which she realized in the end was the next best thing to fear. At dinnertime, she snapped at John when he asked if she meant to have an outing on Lord Mayor's Day, the public holiday that fell next month, with the unexpressed but obvious hope that she might like to share the day with him.

'Hoity-toity,' Margery murmured, and Mistress Noxon said that they would eat in silence if they could not behave with Christian civility to one another.

Cat was desperate to know more from Hakesby. But he and Dr Wren were at work all afternoon. It was not until after six that Cat heard Hakesby's feet descending the stairs. She ran up to the hall and contrived to waylay him before he reached the door.

'Sir, I pray you, a word before you go.'

He stooped over her, his grey hair swaying like curtains on either side of his thin face. 'What is it, my dear?'

It was the first time he had called her 'my dear' — indeed, the first time that anyone had done so for years, even poor Jem. She was not sure she liked it.

'The man, sir,' she said. 'The man who saw the cloak. What was he like?'

'Like? Much like most young men, I suppose. Middling height. Thin as a rake.'

'How was he dressed?'

'I can't recall — no, stay, he wore green, I remember that because it struck me that the colour would have been thought rather lively for a Whitehall clerk in the Lord Protector's time. I was there, you know, at

Whitehall. I worked as a senior draughtsman for the Surveyor General.'

Cat's lips moved but the words made
hardly any sound. 'A green coat?'

'Yes. A green coat. Why do you want to
know?'

'I — I wondered. It seemed so strange.'
She hesitated and then made up her mind
to confide a little more in him. 'John marked
a man in a green coat in the court.'

Hakesby shrugged, settling his own cloak
around his shoulders. 'Is there anything so
very curious about that? Many men wear
green coats, especially young and foolish
ones. I wouldn't let it concern you.' He took
a step toward the door, and then paused.
'Ah — I wonder — I have a suggestion — a
request. A favour, even.'

He looked at her, smiling and moistening
his lips. She recoiled, thinking: Oh no, not
him too.

'You recall that you assisted me the other
day with a little work of my own?'

She blinked as relief rushed over her. 'Yes,
sir.'

'I wonder — if I had a word with Mistress
Noxon and made it right with her — would
you do some more?'

'Yes. Yes, sir.' She swallowed.

'Acting as my amanuensis, you might say.

Just occasionally. Do you know what an amanuensis is?'

'Yes, sir. One who takes dictation.'

He frowned, and she knew she had made another mistake. 'You're full of surprises, Jane.'

When Master Hakesby had gone, Cat stood for a moment in the hall, shivering. The suggestion would have delighted her this morning, and even now it brought her pleasure: this knowledge that Master Hakesby, having seen her work, wished her to do more.

But now she was too afraid to enjoy it.

A thin young man in a green coat had followed John when he brought Jem's box from Barnabas Place. A thin young man in a green coat had noticed her cloak at St Paul's, and this young man worked for Lord Arlington.

In terms of logic, it did not necessarily follow that the first thin young man in a green coat was the same as the second.

But if he were . . . How could he have known that it was her cloak, the stolen cloak, hanging in Convocation House Yard? No one at Barnabas Place could have told him that, because no one there had known that she had had it. Only Jem had known, but he was dead.

The young man had recognized the cloak. He had said it was his. There was an obvious and simple explanation for this: that he was speaking the truth.

In which case, Lord Arlington's clerk in Convocation House Yard was none other than the man whose hand she had bitten on the night that the Fire destroyed St Paul's. The thin young man in a green coat was identical to the thin young man who had dragged her away from the flames.

Was he therefore a government spy? Had he known why she was at St Paul's that night?

It was raining hard. The clocks of the neighbourhood had struck midnight some time ago.

Mistress Noxon was in bed and presumably asleep. John slept beyond the kitchen. Margery was in the attic, with Cat; but she slept like the dead and snored like the Last Trump.

Cat would be undisturbed, so long as she were careful.

Cat's candle was still burning. She got out of her bed, a straw mattress near the window, and wrapped a blanket around her shoulders. Her box, Jem's box, was at the head of the bed. Cat kept it beside the mattress she slept on, with its key concealed in the crack where the boards of the floor met the wall. The box contained her few clothes, the bag she had brought from Barnabas Place, the box of drawing instruments from Great Aunt Eyre, and the pieces of paper that she gathered as and when she could from Master Hakesby's scraps, to be hoarded for times like this.

She knelt down, turned the key, lifted the lid and took out paper and pencil. She smoothed out a sheet on the top of the box, weighting it with the candlestick, Hepzibah and the key. Working rapidly, and shielding the stub of the candle with her left arm, she sketched in freehand the outlines of an elegant open space, a hexagon, into which avenues entered in the centre of each of the six sides. There would be a public garden in the open space, laid out with statues and at least one fountain.

As the lines glided across the paper, the buildings and streets rose above them in her mind, the parts perfectly in balance with each other, forming the heart of a magnificent city empty of people.

This work was the only effective distraction from the incessant interior interrogation that Master Hakesby had unwittingly set in train in the afternoon. No wonder,

Cat thought, that they called God the Great Architect. If you were omnipotent and had all the time in eternity, what better way to use these blessings than to design an entire universe and all it contained? What better way to forget yourself?

The wind was rising, throwing squally gusts against the window. She worked on and the candle burned lower. Margery snuffled in her sleep.

The door latch cracked up.

Cat swung round. Mistress Noxon was in the doorway, wrapped in her bedgown and wearing a shawl and a nightcap.

'What are you doing?' she hissed.

Cat pushed the paper aside, trying to conceal it with a fold of the blanket.

'Mistress, forgive me —'

'I thought you'd fallen asleep and left your candle burning. For all I know, you'd burn the whole house about our ears.'

Cat shook her head violently. She had dreams of fire and falling houses and, worst of all, the ferocious crackle of the flames as they devoured whatever lay in their path.

'I'm sorry,' she whispered, and meant it, for everyone was afraid of fire now.

Mistress Noxon advanced into the room and held up her own candle. 'What's this? The paper?'

There was no help for it. Cat pulled the blanket aside.

Mistress Noxon took the paper and held it to the candle flame, tilting it this way and that to see it better. She frowned. 'You strange, unnatural girl,' she said softly, but the anger had left her voice and was replaced with a sort of wonder. 'Why do you draw such things?'

'They interest me, mistress. I — I cannot help it.'

'You're mad. Mad as a March hare.'

Margery snored on.

'I have an aptitude. A desire.'

'An aptitude?' Mistress Noxon snorted. 'More like a moonshine fancy. I never heard of such a thing. As for the rest —'

'Yesterday, I did some copying for Master Hakesby and —'

'I know you did, and took yourself away from your work. Your proper work.'

'And Dr Wren saw what I had done as well, and he thought it was passable. Today, Master Hakesby asked me if I would do more for him.'

'He's a single gentleman,' Mistress Noxon said. 'He's a widower, you know, so he was accustomed to his comforts and doubtless wants them still. So you'll do no such thing. I know what he's after.'

'No, mistress — it's not that, I think. He wants me to help him with his drawing. He has the ague and his hands shake.'

'His ague? Is that what he calls it?'

'He said he would talk to you about it.'

Mistress Noxon sighed. She handed the sheet of paper to Cat. She was silent for a moment and then she said, very quietly, 'You were never easy, even as a child.'

'But you didn't know me then, mistress.'

'My uncle did,' Mistress Noxon snapped. 'Better than your own father and mother, maybe. He said you were like a changeling. Something the fairies left behind.'

Cat's eyes drifted back to the paper. Instead of a public garden, should there perhaps be a church in the middle of the piazza? A church of six bays with a spire rising by stages from a square tower.

'Why are you doing this nonsense now?' Mistress Noxon said.

'I couldn't sleep. I — I was fearful.' Even the piazza would not take that away. 'The man who was in the yard yesterday. The one John said was following him from Barnabas Place. I think he's looking for me.'

'You're mad. Why should he be doing that? Put that rubbish away and go to bed.'

When she was alone, Cat blew out the candle and lay in the comforting darkness with Hepzibah growing warmer in her hand. Margery's snores mingled with the tapping of the rain on the window.

She would not let them take her back to Barnabas Place. She would sooner die. At best, her uncle would force her to marry Sir Denzil, condemning her to a living nightmare and losing all control of her aunt's estate in the process. At worst, they would lay information against her and put her on trial for the attempted murder of her cousin. Uncle Alderley had probably talked in confidence to one of his Whitehall friends already. But whom did they really want? Her father or herself?

Slowly Hepzibah worked her old magic. The clerk might have followed Jem's box to see where it was taken, but he could not have discovered that Cat was living at Three Cocks Yard. Even the grey cloak at St Paul's could have told him nothing about her for certain. If she kept herself to herself, she could be safe.

In the meantime she would wait for the future to show itself. In a perfect world, she would kill her cousin Edward, for had he not killed something in her? In a perfect world, she would work for Master Hakesby. In a perfect world, she would not be obliged to go into exile with her father, assuming she ever found him, for she would always be a poor second best to his God.

A nameless emotion rippled through her at the thought of him, and Hepzibah's reassurance was powerless to fight it. He was her father, after all, and that meant something, though she was not sure exactly what. She could not abandon him.

CHAPTER TWENTY-ONE

In the morning, it was raining more heavily. I settled my father by the fire with strict instructions not to ramble in the garden or to bother Mistress Ralston. I walked down to the river and hired a tilt boat to take me downstream to the public stairs at Whitehall.

Master Williamson was not at Scotland Yard. I went to his room at Lord Arlington's office in the Privy Garden. A supercilious clerk directed me to the Matted Gallery. The gallery was crowded with people strolling slowly up and down, bowing to their acquaintance. It was a favourite resort at the palace, especially when the weather was too bad for the park.

I found Williamson standing by a window at the far end, looking down on the garden below. He was humming a tune under his breath, as he often did when wrapped in thought.

'His lordship is in the Duke's closet,' he

said without preamble, having realized that I was almost at his elbow. 'It's mighty inconvenient. He commanded me to wait for him here, but I have a thousand things to do.'

He took me by the arm and drew me into an alcove in which was a table displaying a clock of great antiquity. His eyes were everywhere apart from my face, constantly searching the throng of people in the gallery.

'But it's well you're here,' he went on. 'I need to be quite sure about something. This Coldridge you mentioned. You're sure this was the name you saw in the manservant's box, and also the name that Sneyd's comrade was using?'

'Beyond all doubt, sir. "Coldridge PW" was written on the paper enclosing the guineas in Layne's box, though the handwriting was not his.' I wondered why it was so important for Williamson to check what I had told him yesterday. 'And Mistress Sneyd certainly told me that her husband's comrade was called Coldridge.'

'Did you ask your father about him?'

'Yes. He didn't know the name.'

'Did not?' Williamson said sharply. 'Or would not admit it?'

'I caught him at a lucid moment. I believe

I know when he tells me the truth.'

Williamson grunted. 'And you've learned nothing more about this Coldridge?'

'Only this, sir.' I decided to tell him of the speculation that had come to me in the cathedral. I had not mentioned it yesterday as it seemed far-fetched. But now I wanted to divert Williamson's attention from my father. 'It struck me that "PW" might refer to Paul's Walk. In which case the paper gave a name and a place. Could that have been the reason Layne went to St Paul's on the night the Fire destroyed it?'

'To meet Coldridge?'

'Or to spy on a meeting between Coldridge and another person — Jem Brockhurst, the servant who was flogged to death?'

Williamson chewed his lower lip. 'It's possible,' he conceded. 'I'll turn it over in my mind.' All of a sudden, he snapped out of his reverie and became his usual self. 'I'm engaged here, Marwood, but there's no need for you to be idle. I want you to complete the current list of my news correspondents. It shouldn't take you long. Then take the *Gazette* proof back to Master Newcomb. Tell him —' He looked past me, and suddenly his face creased into a smile. 'Sir Denzil — your servant, sir.' He swept into a low bow. 'And yours too, sir.' Another bow, even lower. 'What a pleasure to see you at court again.'

I turned. Master Alderley and Sir Denzil Croughton were approaching, arm-in-arm. They separated themselves and bowed to Master Williamson. I bowed as well, but their eyes slid over me, and they did not return my courtesy.

'We are come to wait on the Duke of York,' Sir Denzil said in his high, weary voice. 'By his express command. But my Lord Arlington is with him.'

Williamson bowed again, acknowledging the manifest importance of this. 'He wishes for your assistance, sir?' he said to Master Alderley.

'Yes. A small matter, but urgent. To His Royal Highness, at least.'

'Small?' Sir Denzil laughed. 'Small?' His voice dropped almost to a whisper. 'By God, sir, there are few people in this gallery — few people in England, indeed — for whom two thousand, four hundred pounds is a small sum. And fewer still who could lay their hands on it at the drop of a hat.'

'You flatter me, sir.' Master Alderley smiled. 'It is not ready money, after all — merely a matter of credit at short notice. A trifle.'

'Ha!' Sir Denzil cried. 'If that's a trifle, sir, then I'm a poxy Dutch whore, sir, and be damned to me!'

I stared at the muddy matting on the floor, knowing that I was of so little account to these gentlemen that they saw no need to set curbs on their tongues. How strange to lend a man money you did not have. The currency such people dealt in was not gold and silver: it was promises and dreams.

The three gentlemen began to walk slowly down the length of the gallery, with Alderley in the middle. In the absence of any instructions to the contrary, I followed, two paces behind Master Williamson.

Sir Denzil stopped suddenly. 'Look.'

He pointed towards a door some distance away on the river side of the gallery. It was guarded by two soldiers. One of them had opened it for a gentleman who was about to pass through to the apartments beyond.

The gentleman paused in the doorway and glanced along the gallery. He was a plump, middle-aged man, quietly dressed in dark clothes. I knew him at once by the wart on his chin.

'Ah,' Master Williamson said. 'His master is stirring at last.'

Sir Denzil laughed softly. 'Stirring, sir? The question is, which part of him is

247

stirring?'

The door closed behind the gentleman. At the same moment, a servant in royal livery cut through the crowd towards us. Sir Denzil and Alderley turned towards him.

The servant came to a halt in front of them and bowed in the arrogant manner of his kind. 'His Royal Highness is at liberty to receive you now.'

'At last,' Master Alderley said.

'Let us walk together,' Master Williamson said. 'Lord Arlington will be at liberty too.'

The three of them left me to consider the riddle of the plump gentleman with the wart on his chin.

'Pray, sir,' I asked a servant in livery who was dawdling through the crowd. 'Do you know where that door goes to?'

The servant laughed in the sneering Whitehall manner that suggested he found my ignorance both irritating and amusing. 'Don't you know? You won't go far in this place if you have to ask something like that,' he said. 'It leads to the King's private apartments.'

'Master Marwood?'

I came to a halt under the northern gateway from Scotland Yard to the thoroughfare beyond. I was on my way to

Master Newcomb, the printer, with the marked-up page proofs for the next *Gazette*.

A woman was standing under the outer arch, sheltering from the rain. Most of the light was behind her, and she was reduced to little more than a tall, slender shadow. Her face was partly covered by the collar of her cloak, which muffled her voice.

'Yes?'

She pushed aside the collar of the cloak, revealing a narrow face and thin-lipped mouth.

'Don't I know you?' I said. 'Mistress Alderley's maid?'

'Yes, sir. She bids me give you a message. She is visiting a friend in the City tomorrow, and if you are at leisure after dinner, she begs you call on her there.'

'Why? Do you know?'

'You must ask her that yourself, sir. The house is next door to the sign of the Three Stars in Cradle Alley. Do you know it? Near Moorgate.'

'I thought Cradle Alley had been burned.'

'Only the western end. My mistress goes to dine there, and she will stay until master sends the coach for her.'

'When?'

'You are to attend her at three o'clock in the afternoon.'

'Very well. Pray tell her —'

'It's a private interview,' the maid said. 'She desires you not mention it to anyone.'

Without another word, she walked away in the rain.

Master Newcomb, the printer, was in an affable mood, as he generally was at present.

He had been fortunate. Few of the City's other printers had managed to save their press and to find themselves new premises since the Fire, let alone to continue to work profitably. Newcomb had lost the greater part of his stock and some of his household goods. But he was still doing steady business.

All in all, the court connection had served him well, and not just in the matter of finding new premises. Master Williamson employed him to print the *Gazette,* six hundred copies twice a week. It was steady, reliable work; it paid the rent, and it also went some way to providing Newcomb and his family with bread and meat.

The printer was in the shop at the front of his premises when I arrived, my hat dripping and my only remaining cloak sodden with rain. He was a bluff, fresh-faced man in early middle age. He looked up at the click of the latch.

'Why, sir, a pleasure to see you.' Newcomb waved his apprentice forward. 'Take Master Marwood's cloak and hang it by the kitchen fire. Ay, and his hat too.'

I came forward, feeling for the inner pocket of my coat. 'I have the proof here.'

Newcomb took the two sheets and scanned through the additions and corrections that Williamson had marked up.

'You'll stay for a glass of wine, I hope? We'll have it warmed to keep out the damp.'

He left his apprentice in charge of the shop, gave the proof to his journeyman and led me upstairs to the parlour.

Mistress Newcomb served our wine herself. When she came into the room, I saw that she was with child again. I had lost track of their children, living and dead, but I thought that this was probably her eighth pregnancy.

'You're looking thinner every day,' she said to me as she set the tray on the table. 'You can't be eating properly.'

'Don't worry him, my dear,' Master Newcomb said. 'Let him drink his wine in peace.'

She ignored her husband, as she often did. 'Come to dinner, sir, and I'll feed you up. And your father too, if he is well enough. How is the poor man doing?'

'A little older and a little vaguer, mistress.

Otherwise well enough.'

'I hear you're living as far from town as Chelsea,' Mistress Newcomb said. 'It cannot be convenient.'

I shrugged. 'The air is better. And it seemed wise when — when he came to live with me.'

The Newcombs exchanged glances. They had known my father before his imprisonment, for he had been a familiar figure among his brother printers and stationers and well known at Stationers' Hall. He had been surprisingly popular among them, too, despite holding religious views that condemned most of the human race, apart from himself and a few other chosen ones, to an afterlife of eternal damnation. But, religion apart, he had had a reputation as an upright but kindly man, skilled in his trade and happy to help a friend in distress.

'Does he like living in the country?' Mistress Newcomb asked.

'It matters little to him where he lives now, mistress. He rarely leaves the house and garden. He spends most of his time dozing by the kitchen fire.'

'Will you stay in Chelsea?'

I hesitated. 'We shall be obliged to move very soon — it is no longer convenient for the people of the house to have us.'

Again, the Newcombs exchanged glances, passing information between them in the swift and silent shorthand of the married.

'You should find yourselves lodgings nearer Whitehall,' Master Newcomb said.

Another glance.

'As it happens,' Mistress Newcomb said with an air of abstraction, 'Master Newcomb and I have been discussing the possibility of taking lodgers ourselves. There are two chambers at the side, on the first floor. Not large, but adequate. The apprentice has one of them at present, but he could sleep in the kitchen. And the second one we use only as a store.'

A great wailing of high voices arose from somewhere in the rear of the house.

'Those wretched children!' Newcomb said. 'My dear, can you not make them mute, at least while Master Marwood is here?'

'Usually they are as quiet as lambs,' Mistress Newcomb said, smiling sweetly at me as she glided towards the door. 'But it happens that Mary and Henry both have the toothache, and once one of them starts crying, that sets the other one off.' She shouted downstairs to an invisible servant. 'Margaret! Stop those children making that din. At once, do you hear?'

'The apothecary makes up drops for them,' their father said. 'It's the only way, and the expense of it can go to the devil. A man cannot set a price on domestic peace.'

Mistress Newcomb was lingering in the doorway, her colour high. 'Margaret lets them run wild, the foolish woman. She's too kind to them. If I've told her once, I've told her a thousand times.' She moderated her voice and gave me another smile. 'If you liked, sir, you could come to dinner tomorrow and see if the rooms would suit your purpose.'

The wailing increased, and Mistress Newcomb slipped away.

'She has it all arranged,' Master Newcomb said in a low voice. 'She always does.' He sipped his wine. 'Mind you, you could do a lot worse. And it would be a convenient arrangement for all of us. But don't let our convenience affect how you decide.'

'Thank you, sir.' I found myself unexpectedly moved. In the last few years, I had received little kindness from others. The suggestion was kindly meant, even if it was tinged with self-interest.

Newcomb's eyes considered me over the brim of his glass. 'And she's right about the other thing, too, you know. Come to dinner. You look nothing but skin and bone, if you'll allow me to say so. As if you're living on air and not much else.'

The rain stopped while I was at the Newcombs'. When I returned to Whitehall, I found a message from Williamson at Scotland Yard, commanding me to attend him at Lord Arlington's.

He was not there, but I found him taking the air nearby in the Privy Garden. He was pacing along one of the straight paths that ran parallel to the range of buildings containing the Matted Gallery. If he came to a puddle, he walked through it rather than alter his course by a single degree.

He looked up as he heard my footsteps on the gravel. 'You were a long time with Newcomb.'

I bowed. 'Your pardon, sir. As it happens, he has two rooms to let above his press.'

Williamson raised his eyebrows. 'How fortunate. Will you take them?'

'I haven't seen them yet. But I am hopeful.'

He walked on. I walked a pace behind, following him to the far side of the garden, to the wall that divided it from the bowling green, and then along another of the paths. He did not speak until he stopped by the King's great sundial. He looked about him to make sure there was no one in earshot.

'This business at Barnabas Place,' he said abruptly. 'There's something you'd better know. It may not matter, but I cannot be sure.'

He took a sheet of paper from his pocket and handed it to me. It contained a list of names, arranged in a column.

John Bradshaw — obit
Lord Grey of Groby — obit
Oliver Cromwell — obit
Edward Whalley — fugit
Sir Michael Livesey — fugit
~~*John Okey*~~

The hairs prickled on the back of my neck. I looked up after reading the first six. 'But these are —'

'Yes. These are the Regicides. The men who presided over the murder of his late Majesty, and those who assisted them.'

I knew then why Master Williamson preferred to talk to me in the privacy of the garden. At the King's Restoration, six years ago, Parliament had passed the Act of Indemnity and Oblivion, a necessary measure to heal the wounds of the long Civil War. It granted a general pardon to those who had taken up arms against the King and his father. The only exceptions to this pardon were the Regicides and their helpers, together with a handful of others whose treason had been considered too foul to excuse.

My eyes ran down to the foot of the list. The annotations after the names told me the men's fates. 'Obit'; these were the lucky ones, who had died. Those who had escaped and were still alive were labelled 'fugit'; they lived in fear of death at the hand of the King's agents. Others had been imprisoned or even pardoned. And the rest —

'The ones crossed out have been executed or otherwise killed,' Williamson said. 'Read on.'

I turned the paper over. The list continued on the other side. My eyes snagged on a name near the bottom.

Thomas Lovett — fugit.

'There's nothing against Catherine Lovett personally, or Sir Denzil would not have betrothed himself to her.' Williamson coughed. 'Her father's goods and lands were confiscated when he fled abroad, including his house and business in Bow Lane. But I am informed that the young lady is an heiress in her own right, by her mother's family, so she still has her own fortune.'

'Pray, sir,' I asked, 'why are you telling me this?'

'Because this business is about more than a murdered servant. More than an insignificant Fifth Monarchy man ending up in the Fleet Ditch. Henry Alderley's niece is the daughter of a Regicide, who has so far escaped capture. You must tread very carefully, Marwood. We must all tread carefully. Do you understand me?'

I understood many things now. One of them was that Master Williamson was scared. Another was that he was perhaps a kinder man than I had thought him to be.

CHAPTER TWENTY-TWO

On Sunday morning, I took a boat down to the stairs by Charing Cross and dined with the Newcombs at the Savoy. My hostess fed me well, and I took more wine than was altogether wise. No doubt she wanted to ingratiate herself and her husband with me. I liked Master Newcomb well enough, but I was less sure of his wife, a dark, sharp woman with darting eyes. She was charm itself to me but she was curt with her servants and quick to chastise her children.

After dinner, they showed me the two rooms on the first floor of their premises. The apartments were small and overlooked a common way leading to a yard with a pump. But they were clean and they were available now. It would be possible for my father and me to have our own rooms, something I devoutly desired. The sounds of the press in the workshop downstairs might deter many prospective tenants, but they would have a blessed familiarity for the old man. Moreover, I had learned during dinner that Mistress Newcomb had nursed her own father in his last years; she was used to dealing with the vagaries of the aged. As a final advantage, the lodging was retired in situation, yet convenient for both Whitehall and the City.

I took the lodgings on the spot. The Newcombs already knew my father's history, and so there would be nothing to conceal from them. Perhaps, I thought, as I walked a little unsteadily up to the Strand, the tide is beginning to run in my favour.

I turned east and walked towards the black stump of St Paul's and the city of ashes.

Cradle Alley was a narrow but straight street that ran east from Coleman Street in the direction of Austin Friars and Broad Street. The western part of it was lined with heaps of ash and rubble, some of which still lay on the roadway, stretching down to the choked kennel in the middle.

I picked my way along the alley, holding my cloak to my nose. I was late. It had taken me longer to get here than I had expected, for the streets were still clogged with debris. I wished now that I had not lingered at the

Newcombs'.

Tendrils of smoke from trapped fires mingled with the misty vapour of the rain and the gritty coal smog that had covered so much of London even before the Fire. The ruins gave way to a variety of houses and workshops huddling on either side of Cradle Alley.

The house next to the sign of the three stars was on the left, near the end. The building was narrow and spread itself over four storeys, the upper ones jettied out above the street. There was no trace of a business or trade being carried on there, and no clue to its occupants. But the windows were clean and the plaster on the gable had been whitewashed since the Fire. It looked well cared for, which could not at present be said of most houses that remained in the City.

An old woman, her eyes closed and her face the colour of grubby chalk, was squatting in a doorway on the other side of the road, her hand held out for alms. I dropped a penny into her palm. The eyes opened at once. The fingers closed over the coin and thrust it out of sight beneath her filthy cloak.

'God bless you, sir,' she mumbled.

'Who lives over there? In that tall old house?'

She looked up. One of her eyes was covered with a grey film. 'That's Quincy's, master.' She held out her hand again, palm upwards. The penny was no longer there.

I gave her another penny. 'Master Quincy?'

'Old man's dead and in his grave. But it's still Quincy's.'

'Who lives there now?'

'They come and they go.'

The eyelids closed, and I gave up the struggle to extract information from her. I jumped over the kennel to the other side of the lane and knocked on the door of the tall house. It opened almost at once. The porter ushered me into the hall even as I was stating my name and business.

The interior took me by surprise because it did not match the exterior of the house. The hall was spacious and well proportioned. Clocks ticked away the seconds. The flagstones were marble, chequered black and white.

Another manservant appeared, bowed and asked me to follow him. He was a tall man, with a pox-scarred face and the carriage of a soldier; there was nothing servile about him. We went up a wide, shallow staircase to a galleried landing on the first floor. He tapped on a door and, without waiting for a reply, opened it and stood aside for me to enter.

Mistress Alderley was seated by the fire in a tall armchair with a caned back. As I came in, she laid aside a book on the table by her chair. She was more plainly dressed than usual, though her clothes were of the finest quality. To my surprise, there was no sign of her maid or her hostess.

I bowed low. As I raised my head, I made a rapid survey. The room was large, high-ceilinged and surprisingly modern. Opposite the door, two large windows gave a view north over the rooftops to the City wall, punctuated by the stumpy tower of Moorgate.

The apartment was furnished in the French style as a withdrawing room or private parlour. It was as luxurious as the parlour at Barnabas Place but very different in its manner of expressing it. Barnabas Place looked to the past in its furniture and fittings: this room could hardly have been more modern. There were many pictures on the walls, most of them on classical themes and many with goddesses or perhaps nymphs displaying their charms.

Only a heavy leather screen struck an old-fashioned note. It was placed across one corner of the room; the lintel of a second doorway was visible above it. The leather had been painted with a hunting scene, but the reds and greens had darkened with time and smoke into a mottled brown.

Mistress Alderley indicated that I should sit on a settle facing the fire and at right angles to her chair. 'It is kind of you to come, Master Marwood. You must forgive me for asking you here. And you must be curious about the reason.'

For a moment, neither of us spoke. In repose, her oval face looked almost sullen. The brown eyes were hooded with heavy lids. How old was she? Thirty? Thirty-five?

She gave a sigh, as if something were troubling her, and stirred in her chair. 'First,' she said, 'is there new intelligence about the murders? Now we have two of them, I understand.' She noticed my puzzled look. 'Master Williamson told my husband about the second man, when they met at Whitehall yesterday.'

'I've heard nothing more, madam.'

Her long fingers toyed with a tassel on the arm of the chair. 'My second question is this: may I put a private proposition before you? And, whatever your answer, may I depend on your discretion?'

Did she know, I wondered, that I would find it hard to deny her anything, especially if she asked in that confiding tone?

'Yes,' I said.

Mistress Alderley looked searchingly at me. 'Will you help me find my husband's niece?'

I stared at her in surprise. 'But isn't she in the country? You told me she was staying with friends because of her health.'

'I told you an untruth. Well? Will you help me?'

I tried to retain at least a little caution. 'As far as I can, madam. But Master Williamson must —'

'You need not trouble yourself about Master Williamson. But remember this: he does not know what I wish you to do, or why. And he must not, unless I decide otherwise.'

'And Master Alderley?'

'He does not know of this, and at present I wish him to remain in ignorance.'

'But, madam,' I said, 'I must know more of this before I can decide how to proceed.'

Her mouth tightened. But she nodded. 'Very well.' Then she smiled, the merest twitch of the lips. 'First, how did you like the lodgings you saw today?'

'In the Savoy?' Yet again she had taken me unawares. 'Very well, madam. I have taken them.'

'Your father will find the business of the place reassuring, I dare say,' she said. 'As a printer, I mean. And of course you needed to find somewhere quickly. Lodgings are hard to come by since the Fire, especially for men like your father. How fortunate for you.'

'You — you knew?'

'Yes. You might even say I played the part of providence.'

I found I was on my feet, full of rage and fear for my father, and for myself. 'Why, madam?' I demanded. 'Why?'

'Sit down and I shall tell you.'

I sat down again. As I did so, I heard, quite distinctly, a board creaking nearby. The sound came from behind the screen in the corner of the room.

Mistress Alderley cleared her throat, perhaps in an attempt to mask the sound. 'I made enquiries. And I thought I would do you a service beforehand, so you would understand that you will not be the loser by helping me.'

I understood more than that. She knew who my father was, and how precarious our circumstances were. If she had the power to help us, she also had the power to harm us.

I heard the scrape of a chair behind the screen and then heavy footsteps. I leapt to my feet. A gentleman appeared. He was middle-aged and well-fleshed. His clothes were sober, though his face had the flush of good living and there was nothing of the Puritan of him. There was a wart on his chin.

'I am Master Chiffinch,' he said.

I bowed low to him, hoping my fear did not show. One mystery was solved, the identity of the man I had seen visiting Master Williamson. I knew Chiffinch by reputation, if not by face, as did most people who worked at Whitehall. He was the Clerk of the King's Closet, like his brother before him — the man who controlled the private access to the King.

'We want you to go to Coldridge,' he said.

'Coldridge, sir? But where is he?'

'It's a place, not a man.'

I gaped at him. 'I don't understand.'

'It is simple enough. We want to find Catherine Lovett, Mistress Alderley's niece, and restore her to her friends. It must be done discreetly, for the young lady is about to be married, and we must safeguard her reputation from slander.'

I bowed again.

'Coldridge is a property in Suffolk,' Chiffinch continued briskly. 'Mistress Lovett owns it now, and it's where she passed some of her childhood. It lies not far from the village of Champney Crucis.'

'We cannot be sure that she's there,' Mistress Alderley said. 'But she may have fled there as . . . as a sort of refuge.'

'A refuge from what?' I said.

'She has maidenly doubts about her fitness for the married state, as so many girls do. I need hardly say that this alliance with Sir Denzil is entirely suitable. Her family wish it, and her betrothed could not be kinder or more attentive to her. But it is this childish scruple that must have temporarily disordered her wits.'

'It is natural that a girl should seek refuge in the place where she was happy as a child,' Chiffinch interrupted. 'And you found evidence of it too, did you not, madam?'

'Master Marwood did, sir, not I.'

'The paper,' I said. 'In Layne's box: "Coldridge PW".'

She nodded. 'In the other servant's hand. That villain, Jem. You were right about that. Layne must have broken into the box and taken it.'

'Six guineas with it,' I reminded her.

'Blackmail,' Chiffinch said. 'Layne probably got wind of her intended escape and tried to extort money for his silence. Mistress Lovett bribed him to keep his mouth shut. But Jem decided to make sure of his silence and lured him to St Paul's instead. In all the confusion that night it can't have been difficult to conceal a murder there. All it took was one thrust of a dagger.'

'But to kill a man for so small a reason —'

Chiffinch waved me to silence. 'The rogue was possessed by a devil. If we accept that Jem killed Layne, it explains a great deal, I think, including the attack on your stepson. Jem was vicious by nature, and fanatical in his attachment to Mistress Lovett.'

'Of course my niece knew nothing of it,' Mistress Alderley said.

I kept silent. Chiffinch regarded me with large, moist eyes. I thought of the ragged little man I had seen flogged to death at Barnabas Place. He had not seemed vicious then, but perhaps no man did when he was under the whip.

'There you have it, Marwood,' he said, speaking more slowly than before as if in emphasis. 'There you have the whole story.'

'You must go to Coldridge and see if Catherine is there, Master Marwood,' Mistress Alderley said, looking earnestly at me. 'The estate has been leased, I believe, but perhaps she is lodging in seclusion with a childhood acquaintance, or an old servant.

Tell her I sent you, and all is forgiven. Bring her home. Reason with her, but if necessary compel her. You may hire a woman to attend her on the journey. Master Chiffinch will arrange money and letters of authority for you.'

'There is a complication,' Chiffinch said. 'It is just possible that if you search for her, you may also find her father.' He stared at me and he must have seen the bewilderment on my face. 'Thomas Lovett,' he went on. 'The Regicide. In which case you are to forget the girl for the moment. You must go at once to the nearest justice and have Lovett seized.'

Chiffinch had business elsewhere and left me alone with Mistress Alderley. We sat in silence, wrapped in our own thoughts.

'Catherine is a strange girl, Master Marwood,' she said after a moment or two. 'Small in stature, and in many ways more like a child than a woman. Her father has left his mark on her.'

'She's of the Fifth Monarchy persuasion too?'

'Nothing like that. What they share is very different. Thomas Lovett was a master mason, like his father before him. His work was much valued in the old King's time. He had travelled on the Continent as a young man and he knew the latest styles of the Continent. Master Inigo Jones himself thought highly of him. I believe that's what she thinks of most, in her heart of hearts. This vulgar, mechanical work of building.'

'A woman can't wield a chisel,' I pointed out. 'She can't be a mason like her father. The very idea is absurd.'

'I suppose a woman could wield a chisel as well as anyone,' Mistress Alderley said, to my surprise. 'Should she wish to engage in such a low, dirty business. But it isn't that I mean. At Barnabas Place, Catherine was forever scribbling plans and designs for buildings. Not in public, of course — only when she was alone. I caught her at it once. And my maid brought me discarded sheets that she had thrown away. I think her aunt in Coldridge had encouraged her to take an interest in such things. Mere castles in the air, but harmless enough, though I doubt Sir Denzil would approve. Such a strange, unwomanly taste . . . She looks like a child and thinks like a man. Indeed, I think she would have been happier if she had been born a boy.'

CHAPTER TWENTY-THREE

'You were at Cradle Alley yesterday, I hear,' Master Williamson said. 'Master Chiffinch told me.'

There was a strange intonation in his voice. His face gave nothing away — it rarely did — but I realized that something between us had changed.

'I'm told it's a charming house,' Williamson said. 'And mercifully spared from the Fire. Are — are the new rooms very fine?'

'Yes, sir. From the street, the house is nothing out of the ordinary, but it is quite different inside. One might almost be here at Whitehall.'

'That's not so very surprising.' His eyebrows drew together. 'Bearing in mind Mistress Alderley's tenant.' He saw from my face that I had no idea what he was talking about. 'Why, it is Master Chiffinch himself. Did you not know?'

It was not only the words that told me his

meaning but the prim little smile that accompanied them. It was unlikely that Master Chiffinch himself would have need of a lavishly appointed house in the City. But his royal master was another matter.

'Mistress Alderley,' Williamson went on, 'has court connections. Her first husband, Sir William Quincy, joined the King in exile.' Another prim little smile. 'And Lady Quincy herself, as she was then. But Sir William died just before the Restoration. The King did not forget the young widow of his loyal friend.'

The words were perfectly proper, but there was a wealth of possible meaning to be glimpsed in the murky depths beneath them. How far had Lady Quincy's loyalty to the monarch allowed her to go when the King was in exile? I knew well enough she was an attractive woman, and the King was certainly a man who loved women. When her first husband died, perhaps the King had encouraged a complacent and conveniently rich husband to court her, in the shape of Master Alderley? As for the house in Cradle Alley, it was not hard to guess the uses that the King and Master Chiffinch might find for a discreetly luxurious residence in the City, away from the prying eyes and wagging tongues of Whitehall.

'Master Chiffinch has requested that I give you leave to go down to Suffolk for a few days,' Master Williamson said. 'He has explained the nature of the errand.'

'My father —'

'You leave tomorrow morning. As early as possible. You are to travel as a supernumerary clerk of the Office of Works, carrying a letter from the Surveyor General to the Harbour Master at Harwich, which I understand is conveniently close to Champney. The Office of Works will provide you with the loan of a horse. You will so arrange your journey that you visit Champney, and make your enquiries there.' He waved a hand. 'There's a brick-making works nearby, and if anyone questions you, you are examining the clay in the neighbourhood. If we know nothing else about what will happen to London, we can be sure we need bricks to rebuild it. As for the rest' — he left a pregnant pause — 'Master Chiffinch has already explained everything you need to know.'

I sensed his frustration. Williamson did not like to be kept in the dark, and he hated the idea that I knew more about something than he did.

'The only difficulty is my father, sir. I must move him and our effects to the Savoy as soon as possible.'

'Oh yes. That. The Office of Works will loan you a small wagon for a few hours. You shall have this afternoon off. That should give you ample time to change your lodgings. Come to me if you need anything.'

For the first time in my life, I felt the beneficial effects of proximity to power. Yesterday all these things had been impossible. Now they were mine at the stroke of someone else's pen.

The following morning I rose early in our new lodgings in the Savoy and rode east and north. I left my father at breakfast with a small child perched on either knee, for Mistress Newcomb had decided to make him useful; both he and the little Newcombs seemed happy with this arrangement, at least for the time being.

The day was cloudy but dry. At first my way took me through the ruins of the City to Leadenhall Street, a quarter that had escaped the Fire. My spirits lightened once I had passed through the City walls at Aldgate, and they continued to rise as gradually the houses dropped away.

Gardens, orchards and paddocks appeared, even at the roadside, and at last the road ran through open farmland. The air changed, too, as the smog of the city thinned and then disappeared. Colours grew brighter. The green of grass, trees and bushes was almost unbearably vivid. I had not realized that the colours of London, Whitehall, Westminster and even Chelsea had become so tinged with ashy grey, for my eyes had adjusted to it.

The hours passed. The roads were in better condition than I had expected, despite the autumn rains, for the heat of the summer had baked them hard. I felt increasingly cheerful, as if I had been granted a holiday. If my father had a fit or wandered away, I would not even know of it. If Master Williamson needed someone to take his dictation long into the evening, I would not be there to sit at his elbow, my quill at the ready. Indeed, on that first day away from London, I should have been entirely happy if it had not been for my aching calves and the chafing of the saddle on my thighs.

At Harwich, the Harbour Master gave me a lavish supper and offered to make arrangements for the morrow. I lay that night at an inn near the quayside, where the bed was good. I slept like the dead and woke to find myself bitten by bugs, and my muscles so painful that I could barely stand.

After breakfast, I was ferried over the estuary of the Stour. The Harbour Master had arranged for a guide and a hired horse to be waiting on the other side.

The country was flat and bleak, ravaged by the winds from the sea. The guide and I rode steadily — and in my case most uncomfortably — through a network of muddy lanes in a roughly westerly direction.

The tower of Champney Crucis church was visible from miles away. We reached the village by midday. I ordered dinner and arranged for the extravagance of a bedchamber to myself, as I had the previous night; for Master Williamson had provided me with a purse for expenses and I did not wish to share a bed with strangers.

The village was not large, and I was not surprised to find myself an object of mild curiosity. As I was waiting for my dinner, I allowed the landlord to extract the alleged reason for my visit from me.

'Brick-making, sir?' he said. 'There are several brickworks between here and Ipswich. We have no native stone, you see. In our neighbourhood, we are obliged either to make our own bricks, or import them from the Low Countries.'

'The King will need to do both,' I said. 'There is so much that needs rebuilding, and they will want to do it in brick and stone now, to lessen the risk of another great fire.'

'Is London such a very great city?' the landlord asked, with a wistful note in his voice. 'I have never been there.'

'Enormous. And at present most of it is a great heap of ash. Do you know of any clay pits in the parish?'

'None that I know of.'

'I shall make enquiries. What are the principal houses of the parish?'

'There's only one of any size, sir. Coldridge.'

'Who lives there?'

'Master Howgego — a most pious gentleman, and open-handed to the poor. Now he's bought the place, he plans to rebuild the house. So I dare say he may know —'

'He owns Coldridge? He doesn't hold it on a lease?'

The landlord looked puzzled by my surprise. 'He bought the freehold in the spring. The family that had it had quite died out, apart from a niece in London who has not been here for years. In any case, she's hardly more than a child, and we haven't seen her down here since her aunt died.'

'I shall call on Master Howgego this afternoon,' I said.

'Do so, and he will thank you.' The landlord waved the maidservant over to serve the food. 'For the pleasure of your society, sir, as much as anything else. I scarce think we've seen a stranger for months. Not since Master Alderley came down about the sale.'

'The trustee you mentioned?' I said.

He nodded. 'Yes, sir. He's a London goldsmith, a man of extraordinary wealth. Perhaps you've heard of him?'

CHAPTER TWENTY-FOUR

I walked up to Coldridge, glad to be on foot rather than on a horse. I needed time to think. Something was clearly amiss, for Mistress Alderley had been under the impression that the estate still belonged to Catherine Lovett, and that it would go with her as her dowry when she married Sir Denzil.

Besides, it had been a terrible dinner, with a chicken that must have been older than Methuselah, and exercise would help me digest it more quickly.

The house stood in a small deer park on the edge of a low, north-facing hill; there were few hills in this part of the world and it must have been the highest point for miles around. To the front was a low range built of brick, from which tall chimneys sprouted into fantastical shapes. As I drew closer, a huddle of older buildings appeared behind it, with a farmyard butting against them.

It was a more modest establishment than I had expected. I had thought that Alderley's niece would own a grander house, something more in keeping with Sir Denzil and his pretensions. But perhaps Mistress Lovett's fortune had been in her acreage, and she had no need of a mansion.

In the paved court in front of the house I encountered a groom leading a horse round to the stables. His master had just returned, he said in an accent I found difficult to understand, and he was now talking to one of the gardeners in the lower garden.

I went where his finger pointed and found Master Howgego himself at the entrance to an overgrown maze, in conference with a man dressed in rusty black and clutching a scythe.

'It must all go,' Master Howgego was saying. 'Grub the damned thing up, root and branch. I will have a fountain here within a twelve-month.'

He turned as he heard my footsteps. He was a fresh-faced old man with blunt, amiable features under a periwig that had not seen a comb for some time. I bowed and introduced myself. He read through my letter of introduction, raising bushy eyebrows when he came to Lord Arlington's signature.

'Clay pits, eh? Not on my land. By God,

that would be a fine thing to have here — a pretty source of income, eh? And convenient, too — I mean to extend my house.'

'Then perhaps the family who were here before might know of any clay pits. Do they live in the neighbourhood still?'

Howgego shook his head. He turned to the gardener. 'Did you ever hear of clay pits nearby? Or clay that might be capable of being fired?'

The gardener said he hadn't and added something in an accent so thick that he might have been speaking in Low Dutch for all I knew.

'What?' Howgego said, raising his voice. 'Who?'

The gardener said something else.

Howgego turned to me. 'He says Mother Grimes would know if anyone did. Her husband was the bailiff here, years ago, long before the war.'

'Where can I find her, sir?'

'She lives in a cottage over in Baynam's Wood.'

The gardener sucked in his breath. He crossed two fingers, one over the other, making the sign to avert evil that needed no translation.

Howgego scowled at him and said to me, 'We could walk over there now, if you like.'

The gardener muttered something.

'I shall do as I please, damn you,' Howgego roared. 'Now back to your work.'

We left the fellow leaning on his scythe and contemplating the condemned maze. Master Howgego took me down the slope to a small lake.

'I've met Mother Grimes only once,' he said. 'And that was when we considered coppicing the wood last year. It hasn't been done since long before Cromwell's time, so it's in a sad state. We decided to leave it. The wood's said to be haunted and the villagers won't go there.' He shot me a glance, probing and wary. 'They think she's a witch, of course.'

I didn't say anything, for witchcraft was one of those subjects like religion and politics where the less said the better, unless you knew who you were talking to. We passed through a gate in a paling and went into a meadow that sloped down to a brook fringed with alders and willows. The wood was on the far side, reached by a footbridge. It was bigger than I had expected and must have covered at least ten or fifteen acres.

Even I could see that the place was a sad tangle of branches and bushes and fallen trees. The air smelled of rotting vegetation. The path we followed was muddy underfoot, and slippery with dead leaves. It looked as if deer and foxes used it far more than humans.

'A lonely spot,' I said, casting about for a way to enquire if there had been recent reports of strangers. 'Do you get beggars down here?'

'No. We hardly see a stranger from one month to another. Not that I'd notice if they were here. But Mother Grimes would.' Howgego was sweating, though we were walking slowly and the day was not warm. He wiped his forehead with the back of his sleeve. 'I shall grub all this up too, one day,' he said. 'Sell the best of the timber and burn the rest. Turn the land to pasture.'

'And the cottage?'

'That will go. It's little better than a cowshed with a chimney. But — but not a word of that to Mother Grimes, eh? She — I'm told that she becomes agitated at the most foolish things.'

We came to a clearing, in the middle of which was a small, low cottage. The roof was green with age, and in places saplings and weeds sprouted from the thatch. At one end was a crude chimney built of brick and flint, from which a wisp of smoke rose into the dull grey air. The door was made of rough planks nailed together, the wood dark and fissured with age. A stream ran along the side of the clearing behind the cottage.

'It is a mystery how she survives,' Howgego whispered in my ear. 'They say she feeds on roots, leaves, nuts and berries like the creatures of the wood. But I think the villagers leave food for her under cover of darkness.'

'From charity?'

'No. In the hope of winning her good will. Or at least of averting her ill will.'

Howgego lingered on the edge of the clearing. I glanced towards the stream. At one point the bank sloped down to the water, and the ground was muddy. The earth at this point was much trampled. Close to the water's edge, something white had been pegged to dry on a bush. The old woman's shift? I took a step closer. It could almost be a shirt.

'Master Marwood?'

Howgego was at the door now, his hand raised to knock. I joined him. He knocked. Nothing happened, and after a moment he put his clenched fist to the door and gave it a solid double rap.

We heard the raising of the latch within. Howgego stepped back, bumping into me. The door opened outwards, and a foul, stale smell washed over us. In the doorway was a small, round woman. She made no attempt to curtsy to her landlord, but merely stared at him — not at his face but at the silver buckle on the belt around his waist.

'Mistress Grimes, good day to you,' Master Howgego said. His voice was softer than before, and the words flowed jerkily. 'How are you?'

She said nothing in reply, though she allowed her hands to flutter at her sides in a gesture that might have meant 'I am as you find me' or 'I am as well as can be expected' or even 'Why should you care?'

'We're come to beg a favour,' Howgego continued. 'This, by the way, is Master Marwood, all the way from London.'

He paused but still she said nothing. A shiver tickled my spine. There was something not quite human about Mother Grimes. She wore a dress of sackcloth and a stained apron. On her head was a rumpled cap above a wrinkled face. Her nose was an upturned snout. A scattering of grey hairs grew on her chin and cheeks. Her eyes were brown, small and deep-set. I could not put an age on her: she might have been anywhere between forty and eighty.

'Have you heard that London was destroyed in a great fire at the end of the summer?'

At last she spoke in a faint voice that creaked, as though with disuse: 'You must burn the stubble, when the harvest is in. Then you plough the earth. Only then may you sow the seed for the harvest that is to come.'

'Yes, mistress, indeed.' Howgego wiped his forehead again. 'The city has been reduced to ashes, and the King has ordered that it must be rebuilt in brick and stone, so such a blaze should never take hold again.'

'The King has no need of brick or stone,' Mother Grimes informed him. 'In His father's house are many mansions.'

A thousand devils, I thought: she means King Jesus. She's another of these damned dreamers, like my father. And a witch as well. Was that possible?

'To make bricks, one must have clay.'

She shook her head. She stretched her hand to the latch, as if intending to shut us out. 'Leave me,' she said. 'I'm weary.'

'Pray, mistress, stay a moment,' Howgego said.

She mumbled something that had a rhythm to it, like a prayer or a curse. I could not catch the words, but I sensed the irritation behind them. Howgego took a step backwards.

'Mistress,' I said, 'you and your husband

must have served the family who lived here before Master Howgego. Did you ever hear them talk of clay pits in the neighbourhood in their time?'

'No,' she said, looking straight at me for the first time and no longer mumbling.

'Perhaps I might speak to them myself. Do some of them still live nearby?'

She shook her head. 'All gone.'

'Is there not a young lady? I thought the landlord of the inn told me —'

'No.'

She was looking into my eyes and her lips were moving silently. The shiver glided along my spine again. I am not superstitious, but no man liked to be cursed.

Howgego touched my sleeve. 'Come, sir. Mistress Grimes cannot help us and . . . and we must not outstay our welcome.'

He bowed to Mother Grimes. I let him draw me away. As we crossed the clearing, I noticed two things.

The eaves of the thatched roof came down to within two feet of the ground. An untidy pile of logs and brushwood had been stacked in their shelter beneath the wall of the cottage. There was a large footprint in the muddy ground beside it.

Second, the shift had gone. Or the shirt.

My first task was to reassure Master Howgego. He was twenty or thirty years older than I, a wealthy, vigorous man and on his own land; yet he needed reassurance. Not that he gave me a chance to say anything for the first few minutes. We walked in silence through the woodland, with him taking the lead and setting a fast pace.

'Thank you, sir,' I said as we emerged from the trees. 'It's at least useful to know that she knows nothing of clay.'

He paused in his flight. 'Mother Grimes is — well, most strange, isn't she?' he said, panting slightly. 'The villagers are quite terrified of her, and even the Rector treats her with circumspection.' He moistened his lips and tried to smile. 'I could have her evicted at any moment, of course, but I don't care to. She's an old woman, after all, and the widow of an estate servant. Besides, I don't need to clear that wood at present — I have my hands full enough as it is.'

We walked back towards the house. By the time he had shouted at the man with the scythe, who was grubbing up the maze far too slowly for his master's satisfaction, Master Howgego had regained his former spirits. He insisted I come to the house to take a biscuit and a glass of wine.

He took me into his library, where there was a fire burning, and went away to give orders to his people. I looked about me. Two walls were lined with presses, on top of which were busts of philosophers, emperors and generals from the ancient world. Over the fireplace hung a large painting showing a landscape strewn with ruins. My host had unexpected tastes.

A large board stood, tilted on a stand, at right angles to the window. It looked familiar, though I had not been in this room before. I closed my eyes and suddenly my memory produced an image: a grey cloak hanging from a nail fixed to a stone wall. The cloak I had given to the strange girl at St Paul's on the night it was destroyed. There had been another board near the cloak — the draughtsman's. In my mind I saw the man's thin, lined face, and the bony finger he had waved at me when he prevented me from taking away my own cloak.

Howgego came back into the room, rubbing his hands, with a manservant carrying a tray of wine and biscuits. 'Everything is in train, sir — you will stay and sup with me, will you not? The servants are so idle that it will do them good to bustle about for a change.'

'I shall be glad to, sir.' Dinner at the inn had been so bad that I was glad to have his invitation. I nodded at the drawing board. 'Is that yours, by the way?'

'No, no. It came with the house.' He must have seen the puzzled look on my face, for he rushed on, 'I bought most of the contents — Master Alderley was anxious to dispose of them, and he did not wish to have the trouble and expense of transporting them to London. His niece had no use for them — they had belonged to her aunt, I believe. He sold them to me for a very reasonable price.'

Master Howgego's Ipswich house had been very small. Being for many years a widower, he said, he had not troubled to furnish it with any care, so Master Alderley had done him a considerable service.

'There are scores of books to be read,' he went on, 'though many of them I do not much care for.'

'They were Master Alderley's?'

'No, sir — they belonged to the Eyres, the previous owners. Master Eyre and his wife spent two years travelling in France and Italy after their marriage.' Howgego waved a dismissive finger at the busts that loomed over us in the shadows. 'Hence all this, and much else. They were interested in architecture, and I believe if Master Eyre had been wealthy enough they would have razed this house and built a pagan temple to live in. Mistress Eyre was quite as bad as he. They designed imaginary cities together when they would have been better employed in studying their Bibles. And when he died, she attempted to train up her great-niece in these matters.'

'Mistress Lovett?'

Howgego nodded. 'But Mistress Eyre died, and that was an end to it. Just as well for Mistress Lovett, perhaps — I hear the young lady is to be married, as is fitting for a maid, and what need would a wife have for all this?'

The food we were served was admirably plentiful, and so was the wine. The hours passed agreeably. I was not surprised to learn that Master Howgego was a widower. I had come as a godsend to him. He grew lonely in the evenings with only the servants for company, and the neighbourhood offered him little society apart from the rector.

He had been a merchant in Ipswich, he told me, importing timber and iron from Scandinavia, hemp from Latvia and coal from Newcastle. He had sold his business with the plan of retiring to the country. One of his fellow importers dealt professionally with Master Alderley, and had passed on the news that the Coldridge estate might be for sale.

'I was fortunate,' Master Howgego said, swirling the wine in his glass and peering into its depths. 'And so was Master Alderley. Once I had seen the estate, we concluded the matter very quickly, and at a price that was not unreasonable.' He peered earnestly at me. 'I think you said you were not personally acquainted with him?'

'No, sir. I'm not.'

'In that case, I hope I may say without offence that I did not much take to his manner. These grand London folk give themselves airs, but in truth the Alderleys are no better bred than me or a score of merchants in Ipswich.'

I stayed late. Master Howgego asked me to spend the night, but I declined, saying that I hoped to make an early start for Harwich in the morning, and I needed to give orders at the inn. He let me go with reluctance, and sent me back to the village with a servant to light my way.

I was glad of the guide. There was no moon, and I had taken more sack than was altogether good for me. The air was chilly with a foretaste of the coming winter. The servant plodded ahead with the lantern swinging from the end of a pole. A cutting wind had sprung up while I was in the house, sweeping across the flat landscape from the German Ocean.

By the time I reached the inn, I was shivering with cold. I did not wish for the company of rustics in the taproom, so I ordered a fire to be lit in my chamber.

'A drop of mulled wine, sir?' the slatternly maid suggested. 'That'll warm you.'

I agreed, on the principle that by this stage a little more wine could hardly affect me one way or the other. She took a long time to bring it to me, and I snapped at her when at last she appeared. She cowered from my irritation, and her hands were shaking as she set down the wine on the table by the bed. I drank it for the warmth it gave, but my desire for wine had passed and it tasted sour in my mouth.

I undressed to my shirt and climbed into bed. A great tiredness washed over me. I watched the candle flame casting its wavering light around the chamber. I knew I should blow it out and draw the curtains around the bed. I lacked the strength to do either. In a matter of seconds I fell into a sleep too deep for dreaming.

When I woke, rushing up from the depths of slumber, it was pitch-black in the room. Griping pains were ripping my belly apart. My stomach muscles convulsed. I leaned over the edge of the bed and vomited copiously.

CHAPTER TWENTY-FIVE

From the small hours of Thursday morning to the point when the light was fading in the afternoon, I emptied the contents of my stomach by one route or the other. The process was relentless and seemed to have very little to do with me. It was as if I were a wet cloth and a giant hand were wringing me dry, methodically squeezing out every last drop.

I was feverish, for I dreamed that I walked among smouldering ashes that stretched as far as the eye could see under a leaden sky. It was mysteriously essential that I should reach my destination, not that I knew what or where it was, only that it was so far away that I could not possibly succeed. All this was so vivid that I understood that it was no dream, but real life, and that therefore everything else had been a dream; so I had been mistaken all along about the nature of terrestrial existence.

People came and went. Servants, the innkeeper, a clergyman and Master Howgego. Sometimes they tried to give me water. Master Howgego was in a great passion about something, and the sound of his voice made my head ache even more than it was aching already.

A man in a dirty smock put leeches on me. It had not been a shift on the bush, I thought, suddenly certain. A shirt.

The leeches lay like slugs on my skin and their nibbling was oddly soothing. Afterwards, I slept.

A little later, a large man smelling of pigs carried me downstairs and laid me in a dark box. The box moved, and so did I, jolting up and down. I heard the hooves of horses and thought it possible I was being conveyed to my grave. This failed to interest me very much, though I wished the motion would stop. Then I was distracted, for I retched painfully, bringing up nothing but a little sour spittle. Someone swore.

Later still, I was in a bedroom. Flames flickered over a plaster ceiling, consuming the animals and plants I saw there. 'Help!' I cried. 'Fire! Fire!'

Someone gave me a drink that tasted bitter. A few seconds later, I brought most of it up again. I lay back exhausted, staring at the flaming ceiling. I saw the footprint of a man among the animals and plants, which struck me as important.

Perhaps, I thought, it is the Garden of Eden above me, and that is Adam's footprint in Mother Grimes's wood, which is part of Eden. Perhaps Adam set it on fire and burned it to ashes. That was the original sin.

Even children bear the weight of original sin. We are all sinners. I remembered my father telling me so, all those years ago.

'It's not a stage, James,' my father had said. 'It's a scaffold for a sinner. We are all sinners, but some are worse than others.'

He lifted me on to his shoulders. Only the men on horses were higher than I was, I thought, though of course God was higher than everyone. God had my father's face and his strong, rough-skinned hands, but He lived above us all in Heaven.

Another soldier came through the doorway onto the stage. He carried a great axe whose blade shone like silver. He set the axe against a wooden rack near the back of the scaffold.

A sigh rippled through the crowd.

The stage filled with people. More soldiers. A clergyman. Several private gentlemen. Two burly men dressed all in black with black hoods on their heads that fell to their shoulders. Their faces were entirely obscured.

I lowered my head and whispered in my father's ear: 'Are they dead? The men with no faces?'

'No. They're alive as you or I.'

Another gentleman came onto the scaffold. He was smaller than the others but held himself very erect. He was bearded and his face was very white and very sad. For a moment he looked out over the crowd, turning his head from side to side.

Afterwards, it seemed to me that the man had looked at me for a moment: as if to say, 'I'll know you again.'

But perhaps that was not a true memory but merely the memory of a dream.

I fell into a sleep as deep as death.

When I woke, daylight was slicing through the crack between the curtains on the window. But there were neither curtains nor canopy on the bed, only an unobstructed view of the plasterwork of the ceiling. The animals and plants were undamaged.

I no longer felt feverish, only thirsty and very weary. My right hand was lying on the blanket and I commanded it to move. To my surprise it obeyed. The hand floated in front of my eyes, looking somehow less substantial than usual. I let it fall.

There were footsteps. I turned my head towards the sound. A manservant hovered over me.

'Water,' I croaked.

The servant seemed not to hear me. 'I'll fetch his worship,' he said, and almost ran from the room.

In a moment, Master Howgego was there, minus his wig, his head bound in a kerchief. He was wearing a thick, quilted gown. 'Good, you're awake. How do you feel, sir?'

I did my best to explain, though my voice sounded strange to me. It creaked like a hinge that has not been used for some time. Howgego ordered the servant to prop me up, and gave me water by his own hand, allowing me only sips.

'Better and better,' he said a few minutes later. 'You have retained the water. That was more than you could do yesterday.'

'What day is it, sir?' I croaked.

'Friday.'

'But I should be in London by now.'

'So you shall be, but not today.' Howgego peered down at me, a frown creasing his forehead. 'At first I thought it must have been something you had for supper here.

But I ate from every dish that you did, and I have been as fine as a fiddle. Did you have something at the inn, perhaps?'

I raked my memory. 'A chicken at dinner. It was very tough. But it was cooked to leather, and there was no bad smell about it.'

'Anything else?'

'Only a cup of mulled wine when I got back to the inn.' As I spoke, I remembered that the girl had taken a long time to bring it, and the wine had tasted unexpectedly sour.

'A little wine shouldn't harm a flea.' Howgego rubbed his nose. 'But I wonder.'

We stared at each other. Mother Grimes had not liked my questions. She must have guessed that I had seen the shirt and per-haps the footprint as well. A witch knew how to poison a man by stealth. She had cursed me. It was possible that she had cast a spell on me. Or, more prosaically and more likely, she had bribed the terrified chambermaid to slip something into the mulled wine.

'The cesspit at the inn overflows into the well in wet weather,' Howgego said hastily. 'Perhaps the miasma in the air afflicted you as you slept. That must have been it.' He sounded relieved. 'Still — we must look to

301

the future now, and restore you to health.'

'I've made a great deal of trouble for you.' I remembered the jolting box and the sound of hooves. 'You must have sent your coach for me the other night.'

'It's nothing.'

Master Howgego stayed while his servants rebuilt the fire and fed me a few spoonfuls of broth with his own hand. 'I must apologize for my inhospitality,' he said. 'As you see, you have been sleeping in a naked bed — there was simply no time to hang the curtains. Indeed, I fear the whole chamber is sadly topsy-turvy. We shall set it to rights when you are feeling stronger.'

Afterwards I dozed for a couple of hours and found when I woke that I was capable of leaving my bed and walking, rather uncertainly, to the window. I sat on the window ledge and looked down at the garden and the remains of the maze, at the park and the dull pewter gleam of the lake, and at the dark green smudge of Baynam's Wood beyond.

I was still weak. I was worried about the length of my absence from London. My father could not be trusted by himself, and the Newcombs did not know him as I did.

In the evening I kept down a small bowl of broth. That night I slept well. The following morning, I made arrangements to leave for Harwich, pass the night there and then travel on to London by easy stages, spending another night on the road. If I were well enough, I should leave Coldridge the next day, which was Sunday. My guide had already left but Master Howgego promised to send one of his own servants with me to the ferry. I believe he would have lent me his coach as well if I had expressed the slightest desire for it.

I dined with him. He ate early, as country people do, and afterwards his steward called to discuss a troublesome tenant on one of the outlying farms. The afternoon was fine, so I left them together and went outside.

Leaning on a stick, I walked slowly through the gardens and inspected the gardener's attempts to destroy the maze, which was proving unexpectedly unwilling to be grubbed up. He said something to me but his accent was so strange that he might have been talking in Greek for all the communication that took place.

I went on, walking as briskly as I could, for the air was keen. On the far side of the lake was the dense, dark green of Baynam's Wood. A delicate strand of smoke rose from its depths. In my dream on Saturday night, the wood and Mother Grimes had been tangled up with the Garden of Eden and original sin.

I crossed the brook that fed the lake by the footbridge and walked into the wood. The silence of it wrapped around me. I was growing tired now, but I forced myself onwards. In the clearing, the cottage door was closed. I went over to the stream. Nothing had been hung out to dry.

The footprint had been by the woodpile. That was gone too, and in its place was a log.

I turned, meaning to retreat discreetly. But I found Mother Grimes was not six feet away. She was staring at me.

I was so surprised that I pulled sharply back, tripped on the log, and almost fell.

'Well,' she said. 'So you are better now, and you will soon leave Master Howgego's.'

Her stare unnerved me. To cover my confusion, I took three pennies from my purse and held them out on my palm. Once again, the grubby paw emerged from her cloak like a small nocturnal animal lured into the daylight by the prospect of prey. I felt her fingers on my skin, fluttering like wings. Then the paw disappeared. But the pennies still lay on the palm of my hand.

'Go back where you came from, young master,' she said, in a low but grating voice.

'There's nothing for you here. If you come again, you may not leave.'

I held her gaze for a moment. Before I looked away, I no longer doubted that by one means or the other she had poisoned me. Probably she had not wanted me dead, not this time, only kept to my bed for a few days. If she had been sheltering the owner of a shirt, that person had left Coldridge days ago.

I moistened my lips, forcing myself to continue. 'I'm searching for someone, mistress.'

'I know you are. And you're wasting your time.'

'Why? Was he — or she — not here?'

'You are wasting your time because you should be searching in your heart for Jesus.'

'Yes, but at present —'

Mother Grimes hissed, and the sound was broken and jagged, like a snake laughing. 'As for whatever else you want, you will find it — or them — when you least look for it, whether you search or not.'

She went into her cottage. She barred the door.

I waited a moment. It was very quiet in the clearing, as if the wood around it, and all the living things it contained, were holding their breath to see what would happen next.

I stooped and placed the three pennies in a line on the doorstep. They sparkled in the weak autumn sunshine.

CHAPTER TWENTY-SIX

I rode slowly through the bustle and clamour of the Strand towards Charing Cross and the slovenly sprawl of Whitehall beyond. The muscles in my legs were shrieking to high heaven. A grey sky, smudged with smoke from hundreds of chimneys, rose above the brick buildings of the palace. To the west, the trees of the park were beginning to lose their leaves.

At the gate, the guards were growing used to my face, and they did not have to check their lists every time I passed them. My horse and I parted company at the stables in Scotland Yard, with mutual relief.

I did not dare go directly in search of Master Chiffinch himself. Instead I looked for Master Williamson. He was not in either of his offices, but I found him at last in the Matted Gallery. He was walking with Sir Denzil Croughton again.

When he saw me approaching, Williamson

gestured to me that I should attend him at a distance. He continued his conversation for another turn up the gallery. At the far end, Sir Denzil sauntered through the doorway leading to the Duke of York's apartments. Only then did Williamson beckon me towards him.

'You've taken your time,' he said.

'Forgive me, sir. I've been ill. But I sent word. Perhaps the letter has not arrived?'

'No. But never mind that now. Have you found the girl? Sir Denzil was talking about her only a moment ago.'

'I found no trace of her.'

He glanced about him, making sure we were not overheard. 'And the other?'

I shook my head.

'Master Chiffinch left word he wants to see you,' Williamson said. 'I'll see if he's at leisure.'

He walked across the gallery to the two guards at the doors that led to the King's apartments. He said something to one of them, who summoned a third soldier. There was a whispered conversation. They glanced in my direction.

Williamson returned to me. 'Stay where you are. Someone will come for you, though you may have to wait for a while.' He looked me up and down. 'You should really take the trouble to dress better when you attend me here. It reflects badly on us.'

Having vented his irritation, he walked away. I prepared myself for a long delay. But, only ten minutes later, a servant approached and told me to accompany him. He led me out of the Matted Gallery and down the stairs to a doorway in the northeast corner of the Privy Garden. There were two guards here, one of whom opened the door for us; but otherwise they seemed not to see us.

I followed my guide down a flagged passage, up a flight of stairs, into a gallery overlooking a dank courtyard. We waited here for a moment until a guard motioned us forward. We went down another flight of stairs and through a chamber where four soldiers were playing dice by the fire, and two more were standing guard at yet another doorway. They stood aside to let us pass. We might almost have been invisible.

We came at last to a shadowy vestibule, square in shape and lit by candles as well as a tall window. A richly carved staircase rose from it, cantilevered against the four walls.

'You are to wait,' he said, and left me abruptly by a door under the stairs.

I stood there, feeling foolish, not knowing what to do with myself. I seemed alone, but

I could not be sure of it. Indeed, I had a sense that I was watched.

Another door opened, somewhere above my head. Footsteps clattered down the stairs. For a moment, I thought that two people were approaching. But only one appeared — Master Chiffinch, bringing with him a tang of wine. He nodded to me and went to stand by the window.

If there was a second person, he lingered out of sight on the stairs. I was reminded of my previous meeting with Master Chiffinch, and the way he had stood behind the screen while Mistress Alderley prepared the ground for him. Whitehall manners, I thought, and then I made the obvious deduction.

My mouth dried and I began to tremble. It was common knowledge that Master Chiffinch served only one master, the King himself.

'You may speak freely,' Chiffinch said. 'Any sign of them? Father or daughter?'

'No, sir.'

'So your journey was useless. Why were you so long?'

'I was taken ill.' Suddenly angry, I raised my head and looked at Chiffinch, who was fiddling with his wart. 'Besides, I did not say the journey was useless. There is an old woman at Coldridge, the widow of a former bailiff. She lives alone in a cottage in the woods and is reputed to be a witch.'

He shrugged. 'Every village has one of those.'

'I swear she was hiding something. And a man had visited her — I saw his footprint and, I think, his shirt drying on a bush.'

'No mystery there.' His features twisted into a lascivious mask. 'Age is no barrier.'

Perhaps I imagined it, but I thought I heard a faint, deep chuckle somewhere in the gloom above us.

I persevered: 'You would not say that if you saw her, sir. And there was some mystery about it, for she sees no one at her cottage. They are too afraid to approach her, even the man who owns the land she lives on. When I went back a second time, there was no trace of him.'

'Very well. Is that all?'

'After my first meeting with her, I fell ill. I should have been here last Thursday — Friday at the latest — if it had not been for that. I took some mulled wine at the inn, and I think it was poisoned in some way. She meant to keep me in the village, to give this man time to escape.'

'This is speculation,' Chiffinch said coldly. 'And far-fetched at that. An attempt to excuse your delay.'

'Let me give you a fact then, sir,' I snapped.

'Mind your tongue,' he said.

'I ask your pardon, sir.' I swallowed my anger, for it would not help to antagonize him more, let alone the possible listener in the shadows. 'Coldridge — the house and the land — belongs to Mistress Lovett, does it not? It comes to her from her mother's family, so it has not been confiscated with the rest of Lovett's wealth. And Sir Denzil Croughton will have it as his dowry when they are wed?'

He nodded. 'Mistress Alderley tells me that the estate is at present leased out. The lease expires next year, so there will be no difficulty for Sir Denzil when he takes possession.'

'No,' I said.

'Don't be —'

'No,' I repeated. 'No, Coldridge is not leased out. The whole estate has been sold, sir — to a Master Howgego. He held the lease before, and now he owns the freehold.'

'That cannot be right. You've been misinformed.'

'Then so has Master Howgego. And the entire village. Master Alderley went down to Champney earlier in the year to conclude the sale.'

'That,' Chiffinch said slowly, 'is not possible.'

'Master Howgego even owns the books, the furniture, the carpets that belonged to Mistress Lovett's family. I stayed with him at Coldridge when I was ill. There is no possibility of mistake.'

'Mistress Lovett is not of age. She could not sell Coldridge.'

'Her trustees could.'

'True.' Chiffinch touched his wart again, delicately, as if for luck. 'I believe the estate was not entailed in any way. So in theory they would have the power to convert it into some other form.'

'Then that's what they've done, sir. But no one in London appears to know of it.'

'But it could only be done with Mistress Lovett's knowledge. And for her sole benefit, of course . . .' Chiffinch paused. 'And Sir Denzil would have been told in the normal run of things. After all, he would expect to have the use of it when they are married. Have you spoken to Master Williamson about this?'

'Not about the estate. Or about the bailiff's widow. Only the bare fact that I found no trace of the Lovetts.'

'Good. Keep it that way.'

Something had changed between us, a

shift in the nature of our relationship. Whatever Master Williamson might think, I had a different master now.

Chiffinch turned to look out of the window. He scratched the glass with his fingertip. There wasn't much to see out there — just a long, tiled roof spotted with moss, a smoking chimney and a slice of the river, grey and broad.

His silence emboldened me. I said, 'I assume Master Alderley is her trustee?'

'Yes.' He glanced back. 'One of them. There are two.'

'Is Master Edward Alderley the other?'

'No.'

Chiffinch studied my face for a moment. I sensed he was coming to a decision.

'You might as well know, I suppose,' he said at last. 'You would not be so foolish as to blab about it. I have seen a copy of the deed. The second trustee is Thomas Lovett.'

For the rest of the day I went about my duties for Master Williamson like a sleepwalker.

Thomas Lovett was a traitor, a Regicide, whose possessions were forfeit to the Crown. I did not think it likely that he could legally exercise his duties as a trustee of the estate that his daughter held in her own right. Even if he could, he could only transact business with the collusion of the other trustee, Master Alderley, that eminently respectable goldsmith, whose list of debtors had the names of the King and his brother the Duke at its head.

The alternative was just as bad: that Master Alderley had by some fraudulent means cancelled the trusteeship of his former brother-in-law.

Whichever of these was true, the fact remained that Sir Denzil appeared to be under the illusion that when he married his betrothed, she would bring him the estate of Coldridge as her dowry.

In sum, Alderley had lied to his niece's future husband. He might also have committed forgery and embezzlement. He might even be guilty of aiding and abetting a Regicide.

A very different aspect of the matter struck me: how convenient, I thought, if Alderley were found guilty of high treason. His possessions would then be forfeit to the Crown. The debts of the King and his brother would be wiped out at a stroke.

Where did this leave me? I was involved in this business, whether I liked it or not. The King, I thought, must have the power to investigate these matters in public, and with all the instruments at his disposal. But he — or rather his creature, Chiffinch — had chosen not to. Instead they employed me to ferret on their behalf.

It was not safe to know these facts. It was not safe to speculate about them. Most of all, it was not safe to be Master Chiffinch's ferret.

■ ■ ■ ■

III
ASHES AND EARTH

28 OCTOBER — 10 NOVEMBER 1666

■ ■ ■ ■

CHAPTER TWENTY-SEVEN

Sunday meant church once a day, and sometimes twice if Mistress Noxon felt inclined to be godly. At church, you encountered half the neighbourhood, and anyone might catch a glimpse of your face.

The following Sunday, Mistress Noxon marshalled the servants, inspected their appearance and marched them from Three Cocks Yard to the crumbling church of St Clement Danes in the middle of the Strand. Cat walked beside John, knowing his bulk shielded her entirely from the world, at least on one side, and she had the wall on the other. Margery walked behind with the kitchen boy. Cat couldn't see Margery, but she knew that she was casting malign looks at her. She imagined them like poisoned arrows, sticking out of her back like the quills of a hedgehog.

Mistress Noxon had her seat in the nave, not far from the pulpit and paid for on an annual basis. But the rest of them from Three Cocks Yard trooped up to the gallery reserved for servants, where they could watch the heads of ladies and gentlemen below and speculate about which of them would fall asleep first during the sermon. Since the Fire, the church's congregation had become much larger, for the parish was packed with strangers from the burned-out areas. The tower was still used as a depository for some of the refugees' possessions.

They were a little late, and so Cat was spared the milling around outside beforehand. The balcony was crowded and there was only standing room for the four of them at the back. A pillar obscured their view of the pulpit and the congregation in the nave.

For Cat, this was a blessing. She spent the service with her eyes cast down, distracting herself by thinking about the Vitruvian virtues, namely that a well-made building should be characterized by *firmitas, utilitas, venustas* — that is, it must be solid, useful, beautiful. 'Like the nests of birds and bees,' Aunt Eyre used to say. 'We should build our own nests according to the same principles.' Vitruvius would not have approved of this untidy, inconvenient and ill-designed church.

Afterwards, the congregation below left

first, as befitted the status of those who paid for their seats — they were lower in the church, but superior in everything else. Cat was one of the last to leave. From habit, she lingered for a moment in the porch to give the crowd outside more time to disperse, pretending to study the latest Bill of Mortality that was displayed there. On her first Sunday at Three Cocks Yard, she had been convinced that one of the number murdered that week must be Edward Alderley: and she had both longed and feared that it might be so.

She heard John's heavy breathing behind her. He cleared his throat. 'Would you like to watch the procession on Lord Mayor's Day?'

She turned reluctantly to him. 'I don't know.'

'I thought we could go together.'

'Perhaps there won't be one. No point in having a procession in an ash heap, is there?'

She turned back to the Bill of Mortality to avoid his beseeching eyes. Beside it was a list of burials in the parish. That was when she saw a name she recognized.

Jeremiah Sneyd.

A dizziness mounted to her brain. Her legs trembled, and she leaned against John for support. He said something to her but the words were bereft of meaning.

'Mistress, did you know a man named Sneyd?'

Mistress Noxon frowned at Cat. 'What maggot's in your head now, girl?'

'Have you heard his name, I mean? Recently.'

'No. Should I have?'

They were walking back from church, a little ahead of the other servants, for Mistress Noxon had wanted to upbraid Cat for distracting John from his duties.

'The name was in the church porch,' Cat said. 'On the list of burials. Jeremiah Sneyd.'

'What's it to you?'

'I knew a man called Sneyd.' Cat drew closer, glancing about her to make sure they could not be overheard. She lowered her voice. 'A comrade of my father's. He might know where my father is.'

Mistress Noxon snorted. 'If he did, he can't tell you now, can he?'

'But he was married. If his wife's still living, I could ask her. Perhaps he's gone abroad again.'

'What can your father do for you now, even if he is still alive?' Mistress Noxon whispered. 'He's wanted for high treason.

He's a Regicide. You're better off without him.'

'I need to see him first, to be sure. I owe him that.'

'You're a fool, girl.'

'Can you find out where this Sneyd lived? He used to be a tailor by trade.'

'Why should I trouble to do that?'

'Because you can't wish me to stay with you for ever.'

Mistress Noxon screwed up her face. 'That's one thing you're right about. The sooner you go from us, the better. You're born to trouble as the sparks fly upwards.'

She smiled at Cat as she spoke, which took at least some of the sting from her words.

Jeremiah Sneyd had served with Cat's father throughout the war. He had stayed in the New Model Army for several years longer than Master Lovett, but when he came out the two men had renewed their acquaintance and he used to call at Bow Lane and even dine there. As a child, she remembered watching the two of them pray together — her father tall and thin, and Sneyd small and round.

Cat had observed him carefully, for they had been starved of strangers, and each one became food for speculation. For all his piety, Sneyd was a greedy man, tearing at his bread and meat with the ferocity of a wild beast, and sucking quantities of beer into his large, fleshy mouth.

She should have thought of him before. Sneyd had proved his loyalty in the past, and he had seemed as devoted to the cause of King Jesus as her father himself.

On Monday afternoon, Mistress Noxon waylaid Cat on the way to the necessary house in the yard.

'Sneyd was working as a jobbing tailor,' she said, without looking at Cat. 'I talked to the parish clerk, and his mother used to know them. They lived in the Strand once, but they moved up Cursitor Street way. Ramikin Row, wherever that is.'

'But he was a Dissenter, a Fifth Monarchist. Why was his funeral at St Clement Danes, not in Bunhill Fields?'

'Because his widow's no Dissenter, and St Clement's was her church before she met him. She thought he'd be closer to God there.' Mistress Noxon rubbed finger and thumb together. 'She'll have made it worth their while or they wouldn't have agreed. Waste of money, if you ask me. Her wits must be addled.'

'May I look for Mistress Sneyd?'

'When I can spare you. But you must understand this: if they arrest you, I know nothing of who you really are. I took you as a maid out of the kindness of my heart when you washed up on my doorstep during the Fire.'

Cat bowed her head. 'I understand.'

Mistress Noxon flung open the door of the necessary house and marched inside. She turned to face Cat, who was already retreating. 'There's one other thing you'd better know,' she said. 'Maybe it'll cure your curiosity. They found Sneyd's body in the Fleet Ditch the week before last. Someone murdered him.'

After the servants' dinner on Tuesday, Mistress Noxon told Cat to collect a pair of embroidered gloves that she had ordered from a tailor's east of Moorfields.

'You may have to wait an hour or two,' she said, loudly for the benefit of the other servants. 'But don't come back without them, Jane. He promised I should have them today. I need them for this evening.'

The afternoon was grey but mild and dry. Cat made her way swiftly through the streets, cutting through the ruins of the city to Bishopsgate and then up to Moorfields.

The gloves were already parcelled up, waiting collection. From Moorfields she made her way west to Chancery Lane and Cursitor Street.

She bribed a little girl to show her Ramikin Row. She knocked on doors until she found a woman who pointed out the house where Mistress Sneyd lodged and told her that she was working in the yard at the back.

Cat walked through the passage to the yard. An old woman was sitting on a log in the corner, her eyes cast down, sorting twigs for a broom. Cat stopped in front of her. 'Mistress Sneyd?'

The woman looked up. Her face was gaunt but she was not as old as Cat had thought. 'What?'

'I was saddened to hear of your husband's death.'

'Why? What was he to you?'

'I think my father knew him. Was he in Colonel Harrison's regiment in the war?'

'Perhaps. Who is your father? Coldridge, is he?'

The familiar name caught Cat unawares. Coldridge the man, not Coldridge the place? It must surely be her father, using an assumed name. She glanced about her. She and the old woman were alone. If she could trust anyone, it was someone like this. 'Yes.'

The woman was looking down at her twigs, her face invisible under her hat.

'Have you seen him lately?' Cat said.

Mistress Sneyd shook her head, the hat swaying from side to side.

'Or had your husband?'

There was no reply.

'Mistress? Did you hear me?'

'Go away,' Mistress Sneyd said softly. 'Just go.'

'Please,' Cat said. 'Listen. If he —'

Mistress Sneyd looked up at her. Her face was suffused with blood. She opened her mouth, threw back her head and howled like a dog.

Cat jumped back. She slipped and fell backwards into the gutter. She stood up. Her dress was filthy and damp. She was afraid but she was also growing angry. 'Did your husband see him? Master Coldridge?'

'Who was your father?'

'I told you — a comrade of your husband's.'

'I want nothing to do with those fools, or with their daughters.'

Cat glanced over her shoulder. Half a dozen children had come out from the house and were staring at her.

'Go,' Mistress Sneyd said softly. 'Go while you can and never come back. You keep on with your questions, like that young man the other day, but you do nothing. You and your kind have taken everything from me.'

'But all I want —'

'Go.'

'What young man?' Cat said.

Mistress Sneyd's voice rose and from her lips came a spurt of malice: 'You doxy. I'll tell them you're a witch, and you're trying to put a spell on me. We don't like witches here. We put them on the kitchen fire.'

Cat retreated.

'You devil spawn,' the woman spat out. 'Your father killed my husband. May he rot in hell, and may you rot with him.'

She went into the house behind her, slamming the door.

The children stared at Cat and drew a little closer to her. The oldest of the boys stooped and picked up a stone.

Cat pulled her cloak around her.

The first stone hit the wall behind her.

She broke into a run. The second stone thumped between her shoulder blades. She ran on and on, pushing her way through the crowd. She did not slow to a walk until she reached the bustle of Chancery Lane.

CHAPTER TWENTY-EIGHT

Master Hakesby had not been well during the last few days. The tremor in his hands was worse. He was sleeping badly and, last Friday, he had fallen on the stairs. He was not a drinker, or no more than most men, but Cat could not help wondering if he had the shaking palsy, which had afflicted Great Uncle Eyre in Coldridge.

In the last year of his life, her uncle had crept miserably about the house with very small steps, complaining of pains in his limbs. His hands had trembled so much that his wife had to feed him in the end. Worst of all, he began to see things that were not there, and to mistake the nature of the real things he saw. Mother Grimes, an old woman on the estate, had made herbal infusions for him. The servants said she was a witch or a wise woman, depending who you talked to. Her infusions eased the pain a little, but they also made the visions worse.

Cat prayed that this would not be Master Hakesby's fate. Not for his sake but for hers. She needed him too much. He must not grow ill and die.

On Monday, the boy who brought the milk said that the apprentices of Fleet Street were out, building a great bonfire in a patch of ground cleared by the Fire in Harp Lane, which lay to the east of Fetter Lane. It was Gunpowder Treason Day, the holiday that commemorated the foiling of the Catholic plot to blow up the King and Parliament more than fifty years ago.

The apprentices had made an effigy of the Whore of Babylon dressed as the Pope of Rome, complete with his triple tiara and St Peter's Keys. John begged Mistress Noxon to allow the servants to go out for an hour in the evening, once supper had been served, so they might enjoy the spectacle for themselves.

'You'd like to go, wouldn't you, Jane?' he said, turning to Cat, flushing, and making calf's eyes at her. 'It'll be a rare sight. There'll be stalls and sideshows, I dare say. All the world will be there.'

'I'd like to see it too,' Margery said.

'You can all go, if you must,' Mistress Noxon said. 'But only for an hour, and only when you've cleared away supper and made things ready for the morning.'

In the middle of Monday morning, Master Hakesby's health grew worse. He sent for Mistress Noxon, who went up to see him. Cat wondered if he needed a doctor or at the very least to be bled. But when Mistress Noxon came down, ten minutes later, she told Cat that she should go up to Master Hakesby's room and work for him for the rest of the morning, and possibly for some of the afternoon as well. Mistress Noxon seemed content with the arrangement, though it would mean extra work for everyone else, which made Cat suspect that Master Hakesby was paying handsomely for it.

She found him out of bed, and sitting in his elbow chair. He was still in gown and slippers, though, and his face was even gaunter than usual. His skin was dry, and it was flaking like a shower of miniature snow onto the dark green shoulders of his bedgown.

'I am not quite well, Jane,' he said unnecessarily. His right hand began to twitch of its own volition and he clamped it onto his leg with his left. 'I have asked Mistress Noxon to allow you to assist me. Bring me the paper from the table, will you? The one on top.'

She obeyed. It was a rough sketch of an elevation she noticed — its proportions not unlike those of the Banqueting House in Whitehall, but far smaller in scale. The sketch was in pencil, and the lines had skidded a little erratically over the paper, but the sense of it was perfectly clear. Underneath, written in ink, were measurements of the principal dimensions.

'I must have a fair copy by the end of the afternoon,' Master Hakesby said. 'Can you do it?'

'Yes, sir.' Her voice was low, and she kept her eyes cast down. But she felt a pulse of excitement begin to beat inside her.

'You will work at the table there, and I shall oversee your work. You should prick the measurements first and then pencil the lines in before you use ink. It must be as neat as possible, for it will be seen by the client.'

'The client, sir?'

'A college in Cambridge. This is merely a proposal, which may nor may not lead to a commission. Here you see a side elevation for their new chapel.'

'That Dr Wren is designing?' she suggested.

Master Hakesby snorted, and spots of colour appeared in his cheeks. 'It is more accurate to say that he and I are engaged together on this project.'

She curtsied and busied herself with her preparations, watching Master Hakesby surreptitiously. He sat back in his chair, rubbing his forehead, which caused another shower of snowflakes. A muscle jumped in his cheek. A moment later, he rose from his chair with some difficulty and shuffled with unsteady steps into his closet. After a long silence, she heard him relieving himself.

When he came back, he inspected her progress so far and seemed satisfied with it. While she continued, he took up a well-worn book and rested it on the arm of his chair. He appeared to be reading, but did not often turn a page. When she was passing his chair to fetch a knife to sharpen the pencil, she glanced down at the volume. She saw without surprise that it was the *De Architectura of Vitruvius,* Aunt Eyre's favourite book. It was a good omen.

Firmitas, utilitas, venustas, she thought. Buildings should be like the nests of birds and bees.

The rest of the morning passed pleasantly. The work absorbed Cat, drawing her into a place where both worries and duties evaporated, leaving only the whisper of the pencil on paper, Master Hakesby's breathing, and the plan taking shape on the table before her.

At dinnertime, he told her to go downstairs to fetch him a tray. 'You may have your meal yourself, after that, and then we shall start again this afternoon.'

'Sir?' she said as she was tidying the table to make room for the tray. 'Is the cornice a little too ornamented?'

'What are you talking about?' He sounded irritated. He pulled himself up from the chair and came to look at the design. 'What in God's name can you know of such things?'

She took a deep breath, gathering courage. 'You said the pilasters between the bays are to have Corinthian capitals, sir. But will the carving on the cornice distract the eye from them and confuse the mind?'

He stared down at the paper, screwing up his face in concentration. 'Yes,' he said at last. 'As a matter of fact I was uncertain about that myself. I shall raise it with Dr Wren.' He glanced sideways at her. 'I was intending to do that anyway.'

'Yes, sir. I beg your pardon.'

'But you have an eye, Jane, and that is invaluable.'

He dismissed her, and she floated down the stairs, as happy as she had been since those far-off days at Coldridge.

The clocks were striking nine, a conversation of bells that lasted for several minutes. The three servants walked down to the Strand. John carried a lantern and a stick tipped with iron. There was rowdiness on public holidays, as well as the usual perils of the night. Margery was next to him, and Cat between Margery and the wall.

'It's not very busy,' Margery said when they reached the Strand.

No one replied. But she was right, Cat thought. The street was scarcely empty — the usual pleasure-seekers were about, and some shops had not put up their shutters yet. Coaches and carts passed to and fro, as well as the occasional horseman. But there was no sign of the crowds she had expected, and no sense of that heaving, restless excitement that the mob brought to the streets on public holidays.

The three of them walked under Temple Bar and into Fleet Street. The desolation of the City lay in front of them, with the hulking shadow of St Paul's just visible against the sky. The ruins were in almost complete darkness. Few ventured there by night.

'Where's this bonfire then?' Margery demanded.

'I told you — Harp Lane,' John said with a hint of anxiety in his voice. The outing had been his idea, and its success or failure was his responsibility. 'You'll see in a moment.'

But they didn't see. Beyond Fetter Lane, the ruins stretched down to the Fleet Ditch and then up the slope to the City wall. No torches milled about them, no hubbub rose into the air, and above all no bonfire burned the triple-crowned Anti-Christ of Rome into a heap of ash.

Cat had not wanted to come on this outing. But now it had lost its purpose, she felt disappointed.

'They said it'd be here,' John said; he sounded sulky, a boy deprived of a treat and made to look foolish into the bargain. 'They must have moved it.'

Margery stopped a maidservant coming out of a pastry-cook's with a covered basket on one arm. 'Where's the bonfire then?'

The girl shrugged. 'No one came.' She waved her free arm in a gesture that embraced the City and its environs. 'There's no bonfires this year. No one wants another fire, do they? We've had enough of that.'

John bent his head towards Cat. 'What do

you want to do?'

'Go home,' Cat said. 'I've got a headache.'

Simultaneously, Margery said, 'Let's have some oysters first. It's only a step to Fleet Bridge.'

'We've not got long,' John said. 'Jane, what do you —'

'Come, you will not deny us this? We deserve a treat. And I know a short cut.' Margery snatched the lantern from him. 'Follow me. I'll show you.'

'There's not time,' he said. 'And Mistress Noxon —'

'There's always time for oysters.' Margery marched into the lane running parallel to Fleet Street, taking the light with her. She called back over her shoulder. 'Or what do you say to gingerbread?'

Automatically the others followed. The lane had been cleared since the destruction of the Fire. Cat stumbled on the uneven cobbles, and John took her arm to steady her. She did not snatch it away. This, she realized when it was too late, gave him courage. He stopped suddenly and swung her round, so her back was against the wall.

'Jane, I can't help it,' he whispered. 'I must speak. Or I swear I'll burst.'

The light disappeared round a corner. The darkness descended.

His hands clamped themselves onto her shoulders. She fumbled in her pocket.

'Let me kiss you. Be my sweetheart. I beg you.'

He brought his face down to hers. His sweat smelled acrid, indisputably masculine. Nausea rose in her throat. He pushed her against the wall. His cheek brushed her lips. She heard her cousin Edward's voice rasping in her ear.

Scream all you like, my love. No one will hear.

She eased the little knife from its sheath.

'Sweet Jane. Forgive me. One kiss. Please. Just one.'

Part of her had time to think that John was not like Cousin Edward, that he was a kind, stupid man who was foolish and strange enough to desire her, whereas Edward was a monster who deserved to be hanged for all his fine airs.

But the distinction between the two men didn't matter. John had triggered something within her, and she had no more control over what followed than a ball did when it emerged from the muzzle of a pistol.

His lips had found her face. His mouth was open and moist. One of his teeth jarred her chin. He found her lips.

The light returned. 'Hey — you!' Margery

said. 'What are you —'

She broke off in mid-sentence. Cat pulled out the knife and stabbed John's thigh. She felt the tip snag for an instant on the kersey of his breeches. Then the blade pierced the skin beneath and dug into flesh and muscle.

John screamed. He jerked back from her, clutching his leg.

Cat broke away. She ran through the darkness towards Fetter Lane.

The streets were full of terrors.

Cat took shelter near Harp Lane, not far from the place where the bonfire should have been, pressing herself into a corner where two walls met. She had hoped to find solitude here but she soon discovered her mistake. There were invisible people among the ruins — some living there, perhaps in the ruins of their homes, others roaming through the rubble. For a moment she glimpsed what it must be like to be truly poor, to have even less than a maidservant in Three Cocks Yard, let alone a young heiress of Barnabas Place.

In a perfect city, she thought, desperate to distract herself, there should be modest but airy houses for the poor. They should be built of brick and set in straight, well-drained streets with a pump at every corner.

Not these sooty holes in the ground.

Firmitas, utilitas, venustas. She clung to the words as if they were an amulet to keep her safe. *Firmitas, utilitas, venustas.* The houses of the poor should be solid, useful, beautiful.

It started to rain. She kept the knife in her hand and moved as stealthily as she could, retreating to Fetter Lane and then, because she did not know what else to do, back to Three Cocks Yard. She knocked hesitantly on the door.

Mistress Noxon let her in, once she was sure of Cat's identity. In the hall, only one candle was burning. The housekeeper barred, bolted and locked the door. When she turned, one look at her face was enough to tell Cat that she knew what had happened.

'Are — are they back, mistress? Margery and John?'

Mistress Noxon nodded. 'I'll deal with you in the morning,' she whispered. 'Now go to bed, Jane.'

She spat out Cat's assumed name as if it were a mouthful of bad meat.

Cat curtsied. Her cloak was wet through, and the bottom of it was smeared with ashy mud from the ruins. The skirt of her dress was equally filthy. More trouble for the morning, she thought, and more work.

She went down to the kitchen to fetch her candle and then climbed the stairs. The higher she went, the cooler the air became.

To her dismay, a line of light showed beneath the door of the attic she shared with Margery. She paused on the landing. There were sounds within — footsteps, a ragged gasping, and a scraping noise, as if something were being dragged across the bare boards of the floor. She would have to face Margery at some point. Better to do it sooner than later.

Cat raised the latch and pushed open the door. Cold, damp air swept towards her. The window was wide open. A candle stood on the stool beside the straw mattress where Cat slept. Its flame flickered wildly in the draught, and shadows glided to and fro over the sloping ceiling. Margery was by the window with a roll of papers in her hand.

Cat saw a box — *Cat's box* — standing open on the floor. The shock of it felt like a blow to the stomach, and for a moment she gasped for air like a landed fish.

As the door opened, Margery turned. Her face glistened with rain, or perhaps tears. She ripped away the ribbon that secured the papers and threw them out of the window.

For an instant, the papers fluttered in the air, faintly illuminated by the glow from the window. Then the unbuilt buildings and the unmapped streets vanished into the night.

Lost cities. *Firmitas, utilitas, venustas.*

'I hate you,' Margery said, in a voice that was quiet, almost conversational.

CHAPTER TWENTY-NINE

In the morning after the disasters of Gunpowder Night, the work of the house continued. Fires had to be lit, beds to be made, meals to be cooked. Cat, John and Margery went silently about their work, avoiding eye contact with each other. John limped slightly and slunk against walls, like a dog fearing a whipping. Margery's face was red and the skin around her eyes was puffy from weeping. Cat had listened to her snuffling and sobbing all night.

Mistress Noxon said nothing to any of them, apart from giving orders. All morning, her wrath hung over the household like a black, threatening cloud.

The attic window overlooked the front of the house. Early in the morning, Cat went outside. A grey half-light filled the court, enough for her to see that her papers were long gone, the victims of the wind and the rain. Her leather bag and her spare clothes had also disappeared.

Aunt Eyre's box was just outside the front door. It had been a delicate thing, and the impact of the fall onto flagstones had smashed it beyond repair. Its contents had vanished. There had been compasses, a set of dividers, a protractor and a short ruler, all of brass, together with a pencil enclosed in a silver case.

Her worldly possessions were now reduced to the contents of her pocket: a few shillings, a handkerchief, Hepzibah the doll, her knife, the key to Jem's box and the box itself. This was now empty, apart from the stolen grey cloak, which had been hanging on the back of the attic door.

She did not mind much about the loss of her clothes. But she minded bitterly about the destruction of Aunt Eyre's inlaid box and the theft of its contents.

Cat expected a beating for her part in the affair, and she felt that Margery deserved one for hers. It was possible, even probable, that they would lose their positions.

She wasn't sure what would happen to John — he might escape corporal punishment, or even any punishment. But this would be at least partly because he was a man, and because a woman had tempted him. It was well known that young women were lascivious creatures, desperate to slake their lusts, who preyed on innocent young men. Cat herself was not aware of these lusts within her, but she accepted the possibility that they might be there, somewhere, since everybody else took their existence for granted. Since her mother's death, she had felt much the same about God: possible but by no means probable; but one had to take into account the feelings of other people.

Dinner was cooked, served and cleared away. Afterwards, Mistress Noxon talked separately to each of the three servants. One by one, she drew them aside into her room and interrogated them with calm, impersonal efficiency. At this stage, she did not pass judgement or mete out punishment. She merely gathered information. By the time she had finished she had constructed a pretty accurate narrative of the events of the previous evening, from the non-existent bonfire to the attack on Cat's box.

Still Mistress Noxon said nothing, but went about her work as silently as they did, apart from when she gave them orders.

Later in the afternoon, Dr Wren called on Master Hakesby, and the two men remained closeted together in Master Hakesby's apartment. Dr Wren was grim-faced, and

Cat guessed his plans for the City had received another setback. Since it was a Tuesday, he had attended a meeting with the other Commissioners for rebuilding London. Cat hoped they might send for her, but they did not.

Then it was time for supper. Master Hakesby and Dr Wren ate theirs in Master Hakesby's room. Mistress Noxon herself took the trays upstairs, which gave Margery a chance to knock Cat's spoon into the ashes, accidentally on purpose.

Meanwhile, John limped about the kitchen, silently reminding the two young women that he was wounded and inviting their sympathy. Perhaps he even wanted to make them feel guilty. He was nothing but a great baby, Cat thought, like all men. The knife had barely scratched his thigh but he was acting as if he had lost a limb.

When supper was finished, Mistress Noxon looked around the table and said coldly, 'I'll see each of you again now. John first.'

He followed her into her room. He wasn't long. When he came out his face was as red as a guardsman's coat and his lips were trembling.

Margery sidled up to him. 'What happened?' she whispered.

'Three months' wages in the poor box. Either that or I'm on the street. Tonight.' He sniffed and turned his head away; he was clearly on the verge of tears. He added in a muffled voice, 'She wants you next.'

Margery smoothed her apron and hurried away.

John glanced at Cat, who was standing near the fire. He swallowed. 'I wanted you to enjoy it, Jane. The bonfire. Everything.'

'I didn't,' Cat said. 'And that's that.'

He blundered into the scullery, and from there to the yard to escape her.

When Margery came out, she was crying again, her apron held to her eyes. She pushed past Cat and ran upstairs.

Cat knocked on the door of Mistress Noxon's room. The housekeeper was sitting at her table.

'Close the door,' she said. 'Then stand there.' She pointed to a spot in front of her table.

Cat obeyed. She stood, head down, her hands clasped in front of her.

For a moment Mistress Noxon did not speak. Then: 'I should have you whipped and then put you out on the streets.' She waited, perhaps expecting Cat to speak, before going on: 'You stabbed that great booby. How could you?'

'He attacked me.'

'He tried to kiss you. That's not the same thing.'

'But it is.' Cat looked up and swallowed. 'Mistress.'

'Men always try to kiss a girl. You should have slapped his face. That was all you needed to do. But a knife — dear God, what possessed you?'

Cat said nothing. How could she explain that the last man who had forced himself on her had been Cousin Edward, and that he had raped her on her own bed?

'And now I've got John making even more of a fool of himself than nature intended. Margery's burning up with spite and jealousy. And then there's you. The cause of all this.'

'I ask your pardon,' Cat said stiffly. 'I shall try to mend my ways.'

'Maybe you would try. But it wouldn't do any good.' Mistress Noxon sighed. 'You're a strange little thing. You've tried to settle in. You do your work without complaint — I'll give you that. But, however you look at it, you've brought trouble into this house. And I haven't even mentioned poor Master Hakesby. That's another thing.'

'What about him?' Cat said, suddenly

alarmed. 'There's no quarrel there, mistress, or —'

'Be quiet,' Mistress Noxon said. 'He's a strange man, and God knows what's wrong with him. But he's taken a fancy to you. And it won't do: a dog can't have two masters, and no more can a servant.'

'Shall I not work for him any more, mistress?'

Mistress Noxon shrugged her ample shoulders. 'It doesn't matter what you do in this house. You're still going to cause trouble. And that's why there's no help for it: you'll have to go.'

The kitchen fire was out but the bricks of the hearth still gave off a little warmth. Cat sat on a stool by the grate with the grey cloak about her shoulders. She was perfectly still, and her eyes were half closed.

By tomorrow evening, Mistress Noxon had said, Cat must be out of this house. It was a harsh decision but Cat understood it. She even admired it.

Mistress Noxon had a house to run, and that mattered more than the well-being of an unsatisfactory servant. Two months ago, she had sheltered Cat with reluctance, and she had made Cat work for the privilege. But there had been no trickery about it, no unfulfilled promises, and Cat had known that she was living here on sufferance.

She considered the choices that were left to her. In the end, she sighed and stood up. Taking her candle, she slowly climbed the stairs. She was very weary. The thought of spending another night with Margery was almost unbearable, but there was no help for it.

On the first floor, there was a line of light under Master Hakesby's door. Well, she thought, what is there to lose? She knocked softly. There was no response. She knocked again, a little louder.

A moment later she heard slippered feet shuffling across the floor. The door opened a few inches. Master Hakesby, candle in hand, stared down at her on the landing.

'I thought it might be you,' he said.

Master Hakesby looked like a skeleton. His naked head was bound up in a kerchief. A blanket was draped over his shoulders. The candlelight deepened the hollows in his face and made him look taller and thinner than ever. It seemed impossible that there should be any flesh on him whatsoever. His hand was trembling, so the flame danced wildly, sending his shadow careering around the room.

'Close the door,' he said. He looked her up and down, and seemed to understand her weariness, for he told her to sit on the stool by the drawing table.

He returned to his elbow chair and set down the candle on the bracket attached to one of the arms. There was an open book on the table beside him.

'So you've lost your place, Jane?'

'Yes, sir.'

'There was quite a commotion last night. I heard the wailing and the crashing about. Was that your fault?'

'No, sir.' Cat hesitated, suspecting that Mistress Noxon had already told him at least some of the story. 'The three of us — John, Margery and me — we find that we cannot agree together. So I must go. But I'm sorry you've been troubled by it.'

'Where will you go?'

'I don't know.'

'You have no friends you can call on? No family?'

She shook her head. 'I came to ask your advice, sir. If you would be so good.'

'In that case I have a proposal.' Master Hakesby scratched the stubble on his chin. The silence of the house amplified the sound. 'Dr Wren was here today. He came in part to discuss a scheme he and I have been revolving for some weeks now, since the Fire. The setting up of a drawing office. There has been such a volume of business in the last two months that we cannot go on as we are. We must hire assistants, and they must have somewhere to work. He has found premises near Covent Garden that he thinks will serve. It is a most convenient location, in a street that runs into the piazza itself.'

Cat found it hard to breathe, as if the air had suddenly been sucked from the room. 'Will you yourself move there, sir?'

'No. It is to be a place of business, nothing more. Besides, I am quite comfortable here. When the servants are not at loggerheads with each other.'

She looked up. Master Hakesby had spoken in the same dry tone as before but there had been a hint of amusement in his voice.

'We are considering taking a lease on the attics of the house,' he went on. 'They were used by a weaver for his workshop, and they are already boarded over and admirably well-lit with skylights. There is ample room for as many as four or five draughtsmen if we need them. Dr Wren and I can furnish it with what is wanted.'

Cat said, 'Is there — would there be —'

'A place for you? Perhaps. We will need

someone to keep the place clean and to run errands. It is possible that you could sleep there too. It does not do to leave somewhere empty at night in these troubled times.'

She felt a pang of disappointment. She had hoped for more.

Again, it was as if he sensed her thoughts. 'And,' he said, 'there is one other thing. I am occasionally in want of an assistant. I may call on you for that.'

'Thank you,' she whispered.

Neither of them spoke for a moment. Then he said, 'You puzzle me.' He left the words hanging between them, waiting for her to respond. When she said nothing, he went on: 'You may have noticed that I'm sometimes afflicted by a slight tremor. My physician says it is a palsy.' He scratched his scalp with his long, bony fingers. 'It is of no importance in itself. But when it inconveniences me, I shall sometimes require you to work under my direction at the mechanical part of a design — as you've already done, once or twice. I noted then that you are accurate in measurement and deft with a pen.'

'Sir,' she said. 'I have a favour.'

He frowned and shifted in his chair. 'Is it your place to ask favours?'

'Forgive me, sir, but would you teach me?'

She waved her hand about the room, and the gesture took in the drawing board on its slope, the large chest where plans lay flat in shallow drawers, and the delicately built wooden models on the shelves above. 'I want to learn what I can of all this.'

'Well, I suppose there can be no harm in that.' Master Hakesby's face was in shadow but Cat could tell by his voice that he was amused. 'The more you know, the more you will be able to help me.'

'When will you know about the drawing office, sir?'

'Soon.'

'Mistress Noxon says I must go from here tomorrow evening.'

'As you are such a troublemaker?' Again, there was a touch of amusement in his voice. 'You see your reputation has come before you.' He was silent for a moment. His fingers trembled in his lap. 'I'm tired. Go away now, and I will talk to Mistress Noxon in the morning. And to you. But only if you are not troublesome to anyone in the meantime.'

When Cat reached the attic, the room was in darkness and rain was pattering on the glass of the window. Margery was asleep, or at least pretending to be. Her breathing was heavy and regular. Occasionally she gave a little snore.

Cat blew out her candle and quickly undressed. As she slid under her covers, her hand touched something on the pillow.

Instantly wary, she investigated by touch, feeling the outlines of a sheet of paper, folded over and over again, with something hard inside it. She paused, listening. Margery's breathing had changed. It had become quieter, slower.

Cat unfolded the paper. It contained two coins. Her fingertips explored them. Newly minted half crowns. Margery had paid compensation for what she had done, as well as she could. It was better than nothing.

Time and the night drifted towards dawn. Margery's breathing became heavy and regular, ebbing and flowing in the darkness.

CHAPTER THIRTY

That night, her last at Three Cocks Yard, Cat dreamed again of Cousin Edward. At first she could not see him, for the place they were in was dark. Then she smelled the stench of him, stale sweat and sour wine. Next she heard his breathing, ragged and urgent, growing louder, and the creaking of boards beneath his slippered feet, coming nearer.

The weight of him was upon her, his hand on her mouth and partly over her nose, smothering her. She thrashed beneath him, trying to squirm away but knowing the effort was pointless: he was too strong, too heavy, too determined. In a moment she would feel again the worst pain in the world, stabbing into the heart of her.

She wrenched her mouth from his grip. She sucked in air but the scream inside her would not emerge.

Then — without warning, without transition — she was fully awake and in her bed, pinned down by the covers and soaked in sweat. A shadow thrown by a candle was moving closer. Somewhere behind it was the sound of laboured breathing.

He was here. This was no dream.

A crack like a pistol shot jolted her fully awake. She cried out.

The attic door creaked as it opened, as it always did. The candlelight outlined the doorway, with the small, hunched shadow framed within it.

Margery. Going downstairs to light the kitchen fire, to set water to boil.

Cat lay back in her bed. Gradually her breathing quietened. The sweat cooled on her skin. Her nightshift was damp. The dream did not fade. She was helpless, the victim of her own fear as well as the victim of Cousin Edward.

Tears pricked her eyelids. She could not bear the thought that this would be her condition for the rest of her life: to be the victim of her fear, the victim of Edward.

And if thine eye offend thee, her father used to say, pluck it out: it is better for thee to enter into the kingdom of God with one eye, than having two eyes to be cast into hell fire.

If your cousin rapes you, pluck him out of

his life and yours. If hell fire exists, pray he will be cast into it.

The next day, Wednesday, Cat left Three Cocks Yard after dinner. John followed, trundling her almost empty box on the barrow. He said nothing but she was conscious of his eyes on her.

At Master Hakesby's request, Mistress Noxon had arranged for Cat to lodge for a few days above a coffee house near Charing Cross, where the proprietor's wife was known to her from church. Cat was to pay for the privilege, partly with the help of Margery's five shillings, and partly by making herself useful.

Master Hakesby had promised to let her know when the lease had been signed on the drawing office in Covent Garden. 'A matter of days, I think. Dr Wren is most determined in the matter, and he generally contrives to get his way one way or another.'

The five shillings ensured that she was on a slightly different footing from the other servants at the coffee house, somewhere between paying guest and unpaid apprentice. For two or three hours on Thursday morning, she cleaned, swept and scrubbed. At ten o'clock, however, the mistress of the house said that Cat was free to please herself until five o'clock. It was not worth training up Cat to serve the gentlemen, let alone to prepare such an expensive and delicate drink as coffee.

'Go away,' she said, flapping her apron as if Cat were an impertinent mouse or cruising fly. 'You'll only get under our feet.'

The absence of work and the gift of time should have made these hours a holiday. Instead, the period of enforced leisure unsettled her. It was strange to be neither a servant nor a niece nor a daughter. For the first time in her life, she lacked a place in the world. She was adrift in London.

She walked westwards to Whitehall and then Westminster, relieved to put the ashes and ruins behind her. At first she was cautious, but her fear of being recognized gradually diminished. It was now two months since she had fled by night from Barnabas Place. Her clothes were those of a servant. Not just that: her bearing was different, and she had learned how a servant should respond to her betters. People saw what they expected to see.

That first day gave her confidence. It also gave her time, as she walked, to think about the dream, to think about Cousin Edward.

It was possible that, in a few days' time,

she would begin a new life working for Master Hakesby. She would have the chance to be free of her old self and in a position to invent herself anew. She would have a chance to escape the awkward memory of her father, and the duty he thought she owed to him and his God. Even Coldridge would mean nothing any more — but that would be a price worth paying.

But none of this would be worth anything at all if she were obliged to live with that dream, to live with the knowledge that Edward Alderley was still alive, waiting for her.

The following day, Friday, the mistress of the coffee house sent Cat away a little earlier in the morning. She slipped through the streets with a basket over her left arm, as if her mistress had sent her out on an errand. She kept her right hand in her pocket, her fingers wrapped around the haft of the knife.

She trudged through the crowds, pausing occasionally to look at the wares displayed in the shops and booths along the route. The roar and clatter of Holborn reached her long before she came to the street itself. She was west of the Bars, outside the City Liberties, at a safe distance from the comings and goings at Barnabas Place.

A stall was selling oysters, and she joined the crowd waiting to be served. A servant threaded his way through the crowd, towed by a muzzled mastiff. The dog lunged at Cat, and she recoiled. The servant laughed and hauled the dog away.

Cat stared after them. For the first time in weeks, she thought about the mastiffs of Barnabas Place: Thunder, Lion, Greedy and Bare-Arse. Their names repeated themselves like a benign incantation in her mind. She wished she could see them, and feel their hot breath and moist tongues on her hands. Thunder, Lion, Greedy and Bare-Arse.

Especially Bare-Arse.

Mastiffs needed exercise if they were not to grow fat and slothful. At Barnabas Place, a servant walked them a mile or two each morning. Cat had seen them with him once: gripping four leashes, two to each hand, a whip passed through his belt in case of emergencies, his face red with the exertion of holding them. The passers-by had parted before them like the Red Sea to let them through.

Once a week, however, on Saturday mornings, Edward rode out with the dogs and, accompanied by the servant, took them further afield. Usually they went to Primrose Hill.

Primrose Hill, Cat thought, her mind adrift between memories and desires. Thunder, Lion, Greedy and Bare-Arse.

A man shouldered against her. 'You're blocking the way, wench.'

She stepped back, almost falling into the gutter behind her. She steadied herself. The man stared at her with a frown on his face. He was dressed plainly, a servant probably.

'Don't I know you?' he said.

'No, sir.'

They stared at each other. He wrinkled his forehead, struggling to place her. She didn't recognize him. But that meant nothing. In her old life, she had not much noticed servants, the Alderleys' or other people's, unless they impinged directly on her. But servants always took note of their betters.

'I know you,' he said harshly. 'I'm sure of it.'

It was the voice she knew, not the face. She had heard him through the open window of the parlour, talking to Ann in the garden at Barnabas Place; the fool had been trying to wheedle a kiss from her. It was a grating voice but it had another sound to it, a soft, fluctuating whistle, perhaps caused by missing teeth or a malformed palate.

'You're mistaken, sir.'

Cat ducked away and fled through the crowd.

CHAPTER THIRTY-ONE

My masters, old and new, left me in limbo.

Nor did Mistress Alderley make any attempt to contact me. I should have been relieved, for nothing good could come from another meeting with her. Instead I was disappointed. Desire was like an itch, it seemed to me, for whether you tried to ignore it or you scratched it, it brought you nothing but irritation.

In the meantime, I settled back into my routine with Master Williamson. I assisted him in his correspondence. I took his dictation and I checked his proofs. I dealt on his behalf with Master Newcomb about the printing of the *Gazette*, and I also ran the network of casual workers, mainly women, whom we employed to distribute the newssheet throughout London.

Despite my failure to find Lovett or his daughter in Suffolk, I think my masters were not displeased with me. Williamson announced out of the blue that I should have an extra ten shillings a week. He also gave me a pound and ordered me to find myself a coat that would not shame him and my fellow clerks. He gave me the impression that I had him to thank for these generous gestures, but I suspected that William Chiffinch was behind them.

Two days after my return, I came within three yards of Chiffinch in the Pebble Court when I was on my way to Scotland Yard. I made a hasty bow. He swept past me, his nose in the air, and showed no sign of being aware of my presence.

There was always some difficulty with the *Gazette*'s casual workers. We did not pay them much, and only for a few hours a week. But we needed their services as much as they needed our money, so they occasionally exerted more influence than their lowly position warranted.

Just after my return from Suffolk, there was evidence that one or two of them were not fulfilling the terms of employment, and that copies of the *Gazette* were not reaching certain taverns, coffee houses and private subscribers when they should.

This infuriated Williamson, who attended to the detail of the *Gazette*'s distribution as he did to the detail of all his affairs; it was both his strength and his weakness. He ordered me to monitor individually and secretly each of the women whose work had attracted complaints.

It was unpleasant work, unrewarding by its very nature. But, in a day or two, the mysteries solved themselves. One woman was a drinker, who visited every alehouse on her route and ended each day in a stupor. Another had four children, all under six years of age and one of them a baby, and she could not leave them alone all day.

The third was Margaret Witherdine, the servant whom Mistress Newcomb employed for the heavy work of the house, to be the butt of her own ill humour, and to help with the younger children. Margaret did not live in, because she had a husband and home of her own. She found time enough to increase her earnings by distributing the *Gazette* in the area around Smithfield. It was a tavern-keeper there who laid the complaint against her. I found she was innocent — she had repulsed the man's amorous attentions and he had complained by way of revenge.

Williamson was not a forgiving man. The first two women lost their jobs. He was ready enough to do the same to Margaret, on the grounds she must have flaunted her charms, so the episode was her fault; his real reason was that he did not want to alienate the tavern-keeper. I asked him to reconsider — partly, I am afraid, for the selfish reason of maintaining domestic harmony at the Newcombs. In the end, she was allowed to retain the contract and I arranged for her to be given a different round.

Margaret was not, on the surface, an obvious target for anyone's amorous attentions. She was a thickset woman, broad in the beam but short, with a high colour and black, curly hair. She was grateful for my help — her husband was no longer capable of earning his living, being a sailor invalided out of the Navy and still waiting, after seven months, for his back pay. He had been badly wounded while fighting the Dutch.

Margaret was as kind and honest as a woman could be in her position. The better I knew her, the more I liked her. She was good with my father, too, and so I paid her to take him for an excursion for the good of his health.

My father loved to go along the riverside. When he walked towards the City, he looked about him in amazement, wondering with the wide-eyed curiosity of a child what this ruined place might be, and why its inhabitants did not build it up anew from its ashes.

On this occasion, however, he wanted to walk towards Whitehall. He grew increasingly excited, Margaret told me afterwards, like a child on a holiday. He pointed out to her the square bulk of the Banqueting House, rising among the chimneys and battlements of the lesser buildings that clustered around it.

'That's where we killed the man of blood, my dear,' he had said to her with a smile. 'And made England ready for King Jesus.'

Margaret lived with her husband in Alsatia.

That was the name they gave to Whitefriars, for the area was in constant turmoil, as was the real Alsatia, that troubled province on the borders of Germany and France. London's Alsatia was on the site of a former friary and its environs. It lay to the east of the lawyers in the Temple and to the west of the whores in Bridewell. To the north was Fleet Street, and to the south the Thames. The Newcombs' lodgings in the Savoy were only a few minutes' walk away.

The Fire had passed over the area, reducing many of its buildings to ashes and ruins. But some few remained, for the monastery had been built mainly of brick and stone. Despite the destruction, Alsatia was almost as well populated as it had been before the flames had passed over it. People camped in the ruins, inhabited holes in cellars that were open to the sky, and squeezed themselves even more tightly than before into the remaining buildings.

Alsatia held a particular attraction for its inhabitants that pushed all its drawbacks into insignificance. The entire precinct had been declared a sanctuary in the Middle Ages. Though the monastery had long gone, the right of sanctuary remained. It was a liberty, which meant that in legal terms it was quite separate from the great city that surrounded it.

The inhabitants were rogues, murderers, thieves, beggars, and whores. They united against intruders, fighting off any attempt to infringe the ancient right of sanctuary. No magistrates dared to go there, for they would be beaten or even murdered if they did. Even the King's guards were wary of entering Whitefriars.

Margaret's husband was not a rogue, only a man who had had the misfortune to lose part of a leg in the defence of his country. But he was also a bankrupt, because the Navy owed him eighteen months' worth of back pay, and as such he was liable to arrest if he ventured abroad. That was why they lived in Alsatia, where he was out of the bailiffs' reach.

'People leave us alone now,' she said to me, and there was a note of pride in her voice. 'Alsatia's not so bad when you get used to it. Sam may only have one leg now, but he has a dagger and a pistol. He cut off a man's finger just after we moved there.'

So that was Margaret Witherdine. If I had thought about her, I would have thought her a woman of no importance to me, unless her cooperation were for some reason temporarily convenient for the discharge of my duties. In the same way, I'm sure, I was a man of no importance to her, except insofar as I could help her to earn the few weekly pennies that she took back to her feckless husband.

All that changed when my father went missing.

CHAPTER THIRTY-TWO

My father went missing on Wednesday, just over a week after my return from Coldridge.

Mistress Newcomb gave me the news when I brought the latest batch of corrected proofs to her husband. My father had settled in the parlour after dinner, she told me, as he usually did, and she had left him to sleep. But when she looked in an hour later, she found he had gone.

Her fingers screwed up her apron. 'What could I do, sir? I couldn't stay with him. The children were in a pickle and the maid's ill. Margaret's not here today and the scullery girl's a fool.'

The door had been bolted, but my father had undone it and gone out. Mistress Newcomb had sent the scullery maid and her husband's labourer to scour the streets, but they had found nothing. She had sent them out again, and they were still looking.

I bit back my anger. I knew it was unjust

to blame her. The poor woman had enough to do without keeping watch over my father. She was kinder to him than Mistress Ralston had been in Chelsea, more willing to endure his frailties. But there was a limit to her patience, and I did not want to cross it, for then my father and I would be homeless again. On the other hand, I could not place him in confinement in his own home. After his long years in prison, he hated above all things to be locked in.

'I'll search for him myself,' I said. 'Don't worry, he can't be far.'

I tried to speak cheerfully but I was full of foreboding. My father had the body of an old man and the mind of a child. He would fall easy prey to malice or accident. To make matters worse, I was in a hurry, for Master Williamson wanted to dictate some letters, and he was determined that we should do them this afternoon.

I walked up to the Strand and paused on the corner, where the alley from the Savoy met the main road. The rain drizzled from a grey sky. Traffic roared and clattered past me in either direction, the wheels and hooves throwing a spray of mud and water over the foot passengers.

A cutting wind was coming up from the river, growing more vicious and forceful as the alley funnelled it up to the road. It snatched at men's hats and wigs, and sent women's skirts twitching and flying as if each of them contained a small, manic creature frolicking in the darkness within.

Which way would my father go? I tried to put myself into his poor confused mind. This part of London had been untouched by the Fire. The buildings were much the same as they had been in Cromwell's time. True, there were more people about; their clothes were gaudier; their voices louder. And the women adorned themselves and displayed their charms in a way they would not have dared to ten years earlier. There were more shops as well, and more bustle and excitement.

But the Strand was still recognizable, still part of his London. If he had set out towards Whitehall, to the Banqueting House, I might well have seen him on my way from there. On balance, I thought it more likely he would have followed the long-entrenched geography of habit, and set out for home.

Or rather where his home had been — the house and workshop in Pater Noster Row. It had not been his for six years. After my father's arrest, his landlord, a merchant in Leadenhall, had leased it to another printer, a man who handled broadsides and bawdy ballads. The new tenant had bought from the Crown the confiscated tools and materials of my father's trade — his cases of type, his inks and his stocks of paper.

So I walked eastwards along the south side of the Strand towards the City, shouldering my way through the throng. If I were right, and he had gone there, God alone knew what he would make of the place where he had lived and worked. The flames had burned with particular fury in Pater Noster Row, for it was close to the inferno of St Paul's.

I passed under Temple Bar and entered the territory of the Fire. The ruins stretched away from me almost as far as I could see. Pushing through the crowd, I walked at a fast pace, almost a run, following the slope of Fleet Street down towards the Fleet Ditch and Bridewell.

I felt a hand on my arm. I spun round, my back to the wall, my free hand diving for my dagger.

'Master —'

I let my hand fall to my side. 'Margaret — what the devil are you doing here?'

Her face was red, bathed with sweat. 'Thank God you're come, sir.'

'What is it?' I snapped.

'Your father.' Her hand tightened on my

arm. 'He's here.'

'Where?'

She waved at the ruins behind her.

It was only then that I realized where we were standing. 'Ram Alley?'

It was one of the most notorious thoroughfares of Alsatia. It lay on the western side of Whitefriars, near to the Temple where the lawyers nested like magpies and grew rich from the follies of men. We were standing at its mouth, where its northern end met Fleet Street.

Margaret caught her breath. Two men were waiting in a doorway not fifty yards away. At that point Ram Alley was barely a couple of paces wide. The doorway lacked a door and the house behind it lacked a roof. The men were dressed in rusty black and armed with long swords. They were tall, with great bellies drooping over their belts, and slightly bowlegged. Former Ironsides, I guessed, run to seed and as vicious as scalded rats.

'Is my father . . . safe?'

She touched my arm again, but gently this time, for reassurance. 'He's all right, sir, as God's my witness. At least he was. I left him with my Sam, and he'll deal with anyone who comes close. But Master Marwood can't walk too well. He's hurt his ankle.'

'What happened?'

'He came here to look for me, sir. He . . . he wanted us to go for a walk.' Margaret swallowed. 'To Whitehall again.'

To the Banqueting House, she meant. To the place of blood and ashes where they had made England ready for King Jesus.

'I'm sorry, sir,' she said. 'I'm sorry.'

'You're not to blame,' I said. No one was to blame, not even my poor father. 'We must bring him home. Was he attacked?' I glanced up the alley, at the waiting men. 'By them?'

She shook her head. 'I think not. Someone picked his pocket, I expect, but that's all.'

They would have found precious little there. 'He probably didn't notice,' I said. 'How did he hurt himself?'

'A boy said he was lying in the gutter. He was calling my name. So the boy came for me, thinking he was my father.' She sniffed. 'So I said he was. Safer.'

I took a couple of steps into the alley, but she pulled me back.

'Oh, dear God, please be careful, sir.'

The two men ahead were staring at us, their thumbs hooked in their belts. I said, 'Shall I fetch help?'

'Better not. They might let you in, as you're with me, but if you bring others with you, they'll take you for bailiffs or constables and rouse the neighbourhood.' She lowered her voice. 'They killed a man last week. The body went out with the tide.' She looked up at me. 'I'll tell them that you're my brother, sir. If you don't object.'

As far as I was concerned, she could have said I was the Bishop of Rome if it stood a chance of making those two bullies look kindly on me. 'I must find my father. Then we'll decide what to do.'

'Your pardon, sir, but it will be better if I take your arm. To make us seem friendly. Otherwise they might take you for a law officer.'

Margaret's hand gripped my arm. We walked into Ram Alley. Her arm trembled against mine, but she marched forward, drawing me with her, as if she owned the whole of Alsatia.

There was a screech of metal. One of the two men had drawn his sword. He touched the tip of the long, heavy blade against the wall of the house opposite him, blocking our path. It was an old cavalryman's broadsword with a basket hilt.

'And what have we here?' he asked. His hat was tilted to the left. His right ear had been reduced to a stump.

Margaret dipped in a curtsy. 'This is my brother, sir.'

'We want no riff-raff here,' the other said, fingering the hilt of his dagger. 'We're very particular.'

'He's come to fetch my poor father. He's been taken ill.'

They looked at me with disdain.

'Indeed, sirs,' I said. 'He is not well.'

The second man took the edge of my cloak between finger and thumb and rubbed it, assessing the cloth. It was the one that smelled of fish. 'Poor stuff,' he said, and I could not disagree with him.

'Ill, eh?' the man with the sword said. 'Then we must drink the old gentleman's health. It is our Christian duty to aid the sick. By a lucky chance, young sir, the Blood-Bowl Tavern is but a hop and skip away. We shall be there in a flash.'

'Of course.' I reached for my purse. 'But my father is so ill I must go to him at once, sir. I beg you to excuse me. But would you do me the honour to drink his health on my behalf and my sister's as well as your own?'

It was no time for half measures. I unlaced the purse and held it out to them. The swordsman's friend took it and upturned it over his outstretched hand. I watched in silent agony as my entire stock of ready money — almost thirty shillings in all, more than I had had for months — fell chinking into his palm.

'A pleasure to deal with such an open-handed gentleman.' The swordsman dropped the blade and thrust it into its long scabbard. He swept off his greasy hat and bowed to Margaret with the careful precision of the moderately drunk. 'My compliments to Captain Pegleg, mistress,' he said.

They stood aside, each with his back to a wall, forcing us to pass in single file between them. The man with the dagger put out his boot as I went by, causing me to stumble and almost fall.

'Careful, young sir,' he called after me. 'The ground's as slippery as that whore's arse.'

When we were past them, Margaret squeezed my arm again. 'God be praised, sir,' she murmured. 'It could have gone either way. But they were kind-humoured today.' She snorted, a sort of laugh that had nothing to do with amusement. 'You did well to give them your purse.'

My arm was trembling, and my forehead was prickling with sweat as she guided me through a network of lanes and courts. I lost my sense of direction almost immediately, for there was nothing to help me orientate myself apart from the occasional glimpse of the river.

We came to a small yard surrounded by crumbling buildings of brick, stained with soot. A layer of ashes covered the flagstones beneath our feet. A boy of four or five years was squatting in the dirt and relieving himself. He wore nothing but a shirt, and his arms and legs looked like chicken bones. He held out a cupped hand for alms but otherwise ignored us.

'That door there,' Margaret said. 'Home.'

She led me through an archway into one of the buildings and opened a door into a ground-floor room barely six feet square. The only window was tiny, and a rag had been nailed over it in place of glass. To my immense relief, the first thing I saw in the gloom was my father, sitting on the floor with his back against the wall. Beside him, was another man. His right leg had been taken off below the knee, and he wore a wooden stump in its place.

My father squinted at me in the doorway. 'James,' he said pettishly. 'Where have you been? I wish you'd been here hours ago. This gentleman is Samuel. He and I have been discoursing on the probable nature of Armageddon, and it would have nourished your soul.'

'Is all well?' Margaret whispered.

'Also, on the subject of nourishment,' my

father went on in the same irritable voice, 'I find that I'm hungry.'

'Nobody's been in since you left,' Sam said.

'We met Rock and Captain Boyd in Ram Alley,' Margaret said. 'Master Marwood gave them his purse.'

'Shame. But wise.'

The sailor stared at me. My eyes were adjusting to the gloom. I made out a long, unsheathed dagger on the platform beside him. On his other side, close to his hand, was a shape I took to be his pistol, partly concealed by the folds of his coat. Next to it was a small earthenware bottle.

'Thank you for your kindness to my father, sir.'

'And I thank you for yours to my wife.'

I expected Margaret's husband to be little better than a distressed animal, a drunken wreck wholly dependent on his wife. Samuel Witherdine was certainly a cripple, and perhaps he drank too much, but there was nothing about him that asked for pity.

'You want to get him out of here,' he said. 'This is no place for an old man. Not like him.'

I addressed my father: 'Can you walk, sir?'

He stared at me in surprise. 'Of course I can walk. Is it suppertime?'

'Not without help,' Samuel said. 'He's got a wrench or a sprain to his left ankle. But you'll get him up to Fleet Street between you, and then you can find a hackney or a chair. I'll come with you, just in case.'

'But I don't want to go yet,' my father said. 'We haven't finished our discourse. Could supper be sent for?'

'Another time, sir,' Samuel said, and his voice had become gentler. 'If you would be so kind.'

My father's face brightened. 'We can sing psalms.'

'Indeed we can.'

Margaret helped her husband to rise and gave him his crutch. He stuffed the pistol in the pocket of his long coat and put the dagger in his belt.

When we left the lodging, Samuel hopped behind us. He was marvellously agile, and could have made faster progress than the rest of us despite the crutch. My father was weary, and he hung between Margaret and me, making little effort to help, and squealing with pain when something jarred his injured ankle. Trailing behind us all came the little boy, sucking his fingers as if he hoped against hope to derive nourishment from them.

We took a different, shorter route up to

Fleet Street from the one we had come by. No one tried to stop us, though many watched us go. Perhaps Sam's presence deterred them, or perhaps word had got about that we had already paid our dues to the bullies of Ram Alley.

For the first time in my life, the racket in Fleet Street was a foretaste of paradise. Margaret and I reached the corner, with my father dangling between us. Samuel lingered behind, thirty yards into the safety of Alsatia.

The old man became more lively when he saw where he was. I propped him against the wall, with Margaret to keep him company and stop him from straying. It was only a short distance to the Savoy but I did not think he could manage it, even with our help. I looked about for a vacant hackney coach or chair to take him back. I would have to beg a loan from the Newcombs to pay for it.

Behind me, my father was talking to Margaret, his tongue suddenly unleashed.

'You see, my dear, London is a perfect Gomorrah, another City of the Plain, a place of luxury and sin. Tom Lovett was in the right of it. It is too wicked to last. The Lord will destroy it.'

I turned round sharply. 'What did you say?

Tom who?'

My father raised his watery eyes to me. 'Tom Lovett. Fire and brimstone will not be the half of it, he said. He is a most godly man, in his way, though a little rough in his manner.'

'I didn't know you knew him, sir.'

'He's one of the saved. I used to see him sometimes at meetings in the old days. The room we used was in Watling Street, not a stone's throw from his house in Bow Lane. Tom says the return of this King cannot last. God will blot him out, sooner or later. Charles will go the way of his father, the man of blood.'

I heard my father's words but my understanding lagged a few seconds behind. 'Do you mean you've seen Tom Lovett recently? Since the Restoration?'

His attention was wandering towards two brightly painted prostitutes who were approaching, scanning the crowd for possible customers. 'Recently? Yes — quite by chance. Didn't I say?' He waved behind us, towards the alley where Sam was still waiting. 'I saw Tom in there.'

'This afternoon? Are you saying you've seen him this afternoon?'

'Yes, I told you. Why are you so foolish today?' My father frowned as a memory passed like a shadow through the ruins of his mind. 'Indeed, it was Tom Lovett who made me fall in the gutter. We conversed only for a moment. Then he pushed me down when I tried to follow him. Now why would Tom do that?'

CHAPTER THIRTY-THREE

Next morning, I still did not know what to do for the best.

My duty to my masters was clear enough, that I should reveal what my father had told me yesterday about meeting Lovett in Alsatia; it was up to them to decide what to do with the information. But my duty to my father was opposed to that.

If I told Williamson and Chiffinch, they would interrogate my father to see if they could squeeze more information from him. They might quite possibly imprison him again on suspicion of conspiring with a Regicide. They would comb Alsatia for traces of Thomas Lovett, though I had not the faintest idea how they could do that discreetly.

I left my father in the parlour with strict instructions not to stir until I returned. He would do as I asked, if only because he had no choice — he was still lame from yesterday's adventure in Alsatia, and he could hobble only with difficulty, and with the aid of a stick.

As I had expected, Margaret was in the passage leading to the Newcombs' lodgings, waiting to receive the day's deliveries. I thought it wiser to meet her as if by chance, rather than to summon her, which might arouse Mistress Newcomb's curiosity. Mistress Newcomb was not quite happy with me, because I had borrowed a pound from her husband yesterday to tide me over after Rock and Captain Boyd had taken the contents of my purse.

I drew Margaret aside and gave her two shillings, which drove the colour to her cheeks and prompted a flurry of undeserved thanks.

'By the way, do you remember what my father was saying yesterday just before we found the hackney?' I asked.

'That London was Gomorrah, sir. And that God would destroy it.' She glanced up at me with a hint of a smile. 'If you ask me, God's already done half the job.'

'And . . . ?' I prompted.

She hesitated, her eyes falling. 'And something foolish about the King.'

Instinctively we both looked up and down the passage to make sure we were alone.

'His mind was rambling, of course,' I said. 'He didn't know what he was saying. But do you perhaps recall him mentioning a name?'

'The man who told him about . . . about Gomorrah? Tom something, was it?'

I lowered my voice. 'Tom Lovett. My father thought he'd met him in Alsatia.' It was my turn to hesitate. 'An old comrade, I believe. But Lovett did not wish for his company and pushed him over. That's what caused the sprained ankle.' Another hesitation. 'According to my father.'

Margaret nodded, and I knew that she understood me. My father was too confused, and his memory too erratic, for us to be sure of anything he told us.

'I wonder . . .' I stopped, for her sharp little eyes were making me uncomfortable. 'That is to say, I should like to know whether this Lovett is really there or not. Would you find out for me, if you can? Without his being aware of it, or anyone else.'

'What's this man look like then?' she demanded, as if I'd asked her the most ordinary thing in the world.

I felt suddenly foolish. 'I can't tell you. He's in middle age, I believe, not as old as my father at any rate. He's a Puritan by persuasion, though he may not advertise that.'

'I'll ask Samuel,' she said. 'That'll be best.'

My face must have betrayed what was in my mind.

'Just because Sam's a cripple,' she said, firing up, 'it doesn't mean he's lost his wits. Those Dutch bastards took off his leg with their cannonball, not his head.'

I bowed my head. 'Pray ask Samuel. Whatever you think best.'

I hoped that time and Margaret between them would resolve the matter with the minimum of help from me, that Lovett would betray himself by his actions, or simply disappear. Fear makes fools of us all.

At Whitehall, Williamson had the toothache, which brought out the bully in him. I spent the day copying the letters for his correspondents, the routine ones that went out to the provinces with the *Gazette*. I dined at the palace and continued at my labours for most of the afternoon.

It was a tedious day, and I was glad when it ended. I walked back to our lodgings. It was raining. At this hour, the streets were still busy, and there was a particular bustle outside the arcades of the New Exchange in the Strand, where the rich and fashionable clustered around the shops like wasps around a bowl of honey. The double galleries were packed with customers and their servants. In the road outside, their coaches had almost brought traffic to a standstill.

A servant came up to me as I was making my way through the pedestrians. He bowed very civilly and asked if I was Master Marwood.

'Yes. Why?'

'My mistress desires to speak with you.'

He was wearing livery, I noticed, marked with bold vertical stripes of black and yellow. Alderley's livery. I had a sudden memory of Layne's body in the cellar of Scotland Yard all those weeks ago, and Williamson saying in his grating voice, 'It's the clothes that matter.'

The man gestured at one of the coaches drawn up at the side of the road. I had passed it a moment ago without paying any attention. I saw now that Henry Alderley's badge was painted on the door: the pelican plucking the flesh from her own breast to feed her young. In my family, I thought grimly, it was the other way round.

He led me through the throng and opened the coach door. Mistress Alderley was sitting facing towards the horses, with her maid opposite her. I bowed low.

She inclined her head in reply. 'Master Marwood. A word, if you please. Come out of the rain.' She waved a gloved finger at her maid. 'Go and enquire when the necklace will be ready.'

The footman let down the steps and handed down the maid; she gave me a sour look as she passed. I climbed into the coach and took her seat. The footman closed the door and I was alone with Olivia Alderley in a dim, sweetly scented box. I was obliged to hold my legs rigidly against the door to prevent my knees from brushing the skirt of her dress.

'Well,' she said softly. 'This is a fortunate chance.'

I said nothing. The rain pattered on the roof of the coach.

'Except it isn't a chance at all. I was at Whitehall this afternoon and I saw you leaving.'

'Did you see Master Chiffinch at Whitehall?' I said. Or the King?

'I must see you on Sunday.' She spoke as one speaks to a servant. 'At the same time, the same place.'

'If it pleases you, madam.'

'Yes.' Her voice was brisk, with nothing flirtatious in it. 'It pleases me.'

'I did not find her,' I blurted. 'Your niece,

that is. Catherine Lovett.'

She glanced at me briefly. 'I know.'

She tapped the glass beside her. The footman opened the door. I mumbled farewell. She murmured something in reply but I did not catch it.

My father was dozing by the fire and Mistress Newcomb engaged in preparing supper when I arrived. While I was waiting, the maid came in to tell me that Margaret was outside and begged the favour of a word.

I found her among the shadows in the yard by the kitchen door. It was dark now, and the only light filtered through the cracks of the kitchen shutters.

'What is it?' I asked in an undertone.

Her face was a grey blur in the dusk. 'There was a man, sir.' She spoke in a whisper and I had to strain to catch the words. 'Might be Lovett. Hanging Sword Alley, Salisbury Court end.'

'What's he like?'

'Tall and well set up, wore his own hair. Samuel used to see him in Blood-Bowl Tavern sometimes. Never in liquor, though. He drank a little ale, warmed himself at the fire, read the newspaper.'

'Could Samuel describe him further?' I asked.

'No meat on him.' She spoke in short, jerky sentences, as if words were rationed, were precious in themselves. 'Forty-five, maybe, fifty? Plainly dressed, and wore a sword. People left him alone.'

'Why was he there? Did Samuel say?'

'You don't ask people that in Alsatia,' she said, with a note of scorn in her voice. 'Not unless they want to tell you. Samuel thought he'd fallen on hard times — that he'd known better things. Plenty of men like that in the Blood-Bowl, of course, but he wasn't like them, Sam said — this one knew what he was about. Didn't seem short of money, though. No one troubled him.'

'Where can I find him exactly? Which house?'

'I don't know. He's not there any more. Sam talked to the man who keeps the house.' She paused and sniffed, lifting her chin at me as if to emphasize that Samuel had discovered all this, despite his short-comings in the matter of legs. 'He left last night. No warning.' She snorted with what sounded like genuine amusement. 'He left money with the servant to cover what he owed. Paid up to the last farthing. No more, no less. He'd been keeping his own reckoning. Not many do that, especially in Alsatia.

Not many pay up unless they have to, either.'

I said, 'He must have had a name.'

'It wasn't Lovett. He called himself Master Coldridge.'

I let out the air from my lungs in a rush.

'One other thing, sir.' Her voice became a whisper. 'Sam heard he'd killed a man near Bridewell.'

I felt a prickle of excitement, or perhaps fear. The footbridge over the Fleet was beside Bridewell. The place where Jeremiah Sneyd's body had been found.

At that moment the kitchen door opened, and Mistress Newcomb appeared on the step. Behind her was one of the apprentices, with a staff in one hand and a lantern in the other. 'Who's there?' she demanded. 'Show yourself.'

'It's nothing, mistress,' I said. 'Only Margaret — there was a difficulty with tomorrow's deliveries, but we've dealt with it now.'

I unbolted the yard gate for Margaret to leave.

'That's why they left him alone,' she whispered as she passed me. 'Even Rock and Captain Boyd in Ram Alley.'

Chapter Thirty-Four

On Friday morning I had business for Master Williamson in the City. On my way back I passed along Cheapside. Behind me, the bells of the City's surviving churches were chiming their many versions of eleven o'clock.

Cheapside, once the finest street in London, had been reduced to rubble and ash. A path just wide enough for a wagon to pass had been cleared in the roadway. On either side, labourers were working among ruins. They were not trying to rebuild houses yet, rather to bring some sort of order to the chaos of destruction. Booths selling beer had sprung up at street corners, to slake the thirst of workers and passers-by. When the debris was disturbed, the ashes rose into the air and clung to the back of throats and coated the nostrils.

In a strange fashion, however, Cheapside was busy enough, though not in the way it had been before the Fire. Surveyors were at work, measuring the ground. The task of rebuilding the City was fraught with legal problems, not least that of establishing the precise boundaries of thousands of freeholds which had developed over centuries; and many of the title deeds had been inaccurate, or lost, or destroyed in the Fire.

A few former residents inhabited what had once been their cellars, and troops of scavengers were still picking over what was left. Saddest of all were the men and women who wandered the ruins with dazed expressions on their faces. I supposed that they were searching for their homes or their loved ones, or perhaps for both. Scraps of paper had been nailed to the remains of doorposts or weighted down with stones in the shelter of brick hearths. Messages for lost children, lost parents and lost friends were scrawled on them, some of which were still legible after weeks of exposure to the autumn weather.

On the south side of the street a small crowd clustered around the booth that had been set up among the graves in front of the ruins of Bow Church. I stopped to buy some beer. While I was waiting to be served, there was a stir along Cheapside, caused by three gentlemen walking abreast along the street, with a servant ahead of them to clear the way. All at once I forgot my thirst. The servant was in livery, with broad, vertical stripes of black and yellow on his coat and breeches.

Alderley's colours.

The man himself was behind, striding along as if the street were empty. Mundy, the steward, was on his right. On his left was a younger man, heavy featured and richly dressed, with a sword swinging at his side. He glanced at the beer booth as they passed with a single, baleful eye. He wore a black patch over the other eye.

It could only be Edward Alderley, the son whom Jem had stabbed, set on fire and left for dead.

The party turned into the lane running south beside the church. All at once the co-incidence struck me. This was Bow Lane: where Lovett had had his house and yard before it was confiscated; and it wasn't far from the bridge by Bridewell, where they had found Jeremiah Sneyd's body in the Fleet Ditch, and only a little further away from Alsatia, where Master Coldridge had lodged in Hanging Sword Alley until Wednesday evening.

After a moment or two, I followed Henry Alderley and his party. Bow Lane was still a ravine strewn with ashes and rubbish, with charred ruins rising on either side of it. I picked my way slowly, making a detour to avoid a party of labourers who were making safe the frontage of an inn. Wisps of smoke curled into the air, rising from something still smouldering deep in the ruins. On the corner of Watling Street, a surveyor and his men were measuring the dimensions of a building that had once stood there.

I was in time to see the four men turning right into an alley before the corner. I asked one of the labourers who had lived there before the Fire.

'Don't know, master.' He wiped the dust from his mouth with the back of his hand. 'There's a mason's yard down there. What's left of it.'

I walked down the lane. The alley was partly blocked by a fallen chimney. As for Lovett's house, it no longer existed in any form that resembled a dwelling.

The building had been constructed mainly of wood over a low brick base, an irony for a mason's house. The chimney-stacks had fallen. In the yard behind the house had been a row of wooden sheds and open shelters, whose outlines could be traced by the blackened stumps of the surviving posts that had supported their roofs. There were still stacks of stone within, them. Much of it had been neatly dressed, but the heat of the Fire had cracked and calcined it.

The Alderleys, their steward and their servant were in the yard. Alderley must have heard my footsteps, for he turned and stared at me. Then, to my surprise, he raised his hand and beckoned me over. I had not seen him since that chance meeting in the Matted Gallery at Whitehall.

'I know you, don't I?' He frowned at me across a heap of broken tiles. 'Master Williamson's clerk? Wait — the name's on the tip of my tongue. Marpool — Mardy — no, I have it: Marwood. What are you doing here, Marwood? Have you a message from your master?'

I bowed to him. 'No, sir. I'm on my way to the Savoy.'

The frown deepened. This was not the most direct route to the Savoy. But I did not want to admit my interest in the Lovetts to Master Alderley. As far as I knew, he still believed that the disappearance of his niece was a secret confined within the walls of Barnabas Place. On the other hand, I did want to know what he and his son were doing here. A gull from the river swooped low over Watling Street and gave me inspiration.

'Master Williamson has a share in a warehouse in Thames Street, sir,' I said. 'I had a mind to walk down and see how the work is going on with the clearance.'

Alderley shrugged. 'At a snail's pace no doubt. As it is everywhere.'

Edward Alderley turned and stared at me with his single, baleful eye. 'Not just a snail, sir,' he said, still looking at me, though the words were intended for his father. 'A damned, snivelling, sleeping snail.'

'Very droll, sir,' said the third man, the Alderleys' steward.

'Nothing droll about it in the world,' Edward snapped, rounding on him. 'You should know that as well as anyone, Mundy.'

The steward flushed and turned away, his assurance cracking like an eggshell.

'Does Williamson have a share in the freehold of this warehouse?' Edward asked.

'I believe not, sir,' I said. 'Only the lease.'

'Then he's fortunate indeed.' He swung back to his father. 'I cannot believe those rascally judges should have made such an unjust decision, sir. Everyone knows that that damned Frenchman no more lit the fire than I did.'

I knew then what was on their minds. Parliament had asked the judges to advise on a point of law: whether the landlords or the tenants should be responsible for rebuilding property destroyed by Fire. On Monday it had become known that the judges had decided that tenants should only be responsible if they or their neighbours had started the Fire. But since a Frenchman had admitted the crime and been executed for it last week, it followed that the Fire was due to the action of an enemy. In that case, they ruled, Parliament should ensure that landlords bore the expense. It was openly said at Whitehall and Westminster, and even in the City, that the Frenchman, one Hulbert, was mad and his testimony against himself could not be trusted. But he made a convenient culprit.

Mundy gave a discreet cough and turned to Master Alderley. 'Would you like me to arrange for this site to be measured and cleared as well, sir? It may take a little time — there is so much to be done.'

Before I could stop myself, I let out my breath sharply. Edward glanced at me with his single eye, registering my surprise. I cleared my throat, hoping he would assume that this was the reason for my behaviour.

'It would be wise to do as much as we can before the onset of winter,' Mundy was saying in his droning voice. 'Snow and frost will make the job twice as hard and twice as expensive.'

'Very well,' Master Alderley said. 'Add it to the list.'

I dug the toe of my shoe into a heap of ash beside me, struggling to work out the implications of what I had learned. Little was recognizable among the rubbish. Among the ash were fragments of iron, distorted into fantastical shapes. Once perhaps they had been chisels and axe-heads before the alchemy of fire had robbed them of form and purpose. Here and there were drops of lead, molten then resolidified. I even glimpsed a fragment of china, perhaps from a cup, a sign that the last mistress of the house had had luxurious tastes.

Edward Alderley spat, his spittle just missing my shoe. 'The expense doesn't bear thinking of, sir.'

His father stared at the ruins. 'There's no help for it.' He scratched his forehead, reaching up under his wig with long fingers. 'But there may be a silver lining. Others will be in our position, but less capable of managing the matter.' His lips twisted into a half-smile. 'In which case, they may wish to dispose of some of their freeholds, along with the responsibilities that go with them, at a reasonable price. We must enquire into that.'

I bowed and asked permission to leave

them, knowing that I had no excuse to linger.

But Edward put a hand on my sleeve. 'Stay. Where's the nearest tavern?'

'I can't say, sir. There are booths selling beer in Cheapside. But for a tavern you may have to go up to Smithfield or towards Moorgate.'

'God's teeth.'

'There's no need for a tavern, Edward,' his father said, in a voice that did not invite discussion. 'We shall dine at home. Come — we shall hire a hackney by Ludgate, if you wish, but it will be quicker to walk.'

I bowed. Master Alderley gave me a nod as they left. His son and his steward gave me nothing.

At the Savoy, I glimpsed something red, the colour as vivid as blood against the sooty stone, at the corner of the passage to the Newcombs' lodgings. I walked quickly towards it, my mind full of what I had learned in Bow Lane, and my belly rumbling with hunger.

As I approached the corner, the sound of my footsteps bouncing like balls between the high walls on either side, a soldier in the uniform of the King's Guards appeared. I forgot my hunger for a moment and felt a lurch of fear instead.

They had come for my father.

I broke into a run. 'What is it?' I said, my voice rising. 'What's happening?'

The soldier held up his hand to make me stop.

'My father's ill,' I said. 'He's done nothing wrong, I swear it. If you ask for Master Williamson, at my Lord Arlington's lodging, he will —'

I broke off as a second soldier appeared. It was Lieutenant Thurloe.

'Master Marwood?' he said in a formal, interrogatory voice as if he didn't know me from Adam, though we had parted on reasonably cordial terms at our previous meeting three weeks before, when we had brought the body of Jeremiah Sneyd upriver to Scotland Yard by barge.

'Sir,' I said, 'are you here for my father? His health is not good, and I beg you to —'

'No, sir.' Thurloe beckoned his men. 'I'm looking for you. I'm commanded to convey you under escort to Whitehall. Without delay.'

Chapter Thirty-Five

'Am I under arrest?' I said again.

Thurloe didn't turn his head. But this time he spoke to me at least. 'That's not for me to say.'

'If I'm not, sir, then why are these men behind us? Why you?'

He gave no sign that he had heard me. But still he wouldn't look at me.

He had a barge waiting at the Somerset Stairs. He and I sat under the awning at the stern, with the soldiers on either side. I had left my father in tears. He was convinced that I was to be conveyed to the Tower, and that he would never see me again on this side of the grave.

The tide was with us and we were at Whitehall in ten minutes. I expected us to put in at the common stairs beside the palace, but we went further upstream to the Privy Stairs. A crowd of boats was waiting there already, landing and receiving passengers. Instead of having to wait our turn, however, we were waved directly to the upstream side of the steps, where we disembarked at once.

A manservant was on the watch for us. He and Thurloe had a whispered conversation on the stairs. The two soldiers stayed in the boat, exchanging chaff with the watermen as if nothing of significance had happened.

Thurloe and the servant took me through a maze of passages and chambers, some cramped and ancient, others grand and furnished in the most modern taste, to a small chamber on the second floor. It contained a table, two stools and a chair that looked as if they had stood there since the time of the King's grandfather. A fire burned in the grate.

'You're to wait,' Thurloe said. He glanced over his shoulder. The servant had already withdrawn. For the first time, he looked directly at me. 'I don't know if you're to be arrested, sir,' he murmured. 'But they were so pressing about bringing you here, so damned urgent, and they said I was not to speak to you, nor allow you to speak to others.'

He gave me a nod and left the room. A key turned in the lock. I examined my prison. It did not take long — the chamber measured three paces one way and four the other. The window was small, with tiny leaded panes whose glass distorted the outside world. It overlooked a paved court filthy with bird droppings. I could not see the sky.

I sat at the table. Weariness flooded over me. Nothing good could come of this. The manner of the summons suggested that I was under suspicion. It must surely be connected to my failure to report the presence of Thomas Lovett in Alsatia. Unless it had something to do with Olivia Alderley, in which case I understood even less about this matter than I thought I did.

The hours passed slowly. The light faded beyond the window. Once or twice I rose from the table to feed the fire with another shovelful of coals. I tried to ignore the emptiness of my stomach. Occasionally I heard footsteps, and once the raised voice of a man berating a servant. By this time the only light was the reddish glow from the dying fire. I was slumped over the table with my head resting on my hands, drifting into that place between wakefulness and sleep.

The rattle of the door handle jerked me back to alertness. The key scraped in the lock.

'Marwood?' Chiffinch's figure filled the doorway, with light behind him. 'What the devil are you doing in the dark?'

He turned his head and called to an invisible servant to bring candles. I rose to my feet, blinking as I adjusted to the light. My limbs were stiff and clumsy. I bowed as well as I could.

'How long have you been here?' Chiffinch demanded.

'I don't know, sir.' My mind was as stiff as thick porridge. I groped for the right words. 'They brought me here between midday and one of the clock.'

He shrugged. 'The fools should have given you food and light.'

'Why am I here?' I asked, too weary to be polite, though I knew better than to complain about being kept waiting.

'Because I summoned you, of course.' He glared at me.

'But sending soldiers, sir . . .'

'You were wanted immediately.' Chiffinch stepped aside to allow the servant to enter and place candles on the table. He frowned at me, disliking my presumption in asking him questions. He waited until the door had closed behind the servant. 'But then it became less urgent, so you were obliged to wait.'

And of course he hadn't bothered to let me know, he had let me wait in fear.

I tried to change the subject. 'I saw Master Alderley this morning.'

'What?' The frown deepened. 'You went to Barnabas Place?'

'No, sir — I was in Cheapside, and I chanced to see him and his son. They went into Bow Lane.'

His attention sharpened. 'Where the Lovetts used to live?'

'Yes, sir.' I began to hope that he had heard nothing about my father and Alsatia. 'I followed them. The house was quite destroyed. But Master Alderley and his son were in the yard. They were inspecting the damage with their steward. I hadn't realized that they owned the freehold.'

Chiffinch shrugged. 'So?'

'Isn't it all of a piece with Coldridge? As if Master Alderley has found another way to enrich himself at the expense of the Lovetts.'

'The case is quite different,' he said. 'The Bow Lane freehold was confiscated when Lovett fled abroad. Then the King granted it to Master Alderley.'

He told me this in a voice that did not invite questions. I knew that Alderley had lent the King money. Perhaps it was not unreasonable that there should have been other transactions between them.

But Bow Lane? Why this freehold?

He was still looking at me, his face dancing above the flame of a candle set on the table between us. He said slowly and softly, 'You might say that Master Alderley earned it.' His fingers fiddled with the wart on his cheek. 'But it would not be wise to say it in Master Alderley's hearing.'

I realized then that Chiffinch did not like Master Alderley. 'Earned it, sir?'

'He laid information about his brother-in-law, and he was rewarded. As it happened, Lovett evaded capture. Otherwise the reward would have been bigger.'

Both my tiredness and my hunger were now forgotten for the moment. The information that Alderley had betrayed his brother-in-law as well as stolen from his niece was another fact to be added to the pile, something else to be considered.

'Come,' Chiffinch said.

I followed him along passages, through chambers, up and down steps. Candles burned in sconces on the walls and on tables, lighting our way but leaving pools of darkness between them. I soon lost all sense of direction, just as I had when I had followed Lieutenant Thurloe earlier today. In the interval, the palace had changed under the influence, and not for the better. It had become more than ever like a labyrinth, a place where watchers and monsters lingered out of sight in the shadows or around corners.

This was a part of Whitehall I had never seen before. I was becoming familiar with the areas that the public were allowed to frequent — the Matted Gallery, for example, the courts, the gateways and the great buildings like the Great Hall and the Banqueting House. But we were now among the suites of private apartments where the members of the royal household lived, along with favoured courtiers and their armies of dependants and hangers-on.

The air was dense with the smells of tallow, perfume and drains. Sometimes we passed through apartments full of brightly clothed people and dazzling lights, endlessly reflected in mirrors. People made way for Chiffinch, parting to let him through, but they hardly gave me a second glance. Guards were stationed at intervals, usually at doorways. They opened doors for Chiffinch, but otherwise we might have been invisible. At Whitehall, men saw only what they wished to see.

We came down a flight of stairs. A guard swung open one leaf of a heavy door. As we went outside, the raw night air rushed in to meet us, heavy with the tang of coal smoke from scores of chimneys. I felt raindrops on my cheek. I realized that we were in the Privy Garden, with the Matted Gallery rising somewhere behind us. It was not dark — lanterns hung at intervals from standards placed along the paths between the beds, and light filtered through the glass of dozens of uncurtained windows. In the distance, an orchestra was playing a stately saraband for invisible dancers. Above our heads flew invisible seagulls, their cries mingling with the thin, reedy strains of the music.

Chiffinch led me towards the range at right angles to the Matted Gallery. It consisted of the privy gallery and a long suite of apartments stretching west towards the Holbein Gate and the square bulk of the Banqueting House. We passed through another doorway with guards posted on either side.

There were more guards inside and servants in livery. Chiffinch took me up another flight of stairs to the gallery itself. Its walls were lined with tables on which stood many clocks and other curious pieces of machinery whose purpose I did not know. He tapped on a door on the left, and a voice called out that we should wait.

A moment later there was an explosion. I felt the blast like a wave seconds before I heard it. The door muffled the sound, but the impact was enough to set the chimes tinkling in the clocks.

There were running footsteps on the stairs and men were shouting downstairs.

Chiffinch swore. He flung open the door of the chamber. Smoke rolled out, making me cough. The room beyond was brightly lit, illuminating the smoke so that it looked like sheets of blue-grey gauze swirling and swaying in the draught.

'Sir,' Chiffinch cried. 'Sir — are you hurt?'

'God's fish,' a man said. 'Was ever such ill luck?'

His shape loomed out of the rising smoke, from the ground up. First I saw broken-down leather shoes, sagging stockings, filthy breeches and a long leather apron. The smoke rose higher and higher, revealing more and more of a body that seemed taller than any man's had a right to be.

'It is a fault in the saltpetre,' he said. 'It must be. I'll take my oath that the quantities were exact, so it can't be that. Devil take that damned apothecary.'

At last I saw the long, swarthy face, dark as a black man's, the heavy lips, the folds of skin beneath the brown spaniel eyes. I fell

413

to my knees.

'Your Majesty,' I muttered, and then added foolishly, 'I beg your pardon,' though what I had done amiss I could not have begun to say.

'Get up, man,' he said irritably. 'Open the other windows as quick as you can and clear this smoke.' He raised his voice and shouted at the knot of men congregating in the doorway, 'Go away, you fools, you're not needed. Shut the door, Chiffinch.'

I stumbled to my feet. The King towered over me. I had seen him before, but always from afar. He wore no wig but had a dirty kerchief bound around his head. Sweat cut shining grooves on his forehead. He did not look like a king. He looked like a swarthy blacksmith in a bad temper.

He was saying something to Chiffinch. I crossed the room to the tall windows lining the opposite wall. One of them was already open, which must have lessened the force of the blast by allowing it somewhere to go, thereby preventing the glass from shattering. As I opened the other windows, I looked down and saw that a crowd had gathered below in the Privy Garden, their faces upturned towards me.

Behind me, Chiffinch was speaking to the King in a low and urgent voice. I turned to face them. Now the smoke was ebbing away, I saw clearly the room we were in. This was the Royal Laboratory, a place many talked about but few visited. It was fitted with tables and benches, with shelves on one wall and great ironbound presses against another. There was a variety of instruments, including sets of scales. One shelf held glass retorts and another a row of books, irregular in size.

The King was looking over Master Chiffinch's head at me. His eyes met mine. For an instant, his lips twisted into a half-smile.

God help me, I found myself smiling back.

'Thank you,' he said. 'Come here.'

Chiffinch moved towards the door and waited. I took his place in front of the King.

'So you're Marwood,' he said. 'How does your father do?'

The question took me entirely by surprise. There was no sense of threat to it. It was a courteous enquiry, nothing more, one man to another. Except that one man was a king and the other the son of a disgraced Fifth Monarchist.

'He grows old, sir. And increasingly feeble.'

'He has his wits still?'

'Some of them.'

A line appeared between his eyebrows.

'And does he seem happy?'

'I — I think so, sir. I do what I can for him. He is treated kindly where we lodge.'

'Good,' he said. 'We should care for our fathers when they can care for us no longer, and honour them for what they were. Do you not agree?'

'Yes, Your Majesty.'

I had heard of the Stuart charm, and I felt it then, lapping around me, drawing me towards the King. But there was no calculation to it — or not then, I think, no desire to bend me to his will. He genuinely wanted to know how my father did, and how I treated him.

I felt the colour rising to my cheeks. I had seen the King's father die in front of the Banqueting House, only a few yards from where we were standing. I had seen the executioner hold up the dripping head to the crowd. The King could not know this. Could he?

We should care for our fathers when they can care for us no longer.

'Even,' the King said softly, 'when they are in their graves.'

He gave the last word a faint upward twist, converting a statement to a question.

I looked up at him. 'Yes, sir.'

'You should know that I have a most

particular reason to want Thomas Lovett.'

Of course he did, I thought: Lovett was on the list of Regicides that Master Williamson had shown me. *Thomas Lovett — fugit.*

The King seemed to divine my thoughts. 'Not just the fact he's exempted from the Act of Indemnity and therefore should be arrested and stand trial. There's more. There's worse.'

Worse than a Regicide?

Chiffinch stirred, and the King turned his head towards him.

'Peace,' he said in a low voice that held a hint of anger. 'I know what I'm about, Chiffinch.' He turned back to me. 'You have a quality, Marwood, that may make you invaluable to me. I know what your father was. And I also know that you are not he, and that you've rendered me good service these last few months. When you see Mistress Alderley on Sunday, you must do as she asks.' He smiled, for he must have seen the surprise in my face.

'Your Majesty,' I said, 'pray, what will she ask me to do?'

In the distance, a bell began to toll, quickly but irregularly. I had lost the King's attention. Chiffinch said something, his voice low and urgent.

The King glanced at him. 'Tell them to

bring my coat and hat and wig. At once.'

Chiffinch opened the door. In the doorway he collided with a youthful officer in the Foot Guards, his face as scarlet as his coat.

'Your Majesty,' the young man gasped, 'the palace is on fire.'

CHAPTER THIRTY-SIX

The King strode down the gallery, with a dozen of us trailing after him. He had long legs, and we had almost to run to keep up with him. Chiffinch was close at his heels, along with the young officer and two or three soldiers, as well as servants bearing lights and gentlemen I did not know. I came last of all. The King had not told me to attend him, but nor had he told me to leave.

The bell continued its frenzied tolling. Trumpets were sounding outside. Someone was shouting orders in a voice more like a bull's than a man's. Underneath everything was the steady thump of drums.

The King paused at a window. 'There is no call for panic,' he said in a loud, carrying voice to one of the officers. 'Go down to keep them calm. There will be plenty of time if we need to evacuate. Is my brother here? Send to him to join us.'

Despite the King's orders, you could

almost smell the panic in the air. Outside, men and women were scurrying along the paths of the Privy Garden below, many of them burdened with possessions.

The truth was, we were all afraid of fire. How could we not be after what had happened in September? I still dreamed of crackling flames, houses crashing to the ground, heaps of smouldering ashes, and rats squealing and shrivelling in silver puddles of molten lead. If Whitehall were destroyed as well as the City, what would be left of London?

'Have the pumps been ordered up?' the King asked the officer. 'No? God's body, someone will suffer if they're not outside the Horse Guards Yard by the time we are.'

'If the Court Gate catches, sir, the whole palace will be at risk,' an elderly gentleman said. 'Or if the Banqueting House —'

'The weather is not as before,' the King snapped. 'There's little wind, and this rain must surely help us.'

I followed the others down a wider spiral staircase, with cold air rushing up to meet us. By this time I had lost my sense of direction again, though it was clear that we were in one of the older parts of Whitehall. Sure enough, when I emerged into the open air, the Holbein Gate towered up on my left, an orange glow flickering on its chequered brickwork. To the right was the Banqueting House, whose bulk hid the Court Gate beyond.

Flames were rising above the roofs of the Horse Guards barracks on the other side of the road. As far as I could judge, the wind, such as it was, was blowing off the river. The fire had not reached the Foot Guards House, let alone the Tiltyard to the south or the Duke of Ormonde's lodgings beyond. The flames were curling away from the palace, towards the tops of the trees in the Park further to the west.

The bell rang on and on, while trumpets brayed over the steady pulse of the drums. The roadway was crowded with soldiers and servants. Two engines were already in position, and men were directing thin jets of water into the flames.

The King went as close to the flames as he could manage. The rest of us scurried after him.

'Bring up gunpowder,' he said to one of the officers, raising his voice to be heard over the flames. 'Blow up the south end of the Horse Guards and pray the wind doesn't change. If we're lucky, we'll save the Tiltyard and Foot Guards.'

The commotion continued but there was

soon a sense of purpose about it. More pumps appeared. I joined a chain of men passing buckets of water to refill their reservoirs. Soldiers cleared the area in front of the wall of the Horse Guards and pushed back the crowd towards Charing Cross. The gunpowder arrived in a small wagon, the kegs shielded with canvas sails saturated with water to discourage stray sparks.

I was soon hot and filthy, my muscles aching from the unaccustomed labour. I knew I must be weary and hungry. Nevertheless, I was tireless, working in a trance-like state that made everything, myself included, seem unreal.

Every now and then I glimpsed the tall figure of the King moving among the soldiers and the men manning the pumps. He himself supervised the laying of the charges and gave the order to light the fuses. Four explosions blew up the end of the building, damaging part of the Foot Guards House in the process. The crashes ripped through the air like the worst thunderclaps I had ever heard, quite outstripping the explosion in the King's laboratory earlier in the evening.

By now I had lost all track of time. All I knew was that the fire had been contained and was gradually diminishing. As the flames died, the order was given to rest, though we were not to leave. Other men took our places. We joined the lines of men waiting to be served from the barrels of small beer that had been brought up in a cart. There were still cinders floating in the air, turning to specks of ash as they drifted downwards. When I had my mug, I took it aside to drink in peace.

I leaned against a wall and felt the beer running down my parched throat. My knees buckled. I slid down until I was sitting on the ground and leaning against the wall. There were lanterns nearby, which gave enough light for me to notice that I had grazed myself. Drops of blood oozed from a shallow wound near the knuckle at the base of my right thumb.

In the ruddy half-light, the blood looked black. I stared at it, so weary that I could not drag my eyes away. A flake of ash floated down to my hand and landed beside the blood. I put down the mug and brushed them both away. They left a smear of blood and ash on the hand.

Blood and ash. I realized only then that I was leaning against the outer wall of the Banqueting House, a few yards from the spot where the scaffold had stood. It was here that I had waited on my father's shoulders all those years ago, waiting for them to chop off the head of the old King. Perhaps it was hunger but suddenly I felt faint, my head turning and spinning like a ball gathering speed as it rolled down an infinite slope.

Ashes and blood. The King's nightcap, a scrap of white, falling to the floor of the scaffold. The man in the crowd who wailed and rubbed ashes in his hair. The tall figure of the second executioner wrapping the long hair around his fingers, holding up the severed head to show the crowd. To show me.

'Master Marwood?'

Startled, I looked up, blinking. A soldier was in front of me.

'His Majesty wants you.'

I swallowed the rest of the beer and scrambled up. I followed the man through the crowd to the Court Gate beyond the Banqueting House. The King was outside it, standing at the centre of a knot of gentlemen and talking confidentially to a captain in the Foot Guards. After a few minutes he looked up and saw me.

'Attend me, Marwood,' he said. 'You too, Chiffinch.' He turned to the officer. 'You have your orders. As soon as you have intelligence, bring it to me. But keep it close to yourself until you have seen me.'

The three of us returned the way we had come, up the staircase to the gallery overlooking the Privy Garden. We followed the King to an apartment beside the laboratory. It was modest in size and furnished as a sitting room.

The King flung himself into a chair and ordered wine to be brought, a bowl of water to wash in, and a bath to be prepared for when he was at leisure. Chiffinch stood in the shadows by the door, part watcher, part guard, part confidante.

The King had been dirty before but now he was filthy, his face black from the fire. When the bowl of water came, he washed his face and hands. After he was done, he threw aside the towel and sat back. He drank some wine and ate a biscuit. Only then did he beckon me towards him.

'Your father was a traitor,' he said softly, staring at me with his sad, dark eyes. 'He aided my enemies even after my return. And I have shown him mercy.'

I bowed. Up to a point, I thought. The King or those acting in his name had also imprisoned him for five years, deprived him of his assets and stripped him of much of his reason.

'So now,' he went on, 'you will help me.

You have my word that neither you nor your father will be the loser by it.'

He paused to take more wine. Men said that the King's word was a slippery, negotiable thing, not to be relied on.

There was a knock at the door. Chiffinch stirred. The King looked up and nodded. I was beginning to learn that these two men knew each other so well that much of the communication between them took place without words.

Chiffinch admitted the Captain of the Foot Guards. He saluted the King, who gave him permission to come forward and speak.

'Your Majesty, the fire may have been caused by a groom oversetting a candle in the hayloft above the stables. We have the man in custody.'

The King frowned. 'May?'

'The fire certainly started there, probably at three or four of the clock. But it took a while to establish itself. The groom was drunk and had fallen asleep. He thinks it must have been so.'

A lighted candle, I thought — in the afternoon?

'A candle?' the King said. 'In the afternoon?'

The Captain said eagerly, 'I asked him

that, sir, indeed I did. He said there is no window to the loft. On the other hand, he had no memory of lighting a candle and he knows the way up blindfolded. But he cannot think of any other reason for there to have been a flame up there.'

'He would say that,' Chiffinch put in. 'Wouldn't he? What's his name?'

'Pearson, sir.'

'Then what did he remember?' the King asked. 'Or what did he say he remembered?'

'That he dined at the Blue Posts, where he fell in with a stranger, a man who desired his advice on a lame horse he had in his stable. He was an open-handed gentleman, and Pearson drank a good deal at his expense. He says he recalls feeling sleepy, and the gentleman saying that he would see him safely back to where he lodged.'

The King glanced at me, raising one eyebrow.

Taking this as an invitation to speak, I said, 'Did you ask Pearson what this gentleman was like?'

'Of course I did.' The Captain was clearly puzzled by my presence and irritated by my asking him a question. 'A plain, neat man in middle life. Tall, rather than short. The groom thought his name was Master Coleford. Something like that. He did not quite

427

catch it.'

'Coldridge,' the King murmured, so faintly that only I could hear. 'Damn his insolence. He wanted me to know.'

His heavy eyelids drooped over his eyes. The rest of us waited in a silence broken only by the coals settling in the fire and the muffled sounds from outside. Suddenly he flicked his fingers and looked up.

'Captain, who knows what you've told me?'

'My lieutenant, sir, and my sergeant.'

'It must go no further. Put Pearson under lock and key, and keep him by himself. He'll be questioned again later. Let it be known that the Horse Guards fire was an accident, as indeed it probably was. It is now quite put out, thanks to the prompt actions of my soldiers and servants.'

The King dismissed the Captain. He stared into the fire, occasionally sipping at his wine. The minutes lengthened. From where I stood I saw his face in profile by the light from the candles on the table by his glass. His cheek was like a flap of old pigskin, scratched and red-brown in colour.

'Marwood.' He gestured me to stoop down to him. 'I do not wish it known that Thomas Lovett had a hand in setting this fire. I want to lay him privately by the heels.

You are in a position to help me.'

'Your Majesty has only to command,' I blurted out.

'Really?' The eyelids flickered and I saw that he was looking at me. 'Why do you think you are here?'

'Because — because I may do Your Majesty some service?'

He shook his head. 'I don't mean now, in this room, though there is a service I have in mind. I mean why do you think you have been here at Whitehall these last few months? You cannot imagine it happened by accident. Why did Master Williamson favour you with employment? Why did Chiffinch seek you out? You — the son of a traitor, who is only allowed his liberty through my clemency? A traitor who even took his infant son to gloat over the murder of my own father, the late martyred King.'

These last words threw me into confusion. I jerked myself upwards, away from him. I heard movement behind me as Chiffinch stirred. The King raised his hand and the movement stopped.

'Remember?' he said. 'Do you remember, Marwood?'

'Yes, sir.'

In that instant I understood that I had been living for months in a bubble of illusion. The King had pricked it. Nothing had been quite as I had thought it was. My father's unexpected release, Master Williamson's favour, his choice of me to accompany him to Barnabas Place after the first murder, Mistress Alderley's attentions to me, the provision of lodgings in the Savoy — it was all of a piece. Nothing had been by chance. It had been by the King's design. He had known everything, arranged everything.

Everything? Did he know about my father's abortive expedition into Alsatia? About my father's meeting — so far as I could trust the old man's muddled testimony — with Thomas Lovett?

'You are here,' the King said, 'because Thomas Lovett will trust a man called Marwood.'

Afterwards, when I walked back to the Savoy, it wasn't my meeting with the King that filled my mind, or even the Horse Guards fire. It was what I had seen, nearly eighteen years earlier, on precisely the same spot, between the Horse Guards and the Banqueting House.

I remembered the man on the scaffold. The man of blood. Who was also the little gentleman who tucked his long hair under the nightcap with the help of the clergyman and one of the two masked executioners. Who worried about the keenness of the blade, for he had known how much that could contribute to a swift, clean death. Who had stood before a hostile world in his waistcoat with a nightcap on his head.

The little gentleman should have looked foolish. But he hadn't. He had looked sad.

He knelt and placed his neck on the block, which was no more than six inches high. He said something inaudible. The first executioner raised the axe. The gentleman stretched out his hands before him, as if diving into the air.

The axe descended in a silver arc.

The head parted from the body, fell forward and rolled a few inches towards the edge of the platform. Blood sprayed from both the trunk and the head. The nearest soldier stepped swiftly back, but not swiftly enough: drops of blood spattered his boots and breeches. The body shuddered and slumped to the ground.

The first executioner stood beside it, his head bowed, the axe resting on the block but now held slackly in his hands.

The second executioner had stepped forward. He pushed his colleague briskly aside and picked up the severed head. He tugged off the nightcap and tossed it aside.

The long hair spread out, as if full of life. He wrapped the hair around his right hand. He lifted the head high. Slowly he turned, first to one side and then to the other. Blood dripped from the neck.

The crowd groaned. A man near me held up his hands, which were smeared with ash. He rubbed the ash in his greasy hair. Weeping, he rocked to and fro.

I cried as well.

Blood and ashes. Ashes and blood.

Chapter Thirty-Seven

At the coffee house, all the talk was of the fire at Whitehall.

The long room was thronged, with customers constantly coming and going. Charing Cross was too close to the Horse Guards for comfort — only a few hundred yards down the road. There were rumours of yet another Catholic plot, of other fires and of armed Papists on the brink of a series of coordinated risings.

The mistress kept all the servants too busy to think of very much. Fire or no fire, there was money to be made from so many people, and what better than an endless flow of coffee to keep them alert and stimulate their mental faculties in such an anxious time?

Gradually the atmosphere changed as the news from Whitehall improved. Anxiety gave way to hope, and hope gave way to relief. By the end of the evening the fire was said to be quite extinguished. The mood in the coffee house became one of celebration, which proved equally profitable to the proprietors.

'Good girl,' the mistress said to Cat when she dismissed her for the night. 'You've made yourself useful today. You shall have a holiday tomorrow.'

In Cat's memory, the sun was always shining on Primrose Hill.

She had gone there with her father at least half a dozen times when she was a child. Master Lovett had been friendly with several gentlemen who had owned houses in this direction, particularly in the village of Hampstead to the north of Primrose Hill, where the air was reputed to be especially pure. One summer — 1656 or 1657? — when the plague had been particularly bad in the City, she had stayed with her mother at the Hampstead house of one of these gentlemen, a merchant who had shared her father's religious principles.

Master Lovett had walked up to see them on Sundays, and sometimes in fine weather they would walk or ride through the countryside with him. Primrose Hill lay west of the road to London, near the tavern at Chalcot Farm. It was a wild and lonely place, for all it was so near to the high road and to London itself. It was used mainly for grazing cattle and pigs. There were few lanes, apart from muddy tracks used for driving livestock.

In the summer, Cat remembered, the pasture had been speckled with the bright yellow flowers of gorse, and there had been dense beds of bracken in which adders lurked. It had been, in its way, a sort of paradise, where she could run freely, without the constrictions and prohibitions that hedged her life in Bow Lane or in the houses of her father's friends. It was also one of the few places where her father had briefly put aside his religion, his business and his politics.

As a child she had feared and respected him, more often than she loved him. But on Primrose Hill, at least, she remembered enjoying his company. He had become almost a child again, playing hide and seek in the bracken and telling her stories of his own childhood. She clung to the memory. It wasn't much but it was something.

Primrose Hill was two or three miles out of town. On Saturday morning, Cat walked through familiar streets, following a zigzag course that took her north, away from the river. In Tottenham Court Road, she fell in with a family that were going in the same direction as she was. She was glad of the company. It was not safe for a woman to go alone, for the road was often lonely, even by day.

They parted company in the neighbourhood of Chalcot Farm. She watched them go with a pang of regret. The hill was such a desolate spot that an entire regiment of robbers could lurk there unseen. She found a stick in the hedgerow that would serve her as a staff and set out towards the summit.

The roofs of the farm retreated into the distance. Cattle stared incuriously at her. Four pigs, bent on destroying a field, ignored her altogether. There were no houses up here, only dilapidated shelters for livestock, built of wood and usually squeezed into the corners of the enclosures in which they stood.

Cat did not have a precise idea of the way. She followed whatever path or lane seemed most likely to bring her to higher ground. She met no one. Few people came here in the summer, and fewer still when the days shortened. Once she saw a man several hundred yards away, a farm labourer probably, in a field with cattle huddled against one of its boundaries. She kept her head down and hurried away.

The path she was following levelled out and came to a stile beside a field gate. She was here at last, at the highest point of Primrose Hill, or very close to it. She had been here last in the spring. There had been flowers growing, thousands of primroses especially, among the fresh green grass. All gone now. The grass was coarse, sodden and tussocky. The gorse was blackening as winter approached.

A skylark wheeled above her head, climbing sharply. She walked along the brow of the hill. The din of London had dropped away, and she felt a stab of nostalgia, not for Primrose Hill but for the huge, silent skies of Coldridge.

Automatically she turned to her left. Spread out before her was the great, green sweep that led the eye down to the roofs of London, over the silver ribbon of the Thames and towards the blue Surrey hills on the horizon.

The wind was from the north-east, and the smog that usually cloaked the city had cleared. From afar, London looked almost unchanged: the towers and steeples rose in their accustomed pattern above the streets, and in the middle of them all, towering over the City as it had for centuries, was the dark ridge of St Paul's. She wondered what the view would look like in ten, twenty or thirty years if Dr Wren and Master Hakesby had their way and built a new cathedral, surrounded by a city of such classical elegance that it would rival Rome itself.

Cat's eyes drifted closer, up the slope of the hill. No sign of Cousin Edward or the dogs. He might have changed his routine. But it was relatively early, and he had never been an early riser.

If it hadn't been for the servant yesterday, the man who had jostled her at the oyster stall, she might not have come here. But she was sure she had not imagined that spark of recognition in his eyes, and equally sure that she had known his voice. It made her realize how vulnerable she was, even with her altered appearance. If the servant told Edward, if Edward knew she was still in London, and dressed as a serving maid . . .

She walked further round the hill to a point were the path skirted a ragged copse. She slipped among the trees and crouched in the shelter of a yew tree. She laid the knife on the ground beside her and pulled the grey cloak around her shoulders. She waited.

The sun had climbed higher.

Hooves clattered in the distance. Harnesses jingled.

The sounds grew nearer. Cat glimpsed a plumed hat on the path beyond the gate. Then another. Two riders came into view. Even in the distance, it was clear that they were gentlemen — the periwigs beneath the hats told her that, and the fashionable cut of their cloaks. The taller of the two was in the lead. He was riding a black horse. His cloak was flung back over his shoulders, and there was the line of a baldric across his chest.

An invisible dog barked, a deep, full-bellied sound. Then another dog, and a third and a fourth. She would have known the sound of them anywhere. Here were the great mastiffs of Barnabas Place: Thunder, Lion, Greedy and Bare-Arse, with a manservant to hold them. They were never muzzled when Edward rode out with them. He liked to show his power over them.

Two riders? She had not bargained for that.

They were now near enough for her to make out their faces. The servant and the dogs were still out of sight.

Edward had a black smudge on his face. Not a smudge: an eye patch. She had left her mark on him, just as he had left his mark on her.

Cat was trembling now. She did not know whether it was from fear or rage.

Behind her cousin rode Sir Denzil Croughton, plump as a partridge on a brown mare. Did they still believe that she was betrothed to him? She had hardly thought of him for weeks.

While these thoughts flickered through her mind, she heard the men's voices by the gate, and Sir Denzil's high-pitched laughter, almost a titter. Another sort of panic took her by the throat at the thought of being married to that man-doll.

At this point, her nerve failed her. She had come here in the hope that God would deliver her cousin into her hands, so that she might accomplish what she had begun in Barnabas Place all those weeks ago. She had hoped vaguely that Edward might step aside, perhaps to relieve himself, and that this would give her the chance she needed. Now, seeing him in person on his black horse, with Sir Denzil riding behind him as well as the servant on foot, she saw only the impossibility of achieving anything.

The party from Barnabas Place drew slowly closer. Sir Denzil paused and pointed with his whip at something in the city below. Edward dismounted and unstrapped a saddlebag.

At the sight of him, Cat's hatred welled up, but so did her fear. She could not bear to be so close to him. And it wasn't safe, either.

She stood up and edged behind the trunk of the yew. She retreated through the trees towards the far side of the copse. She could no longer see the dogs but they were giving tongue. They must have seen something or caught a scent, perhaps hers.

The trees gave way to hummocky turf and bramble bushes. The ground sloped toward an ill-kempt hedge that straggled along the line of the hill on its northern slope. She ran towards it.

The barking of the dogs became suddenly louder and more frantic. The men were shouting, even Sir Denzil.

'Bare-Arse!' Edward bellowed. 'Come here, damn ye. Bare-Arse!'

Surely they would not have loosed the mastiffs?

The hedge loomed in front of her. Covering her head with her cloak, Cat dropped down to her hands and knees. She burrowed among the roots and branches of the hedge, struggling to find a way through. Thorns tore her skin.

The barking was louder still. One of them sounded much nearer than before. Bare-

Arse, she thought, he's found my scent and broken free. Dear Bare-Arse, go away.

Cat wriggled deeper into the hedgerow, which was several feet wide at this point. The ground was muddy and streaked with narrow puddles. Damp seeped through her dress and her shift to her bare skin. Her hands were smeared with dirt. She nosed towards the other side of the hedge. A bramble sucker wrapped itself around her shoulder where it met her neck, trapping her as securely as if it were a loop of rope. She wriggled more violently but it held firm.

The dogs were closer. So were the men. Hooves drummed on the turf.

She pulled out her knife, ripped it from its sheath, and attacked the sucker. Behind her there was a snapping of branches and a panting sound as a heavy body crashed into the other side of the hedge. Cat sawed with redoubled force. The blade nicked the skin of her neck. The sucker broke in two, and she was almost free. The cloak had caught on something in the hedge. She wrenched herself away, breaking the clasp that held it around her shoulders, leaving the cloak behind.

She crawled into the field beyond. There was a frenzied scrabbling behind her. Bare-Arse blundered after her, following the hole her body had made. It was a wonder and a misfortune that the leash did not snag on the hedge. He nudged and licked her, dribbling over her arm and her dress. Cat pushed him away but still he fawned around her, his leash trailing behind him.

The hooves were closer now.

She seized the leash.

Then it was too late. A horse and rider cleared the hedge a few yards from where she stood: the brown mare with Sir Denzil, pink-faced and open-mouthed, on its back. He caught sight of Cat and rode towards her, shouting at her to stop.

Bare-Arse tore the leash from her hand and launched himself, snarling, at Sir Denzil. The horse took fright and reared. Sir Denzil toppled from the saddle. The mastiff was upon him at once.

Cat snatched at the dog's spiked collar. Bare-Arse reluctantly allowed her to haul him away from his victim. She looped the end of the leash around a sturdy ash sapling that had sprouted from the hedge. The riderless horse stood watching.

Sir Denzil lay motionless on the rough turf. His wig and hat had fallen off. Someone had lit a fire up here. His shaved head rested on a bed of damp ashes.

She bent down to Bare-Arse and hissed

'Sit!' in his ear. To her surprise, the dog licked her face and obeyed.

'Good dog. Stay.'

The brown mare sidled down the slope of the hill, dipped her head and cropped the grass. Cat was aware on the edge of her mind that there were more drumming hooves, more baying mastiffs, more shouting men. But, just for a moment, nothing counted but herself and the man on the ground.

She stepped closer. His eyes were open, looking up at her. His expression changed. There was confusion in his face, chased away by dawning recognition. His right hand shot out and wrapped itself around her left wrist.

'You,' he said. 'Catherine . . . But you're in the — it can't be.' He dragged her down towards him. 'What the devil are you doing here?'

'Let go, sir,' she hissed.

She tried to wrench herself away but he was too strong, stronger than she would have thought possible. In a moment, Edward would be here.

Bare-Arse growled, showing his teeth. He tried to spring to her aid. The sapling bent but held firm.

She was still holding the knife. She jabbed

it at Sir Denzil's cheek. He reared towards her. The tip missed the face and snagged on the side of the neck. His mouth fell open. His eyes widened. Blue and startled, they stared up at her.

Panic filled her. Edward was coming, Edward would take her —

'Let go,' she whispered. 'Pray, sir —'

Instead, the fingers tightened on her wrist. She dug the blade into Sir Denzil's neck and twisted it. He fell back, shrieking, his grip loosening at last. She tore her wrist away.

A shining ball of blood appeared on his neck. It grew larger and burst, spurting into the ashes, pooling around his head in a red halo so bright it hurt the eyes.

'Good God, there's someone there,' Cousin Edward was shouting. 'Croughton! Croughton!'

Cat turned and ran, her wet skirts flapping about her.

The ground was broken here, a sloping tangle of grass, dying weeds, saplings and bushes. Behind her, the other dogs bayed, catching Bare-Arse's excitement and spurred on by the shouts of Edward and the servant.

Her feet found their way to a winding path, sunken below the level of the ground on either side, and criss-crossed with the roots of stunted trees. The path plunged downwards, and the lower she went, the more the sounds dropped away, the shouting and the barking.

But there were no sounds of pursuit.

She ran on until, panting, she reached a stile to a lane. Judging by the sun, it ran more or less from east to west. To turn right would take her east towards Haverstock Hill and the way she had come from London. But that was the route Cousin Edward must have taken. She turned west, into a desolate and unknown country somewhere north of St Marylebone.

Better the dangers you didn't know than those you did.

It was only then that she realized that she had left behind the grey cloak in the hedge.

By the time Cat reached the coffee house, the light had almost gone from the day. Her clothes were filthy and her dress was torn. She was also soaking wet, because on her way back the fine weather had given way to rain and she lacked even the protection of a thin cloak. Since leaving Primrose Hill she must have walked seven or eight miles. She wasn't sure which had been worse — the wild and inhospitable country she had passed through, or the streets on the outskirts of London, with their roaming population of predatory poor.

Her mind was full of a shifting fog that poisoned thought. Underneath it, she glimpsed from time to time the outlines of a terrible knowledge: the red halo — she had killed the wrong man. She had wanted Cousin Edward dead, not Sir Denzil.

But he should not have kept her from fleeing. He should not have handled her so roughly, as Edward had done.

The front window of the coffee house gave a glimpse of the long room beyond. The candles were lit, and the fire burned brightly in the hearth. Even at this hour, it was full of customers, all men of course, talking, drinking and reading newspapers. The proprietor, his hands folded over his fat belly, was talking with one of his customers. The servants moved up and down the long tables with their trays.

Trembling, she went down the passage at the side of the coffee house to the back door in the yard. The mistress of the house was in the kitchen. She was giving directions to the boy who ran messages and summoned hackney coaches and chairs for the gentlemen. Her eyes widened when she saw Cat.

'Where in God's name have you been? Do

you know what time it is?'

'I'm sorry, mistress. I was lost.'

'You can't see him in that state. Go and make yourself decent. Hurry.'

Fear seized her by the throat and she gasped for breath. Cousin Edward? She forced the words out: 'See who?'

'Master Hakesby, of course. He's been waiting for you nigh on an hour.'

Relief ran through her like wine. She curtsied and went upstairs to the little room she shared with the maids. She tried to brush at least some of the filth from her damp dress, washed her hands and face, tidied her hair, and exchanged her collar for a new one. When she went downstairs, the mistress told her that she would find Master Hakesby in the booth at the back of the coffee house.

'See if he needs anything more,' she said. 'You might as well make yourself useful.'

Her head lowered, she went into the long room and made her way through the crowd. The air was thick with tobacco smoke and the fumes of coffee. As she passed one table, she heard a man say, 'It is difficult to comprehend, is it not? All that blood.' She hugged herself and walked more quickly.

Master Hakesby was alone at his table, tucked away from the noise and the crush.

He was reading a newspaper, huddled in his cloak, his wide-brimmed hat low over his face.

She stood beside him and curtsied. 'I ask your pardon for keeping you waiting, sir.'

'Granted.'

Master Hakesby looked up at her. For the first time she saw his face. But it wasn't Master Hakesby. It was her father.

■ ■ ■ ■

IV
ASHES AND AIR

11 NOVEMBER — 16 DECEMBER 1666

■ ■ ■ ■

CHAPTER THIRTY-EIGHT

I hesitated on the threshold, wondering for a moment if I had been shown into a different apartment from the one I had seen before. Behind me, the servant coughed, as if to nudge me forward. It was the man I had seen on my previous visit, with the soldierly bearing and the face blighted by the pox.

The curtains were already drawn across the windows. The withdrawing room of the house in Cradle Alley had been transformed into a luxurious cave. A large coal fire burned in the grate. Candles added their heat to the fire's — there must have been two or three score of them burning, standing on tables and fixed to wall brackets. The extravagance took my breath away.

Mistress Alderley sat beside the fireplace, with her face shielded from the warmth. The light was kind to her, returning youth to her face. Once again, she seemed alone, without even her maid in attendance.

The heavy leather screen still hid the corner of the drawing room. I could not help glancing at it as I stood in the doorway.

When the servant had retired, closing the door behind him, she looked up at me, and away, as if she needed to be sure of my identity but had no desire to linger on my face for its own sake. 'For God's sake,' she said. 'We are quite alone. You may look, if you want to make sure.'

I took her at her word. There was a door behind the screen, but nothing else apart from a spider's web across the top right-hand corner of the doorway.

'You don't trust me,' she said in a softer voice. I began to protest but she cut me off with a wave of her hand. 'You're wise, Master Marwood. Take nothing for granted in this world. If I've learned nothing else, I've learned that.'

'Madam, I did not mean to doubt you. But —'

'The last time we met here,' she interrupted, 'I was not entirely my own mistress. Pray be seated.'

I took the settle again, which was placed at some distance from that roaring fire. We sat in silence for a moment. The casements rattled in their frames. Mingling with the smell of the fire and candlewax was a hint of the perfume she had worn in the coach on Thursday. She had offered me a seat, so she did not see me as a servant. But she had not offered me refreshment, so she did not count me even approximately as an equal. I was something uncertain in her scale of things. An anomaly.

A clock chimed three o'clock. Silk rustled as she stirred in her chair.

'Have you heard the news?' she said.

'The whole town has heard it, madam. Sir Denzil Croughton murdered.'

'Yesterday morning, in broad daylight on Primrose Hill — and practically in front of my stepson and his servant, and our mastiffs as well. Poor Sir Denzil bled to death in Edward's arms. But no one saw the murderer. Not even a glimpse.'

'Did he speak before he died?'

She shook her head. 'He tried, but the words were unintelligible. He was taken quite by surprise — his sword was still in its sheath, and his pistols in their holsters.'

'Had he enemies?'

'Perhaps. But who would have known to find him there? My husband has offered a reward for the arrest and conviction of the murderer.' Her lips twisted into a smile. 'My maid says the servants think our family is cursed. That death stalks us.'

'It's hard not to suspect a pattern, madam.'

'Behind all these deaths? Yes.' She lowered her voice: 'I know the King has spoken to you about this. He believes Thomas Lovett must be at the heart of it. And my poor niece has been dragged into it. I suspect she knew that he had returned to England. I think she ran away from Barnabas Place to join him, rather than marry Sir Denzil.'

The settle creaked beneath my weight as I shifted my position. This was frankness indeed.

'I hoped you would find a trace of her in Suffolk,' she went on.

'I found nothing certain, madam.'

She looked up sharply, as if catching at a hope. 'But you found something? About Catherine?'

'No — but possibly about her father. I think a man might have been concealed by an old woman, a servant's widow, who lives in a wood near Coldridge. Afterwards I was ill for several days, too sick to move. I believe she had me poisoned, to give the man time to escape.'

'Master Chiffinch knows? And the King?'

I nodded.

'That's all they care about,' Mistress Alderley said with a touch of anger. 'This man Lovett. They don't give a fig for Catherine, except as bait. Find her, they think, and they find him.'

I wondered if Chiffinch or the King had told her that Master Alderley had contrived to sell Coldridge. I dared not ask. I was on delicate ground. However one looked at it, there was something underhand about the sale, even if Alderley had had his niece's best interests at heart.

'I have a kindness for her,' she went on, plucking the words one by one as if they did not come easily to her. 'She is a child still, an innocent. She is not like a girl of her age should be at all — she cares nothing for a new dress or a fine gentleman. All she wants to do is scribble away at drawing buildings that never were and never could be. I cannot help feeling . . .'

'What, madam?'

She glared at me. 'If you must know, I blame myself for her flight.' She took a deep breath and went on in a quieter voice: 'No, that's foolish, of course — I merely meant that I might possibly have prevented it. Catherine tried to confide in me on the evening before she left and I — well, I did not brush her aside exactly, but I turned the talk to other things. I knew she wasn't happy at the prospect of her marriage, and she did not care for Sir Denzil. But I thought time would mend all, and besides it was such a splendid match for her, and her uncle wished for it so much. And now, the longer she is away, the more I feel certain that some terrible fate has befallen her. Indeed, how could it be otherwise? She's so alone. So defenceless. And God is my witness, sir, I know what that feels like.'

Mistress Alderley turned her head away from me.

I thought that she had revealed more of herself than she had intended. 'Perhaps she has found her father and they have fled abroad. Perhaps —'

'Do you think I haven't thought of all this?' she burst out. 'But "perhaps" is not good enough. Besides, her father is no fit guardian for her.'

'What has Master Lovett done, madam?'

'Why, he's a Regicide. Everyone knows that.'

I nodded, as if satisfied, but I knew from what the King had said that there was something more to Lovett, something even worse.

I said, 'What does Master Alderley say?'

Again, her lips twisted. 'Nothing of consequence. He keeps his own counsel but I believe he has no more idea where she is than I do. He — he is very angry with her, I'm afraid. He was quite determined on this marriage, and he feared her running off would ruin all.'

Now of course it no longer mattered. Sir Denzil was no longer in a position to marry anyone. It occurred to me that his death might not be wholly unwelcome to Master Alderley, who would no longer have to account for his unauthorized sale of his niece's dowry.

'Our dogs are savage brutes, you know,' she went on, seemingly at a tangent. 'My husband cannot take chances, not with his strong room on the premises. They have the run of the house at night, and during the day they are mostly chained up. They would kill a stranger they found as soon as look at him. But they are well trained — they are perfectly restrained with our friends, once they know them, and to the family they are as meek as lambs.'

I remembered my first visit to the Alderleys' house, when the mastiffs had licked the blood in the yard with such enthusiasm after Jem's broken body had been dragged away.

She glanced sideways at me through her lashes. 'One of them broke loose on Primrose Hill. Something excited it. Edward had dismounted. The dog wouldn't answer to his call. So Sir Denzil rode after it. When Edward got there, Sir Denzil was dying. The dog was nearby. Its leash was looped over a branch. It must have seen the murder.'

I saw her implication. 'Could the leash have snagged on the branch by accident?'

'How should I know?' she said. 'I wasn't there.'

The touch of petulance took me unawares and made me smile. It made her seem like an ordinary mortal, and I liked her the more for it.

'It's no laughing matter,' she snapped.

'I beg your pardon, madam. So if the leash was looped intentionally over the branch, that suggests . . .'

My voice tailed away. She ran the tip of her forefinger over her forehead. I stared at the floor. Anywhere but at her.

'Yes,' she said. 'It suggests that the dog knew the murderer. More than that, it suggests the dog would obey him.'

Him. The word lay between us and made others. *Or her.*

'But that's obviously nonsense,' she said. 'No one at Barnabas Place would wish Sir Denzil dead. So the leash must have caught on the branch by accident.'

It struck me we were having two conversations now: the words that were said, and the words that were intended to be understood. 'Didn't the dogs pick up the man's scent?' I asked.

Her face was expressionless in the candlelight. 'Edward kept them close in case the assault was the work of a band of robbers. He thought they might return. Besides, mastiffs are guard dogs — they aren't trained for the chase.'

Once again: the words said did not quite correspond to the words meant. She thought her stepson a coward.

'Have they searched the hill?' I asked.

'Yes. The magistrates sent men up — they found nothing out of the ordinary. Master Alderley sent our steward and two servants as well. The only thing of note was the cloak that Edward found. Or rather the dogs found it — it was in the hedge. It's possible it was the murderer's.'

'A cloak, madam? What was it like?'

'Poor quality,' she said. 'Far too light for November. It's rather shabby and there's a tear in the lining.'

'What colour?'

She looked at me, and for an instant the tip of her tongue appeared between her lips. She looked like a child engrossed in a difficult calculation. 'What is it? You look . . . surprised.'

'I've come across a cloak before,' I said. 'That's all. The colour, madam?'

'It's grey,' she said. 'Do you want to see it? Chiffinch sent it over to see if we recognized it. Ring the bell by the fireplace, and I shall tell them to bring it up to us. You might as well return it to him.'

CHAPTER THIRTY-NINE

It was almost dark by the time the porter closed the front door behind me. I stood on the doorstep for a moment, giving my eyes time to adjust, for they were still dazzled by the glare of the candles in the withdrawing room.

Under my arm I carried a bundle containing my own grey cloak parcelled up in an old sheet. My head was swimming, as if I had drunk too much wine too fast.

My own grey cloak near the body.

Sir Denzil's death must surely be linked in some way to the other murders, though his thumbs had not been tied and he had been the last person in the world to nurse Fifth Monarchist sympathies. But he was Catherine Lovett's betrothed and Edward Alderley's friend. His murder could not be a coincidence.

There was no pattern to it. But there must be a pattern.

The heavy sky above the rooftops opposite was streaked with smoke from chimneys and fires among the ruins. A wind had sprung up while I was inside the house, so the streaks slanted eastwards.

Something stirred on the other side of the lane. I made out the shape of the beggar woman hunched in her doorway. There was movement beside her, a scrap of paler grey. She was beckoning me.

I walked slowly across the cobbles, crossed the kennel and stood over her. 'What is it?' I said. 'You've already had a penny from me. I've no more for you today.'

There was enough light to see that her eyes were open, looking up at me. She murmured something in a voice like a sighing hinge.

'I can't hear you,' I said irritably.

'There's men out looking for you.'

I shivered. The wind had an edge to it. 'Who?'

'How'd I know, master? Three men. Asked if I'd seen you going into Quincy's.'

'How do you know it was me they were looking for?'

'They said what you looked like, master. Thin as a shadow, pale as a cloud. Your clothes, too. And they knew when you'd come.'

'Where are they now?'

'I don't know.' She pointed north, towards Moorgate. 'They went that way.'

'Are you sure?'

'Heard them say they'd go back by the wall.'

That made sense, especially at this time of day. The road by the City wall was clear and relatively well-lit; there would be people about. It was the route I had planned to take home myself, instead of going the other way through the ruins.

'What did they look like?'

For an answer, she extended a hand, cupped palm upwards. When I had dropped a sixpence into it, she said, 'One of them was a big man. Dark cloak. Black hat.'

Worse than useless.

I tried to whistle as I walked westwards down Cradle Alley with the bundle under my arm, concealed by my new winter cloak. I wanted it to appear as if I hadn't a care in the world. God knew whom I was trying to fool. Myself, probably.

The men had gone north towards the City wall. As soon as I was out of the woman's sight, I would double back to the south and make my way east to Bishopsgate, un-touched by the Fire. I should have little trouble finding a chair or a hackney coach there. The expense would be ruinous, but it meant I would be able to return to the Savoy in both safety and privacy.

There was no help for it, however — this part of my journey was not pleasant. The area was a maze of blackened rubble. In the gathering dusk you could have hidden a regiment there.

It was growing darker by the moment. My footsteps crunched through a thick slush of ash and mud. They sounded strangely loud to me. I took the noise of the streets for granted — the clatter, the shouts, the hooves, the cries — and I barely noticed it. Here, however, I noticed the silence, which seemed even more profound because of the distant sounds of bells and grating wheels from Bishopsgate and Moorgate.

I was about to turn off Cradle Alley and plunge deeper into the labyrinth of destruction when a nearer sound brought me up short — something small and hard bouncing and scraping over the cobbles, like a stone skittering across the ground when someone kicked it. I peered into the gloom but nothing was visible except the ruined buildings and the darkening grey of the sky.

I stood still and counted the seconds until a minute had passed. In that time, all my courage seeped away. I wanted lights, I wanted people. I turned about to face the way I had come.

In front of me, not three yards away, was a tall, broad man in a dark cloak and hat. He was holding a staff in one hand. His other hand rested on the hilt of a dagger.

There were footsteps behind me. I swung round to face this new threat. There were two other men. The nearer and smaller one was carrying a closed lantern. The larger man behind him wore a sword — the scabbard knocked against a fragment of brickwork as he came forward.

'Shall I shine the light on him, your worship?'

'No, it's him.' Edward Alderley materialized from the gloom. His single eye made his face seem lopsided, something belonging to a creature from a nightmare. 'Good evening to you, Marwood.'

Someone must have talked. I did not suspect Mistress Alderley. She had nothing to gain by betraying a rendezvous she herself had instigated. But the sour-faced maid or the footman at the New Exchange might have been eavesdropping when I had been in the coach with her mistress yesterday.

The thoughts tumbled through my mind

in an instant. I had dismissed Edward Alderley when I met him in Bow Lane as a blustering bully with more money than was good for him. But perhaps I was wrong about that. He — or his father — could easily have bribed his stepmother's servants to spy on their mistress.

I was uncomfortably aware of my vulnerability. If Alderley, father or son, wanted to talk privately to me, surely they could have found me easily enough at Whitehall? Instead Edward had cornered me here. There were no witnesses. He and his men were armed and I was not. It was three against one, and each of those three was taller and heavier than I was. And I was carrying the grey cloak that he must have seen yesterday on Primrose Hill.

'It's damnably cold,' Alderley said. 'Let's walk up to Moorgate and find a tavern with a fire.'

The tavern was by the City wall. He and I sat upstairs, where there was a long room for the better class of customer, at a table by a window with a view of the street. His men waited at the bottom of the stairs, blocking the only way out.

I put the bundle on the table. I noticed his eyes on it.

Gradually the knot of tension in my belly began to unravel. There were lights, noise and people around us. The smells of tobacco and spices and alcohol. This was a public place and they would find it hard to keep me here against my will.

He drank deeply and refilled his glass before I had even touched mine. 'Before she married my father,' he said slowly, 'my stepmother was married to Sir William Quincy. Perhaps you knew of him? Sir William rendered the King many services during his exile, and the King's father before him. That's why His Majesty has a kindness for his widow.'

I nodded. It was not for me to suggest there might be other reasons for the King's kindness. I drank a little wine.

'She is a lady who has suffered much,' he went on. 'Sir William's estate was much embarrassed. Travelling abroad with him unsettled her. And then there was the strain of nursing him through his last illness.' He tapped the side of his head. 'Indeed, she has never quite recovered, though to all outward appearances she seems to have done. She is nervous, Marwood, liable to flights of fancy, and strange, whimsical imaginings.'

'I'm sorry to hear it, sir. But why — ?'

'I mention it to set you on your guard.' The single eye, small and dark, looked steadily at my face. 'She has had so much to distress her lately. First there was the murder of our servant, Layne, and that wicked business with the man who attacked me in my own bed. She misses the company of my cousin, who is away in the country. And now the murder of poor Sir Denzil has unsettled her to the point where we fear for her reason. The point is, you should not believe everything the poor lady says. When these fits are upon her, she grows fearful and sees plots and stratagems everywhere.' He wiped his lips with the back of his hand. 'So what has she told you?'

I shrugged. 'I don't understand, sir.'

'What reason did she give for wanting to see you?' There was a rasp of impatience in Alderley's voice. 'And this is not the first time, I think.' He poked the bundle. 'And what's that? Did she give you something?'

'It's an old cloak — I'm taking it to be mended. You may see if you wish.'

I began to unravel the bundle, exposing a fold of the stained, grey wool. The light was fading and the candles were lit. I gambled on the fact that the colour would look much darker than it had by daylight on Primrose Hill.

But he was already waving the bundle away. 'What did my stepmother want?'

'She asked if we had fresh information about your servant's murder, sir. Layne's, I mean. Master Williamson said I should wait on her. It was she who proposed meeting at Cradle Alley — perhaps she didn't wish to alarm your father.'

He poured more wine and sat back, considering what I had said. 'And have you new intelligence?'

'No, sir. There is nothing.'

He drained the glass again. He took out his purse and removed a gold coin, which he dropped on the table between us. He pushed it across the board towards me. 'If she summons you again, Marwood, send word to me. Will you do that? It's for her own good.'

I looked at the gold piece. 'Yes, sir.'

'Write to me at Barnabas Place.' He rose to his feet. He stood there, swaying slightly, looking down at me. 'You will not be the loser if you do me good service. But I don't forgive those who take my money and fail me.'

Edward Alderley turned away. I watched him walking heavily towards the stairs. I laid my hand on the sovereign and drew it towards me.

■ ■ ■ ■

In the Savoy, I found my father reading his Bible by candlelight. He did not look up when I came into the parlour. I draped the grey cloak over a chair and waited, knowing better than to interrupt him at such a time.

In a moment, he looked up, smiling. 'James,' he said. 'There is good news. "The king made Daniel a great man, and gave him many great gifts, and made him ruler over the whole of the province of Babylon, and the chief of the governors over all the wise men of Babylon." Is it not wonderful?'

'Yes, sir. Have you had supper yet?'

He shrugged the question aside. 'Possibly. But can you recall the passage about the damned? When they are bound and led into the flames? I thought it was in the Book of Daniel too.'

'I cannot bring it to mind, sir. Shall I call the maid, and ask her to bring a little broth?'

My father appeared not to hear. 'I can't see it here,' he said. 'It's so vexing. You must recall the passage, surely?'

I had the Book of Daniel almost to heart because my father had read it to us so often when I was a boy. 'I don't remember it.'

'You must.' He frowned at me. 'The

condemned wear sackcloth and ashes, and their thumbs are bound behind their back, and they are driven like oxen down the broad way that leads to hell, and then —'

'Their thumbs are bound?'

'Eh? Yes, of course. And at the gates of hell, the Devil waits with —'

'Their thumbs are bound behind their back?'

My father looked at me and smiled. 'I knew you would remember.'

'No, sir. I don't. But it's not in the Book of Daniel. I'm sure of it.'

He chewed his lower lip, which made him look like a distressed infant. His face brightened. 'Ah! No — I have it! It's in *God's Fiery Furnace: or The Smiting of Sinners.* An uplifting polemic indeed, sweetly and cogently argued. I printed it as a pamphlet in the year the King lost his head. It was very popular among our brethren. The author was a most godly man whose name escapes me at present. It is a vision of the Last Judgement.'

'Your broth, sir,' I said. 'I will ask them about it in the kitchen.'

My father nodded vigorously. 'Yes, do. Are they late again? I'm very hungry.'

I left him to the Book of Daniel. Bound thumbs, I thought as I went downstairs.

That's where they came from.

With my hand on the latch of the kitchen door, another thought came to me. Sir Denzil's thumbs had not been tied. Perhaps it was simply because there had not been time for it.

The alternative was that someone else had killed him.

CHAPTER FORTY

When her father appeared in the coffee house on Saturday evening, the shock of it had made Cat's head swim and brought her to the brink of fainting.

He summoned a hackney and took them away. In the privacy of the coach, he hugged her, fiercely, laying his cheek hard against hers, so the stubble rubbed her skin. She hugged him back and found that she was weeping.

'Hush,' he said gently, drawing away from her. 'Hush, child.'

They went round by the wall, changed to another hackney at Newgate, to a third beyond Bishopsgate, and finally reached a house somewhere east of Moorfields. Cat had been to the neighbourhood before when, in another life that seemed already remote, Mistress Noxon had sent her to collect her embroidered gloves.

Her father took her to a substantial cottage backing on to a desolate area of waste ground. The owner, Master Davy, was another of the old comrades who supported her father. He welcomed them with open arms. His wife was less hospitable, but she did as she was bid by her husband. There were also three children, who stared wide-eyed at the newcomers but did not speak.

It was clear that the Lovetts — or at least Master Lovett — were expected. Mistress Davy brought them bread, ham and small beer. Afterwards there were prayers, with many thanks for their safe deliverance. After that, everyone went to bed.

The Lovetts slept in the best bedchamber over the parlour.

When they were alone, her father said, 'Have you heard the news? Sir Denzil Croughton is dead.'

She nodded, keeping her head modestly bowed. Her heartbeat accelerated, thumping like a muffled drum against her ribs.

'Murdered, they were saying in the coffee house, on Primrose Hill. This very morning. Your cousin Edward was with him but escaped unharmed.'

She nodded again.

'I heard you were betrothed to Croughton at one time. Had you any tenderness for him?'

She looked up. 'No, sir.'

'I'm glad. He was a sad profligate, by all accounts. And he would have made you unhappy.'

Her father did not encourage further conversation. He told her that she should have the bed. They knelt for prayer before they slept. Afterwards he cupped her face between his hands and stared at her for a moment. He stooped and kissed her forehead. She clung to him, until he pushed her gently away.

He himself slept on a child's palliasse on the floor, his large feet dangling over the edge and swathed in a separate blanket against the cold. 'We'll talk tomorrow,' he said as he blew out the candle. In the darkness she heard him murmur, 'May God keep you safe in the night.'

Cat slept in her shift, but kept her pocket with her. It contained what was still hers: the knife, a few coins and the doll that Jem had made for her. Clutching Hepzibah in her right hand, she fell into an uneasy sleep.

After his years in exile, her father was more like a battered hawk than ever. His high-bridged nose jutted from his narrow face. His dark eyebrows were knitted together, and a deep vertical furrow ran up his forehead. The rest of his hair was now completely grey, but he seemed as upright and vigorous as ever. He was dressed quietly but respectably, like a clerk who had done well for himself or a shopkeeper of the middling sort.

Before breakfast on Sunday morning, but after his private prayers, her father drew her into the chilly closet off the bedchamber and talked to her in whispers.

He had tried to see her early in September, he explained, with the help of Jem. But the speed of the Great Fire's advance had taken them all by surprise and made that impossible. Afterwards he had believed her to be at Barnabas Place. He had gone into the country to avoid the men searching for spies and incendiarists in the aftermath of the Fire. It was only this week, since his return to London, that he had heard from a drunken servant at the Alderleys' that she had gone away from Barnabas Place in September, and that no man knew where.

Jem had written to him about his niece, Mistress Noxon, coming to London, saying that she might offer a refuge in a time of trouble. So her father had gone to Three Cocks Yard, only to discover that he had missed Cat by a matter of days. Mistress Noxon told him that Cat was staying at the

478

coffee house before she took up a position as a maid to Master Hakesby, a draughtsman. He had also learned that she was calling herself Jane.

'You talked to Mistress Noxon?' Cat said. 'Why would she speak to you?'

'Because she once worshipped as we do, and as her uncle did. Because she knows that it is best for a daughter to be with her father.'

Then where were you, Cat thought, these last seven years?

'Did she know you for who you really are, sir?' she said.

Her father smiled. 'She prefers to know as little as possible, child. There are many like that. I don't think she will betray us. She would have handed you over long before if that were the case.'

When he had enquired for Cat at the coffee house, the landlord had taken him for Master Hakesby, and her father had thought it best to allow the mistake to continue.

'The rest you know,' he said. 'Except perhaps one thing. Did your Uncle Alderley tell you that he had sold Coldridge?'

She stared at him. 'But he can't. It's mine.'

'He has.'

She bit down hard on her lower lip. Her eyes filled with tears. She tasted her own blood. 'Does he keep the money safe for me?'

'I doubt it.' Her father covered her hand with his own. 'But don't take it to heart. Coldridge is only a parcel of common clay. To desire it is a mean ambition. In due time, you will have your reward many times over in heaven, and there will be nothing mean or common about that.'

Cat didn't want her reward later in heaven. She wanted Coldridge now.

'But how could he, sir? Is my uncle a thief?'

'Yes.' Her hand still in his, her father sat down on the window seat. 'I trusted him once with my life — with everything. Including yourself. When I went into exile, he could not have been kinder. It was he who arranged everything, he who converted most of what I had to gold. It was only afterwards that I found that he had kept back the greater part for himself. And that was not the worst of it. Money is only money, after all, and usually as much a curse to its possessor as a blessing.'

She saw to her astonishment that his eyes had filled with tears. 'How so?'

'When I went into exile, it was your uncle who betrayed me, and sent the King's soldiers to where I was lodging. Henry Alderley. My dead sister's husband. My comrade. My friend. Even though I escaped arrest, the King gave him my house in Bow Lane as a reward, together with the promise of his favour. If I'd been taken, the King's gratitude would have been boundless.' A note of pride entered her father's voice and unexpectedly he smiled. 'He would have given half his kingdom to lay his hands on me. No doubt he still would.'

'Because you are named as a Regicide, sir?'

He flicked his fingers. 'There are degrees in all things.' The smile broadened. 'To the King, I am not only a Regicide.'

'What else?' Cat whispered.

He ignored her question. 'Your uncle betrayed others, as well as me, and they did not escape.' He drew her closer to him and stared into her face. 'I cannot suffer him to live. Henry Alderley has taken his thirty pieces of silver. Now he must pay for them.'

After breakfast, Master Lovett conducted prayers and gave several lengthy readings from the Books of Job and Revelation with his usual relish. After these he preached an extempore sermon on the text 'And, behold, there came a great wind from the wilderness, and smote the four corners of the house, and it fell upon the young men, and they are dead; and I only am escaped alone to tell thee.'

The whole household was there — the Davys, the undersized maidservant and even a small boy from the yard at the back who did not appear to have any function whatsoever.

Cat felt as if the last seven years had vanished in a flash, leaving her where she had been as a child. For her father, Sunday had always been a day of prayer. This Sunday he praised the Lord for permitting himself, Thomas Lovett, to be God's humble instrument in this wicked city. And he praised the Lord yet again for allowing him to be reunited with his daughter. He prayed that it would not be long before the Last Times began and King Jesus, the only true king, came to reign on earth.

With her father, everything came back to God. Cat wished that he would listen occasionally to someone else. Herself, for example. But there were tears in his eyes when he embraced Cat once the prayers were over. There were tears in hers as well.

After prayers came dinner, which Mistress Davy prepared with the assistance of her elder daughter and Cat. When they had eaten, her father took her aside again.

'I have one more thing to do in London, my dear. Then we shall leave.'

'What thing, sir?' she asked.

'It's better that you don't know.'

'And after that is done, where shall we go?'

'Switzerland first. And then, God willing, we shall take ship to America.'

'But how shall we live?' Her voice was almost a wail. 'How shall we eat?'

'God will provide. We have friends. Consider how the Davys have helped us. There are many such around the world. God's fellowship is a stronger bond than the power of any tyrant on earth.'

She did not want to live in a strange land. Nor did she wish to subsist on the charity of people like the Davys and fill her days with scouring pots and pleading with God. But he was her father. She could not leave him.

'Take comfort, child,' he went on, mistaking the meaning of her silence. 'God will protect us. He will smite our enemies. Did he not smite that sinner Croughton on Primrose Hill?'

Cat lowered her eyes. The colour was rising in her cheeks. It didn't matter. Her father would take guilt for maidenly modesty. She had not liked Sir Denzil, and she would not mourn him. But she had not wanted to kill him.

There was only one person in the world she wanted to kill. Cousin Edward.

Her father talked much with Master Davy, who was chiefly employed on the clearances at St Paul's. Even now, more than two months after the Fire, there was still a quantity of rubble to be moved, and much work to be done on stabilizing the ruins while the authorities debated what should be done with the cathedral. There was a degree of urgency about it all, because the signs were that a hard winter lay ahead, with many storms.

Master Davy ran a team of scaffolders. They had just begun the dangerous job of building a network of poles inside the central tower, whose ruined stump still dominated what was left of the city below. The tower was unstable. Its complete collapse would make either renovation or rebuilding much harder.

On Sunday evening, the two men sat for more than an hour by the parlour fire, their heads close together. The children and the maid were already in bed. As it was Sunday, Mistress Davy had laid aside her sewing and was reading her Bible at the table by the light of the single candle, her lips moving silently. Cat sat opposite her, with another Bible open before her. Occasionally she turned a page but her attention was on the conversation between the men.

They spoke in low voices, their conversation coming in spurts, with silences between them. Her father spoke softly and Cat could catch only stray words and phrases. But Master Davy had a voice that grated like a magpie's.

'When the gentlemen are there,' he was saying, 'we must all stop work in case the noise distresses them. Dr Wren shows them over the church, if he is there, or sometimes the Dean or the Chapter Clerk. Nothing can be done without these gentlemen, they say — neither the City nor the King can bear the whole expense of it, even between them, and they must raise the money somehow.'

The conversation moved to other subjects, but not before Master Lovett said, quite clearly, the name 'Alderley' in the midst of other words she could not hear. Then Mistress Davy distracted Cat with some instructions on the subject of breakfast. By the time she could listen again, the two men had moved to a different subject.

'Yes, sir,' he said. 'We take a wagon in most days. The cost is considerable, but there's always something that needs taking or fetching.'

Her father said something about staircases. Then: '. . . parapet . . . a sad prospect now.' He reverted to his mumble again.

Later, Master Davy said, in reply to an inaudible question: 'Not easy, sir, because of the size. We brace the putlogs diagonally at the corners, of course, so both ends are secure. The supply of poles is another problem, particularly with such a great height to contend with. The Baltic trade is much disrupted because of the war with the Dutch, and after the Fire the demand for poles is immense. So there's a terrible shortage of standards. Ledgers and putlogs can be hard to find, too.'

Putlogs, Cat thought, ledgers and standards: the words slipped into her mind like old friends, trailing memories of the yard behind their old house in Bow Lane. The different lengths of scaffolding poles, each with its own purpose.

Another mumble from her father.

'Two nightwatchmen and a dog,' Master Davy replied. 'Idle sots — they keep by the brazier in their hut in the yard. They hardly ever make their rounds. Not that there's much left worth stealing.'

'It will do very well,' her father said in a suddenly loud voice that made Mistress Davy look up with a start. 'And there is a rightness in it. I told you God would provide, Master Davy, and He has.'

And so to Monday, another day of dreary work and grinding boredom.

Her father changed into the clothes of a labouring man with a leather apron on top. He and Master Davy left the cottage before it was light, leaving the rest of them to the work of the household.

Cat had been used to work in Three Cocks Yard. Mistress Noxon was a hard task-mistress. But, at the Davys' house, everything from emptying chamber pots to bringing soiled linen to the boil was done in the Lord's name. The children worked as hard as anyone. They rarely smiled.

The eldest child had the temerity to laugh when the cat sprang at a sparrow in the yard and ignominiously missed. Her mother boxed her ears so hard that the force of it sent the child reeling against the wall of the house.

The hours of the day elongated themselves. No strangers came to the house to vary the monotony. The men did not return for dinner at twelve o'clock. After Mistress Davy had prayed that they might deserve the Lord's bounty this day, they ate in silence the hard bread and the harder cheese that the Lord had provided.

In the evening, the men returned. It was clear from their manner that they were elated.

But there was no conversation worth hearing after supper, only more prayers and an interminable reading, this time from the Book of Micah.

Cat went to bed first. She was almost asleep when she heard the creak of her father's steps on the stairs.

The door opened. She kept her eyes closed and listened to the slow tread of his feet across the floor. He kicked off his shoes with a clatter. She heard him draping his coat and breeches over the stool. He gave a sigh as he sat down on the mattress. He blew out the candle.

'Catherine?' he whispered. 'Are you awake?'

'Yes, sir.'

'Listen to me. I must go away tomorrow.'

'When will you return?'

'I don't know.' His breath came and went in the darkness. 'It depends on many things. I have changed my plans. You will not come

488

with me when I leave London. But after I'm settled, wherever that may be, I shall send for you or come for you. In the meantime, you will stay here instead.'

'Here? You mean in this house?'

'Yes. The Davys walk in the ways of the Lord. I shall place them in authority over you. They will treat you as their own daughter.'

'But, sir —'

'That's all. You will do as they command until we are together again. Let us say a prayer and then we shall sleep.'

Master Lovett knelt down. She extracted herself from the warmth of the bed and knelt beside him. He whispered a prayer into the darkness. Cat murmured amen when it was time to do so.

Afterwards, she listened to him settle himself to sleep. His breathing slowed and grew regular. In a while he began to snore, quietly at first and then ever more loudly. The sound mingled with other snores from the neighbouring chamber, where the Davys lay with their children.

She wept silently in the darkness.

CHAPTER FORTY-ONE

I was forced to spend Monday morning at Whitehall, copying letters and correcting proofs for the *Gazette.* I had been so little in the office that my work for Williamson had steadily accumulated over the last few days.

I worked mechanically, even carelessly. Most of my attention was elsewhere. I was trying to find a way of linking the three appearances of my grey cloak in a way that did not suggest to an outside observer — Master Chiffinch, say, or Mistress Alderley or even the King himself — that I was a complete lunatic.

If I could argue them away, I would. But I couldn't. The cloak's three appearances were facts, each of them in its own way as unassailable as the mounting block outside my window in Scotland Yard or Master Williamson's habitual ill-temper.

First, my own torn grey summer cloak,

which the boy–girl had stolen from me by Ludgate more than two months ago on the night that St Paul's burned.

Second, and six weeks later, that same cloak, hanging on a nail in Convocation House Yard. When I had tried to take it, a respectable-looking draughtsman prevented me, saying that it belonged to someone else. Whether he had meant himself or some other person, however, it had still been my cloak, with the slash in the lining made by a cutpurse's knife the summer before last.

Third, on Saturday, my cloak again — caught in a hedge on Primrose Hill, a few yards from a man stabbed and left to bleed to death. Not a nameless man, either, but the betrothed husband of Catherine Lovett, Sir Denzil Croughton, whom I had first glimpsed through a window at Barnabas Place.

In the middle of the morning, a servant brought me a note, a few pencilled words from Master Chiffinch. He commanded me to call on him at six o'clock in the evening.

At midday I walked back to the Savoy and dined with the Newcombs and my father.

Margaret was in the kitchen that day, and I noticed she was hanging out sheets on the line in the back yard. After dinner, when I was leaving with the grey cloak wrapped in a bundle, the gate to the yard opened, and she beckoned me towards her.

'There's been men asking about him, sir,' she whispered loudly, her face even redder than usual.

'Who? Where?'

'Master Coldridge. Two men were in the Blood-Bowl Tavern yesterday evening.'

'They came into Alsatia?'

She nodded. 'They weren't bailiffs or anything like that. Free-spending. Big men. Carrying swords.'

'They asked for Coldridge by name?'

'Yes. Sam said they were talking to Rock and Captain Boyd about him.'

I felt suddenly nauseous, with Mistress Newcomb's dinner heavy on my stomach. 'Did they talk to Sam as well?'

'No. But I thought you should know.'

I thanked her and gave her something for her trouble. So here was something else to think about, a formless threat. The trouble was, looking for traces of Coldridge in Alsatia might lead the men to my father.

I took up the bundle, walked up to the Strand and turned east towards the City. Williamson could do without me for a few hours.

■ ■ ■ ■

As winter approached, the battered hulk of
St Paul's looked even more forlorn than it
had at the end of the summer. Rain had
smeared soot and ash on every surface.
Under a heavy grey sky, seagulls circled the
central tower and patrolled the emptiness
where there had once been roofs.

Even in ruin, the cathedral attracted
people. Perhaps they marvelled at it in decay
more than they had done before the Fire. I
joined the group of men filing through the
gate into Convocation House Yard.

The men immediately in front of me were
going to inspect what was left of Bishop
Braybrooke and the other bodies that had
survived the Fire, though time and the
weather was steadily decreasing any resemblance they had to human beings. But they
were still proving an astonishingly popular
spectacle. My neighbour told me excitedly
that the Duke of York himself had come to
inspect the dead bishop this very morning.
Royal patronage increased the bishop's
value still further.

Two men on the gate, the cathedral watchmen, were taking money in the guise of
charity for admitting sightseers to this

carnival of the dead. The watchmen's dog was chained up outside the hut where they spent much of their time. I touched one of them on the sleeve and showed him the general pass that Williamson had given me, the one I had used to gain entry on my previous visit. It vouched for me as a clerk attached to Lord Arlington's office and included an imposing seal.

'You remember me,' I said. 'I was here last month on the King's business to see the Chapter Clerk' — I groped in my memory for the man's name — 'Master Frewin.'

He nodded slowly, his eyes on the seal, swaying slightly on his feet. He was probably illiterate as well as tipsy. He jerked his thumb at the inner enclosure within Convocation House Yard, in the corner by the cloister, the place where I had seen the cloak. 'You're out of luck, sir. Master Frewin's not here today. But if you'd like to see Bishop Braybrooke instead, I —'

'I don't want Master Frewin this time.'

'Just as well, sir.' He chuckled at my expense. 'Seeing that he's in Derbyshire at his mother's deathbed.'

I took out my purse. 'I met a draughtsman when I was last here. I need his name. He's a tall grey man, thin, middle-aged.'

The man stopped laughing. He blinked

with the intellectual effort of this sudden change of subject. 'You mean Master Hakesby, sir? Who works with Dr Wren? Not in today either.'

'That's the man,' I said, hoping it was. 'Where can I find him?'

The watchman paused until I had dropped a shilling into his palm. 'Off the Strand, sir. Three Cocks Yard. Obliged to you, sir.'

I stared at him and blinked. 'Where?'

'Three Cocks Yard. It's where he lodges. It's off the —'

'I know where it is. Which house?'

He shrugged.

'Thank you,' I said, and turned away, with the bundle under my arm.

I had not expected this connection between my missing cloak and a quite different part of this opaque and unsettling affair. As I trudged down Ludgate Hill to Fleet Street, I played out the links of the chain in my mind. Hakesby, the man who stopped me taking the cloak, lived in Three Cocks Yard. I had been there before, when I had followed the servant trundling Jem's box through the streets from Barnabas Place. I had lost sight of the man in the Strand, but possibly he had gone up the alley leading to Three Cocks Yard. I remembered the new houses, brick-built and quietly prosperous, some with shops on their ground floors, arranged around the paved court with a pump.

When I reached the yard, I went into the apothecary's shop and asked the man within if he knew Master Hakesby.

He gave me a swift, assessing glance. 'Two doors up, sir. He lodges at Mistress Noxon's.'

At the house, the outer door stood open, leading to an inner door beyond. I knocked. A scrawny maid answered my knock. She frowned when she saw me, as if trying to remember something.

I gave her my name and asked for Master Hakesby, on cathedral business. She led me upstairs. On the way she glanced back.

'Your pardon, sir. Have you been here before?'

'Never.'

I heard movement below. I peered over the banister rail. There was a man in the gloom at the back of the hall, coming from another room with a chair in his arms. He looked up at me, and for an instant our eyes met. I saw a flash of recognition in his face, and knew it must be mirrored in mine. He was the red-headed manservant who had wheeled the barrow from Barnabas Place. So he had known that I was following him.

On the first-floor landing, the maid tapped on the door. 'Master Marwood for you, sir.'

'Who?' a man said in a low, rumbling voice. 'Come in, if you must.'

The apartment was at the front of the house, with a window overlooking the court below. A fire banked high with coal burned in the grate. The chamber was furnished for work rather than leisure or sleep. A draughtsman's board had been set up by the window with a tall stool beside it. Wooden models of buildings were displayed on shelves, together with rolls of plans and instruments whose purpose I could not guess.

In the middle of this sat Master Hakesby in his dressing gown, with a blanket spread over his knees and a cap of rabbit fur on his head. His gaunt face was unshaven and thinner than I remembered. Beside his armchair was a table covered with books and a pile of papers, weighted down with a handbell.

I bowed to him. 'Your servant, sir.'

He frowned up at me. 'Have we met, sir?'

'Yes,' I said. 'A few weeks ago — in the shed at Convocation House Yard. My Lord Arlington sent me to inspect the work of clearance, and I was waiting to say goodbye to Master Frewin.'

He nodded. 'Yes, yes.' His eyes widened. 'You may go, Margery.'

The maid curtsied, shot me another curious glance and left us alone.

'Forgive me that I don't rise,' he said. 'I've had a touch of ague, and it's left me as weak as a kitten. I recall perfectly how we met.' He sucked in a breath. 'And I cannot understand why you want another meeting.'

For answer, I set down my bundle among his papers on the table and undid it. I took out the grey cloak and held it up. 'Do you remember this, sir?'

'Of course I do,' he snapped. 'That's Jane's cloak. So you found a way to take it after all.'

'Who's Jane?'

He waved a hand, waving the question away. 'Leave the cloak with me, sir. I'll see it restored to its rightful owner. Where did you find it?'

'I know it's someone else's cloak,' I said.

'That's nonsense. Anyone here will tell you that. Ask the servants. Ask Mistress Noxon.'

'Thank you, sir.'

I took up the cloak and bowed.

'Don't go,' he said. 'I haven't finished with you. And put down that cloak. Who are you? I cannot believe my Lord Arlington would employ —'

I closed the door on him. I heard him calling me as I went down the stairs.

The manservant was lingering at the back of the hall, pretending to examine the chair he had been carrying. He lumbered towards me.

'I've seen you before, sir.'

'Yes,' I said, moving down the hall towards the front door. 'I followed you here when you brought a box from Barnabas Place in Holborn.'

My honesty took him by surprise. His mouth opened but no words emerged.

The grey cloak was draped over my arm. I held it up. 'This is Jane's, isn't it?'

A bell jangled above our heads. Master Hakesby was summoning help.

The servant blinked. 'Yes, sir.'

'Is she here? I'd like to return it to her as soon as I can.'

'No, sir. She's gone.' He stretched out a hand and touched the cloak, as if to reassure himself it was real. The gesture was almost a caress. 'Mistress Noxon said she had to go away.'

The bell rang on.

The scrawny maidservant appeared at the back of the hall, passing us on her way to the stairs. She shot me a glance.

'Where can I find Jane?' I said.

The maidservant swung round. 'Jane? She's at that coffee house by Charing Cross.' There was a shrill note of triumph in her voice. 'She's not coming back here, sir, I tell you that.'

A woman's voice called down from somewhere higher in the house. 'Margery! Why haven't you answered that bell? Quickly, girl!'

The maid ran up the stairs. I hurried to the door before it was too late. The manservant followed me and unbolted it. He let me out.

As I ran past him and down the steps, he said, 'Pray, sir, tell her John asked to be remembered to her. Tell her I'm waiting for her. All I need's a sign, sir, and I'll walk to the end of the earth for her. A sign.'

The coffee house was doing a thriving trade. I did not usually frequent such places, because of the expense, but they were springing up everywhere. In general, the view at Whitehall was that coffee houses should be discouraged, because they attracted men of a puritanical cast of mind. They acted as centres of information and encouraged potentially seditious debate. Taverns and alehouses were quite a different matter: men went there for good fellowship and to get drunk.

I went inside, found the landlord, and asked for Jane.

'Who?'

'The maidservant, sir, from Mistress Noxon's in Three Cocks Yard.'

'Oh — her. She's not here now. Why?'

'I have her cloak, sir. I wanted to return it. Where can I find her?'

He called his wife to answer that. She came from the kitchen, wiping her hands on her apron. She was a big woman and in her presence her husband seemed to shrink.

'She's gone, sir,' she said. 'She was only here for a day or two, as a kindness to Mistress Noxon. She left on Saturday.'

'When?'

'Master Hakesby came for her in the evening.'

I stared at her. Then why hadn't Hakesby mentioned this just now? 'Are you sure it was him?'

'Of course I am,' she snapped. 'When he enquired for Jane, I asked him if he was Master Hakesby, and he said he was. Mistress Noxon said he'd call for her, though we weren't expecting him so soon.' She glanced at her husband. 'Jane was out when he came, remember, and when she got back she looked like she'd been rolling in the mud. I told her to make herself decent before she went to him.'

The man nodded at me. 'The gentleman's got her cloak. That's why he's looking for her.'

'She wasn't wearing it when she came back. Did she lose it somewhere?' The landlady frowned. 'Anyway, how did you know to find her here?'

'They told me at Three Cocks Yard,' I said. 'Is that the Master Hakesby I know? The draughtsman? Grey-faced. Very thin, and not in the best of health?'

'He looked healthy enough to me,' the landlady said. 'Tall man, bit of grey in his hair, but vigorous enough.'

'Is he always like that?' I asked. 'Perhaps I saw him when he was ill.'

'I don't know, sir.' She was growing tired of my questions. 'Never saw him before.'

'Big man like that, prime of life,' her husband said, clinging to his grievance. 'You'd think he'd have an appetite to match. All he had was a little pot of coffee. Close-fisted.'

'He paid for it at least, I hope?' his wife said.

'Yes, but nothing over. He took up a whole booth for well over an hour, you know.

Waste of space. It was Saturday, too, and the place was crowded.'

Saturday, I thought: the day of Sir Denzil Croughton's murder. 'Have you any idea where they went?'

The landlady put her hands on her hips and glared at me. 'Why are you asking all this? If you've come from Three Cocks Yard, you'll know Master Hakesby. He lives there, doesn't he? So you can go back and ask him yourself.'

CHAPTER FORTY-TWO

Towards evening, I took a boat to Whitehall. The sky was overcast. There were neither stars nor moon. The river was something to be heard, felt and smelled rather than seen.

There were other boats on the water, their lanterns bobbing up and down, creating globes of light containing shadowy figures. It was raining hard and growing steadily colder. Passengers and boatmen had their hats pulled low and their cloaks pulled high.

At the palace, I walked across from the public stairs to the door of the King's apartments. One of the guards had been on duty on my earlier visit. He recognized me. I asked him to send word that I was here by appointment to see Master Chiffinch.

He took up a sheet of paper. 'You're on the list. You can wait in the anteroom if you want.'

I paced up and down among the other people who were waiting — a restless crowd, all of us wanting something, none of us capable of settling to anything in case our name was called. Chiffinch kept me kicking my heels for nearly an hour.

At last a servant conducted me up to a small office with a view of the river. There was a guard at the door. Chiffinch was behind his desk, reading a letter, his fingers playing unconsciously with the wart on his chin.

I bowed low. 'Your servant, sir. I have something —'

'Be silent.' He looked up. 'I want to show you something.'

He stood up and led the way from the room. He locked the door and set off down the passage with me behind him. I heard the soldier's footsteps behind me. At a brisk pace he took me across the Great Court, through the range with the guardhouse and across to the familiar lodgings in Scotland Yard where Master Williamson had his private office. We did not go upstairs, however, but to the door of a room on the ground floor. It opened off the anteroom where there were always two soldiers on duty. The door had a small opening at eye level, with a shutter across it.

Master Chiffinch stood back. 'Open it,' he said.

I slid the shutter across. I had a view of a room no more than nine feet square, dimly lit by a rushlight on the sill of a window placed high in the wall. A man was lying on the floor. His hands were bound in front of him. His legs were bound, too, but above the knee. I knew who it was even before the man looked up at me.

Chiffinch reached over my shoulder and closed the shutter. 'Samuel Witherdine,' he said in a low voice, too low for the soldiers to be able to make out the words. 'Discharged sailor. Cripple. Bankrupt. The other day, he was asking questions in Alsatia about a certain Master Coldridge. His wife serves Newcomb the printer, with whom you have many dealings and in whose house you lodge. What a curious coincidence, Marwood.'

'Sir,' I said, feeling the sweat break out under my shirt, 'this is not what it seems.'

'The question is, how would it seem to the King? His trust has been betrayed. The son of a traitor is a traitor in his turn. Like father, like son.'

'That's not true.' I turned to face him. 'As God's my witness, sir, I've not betrayed the King.'

'Then what have you done?'

'My father is not himself. His wits go

astray, and his legs follow them. He wandered into Alsatia last week, where he fell and hurt himself. The Witherdines rescued him and brought word to me.'

'So? This is not to the point, Marwood.'

I would have given everything I owned to know what Sam had already told Chiffinch. I couldn't risk being caught in a lie. 'My father had a story that he'd met Thomas Lovett in Alsatia, and that it was Lovett who had made him fall.'

'You didn't think to tell me this?' Chiffinch said.

'Because what my father says is not to be trusted, sir. But I asked Mistress Witherdine to enquire after Lovett in Alsatia. It turned out that her husband had seen a man answering his description in the Blood-Bowl Tavern. He lodged nearby for a few days, using the name of Coldridge. He left the same day my father wandered into Alsatia.'

'Alsatia is but a stone's throw from Bridewell,' Chiffinch observed.

'Yes, sir. Where Sneyd's body was found in the Fleet.'

'Another former comrade of Lovett's.' He poked me hard in the chest, forcing me to step back. 'Dear God. I cannot believe you thought this not worth mentioning to me.'

'There seemed little purpose in telling

you, sir, as Lovett had already gone. And besides . . .'

He poked me again. 'What?'

'My father,' I blurted out. 'I feared you would bring him for questioning, that you'd put the worst construction on his meeting Lovett and see it as a conspiracy between them. I knew it would be the death of him.'

'Ah,' Chiffinch said softly. 'So we come near the truth at last.'

He brought me back to his office. He said nothing on the way. He was a man who knew the power of silence. He did not speak again until his door was closed and he was seated at his table.

'You're lucky in one thing, Marwood. Witherdine told the same story, in essentials at least.'

'Sir, Witherdine is quite innocent of any wrongdoing,' I said. 'Nothing he did was in any way against the King's interests or contrary to the law. I pray you to release him. Whatever you do to me.'

He flicked his eyes towards me and then looked away. 'How I dislike men who make a sacrifice of themselves for others. Let us see what else you have for me first. You saw Mistress Alderley?'

'Yes, sir. We talked of Sir Denzil Croughton's murder on Primrose Hill. And the behaviour of the mastiff.'

Chiffinch nodded. 'Who did not attack the killer.'

'There was one other detail — a grey cloak found near the body. I brought the cloak away with me. I have it at my lodgings still.'

'Why?'

'Because it's mine, sir.'

'God's body!' Chiffinch said. 'Your cloak? You'll drive me stark staring mad if you go on like this. Of course it can't be yours. Unless you were up on that hill yourself. Explain yourself.'

I took a deep breath. 'Sometimes I feel I may be going mad myself, sir. I haven't seen that cloak for weeks. There's only one way I can explain all this — the dog's behaviour and the cloak. Catherine Lovett must have been on Primrose Hill.'

Then at last I told him everything, beginning with the night that St Paul's burned down and the boy–woman who had bitten my hand, and ending with the man who wasn't Hakesby at the coffee house. The one thing I left out was God's Fiery Furnace. My father was involved enough already. I didn't want to make it worse.

There was one way to make sense of at

least some of this. Jane, the maidservant who had worked at Three Cocks Yard, must have been Catherine. And, if the man who had collected her from the coffee house wasn't Hakesby, who else could he have been other than Thomas Lovett?

CHAPTER FORTY-THREE

Chiffinch arranged the release of Sam Witherdine on Monday evening. I took him back to Fleet Street in a coach, and dropped him at the borders of Alsatia. Before we parted, I gave him the gold piece that Edward Alderley had left with me as a bribe on Sunday. I owed Sam much more than that for involving him in this affair.

I heard no more until Wednesday. During the morning I was on *Gazette* business in Scotland Yard. At midday, I left in search of dinner — I had a ticket now that allowed me to dine at Whitehall at a place set apart for clerks and higher servants.

As I came down the stairs from Williamson's office, a man came out of the anteroom off the hall, where the soldiers were on duty. He was not in uniform or in livery but I knew him at once by his bearing and his pox-ravaged complexion. He was the servant who had showed me up to Mistress

Alderley's chamber in the house at Cradle Alley.

'Master Marwood? You're to follow me.'

I didn't ask questions. We were within earshot of the soldiers and of a couple of clerks in the hall. I followed him outside. He led me out of the court, across the street to a set of lodgings built beside the Horse Guards Yard. I had never visited this part of the palace before. It had an air of seclusion about it.

Without saying a word, the servant took me through an inner courtyard and up a flight of steps to a small chamber, no more than a closet, overlooking the Park. No one was there. A fire burned in the grate.

He withdrew, telling me to wait. I stood at the window and stared at the trees and the people strolling up and down the gravelled paths below. I was not in the best of humours — to be frank about it, I was scared. All I wanted was for my father and me to be left alone, and for me to be able to make a living for us.

The door opened and Mistress Alderley entered. I bowed low. She was by herself. She closed the door behind her.

'Master Marwood. You have not been honest with me.' She sat down by the fire, leaving me standing, and went straight to the point. 'Master Chiffinch tells me you knew a great deal about Mistress Lovett that you did not wish to confide in me. That she's been living as a servant near the Strand, and that her father abducted her on Saturday.'

'There were reasons, madam,' I said, 'and also I could not be sure of the identification until Monday — after I had the honour of seeing you last. Did Master Chiffinch also tell you that your stepson and his bullies waylaid me when I left you?'

She nodded. She did not look alluring today. She looked tired and anxious. I felt an unwanted and inconvenient tenderness for her.

'Your stepson was spying on you. He gave me money to tell him if you sought another meeting with me.'

She flicked her fingers. 'Edward thinks gold will solve everything. But he doesn't matter now. I've been commanded to tell you something, and telling you here is safer than anywhere else.'

Commanded? I did not think she would have used that word if the instruction had come from Chiffinch alone.

'It's been decided that you should be trusted with the truth, so you may not blunder into it accidentally and make matters worse. You must not tell another living soul.' She stared at me. 'I warn you, if you do, both you and your father will be shown no mercy.'

'Yes, madam,' I said quickly. 'You have my word.' What else could I say?

'When you saw the King in his laboratory last week, he talked to you about Thomas Lovett. Do you remember?'

'Yes. He said Lovett was worse than a Regicide.'

For the first time she smiled. 'Exactly. Do you know why?'

I shook my head. Then: 'The King knew I had been with my father in the crowd when the late King was executed. He talked of that.'

'You are quick, Master Marwood, and that makes it a little easier. The King has made it his business to know everyone who was there when his father was murdered, everyone who witnessed it, or as near as it can ever be established. Can you remember that day? You must have been little more than an infant.'

'I remember it all. It was hard to forget.'

Mistress Alderley said, 'Master Lovett was named among the Regicides for the part he played in arguing for the King to be tried and executed. He and others of his kind wielded great influence in certain parts of the army. But he did more, and he did it on the day itself. Think back.'

Worse than a Regicide?

I remembered the little gentleman on the stage in front of the Banqueting House. How the Majesty of England, who proclaimed that he ruled by the direct decree of God himself, had been reduced to a man in a waistcoat, with a nightcap on his head. I remembered the two executioners, the one with the axe who severed the King's head from his body with a single blow, and his colleague who held it up to the crowd.

'The executioners,' she said in a voice so low that I took a step nearer to her. 'Who were they, Master Marwood?'

'No one knows for sure.' I was on familiar ground here, because the identity of the executioners had been the subject of speculation for years. 'They were masked at the time to prevent the Royalists hunting them to death afterwards. They say the one with the axe was Richard Brandon, the common hangman, and that he died of remorse not six months later. Certainly, it was a skilled hand that took off the head so neatly with one blow, and his confession is —'

She waved her hand, dismissing Brandon. 'And the second executioner? The one who held up the King's head and showed it to the crowd?'

'Who knows? Perhaps someone brought in to stiffen Brandon's resolve.'

She turned her head away to look at the fire. I listened to the sound of distant hooves in the Park. A drum was beating in the barracks.

'We know who the second man was. Now you do, too.' Mistress Alderley paused, but I did not speak. 'The King wants to find him before anyone else does.' She turned slowly to look at me again. 'He does not want Lovett killed out of hand, for that would be an easy death. He does not want him charged and brought before a court and then executed at Tyburn; or not yet, at least. First, and most of all, he commands that Lovett be brought privately to him. He wants to look him in the eye, to see the man who held up his father's head, and see him without a coward's mask on his face. Then, and only then, he will decide what to do with him.'

I bowed. Still I did not speak. A terrible foreboding crept over me. I did not want to hear this secret. This was something worse than murder, and its darkness touched all who knew of it. Soon after the Restoration, the worst of the Regicides had been hung, drawn and quartered, a punishment so barbaric that even the common people were at last revolted by the spectacle. How would they punish someone who was worse than a Regicide?

'You may have a part to play, Master Marwood.'

My head jerked up. 'Madam, there's nothing I can do.'

I heard a shameful tremor in my voice. I was scared for myself, and for my father, and in a way I had not been before. The King and those who wished to please him would stop at nothing to lay their hands on Lovett. I was of no value to them unless I helped in that. But public opinion had changed in the country since the beginning of the King's reign. There was no longer the same popular appetite to see the blood of Regicides. Quite the contrary: some of those already executed had earned sympathy in many quarters by the quiet heroism with which they met their deaths.

So there would be no public recognition for those who helped bring the second executioner into the King's hands. And if the business went awry, as seemed all too likely, the first people to suffer would be those who had failed.

'You are too modest,' Mistress Alderley

said in a low, caressing voice. 'You have already rendered the King much service.'

'But both the Lovetts have vanished, madam, and this time we have not the slightest clue to their whereabouts. Mistress Lovett knows my face. Her father has never met me and has no reason to trust me. He and my father may have been comrades once, but that's worth nothing now. Lovett has seen my father. He knows he's a broken man.'

'But his daughter doesn't know that, does she? And she could be the key to finding him, just as you could be the key to finding her. As you say, you know what Mistress Lovett looks like, you know where she lodged after she left Barnabas Place, and you've even met this Hakesby who seems to have made himself her guardian. Will you talk to him? He may know something.'

'If you wish, but —'

'You're the son of Lovett's old comrade, and you did my niece a kindness during the Fire. If you can find her, you can make her trust you. We want you to —'

There were heavy footsteps outside and a murmuring of voices. Mistress Alderley broke off, holding up her hand. The door opened without a preliminary knock. Master Chiffinch entered the room. He kicked the door shut behind him.

'Your husband's gone, mistress,' he said. 'God send a pox on this whole devil-damned business.'

Chapter Forty-Four

On Monday night, Cat lay on her back, listening to the concerto of snores from her father and from the Davys, and the faint pattering and rustling of small creatures going about their nocturnal business. Even with the bed curtains drawn, the night air was cold on her cheeks.

It was easier, she thought, to love her father in an uncomplicated way when he wasn't there. In memory, and at a distance, he could be simplified and improved — the blemishes cut out, the stains cleaned, the dirt brushed off, the kinks ironed away, the holes patched. In person, on the other hand, he was as awkward and jagged as a lump of rock.

She heard midnight strike. It was Tuesday already. Today she would make her decision.

She knew she was fortunate to have the luxury of choice. It was not a luxury she had had before. In the past, others had decided what she did and where she went, and with whom. Her husband had been chosen for her. Her virginity had been snatched from her, not freely given. She had fled from Barnabas Place into the night because Edward had made it impossible for her to stay.

But this time she had a choice. To stay or to go. Neither had much to recommend it.

In the morning, she helped serve her father and Master Davy their breakfast. They ate in silence. Master Lovett was dressed as a labourer, as he had been yesterday. But the clothes he had worn at the coffee house, the dark suit and the wool cloak, were no longer hanging in the press in the bedroom; and his hat, his linen and his shoes were gone from the chest.

The boy was already in the yard, seeing to the harnessing of the horses. The wagon was kept in an open shed behind the cottage. The men had loaded it yesterday, working into the evening by the light of lanterns. The poles were bundled according to size — the putlogs, the ledgers and the standards — and roped together with canvas on top to keep out the weather and deter thieves. Beside the poles were coils of hemp to lash them together. There was also a big box containing the hammers, saws and chisels. Cat thought there might be other things concealed among them, but she wasn't sure.

After breakfast, Master Lovett drew Cat into the parlour.

'Remember, you must do as the Davys tell you, and pray for me while I'm gone. Whatever happens, we will not see each other for a long time — perhaps for ever on this side of the grave. But it doesn't matter. We shall be together later, and for all eternity. Kneel.'

She knelt at her father's feet. He blessed her, then raised her and kissed her on the forehead. His beard felt rough and alien on her skin, like the touch of a living animal's fur. For a moment they stood there, he with his hands resting on her shoulders, she with her arms hanging at her sides. His forehead was as creased and weathered as the skin on an old apple. There was a sore on his cheek. For the first time she noticed how folds of skin drooped over his eyes. He's growing old, she thought with a pang of sorrow, and one day he will die.

She followed him into the yard. He climbed up beside Master Davy, who took up the reins and manoeuvred the wagon through the gateway. Neither man looked back.

'You can begin with the scullery floor this morning,' Mistress Davy said to Cat as the yard boy was closing the gates. 'You skimped the corners yesterday.'

Later in the day, Cat was sent to take in the washing as the light was fading. Beyond the yard, with the stable and wagon shed, was a vegetable garden with a pigsty. Beyond that was an orchard, the trees stripped and bare, waiting for winter.

It was already very cold. There would be a frost tonight. The shirts, nightgowns and stockings were almost as wet as they had been when she and the eldest girl had hung them out. Now the clothes were stiff with cold as well.

She looked about her as she piled the washing in the basket. At the far end of the orchard, there was a wall topped with shards of glass. In the wall was a gate secured on the inside by a heavy bar and two bolts.

When the washing was down, she left the basket under the tree and walked over to the door. The bolts were stiff and cold. But she could move them in their sockets. She could also lift the bar. She picked up the basket and returned to the kitchen.

'Hang it to air by the fire,' Mistress Davy said. 'No, not there, you foolish girl. On the other side.' She cocked her head. 'Is that the wagon? Tell the boy to open the gate before you do anything else.'

Master Davy brought the wagon home alone. Now her father was gone, the life of the family contracted. The Davys took their supper in the kitchen. Cat and the children ate vegetable broth with wheaten bread. Master and Mistress Davy worked their way through a stew made of pigeons and chestnuts. Conversation was not permitted at the lower end of the table.

Afterwards, Cat and the children cleared away, put out the fire and made the kitchen ready for the morning. There were more prayers, and then it was bedtime. The Davys had reclaimed the chamber over the parlour. From now on, Cat was to sleep with the children in the other room.

She and Master Davy were the last to go up to bed. As Cat was climbing the stair, she heard movement below and looked back. He was standing at the foot of the stairs, holding his candle high and looking up at her. The light fell on his upturned face.

For a moment, his expression reminded her of someone very different. She had seen her Cousin Edward look at her in just the same way in the parlour at Barnabas Place all those weeks ago, when she had been trussed up in her unnatural finery, in honour of Sir Denzil Croughton coming to dinner.

Oh God, she thought. Not this as well. She took the knife out of her pocket and kept it under her pillow that night, and she did not sleep much.

Master Davy waited until the next day, Wednesday. He came home for dinner. She felt his eyes on her when they were at table. Afterwards, when she took out the scraps for the pig, she heard his step behind her. As she leaned forward to empty the bucket into the trough, his arm snaked around her waist. She twisted, trying to tear herself away. His grip tightened. He planted a kiss on her cheek. She turned her face aside.

'Let me go, sir.' She could not reach her pocket, where the knife was, because of his restraining arm. 'I shall scream.'

'If you do that, I'll say I caught you stealing food, and I'm going to whip you for it. You wicked child.' With his free hand he squeezed her breast. 'Perhaps I should whip you anyway,' he whispered. 'I'm your master here, under God. Remember that.'

She broke away and ran into the scullery. Her face must have been flushed but neither Mistress Davy nor the children commented on it. Perhaps they hadn't noticed anything. Perhaps in this house it was better not to notice.

There was a change in the day's activities after dinner. Master Davy left the house, saying that he was going to Shoreditch to see a man who was rebuilding his house, and that he would take the boy with him. Mistress Davy set the elder child to reading a passage from the Bible to her brother and sister, which she did quite well for her age, though she stumbled over the longer words. Mistress Davy herself went out ten minutes later with a basket over her arm.

Cat was left to clear the table and make all neat in the kitchen. Once Mistress Davy had left the house, Cat put on her cloak, hat and overshoes and left the house. She walked through the yard and the garden to the orchard.

She had her knife in the pocket beneath her skirt and Jem's doll, together with the few coppers swathed in a rag to stop them chinking. She took nothing else with her because she had nothing left to take. The sky was empty of birds and her head was empty of thoughts.

She unbolted the door in the wall and lifted the bar from its slots. The light was already fading. She had no idea what lay on the other side of the door. Only that it was somewhere other than the Davys' house, which made it a good enough reason to go there.

Chapter Forty-Five

Cat watched John's face light up as if the sun had risen over it.

'Jane,' he said, 'oh Jane.'

She touched his arm lightly. She felt unexpectedly moved by his joy. But she did not know what to say to him. She stepped back in case he should construe the touch as an invitation.

He spluttered into speech. 'How — ? Where — ? I —'

'I had to go away but I didn't like it so I've come back.' She looked up at his red face. His eyes were still round with wonder. 'I knew if I waited here you'd come by sooner or later. It's Wednesday.'

Mistress Noxon was a creature of habit. After dinner on Wednesday she wrote her weekly letter to the widowed aunt in Oxford from whom she had expectations, and sent John with it to the Letter Office.

'Was it my fault?' he said. 'I'm sorry.

Margery told that man where to find you. I shouldn't have let her.'

Cat glanced about them. Fleet Street was too public for this. John had stopped in his tracks when he saw her. Pedestrians were eddying around them, and the racket of hooves and wheels on the roadway meant they had almost to shout to make themselves heard. She drew him into a cobbled alley leading to a tavern and turned her face away from the street.

'What man?' she said. 'Who did she tell?'

'The one that followed me back to Three Cocks Yard. Remember? When I brought the chest that belonged to the mistress's uncle. Margery saw him too, hanging about outside.'

'In the green coat?'

John nodded. 'The skinny fellow. He came to the house on Monday. He was looking for you. He had your cloak.'

God have mercy on us all, she thought, shocked into piety. She shivered, not so much from cold as from a suspicion that something invisible and implacable was dogging her footsteps. 'My grey cloak?'

He nodded. 'What is it? Faith, you've gone so pale.'

She leaned against the wall and pushed away the arm he offered for support. She had left that cloak in a hedge on Primrose Hill, a few yards away from the body of Sir Denzil Croughton.

Her head whirled. This nameless man had given her the cloak on the night St Paul's burned down. He had tried to take it back from the shed in Convocation House Yard, but Master Hakesby had stopped him. He had followed John from Barnabas Place to Three Cocks Yard. And now he had found his own grey cloak on Primrose Hill and come to Mistress Noxon's house with it. Had he also seen her with Sir Denzil Croughton? The man appeared to know everything about her, yet his actions were like those of a figure in a nightmare: devoid of purpose, unpredictable, but always malign.

She found her voice again. 'He brought the cloak to the house? To give it back to me? Are you sure?'

John nodded. 'But he wouldn't leave it with Master Hakesby when he found you weren't there. He just walked out, though Master Hakesby called him back. And then, on the way out, Margery said you'd gone to the coffee house, and you wouldn't be coming back to Mistress Noxon's, ever. And I said . . . I said . . .'

'What did you say?'

The colour on John's face darkened still further. 'I asked him to remember me to you, Jane. That's all.'

'He didn't find me. I'd left the coffee house already.'

'I know. Master Hakesby sent me to find you, but the people there said you'd already left, on Saturday. They said Master Hakesby had come for you, to take you to your new lodging. But this man wasn't Master Hakesby. Because Master Hakesby was ill in his own bed on Saturday.'

There was little more to be learned from John, apart from the information that Mistress Noxon had dissuaded Master Hakesby from alerting the authorities to Cat's disappearance on the grounds that Cat wouldn't thank him if he did.

Several clocks were striking five.

'I must go soon,' John said. 'You know what the mistress is like.'

'Where's Master Hakesby? Is he in bed still?'

'No. He's well enough now. You know what he's like. The ague comes and goes.'

She said, 'Tell him you've seen me. Ask him to come to me here.'

'You can't wait in the street. Not alone. Anyway, Master Hakesby's not at the house today. He's at St Paul's. Shall I take you to him? I go so often to him there that they let me pass to and fro in the yard without question.'

'The mistress will punish you if you're late.'

He shrugged his massive shoulders. 'Then let her.' Suddenly he was sure of himself, and of what he should do. His hesitation dropped away. 'Come, Jane,' he said. 'It will be better if you take my arm in the street.'

John held out his arm. For a moment, she looked up at his face, searching for a hint that might tell her whether there would be a price to pay for his protection. But she had no choice but to trust him. She wouldn't be able to get into Convocation House Yard without him, because she didn't have a pass. Besides, what had he ever done to make her doubt him?

'I'm sorry I stabbed you,' she said. 'You shouldn't have tried to kiss me, but I shouldn't have done that.'

Cat watched his face light up for a second time. She took his arm, keeping well away from him, and they walked in silence across the Fleet Bridge and up the hill to Ludgate. His bulk shielded her.

The street was still busy enough at this hour. On either side of the road were ruins and ash heaps, dotted with fires that glowed in the gathering dusk. The cathedral was a black shadow before them. In this light it looked almost undamaged, as if the Fire and everything that had happened since were no more than an unpleasant dream.

In Convocation House Yard, the last of the sightseers were leaving. One of the watchmen was covering Bishop Braybrooke and the other bodies for the night. The second watchman was near the gate, but he was sitting in his shed, huddled over the brazier. He opened his shutter when he heard John's knock. When he saw John's familiar face, he grunted, waved him through and slammed the shutter closed again. Cat slipped unseen into the yard, sheltered by John.

At this time of day, there was no one at all on guard at the gate to the inner enclosure, where the Chapter Clerk, Master Frewin, had caused the shed for the builders and surveyors to be built against the wall of the cloister. The labourers had already gone home but there were lights in the windows of the shed itself.

Cat hung back as John pushed open the door, seized by a fear that she would find Dr Wren and Uncle Alderley inside. But the shed was almost empty. Two clerks were standing at their high desks and working over what looked like columns of figures. Master Hakesby was still hunched over his draughtsman's slope. He did not look up as they came in.

John led the way towards him, with Cat trailing behind, suddenly uncertain of her welcome. Hakesby looked up at the sound of their footsteps. He was wearing mittens and a fur hat against the cold, and his cloak had a fur-lined collar.

'John?' He peered through the gloom. 'Is that you?'

'Yes, master.'

'Why are you here? And who's this?'

Cat came out from behind John and advanced into the pool of candlelight around the table.

'God have mercy!' Hakesby said. 'What the — ?'

'Hush, sir, I beg you,' she whispered.

'Where have you been, Jane?' His face looked even more gaunt than usual. 'What do you want?'

'Refuge, sir. And to work for you.'

'Who took you away? The man who claimed to be me.'

'I can't say, sir. But I had no choice in the matter.'

He lowered his voice. 'Have you committed some crime?'

Beside her, John shifted his weight from foot to foot. 'She's as honest as the day is long, sir. Take my oath on it.'

She did not deserve this loyalty.

Hakesby glanced at him. 'That's not what I asked. Well, Jane?'

'I have done nothing wrong.' She hesitated. 'Only what I had to.'

He stooped, bringing his head within inches of hers. 'I know that laws change over time. I myself have found it possible to fall foul of a change in the laws of men, and yet keep a clear conscience in the sight of God.'

She remembered then that Master Hakesby had served Oliver in the old days, and perhaps would have risen higher if the King had not returned.

'My conscience is clear, sir,' she whispered. But only honesty would do now. She remembered how careless she had been of poor Jem's devotion, how she had bitten the hand of the thin man who had tried to help her when St Paul's burned down, and how she had been cruel to John, who had given her nothing but devotion. 'Or rather, my conscience is clear in regard to the law. But sometimes I have been unkind to those who wish me well.'

'Very well. Stay here a moment.'

Hakesby left her with John and went

across the shed to speak to the clerks. She glanced down at the plan he had been at work on. Not a church or a public building, she thought, her attention sharpening, but a great house in the shape of a stunted capital H, with flights of steps swooping up to the front door. Hakesby had been working freehand and in pencil, and the lines wavered wildly, but there was a grace and a propriety about the design.

If she were rich, Cat thought, and if Coldridge were still hers, she would pull down the old house and have Master Hakesby build this one for her. If he permitted her to assist him in his drawing office, she would make the design as neat and elegant as the house itself would be. Perhaps the design would be even better, because it would be perfect in a way that a house of brick and wood and stone could never be.

The clerks were putting on their cloaks and leaving. The door to the yard closed with a bang and the candle flames swayed in the draught.

Hakesby returned and drew her aside. 'Very well. I will help you. But we must be careful because someone knows there's a connection between us.'

'The thin man who came to the house with my cloak?'

'Yes. He has also been here, remember, weeks ago. At the time he said my Lord Arlington sent him from Whitehall, but I think that must have been a lie. I did not have a sight of his warrant. Do you know who he is?'

She shook her head. 'Only that he haunts me.'

He grunted, and the creases in his forehead deepened. 'You cannot come back to Three Cocks Yard. It's the first place they will look, and besides, Mistress Noxon wouldn't permit it. I shall sign the lease on the drawing office on Monday, but until then I have nowhere you can go. If we find you lodgings for five nights, perhaps a week, there will be questions we do not want to answer. And I can do nothing to protect you if they trace you.'

'I will go anywhere you say, sir.'

'Will you? Truly? Are you afraid of ghosts?'

Startled, she said loudly, 'What do you mean, sir?'

'Hush. What if I found you somewhere here?'

'At St Paul's?'

'I warn you, you would be quite alone. And at night this is not a place for those who are afraid of ghosts.'

Chapter Forty-Six

Better not risk an unshielded light, Master
Hakesby said, though there would be no
one there to see it, because the cloister and
the cathedral itself were sealed off at nightfall. They were quite alone. Master Hakesby
had sent John home.

The Chapter Clerk's room was about
twelve feet square. It was on the first floor
at the north-west corner of the cloister walk.
It had a groined ceiling, two doors and a
window with a shutter but no glass. The air
was still and chilly, trapped in old stones,
and it smelled of burning.

They entered by a door set high in the
wall at the back of the shed, accessible by a
steep staircase behind the desk where
Master Frewin worked when he was down
with the clerks and Master Hakesby. The
second door was in the chamber's opposite
wall. It was barred on the other side and
opened into a gallery above the north wall

of the cloister. The roof of the gallery had been destroyed under the Commonwealth, Hakesby said, and the rest of it was ruinous.

When the shutters were open, the window beside this second door overlooked what had once been the cloister garth, with the remains of the Chapter House in the middle. By day, Master Hakesby told Cat, you saw nothing but ashes and heaps of stone out there. At night, you saw only darkness.

'You won't be disturbed,' he said. 'Master Frewin is away at his mother's, and he won't be back for a day or two. Even so, I'll lock you in, to be on the safe side. But no one comes here at night.'

Besides, he went on, the common people were convinced that the ruins were populated with the ghosts of the dead who had been buried here, thousands of them crawling by night like ants over an anthill.

As for the watchmen, they rarely ventured far from the stove in their hut. They were usually drunk or asleep or both. Even if they did go into the ruins, or the yard, they did not have keys for the shed or for Master Frewin's private chamber.

Master Hakesby left her with a closed lantern, a spare candle and a tinderbox. For drink, there was half a jug of small beer, left over from his dinner. He had no food for her, so she would have to fast until the morning. But at least Master Frewin kept a pot for pissing in behind the screen.

He opened a wall cupboard beside the empty fireplace. The light shone on cassocks and surplices hanging on hooks and bundled in a heap on the floor. The Fire had spared this part of the cloister from serious damage.

'Will you be all right?' he said, peering at her through the gloom.

'Yes, sir.' After the Davys' house, solitude had its attractions. 'When will you come back?'

'About eight of the clock. If I come earlier, people will notice. I'll bring you food.'

'How long must I stay here?'

'I don't know, Jane. Let me turn it over in my mind.'

He went to the door and raised the latch.

She was suddenly desperate to make him stay. 'Sir?'

He stopped. 'What?'

'Why are you doing this for me? You are . . . so kind.'

Master Hakesby's face was reduced to a murky outline. 'Because . . . because sometimes it's as easy to be kind as to be cruel. Or perhaps — no, that's enough, child.

Don't ask me questions without answers.'

Cat knew that his hands were shaking by the way the light from his lantern trembled. He wished her goodnight and left the room. She heard the key turning in the lock and wondered if he would be well enough to return in the morning. The door was thick and she could not hear his footsteps descending the stairs.

Silence crept over her like a mist, cold and clammy. Taking up the lantern, she explored the chamber as best she could. Besides the wall cupboard, there were two chairs, a table and a press, all made of blackened oak, with heavy, bulbous legs. The press was unlocked. When she opened it, the hinges screeched, and she nearly let the lid fall with the shock. Stacked inside were ledgers with heavy bindings, scrolls and bundles of papers. They smelled of must, of things too long undisturbed. The mice had been there, and left traces of their slow depredations.

Cat lowered the lid. She drank a little beer and used Master Frewin's pot. She dragged the cassocks and surplices from the wall cupboard, disturbing small creatures that pattered away into the dark, and shook out the folds of stiff, cold cloth, one by one. She arranged a makeshift bed in the corner of the chamber furthest from the doors, the fireplace and the window.

Then there was nothing left to do. It was still early, five or six o'clock. She was hungry and weary.

She lay down, wrapped in her cloak, and covered herself as best she could with the makeshift bedclothes. She blew out the candle in the lantern and lost both its light and the tiny warmth it gave the atmosphere. She pushed her hands into the folds of her skirt for warmth, her fingers touching the familiar shapes of the knife and Hepzibah the doll in her pocket.

Despite her precautions she could feel draughts on the skin of her face. She closed her eyes, but her mind refused to drift towards unconsciousness. Instead she worried about herself, her father and the intractable problem of the future. Her thoughts followed a circular track that brought her always back here, to this chilly room at St Paul's.

Her father would search for her, she knew, supposing he survived, but she did not want him to find her if that meant a return to the sort of life that he led, let alone to a miserable existence with the Davys. On the other hand, she could not imagine a future entirely without him.

Her hope of living in Master Hakesby's

drawing office and working for him now seemed an absurdly impossible dream. Her situation was worse than it had ever been. Her father and the Davys would be looking for her, and so were the Alderleys and the thin man in the green coat. She had killed Sir Denzil Croughton and left her cousin for dead. There was no arguing all this away, no escaping the consequences, whether they caught her or not. So perhaps, in retrospect, even this miserable refuge would seem like a taste of paradise.

As Cat lay there, the floor became harder, her stomach emptier, and her body colder. The shutters rattled over the window. The shape of the frame was just visible — lines of dark grey that merged imperceptibly with the darkness. She closed her eyes, squeezing them shut, trying by force of will to compel sleep to come to her.

When she next opened her eyes, something had changed. It took a moment to realize what it was. The darkness was not quite as absolute as it had been. The chamber had grown very slightly lighter.

It was far too early for dawn. Cat sat up slowly. There was a puddle of light, faint and golden, spreading under the door leading to the ruined gallery over the cloister. As she watched, it became larger and brighter.

Hairs rose on the back of her neck. She pushed aside the cassocks and surplices that covered her. Before she had time to stand, there was a faint grating noise from the other side of the door.

The sound of a bar moving in its socket.

CHAPTER FORTY-SEVEN

Chiffinch talked in a rapid, agitated voice, directing his words at Mistress Alderley in her chair by the fire. I was still standing by the window overlooking the Park, though he gave no sign that he was aware of my presence. But he must have wanted me to hear as well. That was worrying in itself.

Henry Alderley, Master Chiffinch said, had last been seen in the morning, between ten and eleven o'clock, not far from St Giles in Cripplegate to the north of the City wall. He and his steward had gone out to collect rents from several tenements he owned in St Giles Without, attended by an armed manservant and travelling by coach. Normally he would not have gone himself, Mistress Alderley said, but since the Fire he had had much trouble with these leases: rents had not been paid, and he suspected several of his tenants of illegal subletting and making unlicensed alterations.

'He is not a man who cares to be cheated,' Mistress Alderley said primly.

I thought it would be more accurate to say that if there were any cheating going on, Master Alderley preferred to do it himself.

'But what's happened, sir?' she asked, growing agitated. 'Was he called away? Where's he gone?'

Master Chiffinch cleared his throat. 'He appears to have vanished, madam. He sent the servant and his steward — Mundy, is it? — back to the coach with the satchel containing the rents. He stayed in the yard at the back of the tenement — to visit the necessary house. And when he didn't come back, Master Mundy went to enquire for him. It must have been at least thirty or forty minutes later. Why he didn't go sooner, I simply cannot understand.'

Mistress Alderley coughed. 'My husband suffers from piles, sir, and he is often some little time when he is at his close stool at least home. And he grows very irritable if he is disturbed while he is . . .'

Her voice trailed away to a discreet silence. I suppressed an unseemly bubble of mirth that rose like trapped wind from deep inside me.

'It's a shame Mundy left it so long, nevertheless.' Chiffinch toyed with his wart, which I was beginning to suspect was a sign that he was feeling awkward. 'When he got there, he found the privy occupied by an old woman. Who was deaf, to make matters worse. And there was no sign of Master Alderley.' He threw me a glance, eyebrows raised. 'No one admitted to seeing him in the yard.'

I cleared my throat. 'Was there another way to leave the yard, sir?'

'Yes. They'd left the coach in White Cross Street and walked from there. But the tenement's yard is on the other side of the building, hard by Haberdashers' Square. You know it?'

'Yes, sir. So he could have walked out that way, easily enough. Or been taken.' I heard Mistress Alderley sucking in her breath. 'You could get a coach or cart in there. If you needed one.'

Chiffinch grunted. 'And it's but a step from there to Grub Street.'

For a moment I had the unsettling sensation that he had forgotten who I was, that he was treating me almost as an equal.

'Was Master Alderley intending a journey, madam?' he went on. 'Or was there any sign he might be?'

Mistress Alderley shook her head. 'We were to meet at supper. He was going to the

Exchange today, and dining with friends.' Her eyes widened. 'Is it Lovett who took him?'

'I don't see who else it can have been.'

Her breathing was irregular, and her bosom rose and fell rapidly. 'Why? To kill him in revenge for betraying him?'

'I don't know, madam,' Chiffinch said. 'We don't even know your husband was taken. It's possible he walked away of his own volition for some reason. But we must assume he is still alive. We haven't found . . . anything to make us think otherwise.'

They hadn't found Alderley's body. Not yet.

'If it was Lovett, sir,' I said, 'you would think his daughter would know where Master Alderley is. Assuming she's with her father now.'

'My niece can have had nothing to do with this,' Mistress Alderley said, firing up with anger and glaring at me.

I bowed, as if acknowledging the truth of what she said. But I wasn't so sure she was right. The young woman who had put on boy's clothes during the Fire and bitten my hand was clearly capable of a good deal — including, perhaps, the murder of Sir Denzil Croughton. If that were true, she would take a little matter like abduction in her stride.

'Master Alderley is not as other men,' Chiffinch said carefully. 'It would not be wise to let the fact of his disappearance become known. Or at least we must delay the news getting out for as long as possible. If his depositors and his creditors got wind of it too soon, or in the wrong way . . .'

Mistress Alderley's face lost its colour. 'That would be . . . unwise.' She turned to me. 'You will be discreet, Master Marwood, I know.'

'He will,' Chiffinch said, looking grimly at me. 'I'll answer for it, madam.'

'I must go home. I must talk to Edward, and we must stop the servants' mouths. Pray, sir, have them send for my coach.'

Chiffinch nodded to me, and I went out to speak to the servants and then to wait for the coach to be brought into the street. It must have been held in readiness — it came rumbling out of the gate to Scotland Yard in a matter of moments. Ann, Mistress Alderley's maid, was inside.

The Alderleys' badge, the pelican plucking her breast to feed her young, was on the door. The Alderleys were rich enough to own at least two coaches. But whose wealth was it really?

Ann, carrying her mistress's cloak, came with me to the chamber where her mistress was waiting. I followed them downstairs again. Mistress Alderley did not look at me as Master Chiffinch handed her into the coach. But she beckoned me over when she was settled in her seat.

'Remember what we were saying earlier, Marwood,' she said, too low for anyone else to hear. 'Find her for me. And you will earn my gratitude. It matters more to me than finding her father.'

Grim-faced, Chiffinch watched the coach rattling down Whitehall towards Charing Cross. He glanced at me. 'If any of this gets out, Master Marwood, I'll see your father hanged at Tyburn. Do we understand each other?'

I bowed and met his gaze squarely. 'Perfectly, sir. What would you have me do?'

'You can go to the devil for all I care. As long as you keep your mouth shut and hold yourself ready if I need you.'

Chiffinch's agitation made me wonder whether he himself, like the King, had had financial dealings with Master Alderley. It was certain that his disappearance had complicated this situation in ways I could only dimly perceive. I suspected that Chiffinch was reluctant to act without fresh instructions from his master.

I had missed dinner, so there was nothing left for me to do but to go back to Scotland Yard, and continue with my work. I finished my assigned copying by mid-afternoon. Williamson signed the letters I had written and sent me off with them to the Letter Office.

It was like any other tedious afternoon. The other clerks yawned over their work. Master Chiffinch had succeeded so far in this, at least. The news of Master Alderley's disappearance had not become widely known in Whitehall, which was remarkable in itself, for the palace was such a hive of gossip.

All the while, my head was buzzing with speculation. Chiffinch had forbidden me to speak to anyone about Master Alderley, and I would be a fool to disobey him. Before that, however, Mistress Alderley had asked me to find her niece and, through her, Thomas Lovett.

Nothing had changed that. Whatever had happened to Henry Alderley, the King would still want Lovett brought to him. Mistress Alderley still wanted her niece back — partly, I suspected, because she felt guilty about her treatment of the girl.

There had been no trace of Catherine Lovett since Saturday afternoon in the coffee house. She could be anywhere in London, or even somewhere outside it. She might even be dead. But there was an obvious place to start looking, and no one had told me not to go there.

Why not? In the back of my mind was the fugitive, shameful thought that perhaps, if I did, and if I had even some small success, Mistress Olivia Alderley might smile on me.

It was after five o'clock by the time I knocked on the door of Mistress Noxon's house in Three Cocks Yard.

It was the little maidservant, Margery, who came to the door. I asked her if Master Hakesby was within.

'Yes, sir, but I . . . I'm not supposed to let you in, not without calling the mistress.'

'Show me up to Master Hakesby,' I suggested. 'And then tell your mistress.'

She stared doubtfully at me. I took out my purse and gave her sixpence.

'It's important,' I said. 'As God's my witness, no one will blame you.'

She gave way at that, and led me upstairs to Master Hakesby's apartment. He was standing by his draughtsman's table, which was by the window. The daylight was fading rapidly and two candles burned on the table. He was fully dressed in a sober suit of grey, and he appeared less frail than he had done two days ago. He did not look surprised to see me. I wondered whether he had caught sight of me from the window as I crossed the yard below towards the house.

'If it please you —' Margery began.

'Yes.' Hakesby nodded to her. 'You may go.'

'Mistress Noxon, sir . . .'

'You may tell her it's quite all right, and she is not to trouble us. I'll ring when I need you.'

When the door had closed behind her, Hakesby sat in his elbow chair and waved me towards a stool nearby. 'So you've come back. Well?'

'Is my name familiar, sir?'

'What?'

'Marwood, sir. Did you ever know of anyone else with this name? In the old days.'

'I recall a printer called Marwood.' He put his head to one side. 'In the old days. I believe I had some small acquaintance with him.'

'My father, sir,' I said. 'I'm still looking for Jane.'

He gave the slightest of shrugs but said nothing.

'Except she isn't really Jane, is she?'

'Really? What makes you think that?'

'Her name is Catherine Lovett.' I saw a flicker of movement cross his face, like a wince of pain. 'She lived at Barnabas Place with her uncle, Henry Alderley, and his family until the Fire. She fled here a day or so after St Paul's burned down, perhaps because her uncle would have her marry a man she did not want. An old servant of the Lovetts, one Jem Brockhurst, was thought to have had a hand in her departure and to have attacked her cousin, Edward, on the same night.'

'Alderley?' He raised his head. 'The goldsmith?'

'Yes, sir. He had Jem flogged to encourage him to confess his crimes, but the old man died under the lash. As for Mistress Lovett, Mistress Noxon sheltered her, and gave her another name. She must have known who Jane really is, and I think you did, too.'

'This is nonsense,' Hakesby said. 'Be careful what you say. It's slander. It's better that you go now. Or you'll make matters worse for yourself when I bring you to court.'

'In a moment. Hear me out.' It was an empty threat, and he knew it. 'Later, Mistress Noxon claimed Jem's box, claiming to be his niece. She probably is, which will be easy enough to prove. She sent a servant to Barnabas Place to collect the box, though she gave Master Alderley the impression that she lived in Oxford, not London. The servant brought it here.'

I paused. Hakesby continued to look at me. His face was stern and yet unconcerned, as if he were a judge listening to my evidence as I stood before him in the dock. His left hand lay on his lap. It trembled slightly. A trace of the ague? Fear?

'You were kind to her,' I went on. 'When there was trouble with the other servants, and Mistress Noxon said she had to go, you offered to take her in at your new place of business. She went to stay at a coffee house for a few days first. But on Saturday a man came and took her away. He said he was you. But he wasn't.'

The long fingers of Hakesby's right hand tightened on the arm of the chair. I saw the knuckles grow pale.

'I think that man was her father,' I said. 'Thomas Lovett. The Regicide. Did you know him well, sir? In the old days.'

Hakesby would not answer.

'Sir,' I said, growing desperate, 'my own father suffered for the same beliefs as Thomas Lovett's, and he made his family suffer for them too. Nevertheless I have sympathy for such men. Many of them were upright and honourable in what they did.'

'And you? Where do you stand?'

'I think we must let bygones be bygones. The old days have passed. Times have changed, and we must change with them.'

'Some people never change,' he said wearily. 'They are hard as rock.'

'And Mistress Lovett? Is she as hard as rock as well?'

Then, at long last, Hakesby abandoned the pretence. 'She's not like her father, and I doubt that she shares his beliefs. Though she has some of his gifts. But what is she to you? Why should you care what happens to her? Why should it matter to you if she lives or dies?'

'Her Aunt Alderley asked me to find her and bring her home. She cares for the girl and will not let her come to harm. And she has powerful friends of her own, quite apart from her husband.'

'Are you a government spy?'

'No, sir,' I said. 'I work as a clerk in Master Williamson's office. I help him conduct the *Gazette*.'

'So you dance to the government's tune, Master Marwood?'

'No, sir. I work to live. My father is failing. I must put food on the table for us, and find a roof for our heads.'

Hakesby stirred in his chair. 'Doesn't a daughter belong with her father?'

'Not this daughter. And not this father.' I leaned forward. 'Sir, I don't know what Master Lovett was, but I know what he has become. In the last few weeks he has murdered at least three men, including one of Master Alderley's manservants, who was spying on him, and one of his own former comrades, a man named Sneyd.'

'Sneyd? The tailor. I knew him — he made a coat for me once, in Oliver's time.'

'They found him last month in the Fleet Ditch.'

'Drowned?'

'No, sir,' I said. 'He was stabbed in the brain by someone who knew what he was doing. The manservant was killed in exactly the same way. And, in both cases, the thumbs of the dead man had been tied together.'

Hakesby's face changed. Fear had touched him. 'You said he's killed three men. Who was the third?'

'Sir Denzil Croughton, last Saturday. He was betrothed to Mistress Lovett.'

'The man who was stabbed on Primrose Hill? You're raving.'

'Does it sound as if I'm the one who's

raving?' I stood up and looked down at him. 'Three men murdered, and who knows how many others have died because of this? Lovett was also behind the Whitehall fire last week. God knows what else he intends.'

Hakesby lifted his arms, clasped his long bony fingers together and laid his hands on his lap. 'I fear for her.'

I bent towards him and said in a low voice, 'I wish Mistress Lovett nothing but good. But don't you see? If she's with him now, he will drag her down with him. So if you know where she is, can we not help her?'

CHAPTER FORTY-EIGHT

Cat pushed aside the coverings and slowly stood up. Her fingers wrapped around the handle of the knife. She drew it from its sheath.

The light on the floor increased in size. The door was silently opening. Glowing lines appeared at the top, the bottom and one side of the door, narrow at first but gradually widening into slabs of colour. The light was not bright. She guessed it came from another closed lantern.

She backed into the corner. Her mouth was dry. It was too late to hide. Only the wall cupboard was large enough to conceal her, but that was directly opposite the opening door and she hadn't time to reach it, let alone to reach it without making a noise.

She took a step along the wall to the right. Then another. The movement brought the opening door at least partly between her and whoever was on the other side of it.

She heard a shuffling, faint as a whisper. Attack was the only course left to her. Go for his eyes, she thought, remembering Cousin Edward, or his manhood. Or both.

Her foot touched the jug, which still contained a little beer. It slid, scraping, across the stone floor.

'Catherine. Is that you?'

The whisper reached her through the not-quite darkness. Fear dropped away from her, replaced in that first moment by a stab of anger, sharp as her own knife.

How dare he?

'Sir?' she said.

The door swung open to its full extent. The dark shape of her father almost filled the doorway. She put the knife in its sheath and returned it to her pocket.

The anger diminished, and became a dull ache of despair, a sense that all roads led back to her father, that she would never escape him or the life he had chosen for them.

'Why aren't you where I left you?' he said, almost pettishly.

'I could not tolerate that house any longer, sir. But why are you here? Why are —'

'You were at that house by my command,' he said harshly. 'You had no right to leave it. There's no sin in honest work, only in refusing it.'

'Master Davy is a lecher, sir.' And a bully, and a hypocrite. 'He kissed me and touched me where he should touch only his wife.'

'Your wits are wandering, girl. Either that or you are lying.'

'He threatened to whip me if I did not do what he wanted.'

'You're lying. Master Davy is a friend. He is one of us. I have known him for nigh on twenty years. I entrusted you to his care. He would never betray that trust. He would never do me such a wrong.'

'He did me the wrong, sir,' she spat. 'Not you. And I tell you I will not stand for it. Not from any man. Ever.'

He took a step towards her. 'You were always headstrong, Catherine.' His voice was gentler, almost conciliatory. 'Come. We will talk about this later. Perhaps there is something in what you say, but there's no time to enquire into it now. The Chapter Clerk's away, but others may come to the room.'

'How did you know to find me here?' She paused but all she heard was his breathing. 'You saw me come? No, not that. You know about the Chapter Clerk.'

The knowledge that she had been betrayed swept over her. Something shifted in the relationship between her father and herself. Something was broken. No man could be trusted. Not even her father. Not even Master Hakesby.

'Come,' her father said again. 'We will talk later.'

'Where are we going?' She didn't want to go with him at all. But she didn't want to stay in this place, either. 'Can we leave St Paul's?'

'No. There's no way out tonight. We must wait for the morning, for Master Davy and his wagon.'

'I won't go with him.'

He slapped her face, causing her to stagger and almost fall. 'You will go where I tell you.' He steadied her and his voice became gentler again. 'We shall go up,' he said. 'We shall go higher, closer to God. It's safer there, because once in a while the watchmen come into the church itself. Besides, there is something up there I must show you, and something I must do.'

Her father wasn't mad, Cat decided, not if you knew his beliefs and started from those; given that, there was nothing foolish about him or his actions.

He insisted on returning everything in the chamber to where it had been when she had first come into it. He made her open the shutter and empty the pot and the beer jug out of the window into the darkness of the cloister garth below. The surplices and cassocks went back into the wall cupboard.

When she had finished, he checked the room, as carefully as he could by the poor light of the lantern. His movements were methodical and unhurried. She waited, shivering in her cloak, for him to finish. Only when he was quite satisfied that she had left no trace of her presence did he take her by the arm and draw her through the doorway.

The gallery on the other side stretched above the north walk of the cloister. Most of the roof had gone, and one of the stone window frames had collapsed outwards, taking with it some of the wall on either side of it.

'It's safe enough if you go carefully and stay to the left,' her father said. 'Keep hold of my arm.'

He put the bars across the door and drew her down the gallery to an archway. This led to another chamber that ran down to the corner of the cloister. Here, in the angle where the cathedral's nave met the south transept, there was a small doorway. The door, blackened by the heat but still intact, was standing open.

The beam of the lantern played briefly and faintly on the spiral staircase beyond. The steps curled through the thickness of the wall into the darkness above.

Cat touched her father's arm. 'Sir? Must we go here?' Neither high places nor darkness scared her. But she had a fear of being trapped, of being powerless.

'Be not afraid,' he commanded. 'For I am with you.'

He pushed her ahead of him. She began to climb, stretching her arms so her hands could touch the wall on the left and the central post on the right. He closed the door behind them and followed, his footsteps steady and firm on the stone treads as if he were climbing in broad daylight.

The light danced around her, throwing her shadow ahead. A current of air rushed down towards them. Here, encased in the stone skeleton of the building, it was much colder even than in the chamber where she had tried to sleep.

'Faster,' he whispered behind her. 'Higher.'

The staircase levelled out into a passage that ran between blank stone walls.

'Quietly now,' her father murmured behind her. 'We're at triforium level. Have no fear — the floor is sound and level. There's another stair at the end.'

She felt his hand on her shoulder. He nudged her gently through the archway. She was calmer now, responding to the precision of his knowledge and the authority in his voice. The triforium was the middle storey of a church interior, the arcading above the aisles. She had her bearings now: somewhere to the left must be the central tower.

At the end was another spiral stair, at the top of which they entered what at first seemed like another passage. Cat had taken only a few steps along it when she realized that this passage was different. The air was fresher and more turbulent. There was suddenly a pallor to the darkness, a sense that it was not quite as deep as it had been. She stopped and stretched out her right hand. She touched the rough stone of the wall. She stretched out her left hand and touched —

Nothing.

'Keep to the right,' her father hissed at her shoulder. 'Don't look down. Walk.'

Her legs ached. She felt weak. She took a step forward. Then another. Her left hand brushed something. A pillar. Then nothing again.

'Good,' he said. 'Only a few paces.'

Her knees were somehow dissolving, the solid matter of bone and tendon losing form and density, becoming jelly. The light from the lantern flickered ahead, showing ash and stone and, to the left —

Nothing.

'Look to the right, at the wall. Walk. In a moment you'll be at the tower staircase.'

Again, knowledge steadied her. They were still inside the cathedral, but high above the crossing, with the central tower above them. A narrow passage with the wall on one side and the arches on the other, framing —

Nothing.

She was inside the empty heart of the tower. Somewhere far below this dark vacancy — eighty feet below? A hundred? — was the floor of the cathedral.

Then — a moment later? An hour? — an archway loomed before her. She stumbled through it and collapsed on the lower steps of the staircase beyond.

'Put your faith in me, and the Lord our God, Catherine,' her father said. 'I've worked in this place since I was a boy. Your grandfather was a mason here too. I won't let you fall.'

She felt a rush of love for him, its force taking her by surprise. Then loathing.

566

How could you?

After that it was easier. Her legs still ached. She was still faint with hunger. But she climbed steadily, with him keeping pace behind her. This staircase was rising through the tower itself, she realized, near its south-east corner. There was a slit window at every few turns of the stair.

Once they were above the level of the choir, she caught glimpses of London below them, of a wasteland of ashes and ruins, speckled with the occasional fire, unimaginably far away. To the south was the broad black stripe of the river, with the boats passing to and fro, their lanterns bobbing on the water. Once she heard a dog barking.

Sometimes they passed empty doorways. Her father said they had once led to vanished chambers above the vaulting of the tower.

'Not long now,' he said. 'Almost there.'

They came to a low doorway, not more than four feet high. It still had a door in it.

'Let me go first,' he said.

She stepped back, allowing him to push past her. He took out a key and, holding the lantern to the door, unlocked it and threw the door open.

There was a rush of air towards them, bringing the smell of the river. She heard a sound, a long, faint moan; a trick of the wind.

Master Lovett scrambled through the doorway. He turned back. 'Come,' he said impatiently. 'Keep to the right, by the wall.'

She followed him outside. Above their heads was the sky, heavy and dark, with a handful of stars burning far beyond the clouds. She stood there for a moment, allowing her eyes to adjust to the light. The air was fresh and had a tang of salt. Apart from the buffeting of the wind it was almost silent. From the Tower in the east to the distant lights of Whitehall and Westminster in the west, the noise and bustle had dropped away. Cat had never been so high above London, not within the City itself.

Another moan. Not the wind. Something nearer.

'I've a surprise for you, Catherine,' her father said. He sounded almost merry. 'Your Uncle Alderley is waiting to greet you.'

The moaning was close to her, little more than a hand's reach from where she was standing, just outside the doorway from the stairs. She recoiled from the sound, jarring her spine against the stone of the parapet. Her hand flailed out, searching for support. It collided with her father's arm. He gripped her wrist. She heard him exclaim.

Something small and metallic skittered across the stone ledge they were standing on.

Then — suddenly — there was silence again, except for the wind, a silence where there should not have been silence. All three of them — Cat, her father and Uncle Alderley — held their breath and waited, without knowing precisely what they were waiting for.

Waiting, it turned out, for the sound of metal hitting stone two hundred feet below the empty heart of the tower.

CHAPTER FORTY-NINE

Hakesby and I passed through the gateway and walked up Ludgate Hill to St Paul's. It was gone six o'clock. I had not told him that Alderley had disappeared — it was not my secret to tell, and besides there was no point in risking Master Chiffinch's anger any more than I already had.

The cathedral looked like an abandoned fortress. Its walls were still sheer and high, with high fences blocking the gaps that the Fire had caused. Some doorways had been permanently sealed with brick, others with wooden barriers topped with spikes. The place was dark, without a single gleam of light inside the fabric.

We walked round to Convocation House Yard. I rattled the gate for long enough to set the dog barking. Eventually the watchmen stumbled from their hut and swore at us.

'Damn your impudence,' Hakesby shouted

in a loud, angry voice that took me by surprise. 'You'll be whipped and dismissed if you don't have a care. Don't you know I'm Master Hakesby? Let me in.'

There were agitated whispers on the other side of the gate. The dog continued to bark. It then gave a squeal and fell abruptly silent, as if someone had kicked it. The bar was lifted from the gate, and one leaf opened. One of the men held up a lantern. Hakesby stepped forward so the light fell on his face.

'Your worship's pardon, sir,' the watchman said, sending a waft of spirits towards us. 'Pray forgive us. You wouldn't believe the rogues and beggars we get knocking on the door after dark, you —'

'Be silent. Chain that dog and let us in.'

The yard was almost in darkness. A light burned in the watchmen's hut, and another by the inner gate leading to the builders' enclosure at the side of the cloister.

'We've work to do,' Hakesby said. 'Give my friend your lantern and keep the dog confined.'

The watchman handed him the light and knuckled his forehead. 'How long will your worships be?'

'I don't know. Be off with you.'

The two men dragged the dog towards their hut. We crossed the yard to the inner gate. Hakesby took a key from his pocket and unlocked it.

When we were inside, I said, 'Better bar it, sir. We don't want to be disturbed.'

He hesitated. I saw his eyes gleam. He was looking at me, wondering whether to trust me in this as well as all the rest. I was wondering the same thing about him.

'I won't get far without you, sir,' I said. 'Mistress Noxon knows we left the house together, and so does the maid. Those men must have seen my face, too.'

'Do it.'

I set down the lantern and slid the bar across, sealing us in. 'I should tell you that others know I intended to talk to you.'

Hakesby snorted. 'Then we may trust each other completely.'

I could not see his face but the tone of his voice made me suspect that he was smiling. He led the way to the shed. He used another key to unlock that.

By night, a place changed. I had not realized that the shed was so long and cavernous. In the light of the single lantern, it seemed infinite.

We walked down the shed to the table where I had seen him working. He pointed to the wooden steps running up the back wall. His Adam's apple bobbed up and down his windpipe. 'She's just up there. Beyond that door.'

Hakesby asked me to hold the lantern. The self-assurance he had shown with the watchmen had ebbed away. His hand trembled when he took a key from his pocket and unlocked a chest on the floor. He stooped with obvious difficulty and took out a bunch of keys, some large, some small.

He climbed the wooden steps slowly, clinging to the rail, with the keys chinking softly in his hand. I followed behind him. He knocked at the door at the top, an oddly decorous action, and called out, 'It's me, Jane. Master Hakesby.'

There was no answer. He glanced back at me, selected a key and unlocked the door. He unlatched it and pushed it open. He hesitated on the threshold. 'Jane? Jane?'

Again, there was no response. He took the lantern from me and led the way inside. I heard him muttering under his breath. I followed him in. The air was different here — colder and danker, tainted with the stale smell of burning that still clung to the entire city.

A sense of dread crept over me. 'What is it, sir?'

'She's gone.' Hakesby crossed to a door in the opposite wall and twisted the ring that lifted the latch, but the door wouldn't move. He took the lantern to the window and examined the fastening of the shutters. 'But she can't have left the way we came in. The door and the shed were locked, and so was the yard gate. Then there were the watchmen and the dog in Convocation House Yard. And she didn't go through the window —'

'So she must have gone through the other door,' I said with a touch of impatience.

'We must be methodical, Master Marwood, if we wish to avoid mistakes. Yes, she must have gone by the other door.'

I went over to the second door and twisted the ring that turned the latch. The door didn't move. 'Have you a key? Where does it lead?'

'It's not locked,' he said in his low, deliberate voice. 'It's barred on the other side. It leads to the gallery over the cloister, and then to some stairs into the cathedral itself, near the south door. But the gallery is so ruinous that only a fool would pass through it, even in daytime.'

'Then where is she?'

'I don't know,' he said, spreading his hands. In the lantern light, his face was pitted with deep shadows. It looked like a long yellow skull.

Suddenly the pieces assembled themselves in my head. 'Lovett's here, isn't he?' I said. 'He's in the cathedral. You knew he was there all along, because you let him hide here. Just as you knew that he would come for his daughter. Because you'd told him where to find her. You've led me into a trap.'

'Let me tell the truth,' Hakesby said in a voice not much louder than a whisper. 'The whole truth. This is not a trap. I swear it.'

He pushed aside some of the papers on the table and put down the lantern. He sank down on the chair beside it. He pointed to another chair, nearer to the door to the stairs.

'Pray sit down, Master Marwood.'

'We haven't time to sit and discuss it, sir.' But I too lowered my voice. 'You've betrayed me.'

'I've not betrayed you. I give you my oath on it. Like you, I want nothing but Mistress Lovett's safety. And I fear I've led her into danger.'

'Then we must act. Now. For her sake.'

I took the lantern from the table and went round the room, opening the cupboard and the chest, peering into corners and under the furniture. All the time, I was listening for other sounds.

'For her sake, we must think first,' Hakesby said. 'Sit down, I pray you, sir. It's uncomfortable to crane my head to see you.'

His actions and his words sucked some of the tension from the room. There was nothing aggressive about him. Only a great weariness.

'Talk, then,' I said. 'I'm listening. But talk quickly.'

'These accusations you've made about Master Lovett,' he said. 'The murders, the Whitehall fire. I know nothing of such things. You must believe me. I didn't even know he was in England until yesterday. He told me he had come back for his daughter's sake, to take her out of the country with him.'

I found a chamber pot under the table. It was empty. I said, 'How long has Lovett been in St Paul's?'

'This will be his second night. He was here already, you see. But I didn't bring him.'

I took up the pot and sniffed. It smelled of urine, which was only to be expected. 'Then who did?'

'Another man he used to know, in the old days. One of the workmen. There are scores of them in the building during the day.'

I waited but Hakesby didn't give me the

man's name. I ran my finger around the inside of the pot. I felt a hint of moisture. 'Not a mere labourer, then,' I suggested. 'Someone with a little authority?'

'Perhaps,' he said. 'You don't need to know. We knew each other in the old days, you understand. He asked me to sign a pass to allow him to bring a wagon in.' He swallowed again. 'When there should have been no real need for him to do so. I didn't ask questions. Better not.'

I put down the pot. The old days. The phrase they kept using, as if it explained all and excused all. Perhaps it did, to them, and to my father when he remembered what the old days were. But it didn't explain or excuse anything to me.

'This needn't go further than us, Master Marwood, need it? I have tried to act for the best, indeed I have, and — and nowadays the King, for all his shortcomings, has no more loyal subject than myself.'

'If you tell me everything,' I said, 'if you hold nothing back, and if we can find the girl unharmed — well, in that case perhaps this can remain between us. But if not . . .'

I was beginning to understand how Lovett worked. He had survived in England for at least ten weeks with the support of a network of people who had known and respected him in the old days. People who had shared at least some of his beliefs, who had served him or prayed with him or fought beside him. His old servant, Jem, had been one of them, Sneyd had been another, and probably Mother Grimes a third. Add to that the anonymous workman at St Paul's and Hakesby himself. And God alone knew who else.

I stared at Hakesby, trying to make out his expression in the dim light, my mind turning and creaking fit to break like the sails of a windmill in a gale. 'We must find her, sir. At once. She's not long gone.'

I wasn't sure how much Mistress Noxon knew — probably she had sheltered Cat for her uncle's sake. But, if in the old days she had shared his loyalties, perhaps that was why Master Hakesby had come to lodge with her in the first place.

'A moment, sir. A moment, I beg you.'

You couldn't call these people conspirators. As far as possible, I suspected, Lovett had kept most of them in ignorance of one another, and in ignorance of his real purpose in returning to England. Nor would they have known what he had become during his years of exile, and the means he was willing to adopt in the hope that his actions would bring about the reign of King Jesus.

'We're wasting time,' I said. 'We must look for the girl, not sit here talking.'

'The girl,' he said. He still didn't move. 'You're right, Master Marwood — she's what matters now. Master Lovett said he'd come to London to collect her. After all, she's his child, and a child should be with her father.'

'Not all children,' I said harshly. 'And not all fathers. So Lovett knew she might have gone back to Mistress Noxon's, and that you lodged there as well?'

Hakesby nodded. 'He'd been to Three Cocks Yard already — on Saturday, when Mistress Noxon told him his daughter was at the coffee house. So he followed her there and removed her. But it seems that Jane — Mistress Catherine, that is, but I still think of her as Jane — ran away from the house where her father took her. He thought she might have gone back to Mistress Noxon's.'

I wanted to pick Hakesby up and shake him. 'When did you talk to Lovett?'

'I told you — yesterday. He came up to me when I was inspecting the work in the cathedral. I didn't know him at first — he's much changed, and he was dressed as a common labourer. He thanked me for helping him find shelter, albeit without my knowing it was him I was helping. And then he begged me to say if I had news of his daughter. So today, when she came here, I — I thought it best to search him out and tell him where she was. A child should be with her father . . . But I didn't realize he would come so quickly, before it was night. I thought we'd reach her before he did.'

He raised his face to me and the light from the lantern fell on it. His eyes shone with unshed tears. 'I told Lovett where to find her, that she was here in this room, and how to get here. I was wrong to do that. But I thought a child should be with her —'

'How did he get back in St Paul's?'

'There would be no difficulty if he was with the man who was helping him. The workmen were still passing in and out at that hour.'

I considered. 'At least Lovett's not expecting you back here until the morning. Which means that she may still be here, still in St Paul's. Where would he take her?'

Hakesby raised his arm and pointed towards the high places of the abandoned church. 'Somewhere up there, probably. Unless there's a vault I don't know of. Nobody goes above ground unless they've no choice — the building's not safe, you see, even with the scaffolding we're putting up inside. The tower sways in strong winds. Stones fall every day. But Lovett worked here a great deal before the war — even as a boy, with his father, who was one of Inigo Jones's principal masons. He knows the place as well as anyone does, and he'll know the risks, too.'

I calculated the implications. Lovett must have approached this room from the second door, from the cloister gallery. 'How did Lovett reach this chamber?'

'Assuming he came from the cathedral? It must have been from the gallery beyond that door. It would take a man of strong nerve, though.'

'They're not long gone,' I said. 'The pot has been recently used.'

Hakesby pushed back his chair and stood up with some difficulty, as though his limbs were no longer entirely his to command. He said, in a steady voice, 'Then we must look for her at once, sir. This is my fault, and I must try to set it right as best I can.'

We could not use the door leading to the gallery, because Lovett had barred it on the other side. So I led the way back down the steps to the shed, where the leather curtain still masked the door from the shed to the cloister below the upper gallery. At Hakesby's suggestion, we found and lit a second lantern.

I held the curtain aside while he sorted through his bunch of keys.

'The common people say they have seen ghosts here since the Fire,' he said. 'The people who died, the ones whose bodies weren't found. They are searching for their mortal remains, for how can they rise up on Judgement Day and greet our Redeemer without them?'

I said nothing. A childhood full of this sort of talk had inured me to it, as a dose of pox or measles inures a man to future infection.

A rush of air greeted us as Hakesby pushed open the door. The air was cold and damp, smelling of old fires, stone dust and charnel houses.

'I've never been here by night,' he whispered.

We picked our way along the cloister to the place where the remains of the south door were still propped against the wall. I paused on the threshold. Both of us shaded our lanterns under our cloaks. I waited, listening to Hakesby's breathing at my shoulder, until the darkness was no longer uniform. One by one, a few stars appeared, far above our heads.

I whispered to Hakesby: 'You know the

way. Lead us to the crossing. As quietly as possible.'

It was then, as we advanced slowly into the ruins, I realized how immense and foolhardy was this undertaking. The floor was much clearer than it had been when I was last here, but there were still piles of stone and heaps of rubble scattered about, their outlines hardly visible in the lantern light. Pillars loomed like the trunks of mighty oaks. The jagged outlines of windows were no more than memories of what they had once been.

The cathedral seemed even larger than by daylight. Almost all the roof had gone. You could no longer tell with any certainty where St Paul's ended and the night sky began.

Our progress was painfully slow. I kept the lantern under the shelter of my cloak, allowing only a square of light to fall on the floor before us. I did not know we had reached the crossing until I felt Hakesby's hand on my arm, drawing me to a stop.

Here we were, at the heart of the building, where the nave and choir met the transepts below the central tower. The wind moved above and around us, creating the strange illusion that the cathedral was breathing.

'We cannot search the whole place,' Hakesby whispered. 'They could be anywhere.'

He was right, and we both knew it. You would need half a company of soldiers to comb the whole building at ground level and explore the galleries and staircases above ground, as well as whatever lay beneath. You would need people who knew the cathedral as they knew their own parlour to examine all the places where refugees might hide. You would need to set guards at any possible points of escape. Above all, you would need daylight.

'We must pray for a miracle,' Hakesby said.

It was just the sort of remark my father would have made. Dear God, I thought, my life is haunted by these religious fools.

Perhaps I should go to Whitehall, tell Chiffinch everything, and persuade him to talk to the King. If the King ordered it, the Foot Guards could seal off the entire ruin for the rest of the night and then search it properly by daylight. But Lovett and his daughter might have left by the time the soldiers came, if they hadn't left already. Besides, the City authorities would need to be consulted, and the last thing the King would want was to make public his pursuit of

Thomas Lovett.

At that moment, I heard the chink of metal on stone. Hakesby gasped. I nearly dropped the lantern. The sound was high and surprisingly musical, the chink of impact followed by a brief, scuttling clatter, as the object came to rest.

Everything changed at a stroke. Something had fallen from the sky. It had landed, by the sound of it, about three yards away from where we were standing.

I crouched and played the beam of the lantern over the blackened flagstones until I found Master Hakesby's miracle. It took the form of a small dagger.

CHAPTER FIFTY

'That was my dagger you made me drop,' her father said, releasing her wrist.

Simultaneously, as she regained her balance, Cat said, 'Uncle Alderley? What's he —'

'Henry Alderley is an abomination in the sight of the Lord,' Master Lovett said, his voice acquiring the cadences of the pulpit. 'A coward. A thief. A . . .'

He spat. The wind caught it, and she felt flecks of his spittle on her cheek.

'But how does he come here, sir?'

'Because I brought him, with the help of a friend in Jesus. First we carried him in a wagon, and then persuaded him at the point of a dagger, the one that has fallen. Here, in this high place, he will understand what it is to be a man of such sin: a man who takes so much from Caesar that he forgets what he owes to God.'

She tried to bring her father back from

the divine to mundane. 'Where are we?'

'In the tower of St Paul's, of course. At the very top. At the highest place in this degenerate city.'

'Is it — is it safe?'

'Safe?' he cried. 'Nowhere is safe, child. Not on this earth. But we are in God's hands, you and I, and He will bring us to Him in His own good time.'

'I don't want to fall, sir. Not before my time.' Or indeed at any time, she thought, including God's.

'Then mind your step and trust in the Lord. The roof has gone, of course, but the walls are mostly sound. There's some scaffolding below us but nothing else. Keep close to the parapet and you'll be on the wall-walk. It's about six feet wide, but in places it is partly fallen. Feel your way before you put your weight on anything. The parapet is crumbling, so be careful there as well. We're on the west side now. The east side is particularly bad.'

Cat felt for the parapet and ran her hand up to the top. It was about four or five feet high. She could see over it, but only just. There were no battlements here, she remembered, only a plain line of coping stones that projected slightly from the outer face of the tower.

'There's a chamber at the north-east corner,' he said, his breath warm against the tip of her ear. 'Made of stone and built into the angle where the walls meet. It was built for the roofers when the spire was still here.'

'Are we going there now, sir?'

'Yes. We can shelter there for a time. Alderley? Stand up.'

The moaning grew louder. Her father had covered the lantern. She did not see him stepping around her so much as hear him, and feel the displacement of the air as he passed.

He stooped, dragged her uncle to his feet and propped him against the wall. 'Stop your groaning,' he ordered. 'I'm going to take out the gag. If you shout for help, two things will happen. No one will hear except us. And I will break one of your fingers.'

Her father wrenched out the gag. 'Move along in front of us.'

Uncle Alderley retched. He tried to speak but failed.

'Move!'

'For pity's sake, Tom. I beg you.'

Cat would not have recognized her uncle's voice. It was thin, purged of vitality like an old man's, almost drowned by the wind. It had lost all trace of authority. She could not see him except as a blur, but he was oddly hunched over, as if he had acquired a crooked back since he had last seen her.

'Pity, Henry? Is that what you gave me?'

'Forgive me. For the love of God. For your poor dead sister's sake, my poor dead wife who loved us both.'

'After what you've done? Why should I?'

Her uncle's voice rose to a wail. 'I'm afraid of falling.'

'I know,' her father said. 'You were so scared of heights that you would not go out on the roof of your house with me to see the stars. My sister told me you whimpered like a child at the very thought of it. Do you remember that? Edward was very little then, and Catherine had not been born.'

He prodded Alderley's arm, forcing him to shift along the wall-walk. He prodded again and again, like a farmer goading a reluctant cow. The three of them shuffled slowly along the parapet, with London turning below in time with their footsteps. Uncle Alderley went first, weeping, edging sideways with his back to the emptiness inside the tower; he stopped after every pace and clung to the top of the parapet.

'Go on, you coward.'

'The sky is pressing down on me,' Uncle Alderley cried. 'I shall fall, Tom.'

'You'll fall if you don't move,' her father

said cheerfully, 'because I'll push you off. Two hundred feet down? Two hundred and fifty? And at the bottom the Devil will be waiting for you.'

They came at last to the narrow doorway in the north-west corner of the tower. There was no door. Three steps led down into a small stone enclosure, crudely vaulted with rubble. Uncle Alderley collapsed on the floor in the corner where the walls of the tower met.

Her father uncovered the lantern and placed it in a niche to the right of the doorway. He opened it only enough to allow a dim light to fill the space where they were. It was safe enough, Cat supposed, for there were no windows in the outer walls, and they were probably invisible even from below, underneath the crossing.

Uncle Alderley lay gasping for breath, heaving dry sobs from somewhere deep inside himself. He was lying on his side. His hands had been tied behind his back, which gave him his hunched appearance.

Not his hands, Cat saw, as her eyes adjusted to the growing light. His thumbs.

'You think I'm cruel?' her father said to her. 'I have reason to be, certainly, but I am not. I am the sharp sword in the Lord's right hand. I bring justice in His name. It was your uncle who betrayed me at the Restoration, despite his promises to do all he could to help us.'

'Oh Tom,' her uncle groaned, 'they made me do it. I swear it.'

'I thought your uncle a godly man once, Catherine. But the only god he worships is himself. He told those Royalist scum where to find me. I did not know this until my servant Jem uncovered the secret last year. It was only by the grace of God that I escaped. They gave him my house and the yard in the City for his treachery, and the King has shown him favour ever since and even gave him as a wife one of his own cast-off adulterous whores in place of my sister. Men praised him for taking you in — you, the daughter of a Regicide. It was a proof of his magnanimity, they said, of his sense of justice.'

He turned and kicked the man on the floor in the stomach. Henry Alderley shrieked, straining against his tied thumbs. His body twisted into an untidy, pulsing bundle.

'That's justice,' her father said. 'Mark it well, Catherine. But it is nothing to what will happen to him at the Last Judgement. He served Parliament when it was profitable to do it, then Cromwell, and now he thinks he serves the King. But his true master is the Devil himself. What does it matter that he has stolen Coldridge from you as well? True, it's lost for ever. But it will do him no good, and he will not enjoy the fruit of his evil. We shall see to that at least.'

'What will you do to him, sir?'

'You shall see.'

'Sir,' Alderley whispered. 'I beg you, listen to me. You and my niece shall have gold, all the gold I have and all I can borrow. I'll sign a confession, whatever you ask. But spare me, I pray you.' He was speaking more and more quickly, and the flow of words became a torrent. 'And I sold Coldridge only for your sake, Catherine, because Sir Denzil has debts and we needed to pay them off as a price of your marriage. I —'

'Sir Denzil is dead,' her father said. 'Thanks be to God. There will be no marriage now.'

Cat's mouth was dry. Her stomach heaved. At first she couldn't find the words for what she had to say. When she could, her lips were reluctant to frame them. 'Will you kill him, sir?'

'I need not soil my hands with his death, child,' her father said. 'Unless I want to. I might let the King his master kill him instead. Hang him at Tyburn. Draw out his bowels while he yet lives. Hack him into quarters. Cut off his sinful head and let it rot on a spike.'

'Why?' She stared at him, wondering if his wits had finally run away with him. 'Why would the King of all people wish my uncle dead and dishonoured?'

CHAPTER FIFTY-ONE

The spiral staircase was in the north transept, to the east of the great north door. It
was, Hakesby said, the best preserved of all
the staircases, and it offered the safest way
to reach the tower. In the daytime, the scaffolders also used a system of ladders, whose
position changed according to where they
were working; but these were removed at
the end of the day.

'This dagger,' I said. 'It could be anyone's.
We can't be sure it was dropped by Lovett
or his daughter.'

'But who else could be up there? Lovett
can't leave the cathedral until daylight. The
watchmen never go above ground, so he
would calculate they would not be
disturbed.'

I glanced up into the darkness. 'But
there's nothing left up there. Nowhere for
them to go. The floors are gone.'

'They could be on the stairs. Or at the

top, even. There's a little chamber up there, for the roofers, within the angle of the wall.'

I told myself that it was the cold making me shiver. 'Have you been there yourself, sir? Since the Fire, I mean.'

'No,' Hakesby said. 'The timbers and the leads have gone, of course, but I'm told that the walls remain, and to their full height. Parts of the parapet are a little damaged. Still, I'm assured it's quite safe, if you look alert and move with care.'

'By daylight,' I said.

He gave a little cough, the sort a man makes when embarrassed. 'Of course. By daylight.'

At first it was easy. The treads of the staircase were level, shallow and broad. At the top was a short passage in the thickness of the wall that brought us to triforium level above the vault covering the east side of the transept, where there had once been chapels. Part of the vault had collapsed, but the scaffolders had constructed a walkway of planks supported by poles. It led south, toward the tower at the crossing.

'Pray let me take your arm,' Hakesby said. 'I feel unsteady.'

His fingers trembled on my arm as we picked our way slowly along the walkway to the staircase at the far end. I was half expecting what happened next.

Hakesby stopped at the archway before the stairs. His fingers tightened their grip. 'Forgive me, Master Marwood,' he whispered. 'I'm ill. I lack the strength to climb further.'

'I can't go alone,' I said. 'I don't know the way.'

'I would come if I had the strength, sir. I swear it. I will . . . I will go for help instead.'

'Where?' I said. 'To Whitehall where no one knows you? Will you talk to the King? Will you turn out the Guards?'

He turned his head away. I intended the sarcasm to wound, and it had. 'Consider, sir. Mistress Lovett doesn't know me. It's you she trusts.'

'I can't go up there.' He was squeezing my arm so hard that I tried to pull it away from him. 'Find her,' he whispered. 'Bring her safely to me. I beg you.'

For a moment neither of us spoke. I covered my lantern. The sincerity in his voice was unmistakable. Like Mistress Alderley, Hakesby seemed to care for the girl for her own sake.

I listened to his breathing, which was fast and shallow as if he had just run a race. Apart from that, there was nothing but the darkness, the murmuring wind and the smell of fear.

Fear had one advantage, at least. It sharpened the senses.

I smelled burning. Someone had recently come up or down the stairs with a light. My nose had become so miraculously acute that it could distinguish between the smell of my lantern and this other smell, which seemed to me to have a faint but disagreeable hint of old fish.

The second staircase was narrower and in worse condition than the first. Step by step, I climbed higher in the tower, trying to move as quietly as I could. I shone the lantern only on the tread immediately in front of me. In my other hand I carried the dagger that had fallen at our feet.

I soon lost track of how far I had climbed. Occasionally there were ventilation slits in the outer wall of the staircase, but they revealed little of the world outside. I passed vacant arches which had once led to chambers within the tower, but which now led to nothing whatsoever.

My skin was clammy with sweat, though the air was growing colder the higher I climbed. I was sorely tempted to turn back. But if I did, then Lovett might easily escape arrest, and Catherine with him. And I would be held responsible.

I did not like to dwell on what Chiffinch's displeasure would mean for myself, and for my father. Also, though I hardly dared admit this even to myself, despite the unknown terrors that waited above me, despite my fear, I was dimly aware of my fond, foolish desire to please Mistress Alderley.

The air freshened and grew colder. Then, as I rounded a turn of the staircase, I saw the faint gleam of a solitary star ahead. I had arrived, though precisely where I did not know.

I masked the lantern completely. I paused to listen at each remaining step, feeling with my hand for the next one. I heard nothing except the wind, which was much stronger than it had been below.

I came to another archway, this one so low that I had to crouch to pass through it. On the other side, I risked a flash of the lantern and stood up. The wind caught my cloak and set it billowing inward, towards the empty centre of the tower. I clutched at the parapet to steady myself. The calcined surface of the stone crumbled a little beneath my fingers. But the parapet itself held firm.

Above my head was the dome of the sky, filled with scudding clouds and, here and there, a sprinkling of stars. I was standing at one corner of the tower. I ignored the darkness to my right and let my gaze move along the parapet. It was then that I saw another, even smaller archway, this one filled with faint, dingy light.

Until then, I had thought it possible — likely, even — that I would find no one up here, that even if Lovett had been here, he would have somehow contrived to flee from St Paul's with his daughter. If I were honest with myself, part of me had hoped that it might be so, which would mean that I could return to Hakesby with honour satisfied.

I edged, step by step, along the top of the wall towards this second archway. The wind would mask the sound of my approach, I calculated, but I could not rid myself of the idea that someone was in the darkness, that someone was watching me.

The distance between me and the doorway slowly shrank.

Not too late to turn back, I thought. No one will ever know. I'll say the tower was empty, and they must have fled already.

But I went on and on, one foot following after the other, as if following the implacable logic of a dream that had robbed me of my will.

Then, quite suddenly and inexplicably, I

saw my father's face with my mind's eye: not my father as he was now, but as he had been when I was a child: immense, infinitely powerful, the source of everything worth having in my life; more godlike than God himself.

Save me, I thought, I've lost my wits.

My father would not have turned back. Even now, he was not a coward. In his prime, he would have confronted the Devil himself in the mouth of hell.

I edged closer and closer until I was standing in the doorway, looking into the small chamber that lay beyond. I uncovered the lantern and held it high.

Three people were staring wide-eyed at me as if I were the ghost of Bishop Braybrooke himself. Henry Alderley was on the left, slumped in the corner, his face filthy and haggard, and his arms pulled behind his back.

The thumbs are tied, I thought. The thumbs again. As recommended for the damned on their way to hell in God's Fiery Furnace.

A man I didn't recognize towered over the others in the middle of the room, his head nearly touching the ceiling at its highest point. Thomas Lovett. He was older than I had expected, and dressed in a labourer's clothes, but he was tall and upright; he had a face as hard and sharp as a hatchet, and he was glaring at me.

The third was the boy–girl who had bitten my hand and stolen my cloak on the night that St Paul's burned. She too was staring at me, but without hostility or indeed any expression that I could detect on her face. She was smaller than I remembered, smooth-skinned but somehow ageless, with delicate, clearly defined features that might have belonged to a child or an old woman.

Time passed. A second? Half a minute? Now I had found them, now I had found Catherine Lovett, I simply did not know what to do.

The boy–girl let out her breath in a long sigh, as if she had been holding it too long for comfort.

I took off my hat and bowed. 'God give you good evening, Mistress Lovett. My name is Marwood.'

The frozen moment shattered.

Thomas Lovett was upon me before I had time to move. He gripped my wrist, twisting it, until I dropped both hat and dagger. I tried to clout the side of his head with the lantern but he caught my arm and forced it backwards. Old though he was, my strength

601

was no match for his. The lantern fell, rolling onto its side. The flame died.

Lovett kicked the dagger into the chamber behind him. He wrapped his hands around my neck and pushed me backwards, away from the doorway. I could do little to resist him. He was taller and heavier than I was, and he had the advantage of surprise.

One step back. Then another. A second later, I realized his intention: behind me was the long drop into the empty heart of the tower.

His daughter appeared suddenly beside me. She grabbed his left arm and tried to tug him away from me. 'Father! Father! Let him go, sir!' She hit his arm with the open palm of her free hand. 'He helped me.'

Lovett's hands relaxed, though he kept them lightly laced around my neck. 'Marwood?' he said slowly, as if the name had only just penetrated his mind. 'Marwood?'

I sucked a breath of air, which led me to a fit of coughing. When I could speak, I said, 'Yes, Marwood, sir. The son of Nathaniel Marwood of Pater Noster Row.'

'Marwood, yes,' he echoed, his hands dropping away from me. 'I remember. The printer.'

'You met him in Alsatia, sir. I fear he's not

the man he was.'

'No,' he said. 'I understood that.'

'He suffered much in his years of imprisonment.' I had no other plan than to keep Lovett talking to me. 'He's in his dotage now, come to it early, and quite ruined.'

'He will have his reward,' he proclaimed. 'There is a place in heaven for men like him, on God's right hand.'

This was not the moment to remind him that he had pushed my father down and left him weeping in the gutter.

'But he still has his lucid moments, sir,' I said, 'and he's often urged me to assist his old comrades as best I can.' I decided that I might as well be hanged for an old sheep as a young lamb. 'In the name of King Jesus.'

'But you work at Whitehall,' Mistress Lovett said, her voice sharpening.

'An informer?' Her father's hands reached for me again. 'And a traitor.'

I dared not move backwards. Somewhere behind me was that drop into darkness. 'There are many at Whitehall whose loyalties lie elsewhere,' I said hastily. 'And we are all the more useful there because of it.'

Lovett's hands settled on my shoulders. Once again I felt the pressure he was exerting, pushing me backwards. 'How have you come here? How did you know where we were?'

'Why, sir, because Master Hakesby told me you would be here.'

I felt something shift below my left foot. I flung myself forward. Lovett's hands gripped harder.

Nearer the edge, the walkway was not secure. The stone itself was crumbling under my weight. From far below came the sound of fragments of stone pattering on the ground.

'I nearly lost my footing, sir,' I said, trying to keep my voice low and reasonable, as if this were a minor, everyday hazard of this place, not the result of a potentially murderous assault on me.

The pressure slackened a little.

'Master Hakesby knew you must have taken your daughter from the Chapter Clerk's chamber,' I went on. 'He thought it probable you'd be up here. He would have come himself, sir, but he was not well enough for the climb . . . We must get you away to safety.'

'I don't trust you,' Lovett said. 'And why should I? You are not your father.'

There was no answer to that. The pressure of his hands began to increase again. I tried to divert him. 'I hadn't expected you to have company, sir.'

'Company?'

His attention on me slackened, and so did his grip.

'Master Alderley.'

He frowned, which made me wonder if he had briefly forgotten the very existence of his prisoner. He turned towards the chamber behind him, still dimly lit by Lovett's lantern within. At that instant there was the scrape of metal on stone, followed by a flurry of shadowy movement.

Alderley had freed himself. He threw himself forward — not at Lovett or me, but at Mistress Lovett. He wrapped his arms around her legs and brought her down on the walkway, her head hanging over the drop.

For a moment, none of us moved. The only sound I heard over the wind was Alderley's ragged gasps, part breathing, part sobbing.

Lovett released me. He flung himself on Alderley, who was pushing Mistress Lovett towards the edge. She flailed her arms, trying to reach Alderley's face, but the folds of her cloak impeded her. Lovett sprawled across Alderley, who writhed underneath his weight.

Suddenly free, I backed away. My foot

knocked against something metallic.

My lantern.

Mistress Lovett called out. It was a sound without words and it stopped me in my tracks.

I scooped up the lantern, raised it over my head and swung it down at the two struggling men. I was aiming for Alderley's head but there was so little light, and the men were moving so much, that I struck him only a glancing blow.

But it was enough to distract Alderley. He twitched, shifting his body, which gave Mistress Lovett the chance to curl herself under him so that her head was no longer hanging over the drop. His weight fell back on her almost at once but he no longer had her pinned so securely to the ground.

All this happened so quickly that the events flowed one into the other in a blur of movement. I hit Alderley again, and with better aim. This time he bucked like a restive horse, dislodging Lovett from his back. Mistress Lovett wriggled free.

Alderley pushed himself onto his feet and edged towards the wall of the parapet.

There was a sound behind me. I glanced back. Mistress Lovett was standing now, or rather crouching, as if ready to spring. The light from the doorway glinted on something in her hand. She was holding a knife. There was nothing even remotely meek and womanly about her. Indeed, for an instant she seemed not like a member of the human race but a creature of quite another breed that had more to do with sparrow hawks and cats.

For the length of a heartbeat, I thought of Sir Denzil Croughton dying in a pool of his own blood from a punctured artery, of the mastiff that didn't bark or bite, and of my own grey cloak hanging on a hedge. But there was no time for that, for anything —

'Father,' she cried. 'Have a care —'

Lovett was trying to scramble up, but his cloak tangled itself around his legs. He tore it away from him at once, but the movement sent him slightly off balance. He managed to stand, but more slowly than he had expected. For a second, he swayed, near the edge of the wall-walk, fighting for equilibrium.

He steadied himself but not quite soon enough. Alderley took a step forward, placed a hand on Lovett's chest, and pushed.

It wasn't a hard push. There was no urgency to it. Alderley's movements were unhurried and graceful, like a dancer's in a pavane.

Lovett stepped back. His arms were out-stretched. The light from the doorway was so dim you could hardly see him. His face was a blur, a mask. He might have been anyone.

For the length of another heartbeat, nothing moved. Then his arms flailed violently up and down as if he were trying to fly. He cried out, a sound without words. He fell backwards.

He was no longer there.

There were no more cries. The world held its breath. A third heartbeat.

Then the moist slap of flesh, blood and bone on stone.

Catherine Lovett hissed like a cat.

There was a flurry of movement beside me. She jabbed her knife upwards, under Alderley's chin.

He screamed. She left the knife there. His hands flew to his throat.

Another flurry of movement. Mistress Lovett was behind Alderley now. She pushed him with one sharp shove.

Henry Alderley stepped forward into the air. He screamed as he fell.

Mistress Lovett and I were alone at the top of St Paul's, with the ruins of London around us and no other sound but the wind.

■ ■ ■ ■

At first neither of us moved.

I backed into the doorway, down the steps, feeling my way, and into the chamber. Light, I thought, and a weapon. The other lantern was here. So was the dagger that I had dropped, which Lovett had kicked away from me and into the chamber. It was in the corner where Alderley had been lying. I remembered the scrape of metal on stone, just before he had rushed at Cat. He must have used the dagger to free his thumbs, rubbing the cord that bound them along the edge of the blade, and then dropped it as he scrambled to his feet.

I picked up the dagger first. The lantern was still in the niche by the door. When I raised it the light fell on Catherine Lovett in the doorway, throwing a ruddy glow on her face. She was wrapped in her cloak, hugging herself and weeping. She seemed oblivious to me.

'Mistress Lovett?' I said. 'Mistress Lovett?'

She stared up at me with wide, startled eyes. We were back where we had been when we had first met, all those weeks ago, as St Paul's burned down, when the flames had reddened our faces. When she had spat at me and bitten my hand.

But now I knew she had killed at least two people and maimed a third, her cousin Edward Alderley. At least she had lost her knife.

'Sir,' she said. Her voice was weak but I sensed she was fighting for control, fighting to contain her grief. She swallowed, moistened her lips and gathered strength and assurance. 'Sir. You have come to my rescue a second time. This time I suppose I must thank you.'

CHAPTER FIFTY-TWO

One step down. Another step.

Cat made him lead the way, this thin young man with his high cheekbones and his bright eyes. It was all she could do to put one foot in front of the other. She kept her hand on the outer wall of the staircase, turning slowly and endlessly downwards.

Marwood. That was his name. She had asked him to remind her of it only a moment ago. But her mind seemed incapable of holding information. A few minutes ago she had been possessed of extraordinary energy and felt capable of anything. Now that unnatural vitality had gone, and she felt exhausted, ill and very cold.

The cold made her tremble like Master Hakesby. It made her limbs heavy and uncertain, and filled her mind with grey mist. Is this, she wondered, what it is like to be old?

Marwood held the lantern high so she

could share its light. Every dozen steps or so, he would stop and turn to look at her.

'Mistress . . . ?'

He had stopped again. She blinked at him, thinking how she hated this place, a stone tomb for dead prayers and ruined ghosts.

'Master Hakesby is below. Or he should be.'

'Yes.'

'At the . . . triforium, is it? That's where I left him.' Marwood was speaking in a whisper, just loud enough for her to hear. 'We came to find you. He'll shelter you. If that's what you want. Or we can take you to your Aunt Alderley, not tonight but later, when all this has settled.'

That name took her by surprise. 'You know her? You've talked to her.'

He nodded. 'She wishes you well. I — I think she knows very little of what her husband was.'

'What are you, sir?' she said wearily. 'Why should I trust you?'

He turned away without answering, and they went on, down the endless stairs towards the darkness below.

Master Hakesby was not in the triforium above the north transept but they saw his lantern moving about under the crossing.

Without a word, Cat followed Marwood along the walkway to the archway that led to the last staircase. A few minutes later, they reached the floor of St Paul's.

Hakesby was waiting at the bottom of the steps. 'Thank God,' he said. 'Thank God. I heard the falls and I thought — well, you can imagine what I thought.' He patted Cat's arm, clumsily, as if she were a dog that might possibly bite. 'Poor child. I'm sorry for your father. And your uncle.'

'I want to see him,' Cat said, pushing Hakesby's hand away. 'My father.'

They walked in a file to the crossing. She glanced up. The inside of the tower rose above them, funnelling the darkness towards the paler dark of the sky. She made out one star, then another.

Marwood and Hakesby directed the beams of their lanterns to the crumpled heaps of clothing on the floor. Her father and Alderley lay in a pool of light enclosed by shadows. They were joined in death, with her uncle's head and shoulders resting on her father's legs. Her father's hair had come loose. Strands of grey lay among the ashes that still coated the floor.

'I'm afraid they are . . .'

Hakesby's voice trailed away. *I'm afraid they are dead.* That was what he meant to

613

say. Of course they were dead. What else could they be?

'Who will come first here in the morning?' Marwood said. 'After it's light, I mean. The watchmen?'

'I doubt it.' Hakesby sounded relieved at the change of subject. 'They are such idle devils. More probably it will be the first labourers and their foremen — pray don't step there, sir, there is a — a stickiness on the ground . . .'

'Blood,' Cat said. 'Blood.'

'Mistress Lovett,' Marwood said. 'We should search the bodies before we go.'

'You must do as you like, sir,' she said.

She crouched on the flagstones near her father's body and took one of his hands. It was large, rough-skinned. It still held some warmth. The nails needed trimming. There was a dark halo around the head. More blood.

Her father was lying on his front, with his face turned away from Cat. She watched Marwood lifting aside her father's cloak. He was searching him. What did it matter now?

She closed her eyes and stroked the hand. She didn't want to see her father's face. She heard the chink of coins and Marwood saying something to Hakesby. She was also aware of something scratching and rustling, a long way away. Rats, probably. They had fled from the Fire. But they had returned to St Paul's to see what they could find among the ashes. The rats always returned.

There would be more things in her father's pockets or about his person, Cat thought — letters, perhaps, and other documents. Would Marwood hand them to his masters at Whitehall? But perhaps he wasn't a government spy after all. He had not acted like one tonight, and Master Hakesby trusted him.

On the other hand, people were messy: they were capable of being more than one thing, she supposed; her father had loved her devotedly as his only child, but he had also been a ruthless adherent of the invisible King Jesus.

'Very well,' she heard Marwood say. 'We must go. Mistress, there was a purse of gold in your father's pocket. Shall Master Hakesby hold it for you?'

The words rustled in her ears, as empty of meaning as falling leaves. She raised her father's hand and kissed it.

Chapter Fifty-Three

Master Hakesby and I sat drinking wine in his chamber at Mistress Noxon's.

'Two men dead,' I said after a long silence.

'They'll find them at dawn.' He cupped the glass in both hands, trying to stop it shaking. 'The watchmen will say we were in St Paul's.'

'No,' I said. 'They only know that we went into the yard, into the shed. They don't know we went into the cathedral.'

'Surely they will put two and two together?'

'Why? There's nothing to make them think we stirred from the shed. Besides, they don't know when Lovett and Alderley died. It could have been in the middle of the night, when we were long gone. Do the watchmen ever go into the church itself? During the night, I mean?'

'Not if they can help it.'

'Well then.' I looked at him. The candlelight filled the cracks on his forehead with shadows. He looked fearful, old and very tired. 'So?' I said. 'What is it?'

Hakesby shrugged. 'I don't know what you want.'

'A quiet life, for one thing. This is not our quarrel.'

'I know hardly anything about you.'

'We know we are allies in this, sir, whether we like it or not.'

He said nothing, but sipped his wine, glancing at me over the brim of the glass. I took that for agreement, or even a sort of toast.

'Then what do we do?' he burst out. 'Her father and her uncle. A Regicide and one of the richest men in the country. Both dead, and we are in this up to our necks.'

'We tell the truth, I think,' I said.

'You cannot mean that.'

'We leave out the parts that do not quite suit, sir. Because we don't know where this will go from here. We shall let it be thought that the watchmen or the labourers were the first to find the bodies. But I must confide that you and I found them first to one person, and one only. You must trust me in this, sir — he will keep it close. I will say to him that we found them dead when you showed me into the church. We went there because I asked you to help me search the ruins for Master Lovett, on behalf of the government. So there will be no question about where your loyalties lie.'

'And her?' He turned his head towards the door of his closet, where Mistress Lovett lay sleeping in his bed. 'What in God's name do we do with her?'

'What does she want? Do you know?'

He raised his glass but did not drink from it. His hand was still trembling but less now. He stared at the wine as if the answer to the question lay there. 'I think,' he said slowly, 'she would like to design buildings.'

'What?' I thought I must have misheard him. Then I remembered. 'Yes — I heard she had a taste for such things. Curious, indeed.'

'It's a strange taste, I grant you, for a woman, let alone a young gentlewoman. But she has an aptitude. I think someone encouraged her. She said as much to me.'

I remembered the library at Coldridge, full of the unread books that Henry Alderley had sold to Master Howgego, along with the house and the estate. 'She had an aunt and uncle with an interest in architecture, sir.'

They designed imaginary cities together, Master Howgego had told me, *when they would have been better employed in studying their Bibles . . .*

'I'm establishing a drawing office in Henrietta Street,' Hakesby said. 'Before this happened, I told her I might employ her there. I mentioned this to you earlier. I intended her to work as a maid, but also perhaps occasionally at a drawing board herself, making copies and so on. There will be a great quantity of work in the next few years.'

'You knew who she really was? Even then?'

'I knew what she was, but not who. Safer for everyone.'

I understood what Hakesby didn't say as much as what he did. Since the King's Restoration, there were many who did not find it convenient to live as they had before, or even to use their own names, and there were others who would help them survive in peaceable, unobtrusive ways, and encourage their friends to do the same.

'Mistress Noxon gave me a hint of it,' he continued. 'Besides, it was obvious that Mistress Lovett had lived in a gentleman's house before she came to Three Cocks Yard. But I didn't know she was an heiress.'

'I'm not sure she is now. Master Alderley saw to that. She may have a claim on his estate. But it's another matter whether she would want to press for restitution. Even if she did, she might not get anything.'

'Then what do we do with her?' he said again.

'No one knows that Mistress Lovett was at St Paul's today,' I said. 'Except ourselves.'

'And John. The servant here, who brought her to me at St Paul's.'

'Can you answer for his silence?'

'No one can do that for another man.' Hakesby sniffed. 'But he is . . . attached to her. I believe if we approach him aright, he will keep his mouth shut. For her sake.'

'What about the watchmen?' I asked.

'She said that they did not see her when she went in with John. And you concealed her under your cloak when we left this evening. Anyway, the light was so bad in Convocation House Yard, they could hardly see a foot beyond their shed.'

'Good. No one else has seen her since her father took her from the coffee house last week, or no one who will want to say so. So perhaps it would be best if she stayed lost until this business is sorted out.'

Hakesby nodded. 'If she's agreeable. And in a while, when we all know more, we can decide what's best for her.'

'I think it may be she who decides, sir,' I said. 'From what little I know of her.'

■ ■ ■ ■

The two of us talked until the first cocks began to crow in the back yards of London. Then we went downstairs. The maid came creeping down as Hakesby was unbarring the front door. She stared wide-eyed at us.

'What are you gawping at, Margery?' Hakesby snapped. 'Light the kitchen fire, and set water to boil as soon as you can. I'm as cold as charity, and I must have a caudle to warm me.'

When the maid had gone, he said in an undertone, 'How can I find you if I need to?'

'I lodge at Newcomb the printer's in the Savoy, sir. But it would be better not to call there. Send word instead.'

He gave me a lantern and let me out of the house. 'Fare you well,' he whispered.

Three Cocks Yard was as dark as a tomb. There was no sign of dawn yet. It was very cold. I had drunk a good deal of wine in the last few hours but I did not feel drunk. But there was a hollowness deep in my belly that might have been hunger. More probably it was fear.

I picked my way down the alley to the Strand. There were lights here, and also a few of the early wagons bringing produce into the city. I went into the Savoy. The Newcombs' lodgings were still barred and shuttered at this hour. But the door to the kitchen yard was unbolted. This was Thursday, and Margaret came early to help the maid with scrubbing out the scullery and working in the laundry.

The kitchen windows were unshuttered, and smoke was wisping from the chimneys. I tapped on the back door. Margaret herself opened it. I had not seen her since Sam's release on Monday evening, and I was unsure of my welcome. But she smiled when she saw me, curtsied and let me in.

'Thank you for your kindness to Samuel, sir,' she said as she closed the door. She lowered her voice so the maid at the other end of the kitchen wouldn't hear. 'I don't know when I last had a piece of gold in my hand.'

I shrugged, embarrassed by gratitude that I so ill deserved. 'Is anyone astir?'

She shook her head. 'Mistress will be down soon, though.'

I had no wish to encounter the sharp eyes of Mistress Newcomb. I took a candle and went up the back stairs to the rooms I shared with my father.

He was still asleep. The curtains were

drawn around his bed but I heard his snoring.

I reached into my cloak and took out the portfolio I had found in Lovett's pocket when I searched his body. It was made of pigskin and there was now a reddish stain covering most of one side of it. It was still damp.

I tiptoed to the table, set down the candle and spread out the contents of the portfolio. There were three letters and a bill of credit addressed to a goldsmith in Norwich.

The bill of credit was not negotiable, and so could have no value to Lovett's daughter. That left the letters. Two were written in a cipher or shorthand consisting of characters of the alphabet, numbers and symbols. I knew them as letters only because they were both addressed to Giles Coldridge.

The third letter was clearly older than the others, for the paper was yellowing and brittle to the touch; one corner had crumbled away. This letter was the only one in plain English.

To Master Alderley,
of Leadenhall: London,
31 January 1648/9

Sir, You did this country a great service yesterday, when Thos Lovett fell ill, by taking his part. For all his skill with an axe, Brandon is a mean and cowardly fellow. Yesterday's affair could not have been dispatched without a man of resolution beside him to keep him up to the mark. You cannot receive the public thanks you merit but be assured of my private gratitude. The Lord has directed all to His glory. I rest,

Sir,
Your servant,
Oliver Cromwell

The snoring behind me changed its rhythm. I had a headache. Why in God's name this, on top of everything else? I desperately wanted time to think through the implications of what I had found. How had the letter come into Lovett's possession?

The obvious answer leapt out of the dark at me: Jem Brockhurst. Jem had been loyal to the Lovetts. He had been living at Barnabas Place, so lowly in the household hierarchy that he must have crept about almost unnoticed.

Had Jem been Lovett's spy as well as his messenger boy and his daughter's guardian? I had no proof, but the facts and the possibilities clustered around the speculation, clinging like a cluster of iron nails to a magnet. Suppose Jem had ferreted out the letter and —

But why in God's name had Alderley taken the risk of keeping such a letter, which was as good as a death warrant for him if it fell into the wrong hands? Because he was a prudent man, I thought, and also an arrogant one. Perhaps he had not ruled out the possibility that one day the King would lose his throne and the Commonwealth return. In that case a man with such a letter might turn a profit by it.

Suppose —

The snoring stopped.

I carried the candle and the papers to the fireplace. Suppose that was the reason, the trigger, for Lovett's return to England now, after all these years — the knowledge that he had in his possession the means utterly to ruin Alderley and his family. Suppose Jem had handed over the letter — too precious to be trusted to a third party — on the night before St Paul's burned down. Suppose that was when Lovett had told Jem to send his daughter out to meet him. Suppose —

One by one, I burned the papers — the bill of credit and the two cipher letters. The secrets darkened and disintegrated into fragments on the hearth. I ground them to ash with the poker.

But I kept back Cromwell's letter. Suppose I gave it to Chiffinch and asked him to show it to the King. What would it mean for all of us — for Mistress Lovett, for Edward Alderley, for Olivia Alderley, and most of all for my father and me?

Or suppose I burned the letter with the rest?

My father broke wind. I heard the rattle of curtain rings behind me. I folded Cromwell's letter and pushed it into a crack in the side of the press that held our clothes.

'Who's there?' My father's voice sounded tremulous and full of fear. He broke wind again. 'Who is it?'

'It's James, sir, your son.'

'I was dreaming. I was young again, and you were a little child. I dreamed I was carrying you on my shoulders.'

'I remember, sir. I remember it well. But it's early yet, still dark. Sleep on.'

As I closed the bed curtains again, I held up the candle so the light fell for a moment on my father's face. His eyes were already closed and he was smiling.

Before I left, I threw the bloodstained portfolio on the kitchen fire. Margaret gave me one of this morning's rolls and a mug of small beer. Afterwards, she came with me to the door.

'You're troubled, sir,' she said, in the casual voice of someone commenting on the weather.

'These are troubling times. Tell Samuel I asked after him.'

I took the familiar road to Charing Cross, and down to Whitehall. The Banqueting House rose before me, its windows already alight.

Ashes and blood. How I disliked that slab of stone and glass. It made me a child again, with a child's terrors, sitting on my father's shoulders and watching them kill a king on a stage. Blood and ashes.

Early though it still was, the palace was stirring. There was to be a ball for the Queen's birthday in the evening. The Great Court was seething with servants and tradesmen. There was a sound of hammering from the Great Hall.

At Master Chiffinch's private lodgings, I knocked long and hard until at last a sleepy servant opened the door. I begged him to wake his master and give him a message from me. The knave was puffed up and obstinate, like so many Whitehall servants, and he refused, saying I must wait outside until the house was astir and call again at a more Christian hour. I argued with him, and he threatened to have me beaten about the ears and thrown into the street.

Then I saw Chiffinch himself descending the stairs, candle in hand and arrayed in a splendid bedgown of figured silk and beturbanned like the Turk. 'What's this damned racket, Martin?' he bellowed. 'Who is it? It's the middle of the night. Have you all gone stark crazy?'

'Sir,' I said. 'I must speak to you.'

'What?' He peered through the gloom, rubbing the sleep from his eyes. 'Marwood? Is that you?'

'I've news, sir. It won't wait. For your private ear.'

'If you're wrong, I'll see you both suffer for it.'

I glanced at the servant, who scowled at me. Chiffinch ordered the man to kindle a fire in the parlour and set water to boil. He led me upstairs to his closet, which was well sealed against the draughts and still held a little warmth from last night's fire. He told me to light more candles, took up a blanket and sat in his chair.

'Well? Have you found Alderley?'

'Yes, sir. But he's dead. And so's Lovett.'

Chiffinch whistled, soft and low. 'Are you sure? How? Where?'

'At St Paul's. Lovett had smuggled him into the ruins and forced him up the tower at knifepoint. There must have been a struggle. They had fallen from the top, inside the tower, right down to the floor of the crossing. Lovett's dead as well.'

' 'Sblood.' Chiffinch scratched his scalp under the turban. 'You've seen them? You're absolutely sure they're dead? Both of them.'

'Yes, sir. Lovett had stabbed him before they fell. I don't know if that killed Master Alderley, or if it was the fall. As for Lovett, the back of his head is quite broken apart.'

'The King won't like it,' Chiffinch said. 'He wanted Lovett to himself. He wanted to look the man in the face. When did you discover this?'

'Last night. I fell in with Master Hakesby —'

'Who?'

'The draughtsman who works with Dr Wren. He lodges at Three Cocks Yard, off the Strand.'

Chiffinch nodded. 'I remember.'

'He offered one of the house's servants employment as a maid in his new office because she seemed clean and to have her wits about her. It was Mistress Lovett, though of course he did not know that.'

'Why did you not come to me sooner with the news?'

'Because I had to search the rest of the cathedral, sir. And then Master Hakesby was taken ill, so I took him home.'

He sat in silence for a moment, staring at the ashes in the fireplace. I waited, still wrapped in my cloak but shivering nevertheless. I felt suddenly exhausted, now I had told my news. For good or ill, I had surrendered any power I had. It was out of my hands.

Apart from the Cromwell letter.

Chiffinch looked up. His scratching had pushed the turban to one side, giving him an unexpectedly jaunty air. Stranger still, he was smiling at me. 'Well, Marwood,' he said. 'I always say it's an ill wind that blows no man good.'

CHAPTER FIFTY-FOUR

And then — nothing.

When I was young, after the King came back but before my father's disgrace, we apprentices would sometimes kick a ball about the streets on public holidays, to the great peril of ourselves and any bystanders foolish enough to get in our way. These were brawls by any other name, wars between factions, the printers against the cordwainers, or the haberdashers against the glovers. There were broken bones in our bodies and splashes of blood on the cobbles. But it was a game.

What made it a game was the existence of a pig's bladder inflated with air.

This unlovely object was the prize we fought for with such vigour, and at such a danger to ourselves. Once, however, a group of us strayed into the path of a drunken gallant, who drew his sword and stabbed the pig's bladder repeatedly. He was under the illusion that he was killing a New Model Army trooper because all the while he was shrieking, 'Die, foul lobster! Rot in hell!'

The ball deflated and became nothing worth kicking, let alone fighting for. Later I saw it tossed aside in the kennel, along with all the stinking refuse of the street. Naturally we attacked the gallant instead, but it was not the same.

When Master Chiffinch sent me away that morning, I felt like that pig's bladder — deflated, useless, without a purpose in life. I had hated the fear and worry of the last few weeks. I had also hated the strange excitement that possessed me. I didn't want that sort of excitement back. But I found that I craved it as a drunkard craves wine.

Chiffinch warned me to keep my mouth shut about what had happened in St Paul's on pain of severe punishment. After I had left him, I went to Master Williamson's office, where the servants were lighting the fires, and I waited for the other clerks to arrive. I didn't know what else to do.

I waited all day for Master Chiffinch to send for me. I tried to foretell the questions he would ask me and to work out the answers I should give. I even imagined that the King himself might summon me. Sometimes my expectations were gloomier — at every step on the stairs I heard soldiers coming to arrest me. My mind leapt ahead to an even darker future, with myself rotting in prison and my father dead.

At dinner, I heard a story circulating that a gentleman had died of a fall in the ruins of St Paul's, and that a workman had been killed with him. No one knew the gentleman's name.

I heard nothing from Chiffinch or anyone else that day. Or the next, though by then the gentleman had been identified as Master Alderley, the goldsmith, who was known to be a friend of Dr Wren's and a man with an interest in the rebuilding of the cathedral; the King was said to be much grieved at his death.

Nobody summoned me on Saturday. Or Sunday.

I didn't call on Master Hakesby, either in Three Cocks Yard or at St Paul's. It was safer to pretend our brief acquaintance had never happened. As for Mistress Lovett, there was no news of her at all, and I sought none. A few days later, Master Alderley was buried with much pomp. I heard a rumour at Whitehall that he had not been as rich as the world had believed, and his affairs were much entangled.

As the days of silence became weeks, I

grew increasingly fearful. Fear is an anticipation of evil, akin to a pain of the spirit. Or an emptiness so deep and all-embracing that it sucks your soul into it and leaves you a mere husk of your former self, fit for nothing that matters.

Like the pig's bladder that was once a ball.

Christmas was approaching.

It was already very cold. Everyone said it would be an exceptionally hard winter, which always hurt the poor worst of all. This year, it would be even crueller than usual, for so many people were still refugees from the Fire.

Perhaps it was worst of all for those who had returned to the ruins of their former homes. Here, they lived miserably in the corners of cellars littered with debris and open to the sky. They built sheds and shelters among the frozen ashes, where they waited for spring and hoped that God would smile on them again one day.

On St Lucy's Day, the shortest of the year, I walked past St Paul's on my way to Whitehall. The government and the City were still arguing about what to do with the cathedral — whether to restore or to rebuild — and in the meantime it grew increasingly decayed and forlorn. The roads around it were now cleared of rubble, and there was far more traffic on them during the day than there had been even a month earlier.

At Whitehall, there was a message for me at Master Williamson's office: I was to wait on Master Chiffinch at his lodgings.

I found him swathed in furs and huddled over the fire in his study. He looked unwell, perhaps from too much wine, for his eyes were mere slits and his plump cheeks were pink with sallow patches. He was reading a letter, and he kept me standing before him until he had finished.

'Master Williamson speaks satisfactorily of you,' he said at last, laying aside the letter. 'All in all. A discreet young man, he says, who applies himself to his work with diligence and keeps his own counsel.'

I said nothing.

'He tells me he intends to offer you a permanent clerkship after Christmas. A junior position, of course — he will have a vacancy that needs filling. Perhaps a hundred and fifty pounds a year.'

'Thank you, sir.' I spoke softly but inside I was shouting with joy. This was preferment that meant something — not just for the income, of course, but also for the other emoluments that would come with the position, and the status it would give me among my fellows.

He sneezed violently. 'Do you know the Board of Red Cloth?'

'No, sir.'

'It comes under the Lord Chamberlain. It does very little these days — and never has, as far as I know. But it carries on, as these things do. The members meet every quarter to assess their requirements of the next three months. They have a vacancy for a clerk to record what is decided at these meetings, and I have put forward your name to his lordship.' He held up his hand when I tried to thank him. 'Master Williamson will give you leave to attend to business there on the days when they meet. As there are only four meetings a year, I doubt it will inconvenience him overmuch. It pays about fifty pounds a year, I believe.' He took up his handkerchief and blew his nose very loudly, which turned him pinker than ever. 'I sit on the board myself, as it happens, and I may occasionally call on you to undertake other duties as well.'

I thanked him as effusively as I knew how for his kindness and his condescension, wondering what those other duties might be but deciding it would be unwise to ask.

'One more thing,' he said. 'You're to call at Cradle Alley on Sunday. Three o'clock sharp. Don't be late.'

St Lucy's Day, the thirteenth of December, had fallen on Thursday. I had three long days to wait until Sunday.

In the meantime, I was pleased with myself to the point of smugness. It was not every day, I told myself, that a man was given a position at Whitehall, let alone two of them. I discovered that the news of my advancement had reached the office — my fellow clerks treated me with more respect, and even Master Williamson condescended to nod affably when I greeted him on Friday morning with my usual bow.

I told my father that I had had a piece of good fortune, and that we could, if we wished, move ourselves to a more convenient set of lodgings. But he grew agitated at the idea and begged me to let us stay. He liked the smell of ink and paper, I believed, and the familiar sounds of the press. He even liked Mistress Newcomb, who was firm with him to the point of ruthlessness, but also consistent and never unkind for the sake of it. He knew where he was with her, and after his imprisonment that was luxury indeed.

The Newcombs heard that I was to be promoted, and they made much of me. I promised them a celebratory dinner in the New Year. I put in a good word for Margaret, too, arranging for her to spend several hours a day with my father. At my expense, she was to clean our part of the lodgings, look after our clothes and take him out for air if the weather and his health permitted.

I had another scheme for Margaret and Sam as well: that of bringing them both to live within the Savoy. Like Alsatia, the Savoy and its surroundings were a liberty, a legal sanctuary, in this case under the Duchy of Lancaster. A man might owe a fortune in London or Westminster, but his creditors could not pursue him here. The Savoy was far safer than Alsatia, and there would be a convenience in the arrangement for my father and me.

But there was a worm in my apple, gnawing away at my smugness. A month earlier, four people had gone up the tower at St Paul's, and only two of us had come down alive. I knew the truth of that, and sometimes I relived it in my dreams, even though I tried so hard to forget what had happened.

I wished I could talk to Mistress Lovett about what had happened that night, and about the letter. But I did not enquire after her, though it would have been easy enough to seek out Master Hakesby.

Part of me wanted to burn the letter, as I had the rest of the papers in Lovett's portfolio. But I couldn't bring myself to do it. It was not my secret to destroy. Perhaps, I thought, if I ever saw Mistress Lovett again, I would decide that she should know the truth.

A child deserved to know what her father had been, after his death if not in his life.

Suddenly it struck me that, by a similar argument, the King deserved to know how his father had died, and by whose hand.

I didn't know what to do.

CHAPTER FIFTY-FIVE

'Her ladyship gave orders to admit you.'

The porter stared down from his great height, giving the impression that, in her ladyship's place, he would have kept the door barred against me. He was a different, haughtier porter from the man who had admitted me on my previous visits.

'Her ladyship?' I said.

'My Lady Quincy,' he said, his air of disapproval increasing. He stood back to allow me to enter.

A sign of changing times: Mistress Alderley had reverted to her old name, the name that belonged to her first marriage. I went into the hall. The light was already fading. There were shadowy figures beyond the staircase whose faces I could not see. The house seemed busier than before, full of secret life. I hadn't seen the manservant who took my cloak before, either.

The shutters were up in the drawing

room. The glare of candlelight filled the chamber and brought a smoky warmth to the air. The old screen was still across the corner, and Lady Quincy was in her usual chair. She acknowledged my bow with a gracious inclination of her head and told me to sit.

She was in mourning, as far as her clothes were concerned, but there was nothing sorrowful about her face or her manner. She looked in remarkably fine spirits. As for her dress, black did not suit everyone, but it agreed well enough with her. I began to mutter something about the loss she must have suffered by her husband's death. She cut me off with a wave of her hand.

'There's no need to talk of that now, sir,' she said. 'Let me be blunt, it will save time. Do you know what's become of my niece? Did you find her?'

I hesitated. I had no way of knowing her reason for asking. I had to trust my instinct. 'Yes, madam.'

'Where is she?'

'With friends.'

'Friends whose beliefs are like her father's?'

'No,' I said, trying not to stare at the flame-tinted richness of her skin. 'Loyal subjects of the King.'

'Is she content with her lot?'

'I believe so, madam.'

'That's as well.' Lady Quincy — the name seemed more naturally hers than Mistress Alderley had ever done — took up a fan and toyed with it. 'You see, I can offer her nothing but charity, and not much of that. It turns out that her uncle's estate is much embarrassed.'

I frowned. 'I thought he was rich. One of the richest men in —'

'So did everyone. But he was more than a goldsmith, you understand. His clients deposited their gold and their plate with him for security, on the understanding that he would allow them to withdraw it whenever they wished to have it. In return, Master Alderley lent out the money, and charged interest, or sometimes invested it in a venture, and so made a profit on the transaction.'

So, I thought. A man who makes other people's money breed for him, first cousin to a usurer. It was a strange way to make a living, let alone to become rich.

She seemed to read my mind. 'But he was not a moneylender in the old, avaricious way that we must all condemn. He used to cite the parable of the talents in the Gospel, in which Jesus praised the man who used the money entrusted to him to make more money rather than let it moulder unprofitably in the ground. He told me that everybody gained by this — the depositor, the lender and the borrower. Even England itself, he used to say, from the King downwards — for money must flow safely and easily if a country is to prosper and the government is to have its revenues. Gold is the lifeblood of nations.' She paused. 'At least — that was the theory of it.'

She fell silent, staring down at the fan.

'But perhaps practice does not always follow where theory leads?' I suggested.

'Just so.' She looked up. 'There was a flaw in the logic, it seemed to me, though of course I'm only a woman and cannot understand the matter as a man does.' She glanced at me, and I could have sworn that I saw mockery in her eyes. The woman was like quicksilver; I could never pin her down. 'What if everyone wants his money at the same time? If the depositor wishes to withdraw his gold, and the borrower demands more, while the lender finds that his investments have gone bad and his debtors will not pay him what they owe. All that money is flown away, leaving the man in the centre with nothing. With worse than nothing, if the truth be known, for he still owes his depositors the value of their original deposits.'

'So Master Alderley left nothing but debts?'

There was no mockery in her face now. I thought of another man who was a bankrupt — Samuel Witherdine, crippled in his country's service and denied the pay he was owed. I knew who the better man was.

'It's worse than that,' Lady Quincy said slowly, as if drawing each word painfully from her mouth. 'A little before he died — in order to balance his books . . . my husband was tempted to . . . to use money that was not his to use.'

It seemed to me that, strictly speaking, most of Master Alderley's money had not been his to use, that his wealth had been nothing but a bubble.

'Yes,' I said. 'So he sold Coldridge, which belonged to his niece, and pocketed the proceeds.'

Lady Quincy had the grace to look embarrassed. 'Truly, there is nothing left. Worse than nothing. My late husband's creditors will have every last penny from his estate, and still they won't be even half satisfied. The jointure I brought him on my marriage is safe from them, and so is this house, but I have only a life interest, and on my death they must go to the heirs of Sir William, my first husband. The only persons who have gained by his death are some of Master Alderley's debtors. The ones who gave him no security for the loans he made them, whose word he trusted.'

I remembered Master Chiffinch's words when I had told him that Alderley was dead: *Well, Marwood, I always say it's an ill wind that blows no man good.* 'I wonder, madam, was Master Chiffinch among these debtors?'

It was a question I had no right to ask. Lady Quincy didn't answer. In the silence that followed, I heard, quite distinctly, a floorboard creak nearby. I could have kicked myself. Chiffinch was probably behind the screen again, listening to every word I said. I would not last long in Whitehall now.

I rushed on, desperate to move the subject to safer ground. 'And Edward Alderley? Is he penniless too?'

She shook her head. 'Before he died, his father transferred the ownership of several freeholds to Edward, including Barnabas Place. The creditors can't touch that either. But Edward has no love for his cousin. I fear he does not accept that she has a claim on him. He thinks she must be dead, or fled abroad to be with her father's friends.'

'I don't understand why you are telling

me this, madam.'

She flared up at me. 'Then you are more foolish than I took you to be, Master Marwood. I had a duty towards my niece, and I did not discharge it as I should have done when she was living in my household. I wish to make some small amends, if that's possible. To help her. Is that plain enough?'

'How can you help her?'

'I can give her a little money, if she will take it from me. I cannot have her here to live with me. She's the daughter of a Regicide. And worse. Also, there is the question of Sir Denzil's murder. Edward has made certain allegations. Only in private, so far, but if she appears in public again, or makes a claim on him, it will be a different matter. If that happens, I cannot protect her.'

'The mastiffs,' I said.

'Yes.' Lady Quincy intoned their names like a charm: 'Thunder, Lion, Greedy and Bare-Arse. Especially Bare-Arse, who stood by while Sir Denzil was murdered and did nothing.'

'Her cousin couldn't prove anything, madam.'

'You think not? Edward will think nothing of perjuring himself if he needs to. He says he has found a servant who will swear that she saw that grey cloak in Catherine's chamber on the day before she fled from Barnabas Place. The cloak they found on Primrose Hill. He may be lying, but it's a dangerous lie. And no jury will show favour to the daughter of the Regicide.'

I took a deep breath and jumped into the unknown. 'They say the King himself and his brother borrowed large sums of money from Master Alderley.'

She raised her eyebrows. 'Do they indeed? Well, that's no concern of yours or mine. I think we have finished our business, Master Marwood. I understand you have been rewarded handsomely for your pains. But bear in mind that what the King gives, the King can also take away.'

I stood up. 'Master Alderley committed treason of the worst kind. The King need not repay a debt to a traitor, even in death.'

'What nonsense is this?'

'I'm persuaded that when the King knows all, he will look mercifully on Mistress Lovett and suffer her to live quietly and unmolested, free from any fear of prosecution. He will not visit the sins of the father on the child.'

'The King will do as he pleases. Now, will you —'

I spoke over her. 'Henry Alderley was a traitor and hypocrite. Nearly twenty years ago, he —'

'Pooh!' she interrupted. 'As you well know, many were foolish in those days, and forgot their allegiance to their king. The Act of Indemnity draws a line under that.'

'The Act would not cover this, my lady.' I took out the letter I had found among Thomas Lovett's papers. 'And the King would not wish it to.' I unfolded the letter and said in a voice I tried to keep level, 'Madam, the second executioner of the late King was not Thomas Lovett. Lovett was ill that day. It was Henry Alderley who kept up Brandon's nerve and who held up the King's head to the crowd. I saw him do it myself, with my own eyes, though I did not know it. That's why Alderley prospered under the Commonwealth. Cromwell favoured him.'

Ashes and blood.

The warmth and the colour faded from her face. 'You cannot prove this.'

'This letter does. It's in Cromwell's own hand.'

Another creak from a floorboard. Then another. The candle flames flickered. A tall man appeared from behind the screen.

I flung myself on my knees. Lady Quincy rose and curtsied.

'Give me that letter,' the King said.

■ ■ ■ ■

The King turned aside to read it. I stood in silence. Lady Quincy sat down again. Time stretched out. My legs ached. The coal shifted in the grate. One of the candles guttered and died. How long could it take to read one short letter and digest its contents?

I thought the King might be weeping. But when at last he turned back to us there were no tears on his cheeks, and his voice was as deep and calm as ever.

'You were there, Marwood, were you not? Among the crowd at the Banqueting House.'

'Yes, sir.'

'What — what was my father like? How did he bear himself?'

'No man could have carried himself more honourably, sir.' I thought of that small, sad-faced man in his waistcoat, with a nightcap on his head. I thought how calm he had been, how self-possessed. 'No man could have borne himself more like a king.'

'You were a mere child,' he said softly. 'To see a sight like that . . . What did you think of it then? What did you do?'

'I wept, sir.'

Blood and ashes. Ashes and blood.

■ ■ ■ ■

Afterwards, Lady Quincy sent me home in her coach. It was the one that I had been in before, when she talked to me at the New Exchange, but the device on the door had already been changed. The flames of the servants' links showed that Alderley's pelican feeding her young had been replaced by a widow's lozenge bearing arms I did not recognize, presumably those of Sir William Quincy quartered with her own. The inside of the coach smelled of her perfume, as before.

It was a clear, cold night. The coach was well lit, and the servants were armed. We went round by the City wall, skirting the ruins. The moon had risen, coating the ashes of London with silver.

The King had sworn us both to secrecy. There was nothing to be gained by revealing what Alderley had done, and it would not help Lady Quincy either. Edward would never know the truth about his father. The King was not a vengeful man; he would not visit the sins of the father on the child.

I knew I should feel happy. The King had shown me favour. My father was content enough in his way, and safe from harm. I now had an income to support us and a modest position in the world. Mistress Lovett would live without fear, if she were careful, with the help of Master Hakesby and her father's purse of gold. Even London itself would grow again, phoenix-like, from its own ashes. I had enough.

But enough is never enough. Instead, as the coach swayed and jolted its way to the Strand, my mind dwelled on Olivia, Lady Quincy, and the impossibility that she would ever look kindly on me.

Somewhere among the ashes, a dog barked at the moon.

CHAPTER FIFTY-SIX

In the distance, a dog was barking as if it would never stop.

'Close the window,' Master Hakesby said.

From the wide attic window of the house in Henrietta Street, almost everything in sight was a shade of grey, speckled with faint yellow pinpricks from windows and lanterns. The sky was darkening towards night. The air smelled of coal smoke and the river, a sour blend that caught the back of the throat.

'The draught, Jane! We'll catch our death!'

'Your pardon, sir.'

She closed the casement and drew the curtain across the window. Master Hakesby was sitting over the fire, trembling from the cold or his ague or both. A candle burned on the table at his elbow, and there was another on the mantel. Away from the fire, the long room was a place of shadows, with the draughtsmen's slopes rearing up from the long table.

'Did you fetch more coals?'

'Yes, sir.'

She picked up the scuttle that she had brought up from the cellar and carried it to the hearth.

'You must keep warm,' he said as the coals rattled on to the embers. 'Look at you — chilled to the bone.'

She nodded and smiled, though in truth it was Master Hakesby who looked chilled, not herself.

'And mind you make the room warm for us in the morning, too. Build up a good fire before we come. A man cannot do fine work when he's cold.'

Cat put down the shovel and turned to him. 'Will you not go home now, sir? Mistress Noxon will be wondering where you are.'

Master Hakesby scowled at her but he levered himself up from his chair. He took up the poker and fussed at the fire. When he had finished, Cat fetched his cloak. He allowed her to arrange it around his thin shoulders.

'Would you like me to attend you, sir?' Not to Three Cocks Yard, of course, not to the house, but at least along the Strand, which even on a Sunday evening was thronged with traffic.

'Of course not,' he said. 'You must still keep within doors as much as possible. You must not court danger.'

But it wasn't her safety that concerned him, she knew, so much as the fear that she might think him incapable of managing by himself.

'Are you not afraid here?' he said. 'On your own at night?'

'No, sir.' How could she explain to him that solitude was what she most desired? 'Besides, I'm not alone in the house.'

Master Hakesby and Dr Wren had taken only the top floor, with its huge workshop windows. They employed two draughtsmen, as well as Cat, but they lodged elsewhere. There was a hatter on the ground floor, and a French Huguenot family immediately below the drawing office. A porter guarded the common entry during the hours of daylight and slept in a room off the hatter's back kitchen.

'Up here you are entirely by yourself at night,' he said, worrying ineffectually at the subject like an old dog with a bone.

Cat was standing by the door now, waiting for him to leave. 'I can sit with Madame Charvet if I need company.'

He peered at her. 'I'll be back before it's

light in the morning. We have so much work on hand we cannot afford to lose a moment. Soon there will be even more to do.'

The rebuilding of London would start in the New Year. The government and the City authorities had at last agreed on what should be done and, more importantly, how to pay for it. The necessary Bills were going through Parliament and would soon become law. Master Hakesby hoped that commissions for new projects would pour in.

She opened the door for him, took up a candle and lit his way down the stairs.

'It is a most horrid shame though,' Master Hakesby said as they descended the final flight. 'Posterity will say we threw away the chance to make London a great capital city, fit for all ages. Instead, all we shall do is piecemeal stuff, trying to make good what was there before.'

It was a familiar complaint, and she didn't reply. The porter unbarred the door and summoned a linkboy.

When Master Hakesby was gone, Cat went quickly upstairs. In the drawing office, she bolted the door and lit two more candles, which she placed on the sconces beside the slope nearer the fire. She fetched her private papers from the closet in which she slept. She laid out the largest sheet on the slope and studied the maze of pencilled lines.

Firmitas, utilitas, venustas, Cat murmured. Buildings should be like the nests of birds and bees.

She took up her pen and dipped it in the ink. As she worked, the city rose in her mind from the paper. She saw its towers and bridges, its churches and halls, its avenues and piazzas. Everything was interconnected, the elements combining with each other to work for the whole. In the heart of the city, taller than every other building, drawing the eye from every quarter, was the shining dome of St Paul's.

Here was London. Not London as it was or London as it would be. But the London in her head, displaying the great Vitruvian virtues in all its parts, from the greatest public buildings to the smallest alleys.

Her London.

ABOUT THE AUTHOR

Andrew Taylor is the author of a number of crime novels, including the ground-breaking Roth Trilogy, which was adapted into the acclaimed drama *Fallen Angel*, and the historical crime novels *The Ashes of London, The Silent Boy,* and *The American Boy*, a No.1 *Sunday Times* bestseller and a 2005 Richard & Judy Book Club Choice. He has won many awards, including the CWA Ellis Peters Historical Award (the only author to win it three times) and the CWA's prestigious Diamond Dagger.

The employees of Thorndike Press hope you have enjoyed this Large Print book. All our Thorndike, Wheeler, and Kennebec Large Print titles are designed for easy reading, and all our books are made to last. Other Thorndike Press Large Print books are available at your library, through selected bookstores, or directly from us.

For information about titles, please call:
    (800) 223-1244

or visit our website at:
    gale.com/thorndike

To share your comments, please write:
    Publisher
    Thorndike Press
    10 Water St., Suite 310
    Waterville, ME 04901